The
Violinist
of
Auschwitz

Books by Ellie Midwood

The Girl Who Escaped from Auschwitz

ELLIE MIDWOOD

The Violinist of Auschwitz

GRAND
CENTRAL
NEW YORK   BOSTON

Cover design by Sarah Whittaker
Image of woman © Ildiko Neer/Trevillion; all other images from Shutterstock
Cover copyright © 2023 by Hachette Book Group, Inc.

Grand Central Publishing
Hachette Book Group
1290 Avenue of the Americas, New York, NY 10104
grandcentralpublishing.com
twitter.com/grandcentralpub

Originally published in 2020 by Bookouture in the United Kingdom
First US edition: June 2023

Grand Central Publishing is a division of Hachette Book Group, Inc. The Grand Central Publishing name and logo is a trademark of Hachette Book Group, Inc.

The Hachette Speakers Bureau provides a wide range of authors for speaking events. To find out more, go to hachettespeakersbureau.com or email HachetteSpeakers@hbgusa.com.

Grand Central Publishing books may be purchased in bulk for business, educational, or promotional use. For information, please contact your local bookseller or the Hachette Book Group Special Markets Department at special.markets@hbgusa.com.

Library of Congress Cataloging-in-Publication Data

Names: Midwood, Ellie, author.
Title: The violinist of Auschwitz / Ellie Midwood.
Description: First US edition. | New York : Grand Central, 2023.
Identifiers: LCCN 2022057934 | ISBN 9781538741146 (trade paperback)
Subjects: LCSH: Rosé, Alma—Fiction. | World War, 1939–1945—Concentration camps—Poland—Fiction. | Auschwitz (Concentration camp)—Fiction. | LCGFT: Biographical fiction. | Historical fiction. | Novels.
Classification: LCC PS3613.I3633 V56 2023 | DDC 813/.6—dc23/eng/20221206
LC record available at https://lccn.loc.gov/2022057934

ISBN: 978-1-5387-4114-6 (trade paperback)

Printed in the United States of America

LSC-C

Printing 4, 2023

*To my mom and grandmother, two of the strongest women
I know. You taught me how to be a warrior and
how to write about them. Thank you.*

Prologue

Auschwitz-Birkenau, April 4, 1944

There would be no curtain call tonight. Not for her, at any rate. Her eyes staring fixedly at the crack in the opposite wall, Alma's fingers played with a small, glass vial full of clear liquid. It had taken her a month to secure it from one of the *Kanada* detail inmates. For weeks, he had stalled and grimaced and invented all sorts of excuses—*he'd be glad to help but what she was asking for was nowhere to be had, only the German doctors had it and not their local ones and he didn't know which one of the Germans to bribe; he wasn't quite friendly with them, as she could very well imagine*—in the hope that she would change her mind. Alma had listened and nodded and obstinately replied that *it was all right and she was ready to wait for as long as needed* until she wore him down and he had surrendered at last.

"Here's your goods. The best around, I've been told. Works best as an injection, but you can swallow it if you like. It'll just take a little longer."

"Thank you. You'll get my violin as a payment after—"

"I don't want anything." A categorical shake of the head and a gaze directed at the ground, flattened by the feet of thousands of inmates, most of them now gone and forgotten. "It's mixed with something, so there'll be very little pain before…" He didn't finish, simply staring at her tragically, with his pleading blue eyes, hands thrust in pockets.

Smiling faintly, Alma reached out and gave his wrist a slight pressure, in gratitude for his help.

Pain. If only he'd known the extent of the pain she'd been living with for the past few weeks, he wouldn't have tormented her for so long with this unnecessary wait. This—this would end the pain, not inflict it.

An urgent knock on the door brought Alma out of her reverie. Quickly dropping the vial inside the pocket of her black dress, she clasped her hands and squared her shoulders. "Yes?"

Zippy, a mandolinist, Alma's confidante and a friend she'd grown to love as a sister, stuck her head inside. "Lagerführerin Mandl is here! We're ready to start."

Acknowledging the girl with a nod, Alma gathered her violin case, a conductor's baton, and sheet music from the table. On her way out, she threw a last, appraising glance in the mirror.

The women's orchestra was considered among the privileged prisoners. The so-called camp elite, who wore civilian clothes and were allowed to keep their hair intact. The fortunate ones, who didn't have to break their backs in the quarries or fear the dreaded selections. Nazis' pets, well-fed, and spared the abuse that the others had to endure daily. "A swell arrangement; whatever is there to complain about?" Zippy's words, exactly. But there was little dignity in such a humiliating existence, when one's very reason to live was taken away. Not just taken but snatched, in the middle of the night, in the cruelest of manners; suffocated, burned, dumped into a lake, in a pile of ashes, until nothing remained of it but the memory.

The memory and the pain—dull, never-ending, slowly poisoning her very blood.

Aware of the vial sitting snuggly in her pocket, Alma smoothed her dark locks with one hand and fixed her white lace collar. Tonight, she was giving her last performance. She might as well look the part.

Chapter 1

Auschwitz, July 1943

In the hazy afternoon, Block 10 stood silent and hot. From time to time, an inmate nurse made her unhurried rounds, checking for fresh corpses. Every other day, there were always a few new ones. Not that Alma counted—she had her own fever to worry about—but she heard the nurses pull them from the beds, through her broken sleep, now and then. Some had already been sick when they'd been herded along with Alma onto the train in Drancy, the French transit camp. Some got ill during their journey and no wonder, either, for they'd been packed like sardines, sixty persons per cattle car. Some had died from botched experiments already here, in Auschwitz.

Slowly, Alma roved her gaze over the room. It was rather big, with beds standing so close to each other the nurses had trouble walking between them. But worst of all was the stench, the atrocious, overpowering stench of stale sweat, thick breath, gangrenous flesh, and soiled clothes that made one want to retch.

Unlike the others, Alma's group hadn't been sent to quarantine upon arrival. Neither were they marched straight to gas; instead, they had the doubtful fortune to land here, in the Experimental block—a two-story brick building with windows shuttered closed to guard its sinister secrets from any curious outsiders.

Sometimes, the nurses took pity on them and opened the windows for a few precious moments to ventilate the premises. Though, most of the time, that did more harm than good. Attracted by the smell, swarms of flies and mosquitoes rushed inside and attacked the emaciated bodies with ravenous hunger, spreading more disease and torturing the moaning women with their incessant buzzing and biting. More infected wounds, more corpses taken away by the shaven-headed attendants, one of them invariably marking down the numbers of the deceased in her papers to present them later to their superior, SS Dr. Clauberg. The infamous German order, enforced by the Jewish inmates. Alma was quick to see the irony of such a sad state of affairs.

On her first day in the block, she had naively tried asking for some medication for her fever but was only laughed at. Gathering as much dignity as was possible given the circumstances—a rather difficult undertaking when one had just been shorn like a sheep and given a number instead of her name—she inquired about the X-ray machines she had noticed in two ground-floor rooms, but that question was also ignored by the inmate nurses.

"Mind your own affairs." That was the most she got from Blockälteste Hellinger, a blond woman with a severe face and an armband of a block elder on her left biceps. It appeared that the nurses, even though prisoners themselves, weren't in any rush to make friends with the new arrivals.

"I understand that this is not the Hotel Ritz, but hospitality leaves a lot to be desired here," Alma had noted coolly to her.

Caught off guard, the nurse had looked up from her clipboard and blinked at the new inmate. The entire block had hushed itself instantly. All eyes were suddenly on her. It occurred to Alma that talking back must have been a rare occasion here.

"French transport?" Hellinger measured Alma icily. She spoke German correctly but with a strong Hungarian accent. "I should have guessed. The most stuck-up broads always arrive from there."

"I'm Austrian." Alma smiled.

"Better still. Old Empire ambitions. The SS will adjust your attitude quickly enough, Your Highness."

"You would like that, wouldn't you?"

Much to her surprise, Hellinger shrugged indifferently. "Makes no difference to me. I was appointed as a block elder to mind the order, not bother my head about you lot. Half of you will croak by the end of next week and the other half will be chased through the chimney in the next three months and that's if you're lucky to last that long after the procedure."

The procedure.

Alma was aware of the post-op ward next to theirs, but the access to it had been restricted.

"Sign me up as a volunteer then," she said out of pure spite. Like a cornered animal, she was snapping her teeth in a last attempt at useless self-deception—not so much to injure the enemy, but to persuade herself that she wasn't afraid. "It's all the same to me. The sooner it's all over, the better."

Alma had expected the eruption to follow—the inmates were beaten on the slightest of provocations here—but the block elder remained oddly silent. Hellinger appeared to consider something for some time, then motioned Alma after herself. Eyeing her retreating back with suspicion, Alma followed the head nurse into the dimly lit corridor, where she was standing by the door to the post-op ward, holding it open for Alma. When Alma approached apprehensively, she made a mocking gesture with her hand—*After you, Your Highness.*

In the ward, the air was even fouler. Hellinger stopped at the first bunk, on which a woman lay with a face so ghostly white and beaded with sweat, it resembled a posthumous mask of melting wax.

With a chilling casualness, Hellinger yanked the hem of the woman's robe upward. Alma felt her stomach contracting in revulsion; yet, she applied all her powers to prevent the emotion from showing on her face. Black crust covered the raw, red skin where the blisters had burst on the woman's abdomen. Just above her pubic bone, a long, crudely sewn cut rose in ugly bumps, emanating a sickening stench.

"Bloodless sterilization," Hellinger explained in the dispassionate voice of a college professor. "An extreme dose of radiation applied to the ovaries, followed by their surgical removal to see if *the procedure* was successful. The X-rays are so powerful, they cause extreme burns. The surgery itself is performed mostly without anesthetics. As you can see, this case is badly infected; not that Dr. Clauberg is concerned about it. They're trying to calculate the optimal dose that won't cause such burns, but so far, this is what we're ending up with." She covered the woman's abdomen and gave Alma a pointed look.

For a long time, Alma stood motionless. "Is there a system to it?" she asked at last, finding her voice again. "Their method of selection of inmates, that is."

"They're Germans." Hellinger smiled for the first time. Though, to Alma, it appeared to be a grimace. "Everything's in perfect numerical order. So far, they've completed it on numbers 50204 to 50252."

Alma looked at her left forearm, where her own number, 50381, was tattooed in pale-blue ink.

Hellinger looked at it also. Her features softened a little.

Alma glanced up sharply. Determination was back in her black eyes. "Could I ask you for a favor, perhaps?"

Hellinger gave a one-shoulder shrug.

"Is it possible to get a violin here?"

"A violin?"

Apparently, asking for a musical instrument in Auschwitz was just as unheard-of as talking back to one's superior.

"Are you a violinist or some such?"

"Some such. I haven't played in eight months. I understand that I don't have much time. I should very much like to play one last time, if it's at all possible. If such matter as the condemned person's last wish is still respected in this place."

Hellinger promised to see what she could do. She stole a glance at Alma's pale hand, as if considering taking it into hers for an instant, but changed her mind at the last moment and left the ward abruptly. Giving hope to the condemned was simply cruel.

Alma remained standing before that unmoving ghost of a woman and envied the ones who were gassed upon arrival.

Same endless days. Same block routine that drove one to distraction. Muddy water for breakfast—the Germans called it coffee. Dr. Clauberg making his rounds—"Open your mouth, show me your teeth." A French woman praying in Latin in the corner, rocking back and forth with her hands clasped so tightly, her knuckles turned white.

More muddy water for lunch—the Germans called it soup. The fortunate ones discovered a piece of a rotten turnip in theirs. Sylvia Friedmann, a Jewish prisoner-nurse and Dr. Clauberg's first assistant, reading out the numbers from her list. The woman in the corner rocking faster; thrashing and howling as the two orderlies dragged her out of the ward and along the corridor. Stifling, oppressive silence.

Hellinger collecting the bedsheets and nightgowns for disinfection. Naked, shorn women standing to attention—Dr. Clauberg again, squeezing at their breasts this time. Someone must have reported a pregnant woman. Dr. Clauberg, grinning like a vulture, rubbing his fingers in front of the woman's face—"Milk!" She went quietly, no orderlies this time.

Dinner time. A piece of sawdust bread and a smear of margarine on their palms, licked apathetically by the women. A Belgian girl on the neighboring bunk, her head covered with the blanket, crying for her mother softly—suppressed, pitiful whimpers into the wool, as though so as not to disturb anyone with her grief.

Night. Tears, tears from every bunk around her, hushed prayers, names of the loved ones repeated for hours on end—in endless Kaddish she could no longer bear to hear.

Stillness at last. Silver moonlight spilling from the shuttered window onto Alma's arms. An invisible violin at her shoulder. Her fingers fluttering over the fingerboard like the wings of a butterfly. A bow in her right hand, kissing the violin's strings. Outside, the *Sankas,* camouflaging themselves as Red Cross trucks, taking the bodies away from the neighboring Block 11; Alma had seen them briefly through the cracks in the shutters, setting off in the direction of the crematorium. Inside her head, Strauss, *Tales from the Vienna Woods.*

Music.

Peace.

Serenity.

A world, in which a place like Auschwitz didn't have the moral right to exist.

"Alma? Alma Rosé?"

The young nurse with a fresh, pretty face, whom Hellinger brought to the ward, spoke German with a strong Dutch accent. A warm wave of memories, of happier times in Holland where several Dutch families sheltered her from the Nazis, washed over her. Seasons changed in war-ravaged Europe, but not her hosts' loyalty. Risking their own lives, they had concealed Alma from the Gestapo and asked for nothing in exchange—only for a bit of her marvelous music. Alma was only too glad to oblige; she owed her life and freedom to those brave, selfless people. Repaying their hospitality with her music was the least that she could do. They had moved her from house to house when the rumors of the Gestapo raids swelled to disturbing proportions, but no matter where she was hiding, she had invariably felt welcome and at home.

Naturally, Alma recognized the young girl's face before her; Alma would never forget the kind smiles of the ones who had kept her safe for so long. Though, it took the girl much longer to recognize her. Alma hadn't seen her reflection in days—or was it weeks?—but she could very well imagine what a sorry sight she presented. No longer a celebrated violin player in an elegant evening gown with an open back; that much was obvious.

"Magda, do you know who this is? This is Alma Rosé herself!" The nurse was beaming at Blockälteste Hellinger in apparent delight. "She's a violinist, very famous in Austria!" Misinterpreting Alma's silence, the nurse rushed to explain, "My name is Ima van Esso. You played at our home in Amsterdam. In 1942, a Telemann sonata; remember?"

Of course, she did. A warm house heated against all German regulations; an illegal gathering of music aficionados; mismatched, elegant chairs assembled in a semicircle; women in evening gowns and men in dress suits, all eyes on her—the woman they had adored and risked the wrath of the Gestapo just to hear her play once again.

"You accompanied me. The flute." Somehow, Alma managed the words. The memories cut. It was strange to be holding Ima's hand in hers again. It was a mirthless reunion for all the wrong reasons. The last time they parted ways, Alma was still a free woman.

Ima presented her with a radiant smile. "Yes! It's so kind of you to remember. I was such an amateur . . . most certainly you felt I was beneath your best effort."

Alma felt the beginning of a quiver in her bottom lip and bit into it, hard. "Nonsense. You played excellently." Alma was proud to hear her voice so calm. The self-inflicted pain worked its magic, as it always did.

Magda Hellinger whistled softly through her teeth. "A celebrity, then? Why didn't you say so when you asked me for the blasted violin?"

"Does a person need to be a celebrity to play the violin in this place?" Alma asked, sharper than she had intended.

"Not necessarily, but it helps while trying to obtain one," Hellinger explained. "To organize things in Auschwitz, it requires a lot of work. It will cost me, getting a violin for you. The only person who knows anything about music is this little *Fräulein*. Don't hold it against me, but I had to verify it with her first."

Ima was already pulling at Magda's sleeve as she searched the Blockälteste's face with her pleading eyes. "Oh, Magda, dear, please, do get it for her! You will fall over with amazement once you hear how splendidly she can play. A true virtuoso; you take my word for it. You'll feel as though you're in the Vienna Philharmonic at once—"

"Vienna Philharmonic, my foot," Magda grumbled under her breath, throwing a glance in the direction of the door. "Even if I get one through Zippy, how is she to play it here in secret? Or do you suggest we stage an open concert here, right under Dr. Clauberg's very nose?"

"Dr. Clauberg and the SS *Blockführerin* leave at six." Ima refused to surrender. "They won't come back till the next morning. The compound shall be all but deserted. We'll put a couple of girls as door watchers so they can alert us at once if someone approaches the block."

"What of Block 11? Don't you think they'll hear her play?"

After a pause, Ima shrugged, a gentle, tragic smile appearing on her face. "They're all condemned men there. Do you truly believe they'll report to the SS the last beautiful thing they heard before going to the wall?"

Much to Alma's astonishment, the very next day Magda presented her with a violin. With the slyest of looks, the block elder produced it from inside the pillowcase and held it before bewildered Alma's eyes with visible pride.

"Zippy sends her regards."

Alma grasped at the violin's neck with hunger other inmates displayed only at the sight of bread. "Who's Zippy?" Alma inquired, out of politeness mostly.

All her attention was riveted to the instrument, to which broken pieces of straw still clung from where it had been extracted from its hiding place. Slowly and with great reverence, Alma's fingers caressed the lines of the violin. It had been eight months, eight excruciatingly long months, since she had held her own Guadagnini—her faithful companion that she had to leave for her lover's safekeeping in Utrecht.

Something caught in her throat when Alma remembered Leonard's warm hands on her wet cheeks and his assurances that *she would surely be back before she knew it and that her violin should be right there, with him, awaiting her return, just like he was…*

With a sudden chilling cynicism, she wondered whose bed her Leonard was warming now, much like Heini before him. In the course of the past few years, Alma had grown used to the men's betrayals. Only violins stayed loyal. Her Guadagnini was with her when first husband Váša asked for a divorce; it was still with her when her lover Heini had fled, leaving her to fend for herself in pre-war London. The idea of Alma being the breadwinner in the family didn't appeal to him, much like the discomfort of having to start from a blank slate with a woman he used to swear he loved more than life just weeks before they left their native Austria, with Alma's father in tow. *Poor Heinrich,* Alma mused with a smirk, *didn't even have the guts to look her in the eye before beating his hasty retreat.* She ran from Austria to save her life; he ran back to Vienna to save his—the life of comfort devoid of any unnecessary hardships.

"Who's Zippy?" Magda snorted softly, a conspirator's look about her. "That's for me to know and for you not to find out. Now, put it away and don't even think of touching it until I tell you personally that it's safe. Understood?"

"Yes."

"You ought to say, *Jawohl, Blockälteste*." When Alma looked up at her sharply, Magda softened the order with an unexpected smile. "You don't have to give me their idiotic military response when it's just us girls here. But you ought to say it when the SS wardens, Dr. Clauberg, or Dr. Wirths are present. And you ought to reply in the same manner to them, too, or you'll get it from them, with a whip across your back. Well, not from Dr. Wirths; he's essentially a reasonable man and not violent by nature. In fact, it's thanks to him that we have bedsheets, nightgowns, towels, and even soap in our block. But the others, they're far from being so charitable. They're big on discipline, the SS."

As though not having heard her, Alma continued to stare at the violin with a blissful smile.

Magda Hellinger had already turned to take her leave when she heard an unexpected, "Thank you, Blockälteste."

In spite of herself, Magda discovered that she was grinning. "You're welcome, Your Highness."

That evening, the setting sun colored the underbellies of the clouds tender-pink. All over the camp, silence lay once the outside gangs had been marched in. Inside their cages, the guard dogs slept, locked up for the night. Only Block 10 was in wild excitement. Women, the ones who weren't bedridden that is, moved their cots to free the space for a makeshift stage in the front of the room. Violin in hand, Alma shifted from one foot to the other in great impatience, her nerves strained to the utmost as though she were to play before Vienna's finest again and not this pitiful, suffering herd.

At last, everything was arranged. Perfect silence descended upon the Experimental block. Stepping in front of her audience, Alma brought a bow to the strings and closed her eyes. The first long, tentative note probed the stillness of the descending night. It cut itself short, hesitated, then suddenly gained force and unraveled in a crescendo of runs and, all at once, the very name—Auschwitz—had ceased to exist for its victims. They weren't here any longer; eyes closed, dreamy smiles on their exhausted faces, the women swaying slightly in time with the music, each immersed in her own world where beauty once again had its meaning, where lovers twirled them in their arms to a Viennese waltz, where their loved ones still lived, despite all, for music is eternal and so are the memories.

In the corner, Ima was weeping soundlessly, holding her mouth with her nurse's kerchief. Leaning against the wall, Magda was rubbing her chest as though it physically pained her, being reminded of the fact that something existed beyond this cruel world where her kind was being slaughtered in hundreds of thousands. Yet, she smiled, for along with the pain, the hope had ignited in her once again—hope that perhaps nothing was yet lost if such beauty could still find its way even behind the Auschwitz walls.

Her fingers abuzz with the music, Alma opened her eyes and grinned mischievously at her stunned audience.

"What are you all waiting for?" Her voice suddenly cut through the reverent silence. "Am I playing for nothing? It's not just rude, it's practically amoral to sit still when the waltz is being played. Dance. Well? Up and dance, ladies! I refuse to believe they made you forget how to dance."

For the first few moments, the girls exchanged bewildered gazes. The very idea appeared outrageous. But then Magda herself made a resolute step toward one of the cots, bowed theatrically, and offered one of the women her hand with a gallantry that would make any Old Empire gentleman proud.

"Madame Mila, would you do me the honor?"

Without any hesitation, the girl whom Magda addressed as Mila, placed her narrow palm into the Hungarian *Blockälteste*'s hand. Giggling with disbelief and delight, they began twirling around the small space near the improvised stage, barefoot and tangling in their long nightgowns. Soon, another couple joined them, and another, as Alma looked on, misty-eyed and finally at peace for the first time in months. With the power of her music, she'd made these women free for a few precious moments. Now, she could die happy.

Chapter 2

August 1943

"Your Highness!" Despite the teasing manner in which Magda had addressed Alma, there was a definite measure of respect in her voice now.

Not only that, the block elder had somehow managed to ensure that Alma would be exempt from the experiments just so the Block wouldn't lose their precious violinist who made them forget the horrors of their incarceration each time she played for them. Alma had a strong suspicion that such preferential treatment had something to do with Sylvia Friedmann, Dr. Clauberg's first assistant, who had become a sort of a permanent fixture at their "cultural evenings" as of late. Most certainly it was she who had agreed to strike Alma's name from Dr. Clauberg's list after Alma played her favorite Slovakian songs, which the nurse had requested.

"What do you say to playing for a slightly different audience tonight?" Magda's voice was bright with an artificial cheerfulness in it, but her eyes, averted in discomfort, betrayed the block elder. Behind her back, two newcomers, scrawny like scarecrows, were shifting from one foot to another. "These two girls are from the women's band," Magda continued. "It's them, whom you hear playing every morning when the outside *Kommandos*—the work gangs—walk through the gates. 'Work sets you free' and all that rot. The SS think marching to work ought to be celebrated with music." An expressive roll of Magda's eyes was a clear enough indication of her attitude toward the infamous slogan that was emblazoned above the camp gates—*Arbeit macht frei*. "That was the reason why they organized camp orchestras in the first place."

Alma remained silent.

"Good afternoon, Frau Rosé." The younger woman stepped forward. A striped dress that hung loosely over her frame only emphasized her emaciated state. Oddly enough, her head wasn't shaved—Alma could see the auburn curls neatly tucked under her kerchief. "It's such an honor to make your acquaintance. We're all huge admirers of your talent."

"My name is Hilde, and this is Karla," her friend introduced them both. Just like Karla, Hilde spoke Alma's native language but with a Prussian accent instead of Alma's soft Viennese. She also wore the same striped dress and kerchief. It occurred to Alma that it must have been the band's uniform of sorts.

At once, they began talking over each other:

"We heard from Zippy about the tremendous success of your cultural evenings—"

"She plays in our little orchestra, you see—"

"I play recorder and piccolo—"

"And I'm a percussionist, but, to be truthful with you, all we can produce is the most atrocious *Katzenmusik* that the local Gestapo can use as a form of torture and brassy marches that are only good enough for the *Aussenkommando*—the outside gangs—to march to."

"Sofia, our band leader, tries to organize us the best she can, but we're like monkeys to an organ grinder."

"And it just so happens that today is one of the SS wardens' birthdays and we thought—"

"No."

Startled by such a categorical dismissal—the first thing to fly off Alma's lips that she kept pursed into a tight, unyielding line—the two girls exchanged anxious looks.

Next to them, Magda only snorted softly with good-natured disdain. "I told you she'd refuse. Her Highness doesn't realize where she is yet. If she were assigned to an outside gang for a couple of days, where they'd make her hurl rocks from one pile to another purely for the SS's amusement, that would teach her fast enough how not to turn her little nose away from such opportunities. But we have spoiled her here already."

"I'm not playing for those Nazi pig farmers," Alma said. Seeing the band girls' faces transform with growing horror from such insults being thrown around with such carelessness, she grinned darkly. "Pig farmers," Alma repeated slowly and with great relish. "That's precisely what they are. The scum of the earth that crawled out of all the crevices and flooded the entire continent with their filth. You wish me to play for them? Why would I waste my talents? They wouldn't recognize good music if it hit them full-on in their faces."

Chalk-white and wide-eyed, Karla was already shaking her head so vehemently her auburn curls came loose from under her kerchief. "You mustn't say such things here! People will report you to the *Kapo*, or an SS *Blockführerin,* for a piece of bread and it will all be over for you!"

"All the better. Report me yourselves, if you like. Makes no difference to me." It wasn't mere bravado; she truly didn't care one way or the other if the SS took her to the wall and shot her for her long tongue.

Magda was outright laughing now. *Have you seen anything like it?* her very face seemed to reflect. "Highness." She stepped closer to Alma's bed. "Don't be daft. Get up."

Alma didn't move.

"Well? Shall I help you find your legs? What's the difference who you play for, us or the wardens?" Magda pressed.

"There's a great difference for me."

"The girls are right; someone will report your refusal to play and you'll land yourself in the neighboring block for your arrogance, where the camp Gestapo will make things hot for you."

"They can beat me to death, if such is their wish. It'll change nothing. They can kill me, but they won't make me play."

"I've seen pigheaded people in my life before, but this is something new entirely." Magda shook her head. "I did what I could," she told the band girls before taking her leave. "That's your problem now. I have my own affairs to attend to."

For some time, the three women observed each other silently. Karla was the first one to clear her throat.

"Frau Rosé, I know you're from Austria...We're neighbors. I'm from Germany. Your family is well-known there, too, among artistic circles. What great philanthropists your father and your uncles have always been..." Her voice trailed off. She was watching for Alma's reaction, almost with desperation.

"What does my family have to do with anything?" Alma exhaled, growing tired of the conversation.

Family. The word had long lost its original sense. The Nazis came to her native Vienna and took it all from them; scattered the Rosé clan all over the world. Some fled, including Alma's brother Alfred and his wife. Some stayed, hoping for that collective madness to pass, her elderly father among them. But the madness was only gaining force; every day, some new anti-Semitic law was added to the endless list, and soon, old friends could no longer visit the Rosé house and Alma's father, Arnold Rosé, the former venerable concertmaster expelled from the Philharmonic, was now prohibited to play music written by German composers under his own roof. Alma was almost relieved that her mother had passed away and was no longer around to see it all. Her heart would have most certainly broken at all the inhumanity and terror Hitler's Brownshirts were unleashing on the population.

Family. In the end, there were only two of them left, Alma and Arnold—her beloved *Vati,* who had turned from a celebrated musician into an old broken man before her own eyes in the course of only a few months. Only when he realized that there was no place for him anymore in his own country did he allow Alma to take him away, to the safety of London.

Family, Alma thought, and suddenly felt profoundly miserable.

For a moment, Karla appeared to search for the right words. "Perhaps, if not for yourself—trust me, I understand your sentiments perfectly well—but for the others, for us, would you consider…"

Another uncomfortable pause.

Alma's brows knitted together.

At last, Karla's fellow bandmate released an exasperated sigh. "What she's trying to say is that if you play for them, along with us, they will give the entire band extra rations. As we've already told you, we're not particularly good at what we do, so we need someone…with education."

"Yes, with education and experience—" Karla added.

"And talent—"

"Yes, definitely, talent."

Hilde continued, "What we're saying is that when we play well, they give us extra bread and sometimes even sausage. And we could definitely use some bread and sausage."

Alma's features softened. A faint smile appeared on her lips. "That's the entire trouble? You should have just said so from the very beginning. I have never refused a charity concert in my life."

"You shall play then?" Karla's entire face lit up, as she clasped her hands in front of her chest.

"Yes, only…" With a disgusted grin, Alma pulled her nightgown—the Experimental Block's uniform—away from her body. "I can't very well perform in this, as you can well imagine."

"We'll get you a dress from the *Kanada,* right this instant! You'll look like a princess tonight."

"What's a *Kanada*?" Alma asked.

"The *Kanada* is…ahh…heaven on earth." Dreamily, Karla drew her eyes to the ceiling. "A place where anything can be had."

"It's a Birkenau work detail, the most kosher in the entire camp," Hilde clarified, seeing Alma's confusion. "The set of barracks where they sort the clothes and personal belongings of the new arrivals. Sort, disinfect, and ship them to Germany, for the Aryan folk to wear. If you ever need to 'organize' something, the *Kanada* is the place to go."

Back then, Alma didn't realize just how prophetic those words would be.

They indeed managed to get her an evening gown in under two hours. It smelled faintly of someone else's perfume and was a size too big, but Alma couldn't care less about appearances. Never before did she dress with such reluctance; never before was she overcome with such profound loathing for her audience. But the girls from the orchestra were hungry and so Alma swallowed her feelings and followed them into the night.

Inside the block she was taken to, a few lone bulbs provided the light for the plywood stage. It creaked, even under Alma's slight frame, as she stepped before her audience, violin in hand. It wasn't a Guadagnini by any stretch of the imagination, but it was tuned just fine and had all of its strings about it and, to Alma, that was all that mattered. "Any instrument is good enough in skilled hands," her father used to say.

As she brought the violin to her shoulder, Alma wondered how her *Vati* was faring there, in England. She had left him in the safety of London and herself, against everyone's advice, traveled to Holland, where work could still be found for Jewish musicians. Despite the threat of the German army digging its claws into war-ravaged Europe, Alma had played tirelessly at every venue that booked her for a few precious months and sent her father the proceeds from her little concerts. But then Germany had invaded Holland, just weeks before her planned return to London, and all the communications were suddenly cut off between father and daughter. Raising her bow now in Auschwitz, Alma imagined him drinking his tea somewhere, in a quiet English village, away from the bombs and all this "scientific antisemitism"—safe, untouched by this filth.

She would play for him tonight. Not for this motley crew of elegant, gray uniforms of the SS and civilian attires of the *Kapos*, but for him. She'd play as beautifully as she could, not to please these lowly creatures she despised with great passion, but to make him proud.

She played all of his favorite pieces that night. All of them, from her memory, loudly and defiantly, and also braved the Jewish composers as well. For the dessert, she served them Tchaikovsky, "The Seasons. December; Christmas," just to mock them with the reminder of the nation to which they were presently losing the war. Almost to her disappointment, the SS wardens didn't recognize the joke and broke into tumultuous applause instead.

For the first time in her entire career, Alma didn't bow to her audience.

After the performance, there was indeed extra bread and a piece of moldy sausage. Alma gave hers away to the other girls.

Inside the *Lagerführerin*'s quarters, to which Alma had been summoned by one of the wardens a few days after the concert, the faint aroma of lilacs lingered. As Alma sat across the desk from Maria Mandl, the head of the Birkenau women's camp, an inmate was arranging the fresh flowers in a vase under Mandl's annoyed look. It appeared to Alma that if it weren't for her presence in the room, Mandl would long ago have shouted at the woman. However, the *Lagerführerin* just sat and stared pointedly at the scrawny figure instead. Only after the inmate had left did she shift her gaze to Alma.

Alma guessed her to be in her early thirties, just a couple of years younger than she; though, it was difficult to correctly identify the wardens' ages here, just as it was difficult to identify the inmates' ages. But whereas the inmates aged much too quickly due to starvation, exhaustion, and disease, the wardens' otherwise beautiful faces were marred by the harsh, premature lines from their constant shouting that distorted their mouths and left severe creases between their neatly plucked brows. Hatred aged them just as fast as suffering aged their victims. Alma thought it to be a form of poetic justice.

"My wardens won't stop talking about your performance," Mandl broke the silence first. "Your father was the concertmaster of the Vienna Philharmonic." It wasn't a question; a statement rather, with a measure of thinly veiled respect in it.

Alma recognized a familiar accent. *A fellow Austrian, then, Lagerführerin Mandl.*

"I'm not from Vienna, myself," Mandl continued, shifting in her seat, "but from the Upper parts."

A town—or village—so small she was ashamed to name it. Alma grinned. Just as she'd said: pig farmers, the uniformed lot of them.

"I heard both you and your father play, just before the *Anschluss*."

Naturally, before the *Anschluss*. After the annexation of Austria, every single Jewish musician was dismissed from their position by the Propaganda Ministry's thugs, to be replaced by an Aryan counterpart. An Aryan, who couldn't play to save his life, but that mattered not, as long as his blood was pure.

Alma kept staring at the camp leader without uttering a word. She would lie if she said that Mandl's somewhat uncomfortable squirming from that silence of hers didn't give her a certain pleasure.

"What luck to have you here with us now, don't you agree?" Mandl even smiled at her. It was the smile of a woman who didn't do it often, uncertain and lopsided.

Alma's brow arched. Was this some sort of a tasteless joke?

"I meant to say, Herr Kommandant himself will be most pleased to hear you play for him and his distinguished guests. I'm a great music lover myself, you see. We share that in common."

That's about all we share in common, Alma wanted to say.

"You would most oblige me if you make something suitable out of those women that I'm currently trying to pass off as an orchestra." Mandl uttered a brisk embarrassed chuckle. "You've heard them play. Such so-called music must insult your ears much more than it insults mine."

"It's difficult to play well when all one thinks about is getting some food in one's stomach," Alma countered.

For a few moments, Mandl sat and blinked at her, caught off guard. It was obvious that the first words out of the famous violinist's mouth were not what she had expected to hear.

"I certainly can teach them how to play Viennese-quality music, but I simply can't live or work in such conditions," Alma went on, her voice full of ice. "I saw where they live now, Lagerführerin, and, with all due respect—" she could only hope it didn't come out too sarcastic, "the conditions are atrocious. If you want me to lead your orchestra, I'll need new quarters, assigned specifically to my girls, where we can have a music room to rehearse, storage for the instruments, and access to showers, so we can look presentable for each performance... We'll need new uniforms, not those striped rags they presently wear. And start feeding them well, for heaven's sake! Regular meals, substantial ones, and not those measly portions you throw at them after each performance, like bones to the dogs. It's degrading! How can one create music when one is constantly humiliated to such an extent? Even I won't be able to play in such conditions if you make me live in such a manner even for a few weeks." Alma motioned her head toward the vase with flowers. "You wouldn't leave those lilacs of yours without water and sunlight and expect them to please your senses with their beauty and scent. Can you really, in good conscience, expect us to please you and your comrades with our music if you deny us *our* water and *our* sunlight?"

Her head tilted slightly to one side, Alma waited for Mandl's reaction, annoyed with the fact that she had to explain the obvious to her compatriot.

*

For a few moments, the leader of the women's camp sat frozen, unsure of how to proceed. Her authority had just been challenged, by a Jew no less and an inmate, and she wasn't called the Beast by her charges for nothing. Birkenau was her kingdom, where she, alone, gave the orders. Here, she was not just a rightful ruler, but the Führer's appointed God, with the right to decide who was to live and who was to die. A gun sat snuggly in its holster on her hip, for that very purpose. She had killed for less before, and still…

…and still, Mandl dared not even raise her voice at this woman in front of her, for she would lose her position of superiority at once with a shout, no matter how contradictory that may have sounded. Shouts and curses were daily occurrences in her own family house, coming mostly from her drunkard father and met with just as crude a torrent of insults from her mother, aimed at him: *the good-for-nothing, the useless hog, let him rot in that gutter from which he crawled.*

No one had shouted in the Rosé house; Mandl would have bet money on that. In the Rosé house, they played music, ate from porcelain plates with silver forks, and kissed the ladies' hands gallantly. No, the crude shouting and—worse still—the demonstrations of the whip would only reveal the differences in their upbringing and that Mandl simply couldn't have. In front of the others, she would remain the Beast. In front of Alma Rosé, she'd remain the civil lover of everything refined.

"I suppose that sounds reasonable enough," she finally allowed, contemplatively. "You shall have a new barrack. And new uniforms.

The showers, though, you will have to share with the *Kanada* inmates for now."

"That's perfectly fine, Lagerführerin. And I thank you for your kindness and understanding."

They shook hands at the door—the very first time that Mandl had shaken hands with an inmate. But Alma Rosé didn't act like any regular inmate; rather, a distinguished guest, who graced their godforsaken quarters with her presence. Long after the famous violinist had gone, Mandl stood and stared at her palm with a stupid smile plastered on her face. She had just shaken hands with Alma Rosé herself.

Chapter 3

The Birkenau Music Block had a number on it—12. A gray wooden barrack, it stood on the very edge of the women's camp, tucked neatly away into the relative safety of the outskirts. Here, the grass wasn't eaten by the starved inmates, and pine trees provided the relief of the shadow in the sweltering afternoon; yet, Alma wasn't easily deceived. A fresh, thin film of soot colored the lawn ashen-gray. The pines concealed the wall of barbed wire, at least four meters tall. And, the most sinister of all, the long body of a building with a tall chimney rising from it lay just beside that wall, like a predator in wait. It was slumbering just then—the chimney wasn't belching greasy, foul-smelling smoke into the bright azure sky, but Alma knew precisely what she was looking at. The crematorium.

"Your new block," Maria Mandl announced in the bright tone of a hostess from some Austrian inn. One of the wardens who accompanied Mandl cleared her throat, indicating that favors bestowed by the camp leader upon them, undeserving inmates, ought to be acknowledged.

"Lovely," Alma muttered, her eyes still fixed on the chimney.

"The girls were transferred here just yesterday but as you can hear, they're already rehearsing." Mandl smiled wider. "Come, I'll introduce you properly."

"Achtung!" the second warden bellowed, stepping inside the barrack.

Wiping her free palm discreetly on her blue dress—the Birkenau women's orchestra's new uniform—Alma followed Mandl and her SS entourage inside, holding her violin firmly in her other hand.

At the sight of the SS and the leader of the women's camp herself, the band members instantly leapt to their feet and froze to attention. Mandl waved them back to their chairs, which stood in a semicircle around the conductor's stand in the middle of the practice area. She turned to Alma, looking immensely pleased with herself.

In ordinary circumstances, Alma would have thought it to be a tasteless joke. But then it occurred to her that for Birkenau, which was an even more overpopulated and vermin-riddled version of the main camp Auschwitz, it must have been one of the decent barracks indeed. Alma had never set foot inside a regular women's camp barracks, but she had heard plenty about them. Birkenau women's camp was one of Magda's favorite threats for the new arrivals and not once did its ghastly descriptions supplied by the Hungarian block elder fail to frighten them into submission:

"Keep testing my patience and I'll make it my business to put your name on the transfer list. You think it's bad here, in Auschwitz? Let's see how you'll like sleeping on a wooden bunk in Birkenau with seven or eight women packed next to you like sardines in a tin, instead of having your own bed with a mattress and a pillow. If there's no place for you on the wooden bunks, you'll have to sleep on the lowest level. Do you know what the lowest level means? A wet brick floor. It's so narrow in there, you'll have to crawl inside as though it's a doghouse. If you're fortunate to squeeze along with seven other women into one of the middle-level bunks, prepare to have human waste drip on your face while you sleep—dysentery is a regular occurrence there and once the door to the block is locked for the night, there are no latrine trips for you, my gentle lambs. Everyone does their business right where they lie. To be sure, there's a top bunk, which looks rather good to those who have to sleep below, but it also comes with a caveat: when it rains, it pours directly onto your silly mugs, right through the planks. And in summer, the heat that gathers under the roof will have you suffocated sooner than any gas chamber.

At night, rats come to gnaw on your tender pink heels, and they love the fresh arrivals."

By now, Alma was aware that Blockälteste Hellinger only used such fear-instilling stories to keep her charges in check and had never gone through with her threats to transfer any of them to the hell of Birkenau, but the image was convincing. Even Mandl's reassurances that Alma would get her new accommodation for the orchestra hadn't been enough to ease Alma's apprehension. It was still Birkenau. It was still the anteroom to the gas chamber.

Slowly, she looked around, taking in the premises. There were typical Birkenau three-tier bunk beds, but those had bedding on them, Alma noted with relief. Actual blankets and pillows, one per each bunk. The floor was wooden and not dirt and stone; there was no ceiling, just the roof, but from it, exposed electric bulbs hung on wires and that was already a luxury unheard of by other inmates, who had to trade their bread rations for candle stubs to provide at least some sort of illumination for their barnlike quarters. It was still a mere pitiful shed, but it was a livable pitiful shed and that was all that mattered for now.

Alma offered Mandl a tight-lipped smile. "I don't know how to thank you, Lagerführerin, for your generosity." It took Alma great effort to keep sarcasm out of her voice.

Mandl grinned broadly. "No need to thank me. Contrary to the rumors, I'm open to rational discussion and you brought up certain arguments that I found to be convincing. I only did what was right in this case."

A regular philanthropist with a horsewhip, Alma thought to herself and forced another smile.

"Oh, and this will be your private quarters." Mandl pushed open the door to the room next to the entrance.

It was a closet; not a room and certainly not "quarters." Just four white walls into which a bed, a table with two chairs, and a small cupboard had been squeezed by some magic. *But that was Birkenau for you and beggars couldn't quite be choosers, could they now?* Alma mused darkly. She ought to be grateful she would have a room to call her own, which afforded at least some privacy.

And yet, her sense of justice was outraged. Why should she thank this woman for this doghouse when she wouldn't have been here in the first place had it not been for that demented Führer of theirs and his proclamation that belonging to the Jewish race was suddenly a crime against humanity punishable by death? Why should she be grateful for at least some human decency afforded to her and her new charges when none of them should be here at all; when this entire extermination factory shouldn't exist?

Just shut your trap if you know what's good for you, Highness, Magda's voice sounded in her mind, much too real and knowing. *You hear the gunshots daily by the Wall. You know how revolts end here.*

"Thank you, Lagerführerin," Alma squeezed the words out of herself through gritted teeth. "It is much appreciated."

Just then, she noticed someone's shawl hanging off the back of the chair.

"It looks like someone lives here." Alma gestured toward it.

"Not anymore." Without ceremony, Mandl pulled it from the chair and threw it into the corridor.

It was a sudden and chilling realization, witnessing firsthand how quickly privileges were snatched away from the inmates.

With the same languid, thoroughly rehearsed grace, Mandl motioned Alma after herself as she moved to the center of the practice room. She stopped at the conductor's stand and clasped her hands behind her back. Flanking the orchestra on both sides, her wardens mirrored her pose like two uniformed, demented reflections.

"Meet your new *Kapo* and conductor, Alma Rosé," Mandl announced to the orchestra.

Next to her, a blond woman with a conductor's baton stood in a stiff position, clutching at the useless stick with desperation.

With some sadistic relish, Mandl motioned to her to surrender it to the new authority.

"Czajkowska, from now on your role is reduced to the block elder's duty. Your room will be occupied by the new *Kapo*. You will vacate it as soon as I'm gone and will occupy the room next to it. You are to listen and obey your new *Kapo* and conductor in everything she says." Slowly, the camp leader roved her heavy gaze around the orchestra as though to drive her point across. "If you work hard enough, Frau Rosé will make something suitable out of you."

Frau Rosé. Alma was aware of stunned gazes directed at her. She wondered if they recognized the name or were astonished that Mandl addressed her with the respectful Frau. She stole a glance in the camp leader's direction; saw how the girls shrank away from her—a frightened school of fish before a great white shark. It must have appeared inconceivable to them that the great white shark had respect for anyone who was not a fellow, gray-clad predator.

"However, if she reports to me that you're sabotaging her work, you'll find yourselves in one of the *Aussenkommandos* turning ground outside the camp for twelve hours straight instead of making music. Am I making myself clear?"

A loud and slightly terrified, "*Jawohl, Lagerführerin*" reverberated around the vast block.

Satisfied with the effect her words produced, Mandl turned to Alma. "I have delegated all of your requests to my wardens. I assume everything should have been taken care of by now. But if you find something not to your satisfaction, delegate your concerns to me through my Rapportführerin Singer or through Spitzer from the *Schreibstube*." Mandl jerked her chin toward a young woman she had addressed as Spitzer from the camp administration office, who held a mandolin and had a somewhat sly look about her. "Spitzer reports both to Singer and to me personally, so either way, your concerns will be delivered to me in a timely fashion."

"Thank you, Lagerführerin." Alma slightly inclined her head in the pause that followed.

For some reason, instead of leaving them to their devices, Mandl appeared to hesitate.

"Does Lagerführerin have any special requests for me perhaps?" Alma inquired, summoning another well-bred smile to her face.

As though encouraged by the violinist's words, Mandl brightened, visibly pleased. "Could you perhaps play something for them? So they can understand at last what sort of music I've been trying to extract from them this entire time."

Alma saw through her—that wasn't the camp leader's main reason. She merely wished to hear Alma play for her own pleasure. The roles had finally reversed for the peasant girl from Upper Austria, who used to stand in the cheapest standing place in the Vienna Philharmonic and for the violin virtuoso, who had played on stage in her elegant silk gown. Now, the former peasant girl could have the virtuoso all for herself, and Alma understood it all too well.

"Would Lagerführerin mind my playing Monti's 'Czardas'?" asked Alma.

For an instant, Mandl froze under her SS wardens' inquisitive gazes.

Alma barely restrained herself from grinning openly. Her thoroughly veiled jab had hit its aim with a wonderful precision: the self-proclaimed sophisticated lover of everything refined had not the faintest idea who Monti was and what that cursed "Czardas" of his sounded like.

Though, Mandl recovered her poise quickly enough—Alma had to give the camp leader that. "Oh, I don't care one way or the other. Whatever you wish to play is fine."

Alma patiently waited for Mandl and her SS wardens to settle in the front row, tucked the violin under her chin and stroked the strings with her bow, plunging the entire block into the depths of the folkloric piece which her father had made her practice when she was still a young girl, for hours on end, in some long-forgotten life of hers. Professor Rosé—her beloved *Vati,* ever the perfectionist, made her play it again and again until she had learned it by heart and could play it with her eyes closed and without any sheet music, much like she did now, to the SS women's astonishment.

She obliterated them with that short and rather uncomplicated piece, just like she had obliterated the entire audience and music critics in the Vienna Philharmonic, rendering them all speechless and forcing them to drop at last their condescending tone whenever they wrote about her playing. *Very good technique, but still much too stilted. Much too masculine; she doesn't let herself be passionate with the instrument as she ought to*...She had already made those self-important ravens in their tailcoats explode in the applause; making these SS women do the same was a child's game. Here they were, clapping their hands off like children, looking at her with outright wonder—however did they manage to catch such a rare butterfly in their ghastly collection?

Regarding them closely and with a carefully concealed contempt, Alma wondered the same. Bowing to her gray-clad audience—but not too deeply—she inquired if they desired to hear anything else.

"Prepare something for tonight together with an orchestra, if you can," Mandl asked, getting up to leave. "We'll invite a few SS officers."

As soon as the door closed after them, Alma found herself one on one with her new charges. There were about twenty of them, not counting the former conductor and two girls—Hilde and Karla—whom Alma already knew. All appeared to study Alma closely, impressed but visibly on their guard. After a quick inspection, Alma concluded that at least one of them, that very Spitzer from the *Schreibstube,* belonged to the so-called camp elite. As soon as the rumors about Alma's transfer to Birkenau had begun to swell, Magda Hellinger had instructed her personally how to recognize such details—if she wished to survive it, that is.

The shorter the number on the prisoner's breast, the more important their status. Short numbers were the early prisoners, the so-called camp VIPs. It was them who were made into the very first *Kapos*—inmate functionaries—and block elders. Most of the administrative positions in the camp belonged to their caste. Easily recognizable among the camp's population, they strutted about in civilian suits and spit-shined boots, not unlike the ones worn only by their bosses in the SS. They wore their hair neatly parted to one side and checked their wristwatches lazily as they smoked imported cigarettes while supervising their underlings. Much like the SS, they had the right to take or save lives—a heavy baton hung attached to their hip as a sinister reminder of such power granted by their uniformed superiors.

"Everyone's corrupted in the camp, to a greater or lesser degree." Magda had taught her the local ways just a few days ago. "It's important to know whom to bribe. The SS will take anything—gold, foreign currency, jewelry—but procuring that very stuff is something only *Kanada* inmates can do. Have you seen their women? Hair done up like for some French fashion show, nail polish, perfume, earrings—*Teufel*," she cursed—*hell*, "some of them fare better here than they did at home! So what that they have the crematorium working ceaselessly? Their fellow inmates are herded inside the facility to be gassed and burned and the *Kanada* night shift sunbathes and sings songs just behind the very wall that separates them from the gas chambers."

Magda shook her head in apparent disbelief, before continuing.

"And *Kanada* men, those are veritable stock-market traders! When I went there to procure sheets and towels for our block on Dr. Wirths' orders, I couldn't believe my eyes at first. Every few minutes, a new transaction was being made. One has silk stockings, just pulled out of some poor soul's suitcase that has most likely been gassed by then, and he offers them to a *Kanada* girl for ten dollars. The *Kanada* girl pulls the money out of her bra—they have underwear there, and what underwear, let me tell you!—and gives it to him like it's nothing. It's a good deal for her, considering, for she will sell it later to an SS warden for thirty and will have twenty for herself. Then another trader appears; he has French lavender soap, still unopened—a treasure! Someone trades a bottle of Hennessy they had just discovered for it. And so it goes between them the entire day as they sort through all those riches, and as long as they hand over part of their haul to the SS on duty—now, the SS only take foreign currency or jewelry because it's easier to hide from their own superiors—it's all safe for them to do so."

Her gaze riveted to the Hungarian block elder, Alma had listened intently, taking it all in, purposely silent in order not to interrupt Magda with questions just yet. Such information could turn out to be life-saving in her nearest future. She could always ask for specifics later; now, it was a matter of paramount importance to acquire as many facts as possible, to memorize them as best she could, to sort them into suitable compartments—the SS, the prisoner hierarchy, the price of an inmate's life in American dollars or dental gold.

"The markings on the inmate's breast are just as important as the numbers," Magda had continued. "In men's camp, Green Triangles—criminals—constitute half of the *Kapos*. Red Triangles—political prisoners—constitute another half. Most of the Reds there are Poles, while the Green ones are mostly Germans, so the Greens are considered higher than the Poles just due to their Aryan status. But the Reds are better organized and so the Greens have to be careful around them if they know what's good for them."

Alma's head had begun to ache. A hungry stomach didn't inspire such mental gymnastics, yet Alma had forced herself to stay focused on the nurse's words.

"With women, it's pretty much the same, but there in Birkenau, asocial prisoners—Black Triangles—mostly function as *Kapos*. They are mostly German prostitutes. Then go Greens, but, naturally, there are few of those. Then Reds and only after them—us, Jews, the Yellow Stars. A rather amusing arrangement, if you think of it—murderers and prostitutes having the unrestrained authority over former professors, doctors, journalists, and artists—but this is Auschwitz-Birkenau for you. Blood is everything. But the connections are still more important than blood."

Now, as she stood before these women, more than half of them Reds, Alma couldn't be more grateful for Magda's instructions. The Reds must have been Polish. Presently, they began to exchange hushed remarks in their language that gradually grew louder in volume. Their lips moved, but their eyes remained on Alma, a mixture of suspicion and hostility in them, and were hard and unblinking.

Emboldened by the fact that their new head of the orchestra appeared to be in no rush to establish any sort of authority over them, one of the girls pointed at Alma's yellow star and made what sounded like a complaint to their former *Kapo*. Alma didn't have to understand their language to understand the meaning: *why was the Jew appointed as their leader?* The situation was familiar by now; she had encountered such attitudes all over Hitler's Europe and had grown perfectly immune to it. What disappointed her was a flash of resentment in her fellow inmates' eyes. Poles or not, surely they should have learned by now that they were all in this together? The SS were the enemy, not her.

Alma shifted her glance toward the Jewish girls. Contrary to the Polish ones, they remained silent and subdued, casting their eyes about without meeting hers, looking guilty for no particular reason.

Only Spitzer from the *Schreibstube*, the representative of the camp elite, regarded Alma with an unreadable expression on her face. Fine-boned and wiry, she possessed two gems of black liquid eyes and a habit of narrowing them now and then, which gave her a cunning expression. Whether it was curiosity or the attempt to size her up, Alma decided to ignore Spitzer for now and instead offered her hand, palm up, to the former *Kapo*.

"My name is Alma Rosé. It's a pleasure to make your acquaintance. Please, accept my sincerest apologizes concerning the manner in which we had to meet and allow me to assure you that it is in no way my intention to usurp your power over the block. You may keep your *Kapo*'s duties and I shall obey you as one of your orchestra members and your charge. The only thing I will ask of you is to allow me to keep control of the musical activities. I don't mean it as an insult to you or your band—"

"None taken," the former *Kapo* interrupted her with a smile and grasped Alma's hand. She spoke German very well, with a very slight Polish accent. "Sofia Czajkowska, political. It's my pleasure to make your acquaintance as well. And you're absolutely right concerning both the band and my conductor's abilities. I have none, but Lagerführerin Mandl has taken it into her head that I'm related to the Russian composer Tchaikovsky—I'm not—and apparently, it was enough for her to put me in charge. I can play a few tunes on the guitar well enough, but none of that sophisticated stuff that you just produced. So, by all means, take over the orchestra and don't spare us. We all have one goal and one goal only—to come out of here alive at one point or another, and it would be utterly idiotic of me, or anyone else for that matter, to stand in your way. It's obvious that out of us all you have the most experience—do what you must, Frau Rosé, just keep us alive."

"Please, call me Alma."

"I will. But it's better if they don't." A discreet nod toward the orchestra. "It'll give you more authority." Turning toward her former charges, Sofia began speaking Polish, apparently, translating whatever had just transpired between the two women to the girls who didn't speak German.

The dissatisfied grumbles subsided. One by one, the band girls began nodding enthusiastically to her words. Soon, a few of them were even smiling at Alma, to which she breathed out with relief. The transition of power had been as smooth as one could have only hoped.

"It was very smart of you." Spitzer from the *Schreibstube* approached Alma a few minutes later. "If you tried taking charge without asking Sofia first, she could have made your life a living hell here, you take it from me."

"I'm not interested in any positions of power," Alma explained calmly. "I'm only here to ensure that we all come out of here alive. That's all that matters to me."

"I can tell." For a few moments, the young girl with those sly black eyes appeared to be considering something; then, suddenly, thrust out her hand and announced her name, a different one from that offered by Mandl. "I'm Zippy. Zipporah, actually, but that's what the local underground knows me as. I don't have to tell you that I must remain Helen Spitzer from the *Schreibstube* for everyone else."

"Of course." Alma took her narrow palm in hers and pressed it with great emotion, touched to the marrow with such an unexpected expression of trust.

She had heard Magda speak of the camp resistance with a measure of reverence and fascination. She had also been warned to stay as far away from them as possible, if she knew what was good for her, for those underground types ended up on the camp gallows with frightening regularity. Smuggling, clandestine radios, handwritten leaflets, minor-scale workplace sabotage—in Magda's eyes, their resistance activities were relatively harmless, but, apparently, the SS saw things differently. For some reason, Alma thought the underground types were all men—perhaps, former Red Army soldiers with at least some formal training in combat, or French militants shipped to Auschwitz by the Gestapo for their Resistance activities. Certainly not orchestra mandolinists with shrewd eyes and the white, fragile hands of an archetypical musician.

"So, it was you who got me my new violin?" She was studying Zippy with new-found respect.

"Is it any good?" Zippy bared her beautiful teeth in a grin. "It must be good, if you extracted such music out of it just now."

"To be truthful, I did it out of spite."

"I figured." Zippy dropped a mischievous wink. "I like you. You'll do just fine here, take my word for it." Before long, she was back in her chair, her mandolin at the ready. "Frau Conductor, command. We're ready."

Chapter 4

The SS concert that evening was a great success, even though Alma pulled it off almost entirely on her own shoulders, letting the girls accompany her only in certain places that all of them could manage. Her back wet with sweat, Alma patiently waited for the camp leader to finish accepting congratulations from her colleagues on such a brilliant addition to her orchestra. Back home, in Vienna, she would have already downed her obligatory glass of water that would have awaited her backstage before rushing back to her audience. But this was Birkenau for you. Thirsty and annoyed, Alma looked on as the SS exchanged pleasantries at her expense, congratulating themselves on her talent.

Afterward, instead of a moldy sausage and a piece of stale bread, the orchestra received an actual meal—potatoes with sauerkraut and even some meat—from the very grateful camp leader. Upon Alma, her new favorite pet Jew, Mandl bestowed an additional favor the very next day: a personal pass signed by Lagerführerin herself and a permission to go to the *Kanada*.

"Take whatever you like," Mandl declared generously when Alma inquired politely what it was precisely that she was permitted to take. "Show the *Rottenführer* in charge your *Ausweis* when you get there and give him my personal oral orders to provide you with whatever you need. And do not lose your pass. Only very few privileged inmates have those, so make sure you keep it on your person at all times whenever you go outside women's camp territory. My colleagues sometimes get overly enthusiastic in their duties and may very well shoot you if they find you wandering around without an Ausweis."

It was an odd and frightening experience, walking through the camp alone. Well-trodden paths, a maze of barbed wire, guard towers, endless rows of barracks and shouts—*Halt!*—coming from above, menacing and invisible, whenever Alma stepped in the wrong direction. Rigid with fear, she held her arms up high with the *Ausweis* in it, screaming at the black muzzles of machine guns directed at her.

"Please, don't shoot! I have a pass!"

"It's a restricted zone!"

"Lagerführerin Mandl sent me to the *Kanada* detail."

"Does it look like the *Kanada* to you?"

"I don't know where it is…Could you perhaps kindly point me in the right direction?"

The muzzle of the gun swung to the left grudgingly. "Along that road, through the men's camp, to the left of the medical barracks."

"Many thanks," she replied, backing away, half-expecting a burst of the machine-gun fire.

"Watch where you're going! Another step and you'll fry yourself on the electric fence. Feebleminded cow!"

By the time she had reached the men's camp, Alma's back was entirely wet with sweat. The sun was rolling westward, but the air was dull with ash. Foul-smelling clouds of it dimmed the dusky sky and turned it into premature twilight. It snowed in great greasy flakes all around her; the remnants of the annihilated humanity landing softly on her exposed skin.

Alma wiped her hand down her arm, but the ash only smeared. Her palm was now a dusty dull-gray. It was in her eyelashes, impossible to blink away, in her nose; she opened her mouth to take a deep breath and tasted it on her tongue.

Tearing her kerchief off her head, she turned it inside out and cleaned her tongue, her face, her eyes, her bare arms. Such was her terror and disgust that it had dulled her other senses to such an extent that another enraged SS shout—"Out of the way!"—had scarcely registered with her. Only when the guard had physically installed himself in front of her, eyes wild with rage, hand raised with a whip in it, did Alma leap back guided by sheer instinct.

"I have an *Ausweis*—"

"Stay out of the way! The men are marching!"

Just now did she see them, led by a *Kapo*, five abreast, a ghostly army of gray skeletons returning from their daily labors.

The outside gangs.

It was a grotesque parade; Dante's Inferno, the ninth circle of hell. They marched and marched, all shaved heads; scaly, weather-worn skin; emaciated frames; black, bare feet; torn rags on which the stripes had long disappeared under the layers of blood and dirt. Their eyes stared fixedly forward, dull and devoid of a single spark of hope. Their shoulders were stooped like those of the ancient men, yet they couldn't have been older than forty.

Caps pressed against their seams, they marched past the SS man, who towered over them like some ancient cruel deity. From time to time, he amused himself with slashing their sweat-smeared cheeks with his whip. They barely flinched, having long lost the ability to feel the pain. They marched on, the tormented, accusing apparitions, reduced to nothing, the former lawyers, civil servants, prominent physicians, university professors, set decorators, bank clerks. It appeared almost inconceivable now, the very idea that they used to be anything but this faceless slave force.

Alma felt herself shuddering. Before that day, she had carried the bubble of self-deception like a sort of a protective cocoon around herself. She was Alma Rosé. The SS wouldn't dare touch her. Now, she was suddenly terrified by the chilling thought that at least some of these men must have nursed the same exact empty illusion when they had stepped onto the Auschwitz ramp.

Moving as though in a nightmare, Alma stumbled her way to the *Kanada* detail. Here, it was a different world entirely. Astounded, Alma stopped and contemplated the rows and rows of warehouses that stood with their doors thrown open. From inside, women's laughter could be heard, brilliant and careless. There were no SS guards in sight; only a *Kapo* offered lazy comments from the pile of mattresses on which he was presently lying like some Oriental pasha, a cigarette in hand. Although, it appeared that inmates only half-listened to his half-hearted instructions. If it wasn't for the *Kapo's* distinctive armband, Alma would have trouble distinguishing him from his underlings—nearly everyone in the *Kanada* was dressed in civilian clothing.

In the distance, a group of girls attired in dark slacks, shoes, and light summer shirts were sorting the luggage. Alma stared at their styled hair, wristwatches, and dazzling smiles and thought she was dreaming. A couple of inmates were hurling the suitcases from the back of a truck onto the ground, their muscular arms straining under white undershirts. Only striped caps betrayed their belonging to the camp population.

The contrast with the men's camp was beyond any comprehension.

An SS man with the *Rottenführer* insignia on his uniform strolled out of one of the warehouses, yawned, and stretched his arms over his head, squinting at the setting sun like an overfed cat. Having approached the group of women, he pointed at something lazily and grinned—one of the girls appeared to have made a joke. Another inmate trotted over to him, took his cap off, clicked his heels and opened his palm. Interested, the SS man fingered at the object. In an instant, it disappeared into his pocket.

The SS will take anything, Alma recalled Magda's words. But in such an insolent manner? Right in the open?

Though who would say anything to that? Perhaps, it was a blessing in disguise that the SS were so corrupted. Just one look at the inmates who supplied them with all of these riches was enough of an argument in the SS corruption's favor. What a difference they made from the lifeless army on its last breath Alma had just seen marching back to their airless barracks.

She approached the *Rottenführer* and showed him her *Ausweis* signed by Mandl herself. He barely glanced at it and signed to one of the women who were presently emptying the suitcases within mere steps from him.

"Kitty will escort you inside." He lit a cigarette and blew the smoke away from Alma's face. "No gold, jewelry, or currency is allowed to be taken. Reich orders."

Alma almost asked him what she would do with that currency here, but stopped herself. "Yes, Lagerführerin Mandl has told me that much."

"Jawohl, Herr Rottenführer," the guard corrected her.

Alma looked up at him; much to her amazement, he was grinning.

"You ought to say, *Jawohl, Herr Rottenführer,*" he explained once again as one would to a child. "We're the army."

"I'm a musician." In spite of herself, Alma discovered that she was smiling too.

"Well, then." He spread his arms in a helpless gesture, looking as though he found her positively amusing just then. Even the SS were different here than in the men's camp, soothed by the abundance of the riches all around them and tolerant toward the inmates, from whom they could profit with such great ease.

The female prisoner whom he had addressed as Kitty was already pulling Alma away by her sleeve. A few hairpins were holding her elegant dark curls in place and she had lively eyes and neatly plucked eyebrows that moved expressively when she talked.

"No fraternizing with the guards in the open," she began whispering as soon as they were away from the SS man's earshot. "In private, by all means. But not in the open. There are rumors that some bigwigs are coming from Berlin with the inspection; if they see you chatting so amicably together, he'll be shipped off to the front. But you, you'll end up over there." She pointed her beautiful, neatly manicured finger in the direction of the chimneys that were towering even over the warehouses next to which *Kanada* women worked. From inside them, columns of thick, brownish smoke were rising. This was where "the snow" was coming from.

Alma made no reply; only gulped a mouthful of smoke when the wind blew in their direction and nearly gagged with the sickly-sweet smell of the burnt flesh.

Kitty arched her brow expressively. She didn't appear to be ruffled in the slightest. They worked next to these monstrosities, and she had long grown used to the scent.

Before long, she was leading Alma through the warehouse, holding an empty pillowcase open and filling it with goods in the view of her "guest" still trailing her in a state of apparent shock.

"Underwear. You definitely need underwear, a few changes. What size do you wear?" She quickly measured Alma's tall, slender frame with her assessing gaze. "European 42. Bra size, 2? This is a B; must have come from the department store! Look at it, there's still a label on it. What luck for you then. Pure silk—here, enjoy. Would you like a slip, too? I imagine so. Here, this one should fit you perfectly."

Yet another item was pulled from a pile of undergarments. Alma stared at the sorting table in horror. It was overflowing with silk, ribbons, and simple white cotton. The owners of all of those beautiful things were being burned just meters away, and this dazzling creature next to her was chirping with the professionalism of a Wertheim top salesgirl, advertising the goods to the stunned Alma as one would to a rich client.

"And now for the stockings...toothbrush...soap; here, a lilac one, straight from Paris! What do you say to that? It's your fortunate day today, isn't it?" Kitty was positively beaming, happy with such a haul.

Alma stared at her through the film of tears and wondered if one day she would also grow used to the smell and to the fact that she was wearing dead people's undergarments and smile about it.

As though reading her mind, the girl's smile suddenly dropped. "Quit staring at me like I'm such a heartless monster. Do you think it does not bother me in the slightest? And what of the *Sonderkommando*, our own Jewish men who burn those very corpses there daily and nightly; do you think it doesn't bother them? Burning their own families, friends, neighbors?"

In the pause that followed, only Kitty's heavy breathing could be heard.

"I came here from Slovakia with the very first transport in 1942," the *Kanada* girl continued. "Back then, these crematoriums didn't exist yet. Only one old one in Auschwitz and that one was good for nothing—the walls of the chimneys kept crumbling after every other use. Back then, they didn't burn them like they do now. They buried them in mass graves right over there, in the fields. Do you think it stinks here now? You should have been here when the ground began rising from all that corpse poison that soon began to seep into our water. You should have been here when they began digging them out and burning them, half-decomposed, on pyres so tall, people in Krakow must have seen the fires. Some of the *Sonderkommando* inmates threw themselves into those pyres because they couldn't take doing such a job for the SS any longer. If you were here back then and saw what we saw, I would have granted you the right to look at me with such disdain. We all had to unlearn how to mourn our people if we wanted to survive. Sensitivity doesn't live long here. Sensitivity gets people killed. I strongly advise you to get rid of it if you wish to make it back into the world. Now, do you want a wristwatch or not?"

The unexpected question sounded almost like an accusation. With a great effort, Alma pulled herself together. Having sentiments about all this rot was fine and well, but life went on, even here in the camp, and she would need the watch as a Kapo in order for her entire barrack not to get shot for missing the roll call. "Yes, please."

"Leather strap like mine or metal? Can't give you gold—not allowed. Those are all accounted for."

"Leather is fine."

When Alma stepped outside the warehouse, a pillowcase bursting at the seams with dead people's belongings, the bright August sun spilled its golden light onto her with astonishing insolence. Perhaps, it had long turned off in itself the ability to feel anything too. Perhaps, with time, so would she.

Chapter 5

It was still dark when Sofia shook Alma awake.

"Don't get used to it," the former *Kapo* said, handing Alma a whistle. "This is actually your duty."

Sitting in bed and trying to blink away the sleep, Alma regarded the whistle in puzzlement.

"This is to wake up the block," Sofia clarified. Alma could only guess that she was grinning. She recognized amusement in the former *Kapo*'s voice, but her face in the pre-dawn hour was a mere shadow. "As soon as they're up, it is your duty to ensure that they make their bunks and look presentable before the *Appell*—the roll call. As soon as they're dressed, you take them outside to line up for the inspection. Wardens Drexler and Grese will come down to ensure that everyone is present."

Alma was instantly on guard—the names rang a bell. The inmates trembled when they whispered them.

Getting possession of herself, she swung her legs from her bed. It would be utterly idiotic to antagonize the wardens with her incompetence on the very first day. It was four in the morning and the barrack was damp and chilly. Alma whistled for the girls to get up.

"Your *Schreiberin*, the block clerk, is in charge of the roll call list you will give to the wardens along with your morning report." Sofia followed her back into her room.

Her presence was reassuring, this camp veteran who knew all the ins and outs, who didn't have to give a damn about Alma's success as a *Kapo*, but who did, with admirable dignity.

"Who's my block clerk?" In the darkness, Alma was groping for her dress, which was hanging on the nail behind the door.

Sofia turned on the table lamp. Now, Alma could see it clearly—the Polish inmate was smiling. "Quit your fidgeting. You'll get used to the routine before long. Zippy is your *Schreiberin,* but when she's at the camp administration office, you can appoint someone else as her replacement."

"Do we have the time to wash up?" Alma was struggling furiously into her dress.

"Only very quickly. We're lucky there's a latrine and running water just behind our barrack for our personal use. The others have to run to the communal latrines. You imagine what madness that is. I lived through it when I was in the regular block. Trust me, you won't wish it on your worst enemy. After standing in line for half an hour, you have ten seconds to squat over that filthy hole and do your business. If you take longer than that, they will simply shove you off, finished or not. God help you if you have filth on your legs after that—the SS who stand outside will beat you and send you to the penal *Kommando* for being 'a dirty pig.' I need hardly add that there's no toilet paper or even a scrap of newspaper in the vicinity. If you wish to organize some, you ought to trade your ration for it." She released a mirthless chuckle. "Good times." The sarcasm in her voice was audible. "Things I will be telling my grandchildren if I ever come out of here."

A whirl of activity followed. With infinite patience, Sofia instructed Alma on the precise manner in which the blankets had to be tucked in. She clipped a couple of girls on their ears for dirty fingernails and sent them back to the latrine behind the block—"Do not return until you've scrubbed yourself pink!" Alma was still checking the last few girls' footwear and Sofia was already holding the door open for the ones who'd been cleared, counted by Zippy and appointed to a day duty *Kommando:* "March, march, march! You have thirty minutes precisely to take these stools and music stands to the camp gate and return. If you're late for the roll call . . ."

Sofia didn't have to finish her threat. The girls burst out of the barrack, weighed down with their load, as though Satan himself was chasing them.

In the morning, the fog rolled in and shrouded the camp with gray. Shivering against the wet mist, the Music Block lined up in neat rows of five in front of their barrack. Someone in the back tried to suppress a sneeze, in vain. Sofia whipped around and gave the offender a glare full of magisterial wrath.

Rigid with fear and cold, they stood and waited.

The wardens made their appearance some twenty minutes later. They walked as though on a stroll, two elegant figures in warm woolen uniforms. The brunette had a dog leash wrapped around her gloved palm. Alma stared at the Alsatian and was suddenly overcome with the stinging sense of injustice at the very fact that this woman before her had a dog, whereas she, Alma, had to surrender hers to family friends before fleeing Austria.

"The brunette is Rapportführerin Drexler," Sofia whispered to Alma almost without moving her lips. "When you give her your report, keep your eyes on the ground. She is known to shoot inmates who have the impertinence to stare at her. It offends her delicate Aryan senses."

The blond—a glacial, impersonal beauty with rolls of platinum hair and porcelain skin—had a horsewhip in her hand. She was playing with it as some socialite would with a fan during a soiree.

"The goldilocks is Irma Grese, Drexler's lieutenant," Sofia supplied in the same manner. "She wants to be in the movies when the war is over. Too bad no one told her that the Germans won't be the ones who shall win it."

Alma was amazed that someone could chuckle so gleefully without moving a single facial muscle.

Rapportführerin Drexler received Alma's report and took the list from her without once glancing into it. Now that she stood so near, Drexler's Alsatian sniffed at Alma's hand and suddenly nudged at it with his wet nose. Before she could stop herself, Alma discreetly caressed the silky, warm ear and all at once felt profoundly and ridiculously happy, even if it was only for a few short instants.

"Whatever did you do that for?!" Sofia was upon her as soon as the wardens dismissed them and cleared the *Stubendienst* girls—the block caretakers—to fetch the Music Block's breakfast: the disgusting camp coffee. The orchestra were given precisely ten minutes to consume it before marching out to the gates, instruments in hand, to see off the outside gangs with a brassy German marching tune. "That dog could have taken a chunk out of your hand!"

"He wouldn't. He's a good dog."

Gloomily, Alma studied the camp coffee in her hand. In her opinion, there was no such thing as a bad dog. All dogs were inherently good. She used to have one just like Drexler's Alsatian, black with tan paws, back home, in Austria. Arno's pitiful whines nearly tore her heart in half when she was saying her goodbyes to him, as though he understood that she wouldn't be coming back. He nearly strangled himself on the leash, trying to get to Alma as she was walking farther and farther away and soon disappeared from his view as she stepped onto the train. Alma's gentile friends, the family who gladly agreed to take him in, were holding him hard as they were seeing her off at the train station, but the dog still cried in such a pitiful manner, and Alma herself had begun to weep inside her compartment. Arno knew she wasn't setting off for one of her scheduled tours. The breed was much too intelligent for its own good.

"I've seen that *good dog* maul people to death here," Sofia said.

"Rot!" Alma looked at her savagely. The morning's pent-up nerves had suddenly snapped.

"Rot?" Sofia appeared almost sympathetic, as though she had long grown used to such outbursts. "You'll see it for yourself as soon as we march out."

The words turned out to be prophetic. They were marching toward the main camp gates along the cinder road in the same military formation, instruments in hand. In the distance, the inmates were taking off the remains of the last night's suicides from the stretch of the barbed wire. There were at least two dozen of them—stiff bodies with their black gums bared in silent screams and fingers twisted as though even in death they were trying to claw their way out of their emaciated shells.

"Stack them stiffs nice and neat, like firewood," the SS warden was pointing at the side of the road in a businesslike manner. "If the clothes are still good, take them off. And make it snappy! The truck shall be here any minute to pick them up. If you aren't done by then, I'll put you into its back instead of these stinking carcasses."

The mist shone on the faces of the dead, accumulating, rolling down their cheeks as though the dead were crying. Alma led her little troop past one of the growing mounds and looked straight ahead, straight ahead only.

Through the thickening fog, endless rows of barracks crept into sight. In front of them, a motionless army of rags and gray skulls. The mist curled and stole along the ground, distorting their features. Only an occasional gray uniform glided through the vaporous clouds, the collector of the souls. The entire camp was one boundless cemetery and it was only by some mistake that some of them arrived here still alive.

Alma felt moisture on her face and wiped it with her hand. It must have been the fog.

A slap echoed resoundingly around the compound.

"...Go on and fetch her then!" The mist carried far Rapport-führerin Drexler's voice. "You know the rules. All dead ought to be present during the roll call."

Alma's troop continued to march. An inmate trotted over in front of them, searching the barbed wire with wild eyes. Someone from the clearing *Kommando* told her that the electric current had been turned off—she could retrieve the dead from her block with her bare hands. Still, the inmate hesitated. Craning her long, thin neck but not quite approaching the heap of corpses, she was trying to recognize her bunkmate in one of them.

It went on for some time. Alma had already marched past her and another ghastly heap that was now thankfully left behind. Then, suddenly, there was panting and the unmistakable sound of dog claws digging into the ground when the animal charged full speed. Alma swung round. It was Drexler's Alsatian, slamming its mass of pure muscle into the defenseless woman and burying her under its weight. There was nothing human in the scream that pierced the eerie silence. The dog's sharp teeth glistened white in the fog for one short instant, then tore once again into the soft human flesh.

Alma realized that she had stopped, but for the life of her, she couldn't force her legs to move just then. Only Sofia's rough shove snapped her out of her stunned state.

"What is there to goggle at? Keep marching. Do you wish to be next? Drexler will see to it fast enough!"

A blood-curdling death rattle replaced the screams. Like an automaton, Alma was putting one leg in front of the other, her knuckles bone-white as they clenched her conductor's baton.

"This is what happens to the dawdling Jewish vermin who are wasting my time," Drexler's voice threatened.

The sound of the claws again, this time trotting leisurely. Drexler's Alsatian caught up with the orchestra troop and was jogging on Alma's left, panting heavily as though after an exhausting play. Once again, the dog's nose dug into Alma's free palm. Frozen with terror, she forced herself to keep calm, at least outwardly. Drexler whistled. The dog took off. Alma turned her palm upward. It was wet with blood.

She didn't remember how they reached the gate. Maybe it was Sofia who helped her onto the small platform on which the stools and music stands had been arranged in a semicircle or maybe it was Zippy. She didn't remember what they played while the outside gangs were being marched out of the gates—some brassy German tune—but what had branded itself into her memory was a curse hissed just loudly enough for the orchestra to hear and not the SS:

"Dirty collaborating bitches!"

"Is it always like that?"

In Alma's room, a table lamp was lit. In its dim light, Alma and Zippy sat, heads diligently lowered over the lined sheets of paper supplied by the *Schreibstube* on Maria Mandl's orders. While the rest of the girls were taking their afternoon nap—another recently bestowed privilege—Alma was writing the sheet music from her memory as Zippy copied it after her.

"What? The hatred?" Zippy moved her shoulder indifferently. "Not always. Sometimes. Today was a bad day. They have no one to take it out on, so they take it out on us. They march to grueling work that will kill at least a few of them by the end of the day and we play cheerful tunes as they go. I can see how it's upsetting for them."

"Surely they understand that we aren't playing at the gates of our own free will. The SS invented that practice, didn't they?"

"Naturally. The SS love inventing things of that sort to amuse themselves with. The service here is boring and particularly for the young SS folk. So, from time to time they tie the wrists behind the inmates' backs and string them up near the gallows in the main camp. While the prisoners are screaming in pain, they order other inmates to bring chairs and tables and install themselves there nicely for the afternoon, drink beer, eat sausage, and bet money on whose shoulder joints will pop out of their sockets the last or who shall faint the first. That sort of thing." Zippy made a disgusted noise. "Or take 'bodily exercise,' for instance. Sometimes, after the work shift is over and the SS man has conducted his roll call, he orders the inmates to do 'gymnastics.' Leap-frog over each other's heads—'to stay fit and healthy.' Those who fall, get beaten by a

Kapo with a baton, either until they get up or until they die. That sort of amusement makes days more interesting for the SS. Just like our playing for the gangs that go to the twelve-hour shift that some of them won't survive. The SS think it's funny, but we're the ones who get blamed." Zippy smiled. It was a melancholy, crooked smile. "I was here even before Birkenau was constructed. The very first women's transport from Slovakia, March 1942. I've seen it all."

"How did you survive?" After what she had witnessed that day, to Alma it seemed almost a miracle. People rarely lasted longer than a couple of months here.

"I made myself indispensable in the camp office." Zippy's eyes had a faraway look in them. "I invented a file system for them. Organized schedules, sorted their mail, typed their reports...You would be amazed how many of those SS women are next to illiterate."

"No," Alma said, "I wouldn't."

For some time, they worked in agreeable silence. It was Alma who broke it first.

"What did you do prior to the deportation?"

"I was a commercial artist in Bratislava. That's another way I made myself indispensable—I have beautiful handwriting that Mandl admires." She snorted softly. "Do you want to hear a funny story? I was typing something at the *Schreibstube* when the runner came from Mandl, summoning me to her office. Now, mind you, I had just returned from the infirmary—someone I knew had a friend there who had dysentery and was asking for some charred bread. I thought, *This is it for you, Zipporah. Someone must have ratted. Get your behind ready, Mandl shall lash you personally in front of the entire camp just to freshen up your principles.* But what do you know? I knock on her door, trembling like a dog expecting a thrashing, and she welcomes me inside with a smile on her face and pushes a book into my hands. 'Helen, could you letter a dedication to my good comrade SS Hauptsturmführer Kramer in your special calligraphy? It's his birthday today, November 10.' Without thinking,

I blurted, 'What a coincidence! It's my birthday also...' And then she smiled even wider and said, 'Go to Block 5, where they keep all the packages and select one for yourself for your birthday.'" For some time, Zippy stared at something in the distance. "The book was called *The River Pirates*. I still remember it clear as day. I ate sardines that day, from the Red Cross. And she didn't beat me." Zippy looked at Alma. "As long as you're indispensable to Mandl, you'll survive here." She pulled closer and lowered her voice confidentially, "She has changed your classification in the registration book. A punishable offense if her superiors find out, but she still risked it."

After Alma scowled uncomprehendingly, Zippy grinned wider.

"She changed it from a Jew to a *Mischling,* a mix-blood. Now, as a mix-blood and a *Kapo*, it automatically excludes you from regular selections."

"How do you know?"

"I work in the camp office besides playing my little mandolin, don't I?" The sly look was back on Zippy's face. "We need to stick it out for the next couple of years only. The Germans are losing to the Soviets and, with the Western Allies, the things aren't peachy for them either. We have clandestine radios here. We know what's going on. Only a couple of years or even less, Alma! With our kosher detail, we'll pull through and that's that. You only need to teach us how to play well."

At first, Alma made no reply. It appeared that she didn't even hear Zippy. Her face an unreadable mask of distant memories, she sat silently for quite a while with her hands folded atop the papers.

"My family also thought that their playing would save them. And then came March 1938," she spoke at last, her voice soft yet thick with emotion.

"The Anschluss?" Zippy regarded her with sympathy.

"Yes." Pensively, Alma's fingers rubbed the stub of the pencil as her eyes stared, unseeing, into the space. "I, myself, had few illusions concerning the Nazis. My father, on the other hand... They had me late, *Vati* and *Mutti*. *Vati* was forty-three when I was born. But he played, played until the very day when Hitler arrived in Vienna with his troops. I'll never forget the day when my father and other Jewish musicians were pensioned off—with due courtesy though. Most of the Aryan musicians had been playing under *Vati*'s charge for years; they had tremendous respect for him and were truly regretful to see him go. But there was that one young Nazi violinist in the Philharmonic...He was the only one who openly gloated. A snooty-nosed sod, who couldn't shine my father's shoes on his best day, strutted into *Vati*'s dressing room, from which he was collecting his personal belongings and declared, 'Herr Hofrat, your days here are numbered.' Herr Burghauser, who occasionally played chamber music with *Vati* as a guest of *Vati*'s Rosé Quartet, stopped by our apartment later and told me about the entire rotten affair. Said how ashamed they all were when they heard that Nazi insult *Vati* in such a manner."

Alma paused, her lips pressed tightly together.

"My father was humiliated as it was; he had just lost his position of a concertmaster and, not only that, he was excluded from playing at the gala they had prepared for the Germans that evening. Eugen d'Albert's opera, *Tiefland*. Strange, how I remember precisely what it was...Perhaps, it's because my father kept repeating the same thing ceaselessly after he arrived home that day—'Why can't I play with them? I belong. I am the concertmaster!' Poor old man...He had always had such a dignified, noble look about him and that day, oh how he had suddenly aged. You should have seen him, Zippy. His shoulders stooped at once, but the eyes...It was the look in his eyes that I couldn't bear! Such profound hurt, such childish misunderstanding. The great Professor Rosé, the venerable Vienna Philharmonic concertmaster, the founder of the Rosé Quartet, reduced to nothing in one day, on some madman's orders. A Jew. A stateless person. A drain on the Aryan society."

"Is he . . . ?" Zippy searched her face, afraid to finish the question.

"On no, he's alive." Alma permitted herself a brief smile. "He's presently in England, a friendly alien with a full right to perform. Émigré artists in Britain and the United Stated established a special Rosé Fund for him, in addition to the money my brother and I were sending to support him financially. He insisted that he wished to perform, no matter the bombs raining on the capital, but a family friend whisked him away into the countryside, for which I'll be eternally grateful. It's nice, knowing that he's safe there." Alma paused and finished, as though not fully believing her own words, "Perhaps, one day I shall come back to him."

Chapter 6

Attired in a thin slip supplied by Kitty from the *Kanada*, Alma was brushing her teeth with the small amount of the precious white powder smelling faintly of mint. It came in a round box that featured a blond woman with a dazzling smile and some unreadable words in Polish or Czech, but, apparently, Kitty was well-versed enough in all languages to know to give it to Alma, along with a toothbrush, a bar of soap and even some scented facial cream. In the Experimental Block, she had to make do with a piece of cloth wrapped around her little finger; what pure bliss it was to brush one's teeth like a regular human being again.

After spitting into the rusty sink, Alma lifted her gaze to the cracked mirror Sofia had installed there a few days ago and discovered that she was smiling. Indeed, how little was needed to make a person happy, it suddenly occurred to her.

"Alma!" Zippy's voice echoed around the dingy latrine. She stopped in the door and jerked her thumb in the direction of the camp. "Today is the infirmary day. Every Tuesday and Thursday, we play for the sick in the *Revier*, the women's hospital. Sofia was asking if you wish to join the orchestra or stay here and work... on whatever it is you want to occupy yourself with. Mandl said it's not mandatory for you or me to make our appearances there, if we don't want to."

Alma regarded her incredulously. "Of course, I shall go. Why wouldn't I want to play for the sick?"

For some time, Zippy was silent.

"You've never been to the infirmary before, have you?" she asked softly at last.

"It's just a camp hospital, isn't it?" Alma shrugged and reached for her kerchief. She had washed it the night before, in cold water but with scented French soap, and left it to dry on one of the water pipes on which rust was growing like mushrooms. The entire latrine still smelled like lilacs. "Just how bad can it be?"

Zippy regarded her for an uncomfortably long time. Then she finally asked, in a voice that was oddly toneless: "You don't know much about camp hospitals, do you?"

Alma turned to her, one sarcastic remark or another ready to fly off her lips—*Do you truly suppose your camp hospital can compare to the Experimental Block?*—but the expression in Zippy's eyes was so profoundly forlorn, the words got stuck in Alma's throat. Despite the mounting sense of unease, she reached for Zippy's hand and forced a smile before repeating, with certainty that she no longer felt, "I shall go."

On their way to the Birkenau Women's Infirmary, Zippy noted quietly that one could always recognize Block 25 by its smell. At first, Alma dismissed it as an exaggeration. She'd been inhaling the nauseating stench of the crematorium for days; it had been inconceivable to imagine something more atrocious than that concoction of burnt flesh and singed hair. However, as the over-powering smell reached them—well before they reached the block itself—Alma realized that Zippy wasn't joking. It was a revolting mixture of decaying flesh and putrefying excrement, next to which the permanent stench of the Experimental Block was a child's joke.

Halting in her tracks, Alma brought the collar of her dress to her face to cover her nose and mouth and, all at once, felt guilty for doing so.

Next to her, Zippy clutched at her mandolin, her face sickly green. Only after Sofia prodded Alma gently in the back—"Don't loiter in the middle of the street, the SS are staring"—did she force herself to pull her *Kapo*'s armband up along her arm and proceed forward, straight into the bowels of hell, it seemed.

Inside the infirmary block, it was worse still. A truly frightful sight presented itself to Alma's eyes. Along the long corridor, right on the stone floor, rows and rows of emaciated bodies lay, some still making an effort to move; some eerily still. A mass of bones and gray scabby skin hanging off their limbs like cloth. Sunken eyes that stared without seeing. Rags of some unidentifiable color stiff with grease and dried excrement. Sparse patches of hair sticking out of skulls covered with sores and recently received wounds that no one had tended to.

Swallowing with great difficulty, Alma continued through this purgatory, breathing through her mouth and still tasting that premature rotting on the back of her throat. Putting on her bravest face, she soldiered on through what remained of humanity in this place, next to which Dante's Inferno had lost all its colors.

Women. It was appalling to think that these were all women—someone's mothers, sisters, daughters, wives. Beautiful brides that smiled out from the photos that she had a chance to glimpse in the *Kanada*, all piled, along with birth certificates, passports, certificates of military awards, and bank accounts, into one big heap of useless paper later to be burned by a former Rabbi just behind the warehouse. Kitty had said he recited Kaddish whenever he fulfilled his duty. Only now did Alma understand why—effectively, they were all walking dead, these Revier women. Doomed, condemned to death, regardless of the exact diagnosis. It was only suitable for the Rabbi to mourn them while they were still alive.

As Alma carefully made her way forward through this human mass, bony hands reached for the hem of her skirt and brushed the bare skin on her ankles. As though revived by the sight of healthy, relatively well-dressed women, the poor wretches reached for them out of their last powers. In their delusion, anyone who walked upright must have appeared as a doctor to them; a miracle worker who had adhesive plaster, sulfa drugs, iodine and, perhaps, even a piece of bread.

Distraught and mortified, Alma turned to Sofia and searched the former *Kapo*'s face in desperation.

Sofia only prodded her slightly again. "Keep going; we play for the ones who can actually walk out of here."

"What about..." Alma couldn't finish, just looked around helplessly, her hand clasping at the violin case with force.

"These shall all be taken away with the transport any time now. Keep going. Half of them are sick with typhus and dysentery; do you wish to catch it too?" Sofia's nudges grew more urgent. She, too, was mortified to be stuck here, with the condemned women whose pleas and moans were growing gradually louder, tearing at the Music Block girls' very souls.

With great reluctance, Alma forced herself to move forward until they reached a ward of sorts, where at least a semblance of an infirmary still remained. Bunk beds were still overflowing with emaciated bodies, but at least these bodies lay on straw pallets with dubious-looking bedding on them, but that was already quite a change from what Alma had just witnessed in that hell's antechamber. Some inmates even had rough blankets covering their legs and double straw-stuffed pillows under their heads.

"Why the preferential treatment?" Catching Zippy's sleeve, Alma motioned her head toward one of the sick women, who was presently munching on a piece of a biscuit of sorts.

"Some inmates receive packages from outside the camp. Nurses here aren't stupid and know where their bread is buttered. They get aspirin for these inmates, clean clothes; fluff up their pillows and take them off selection lists and, in exchange, get their share of the package's contents. Not a bad barter, if you think of it." She went on to explain, her voice becoming confidential, "Some women here aren't sick at all. If they have enough food to bribe the doctors or nurses, they'll get a couple of weeks of vacation. The enterprise isn't without its risks, though—the SS doctors sometimes show their faces and then it's to the gas with such holidaymakers. But people still take their chances. It's understandable, too; they aren't like us. They work outside for twelve hours, hard labor, six days a week. Their roll call is three or four hours. And they get beaten on the slightest of provocations—again, unlike us, the cultured lot. One can't quite blame them in good conscience," she concluded.

Briefly greeted by the medical personnel that mostly rushed about ignoring them altogether—one inspection or other must have been indeed coming, Alma concluded from all that frantic commotion—the orchestra girls crammed themselves into a corner and began tuning their instruments.

"What do you usually play here?" Alma inquired in an undertone.

From Sofia, a shrug. "Anything cheerful. None of that sad classical business. Our official task is to lift their spirits, so any popular tunes should do."

"Will Zara Leander's 'Blaue Husaren' do?"

"Zara Leander will most certainly do."

"You know, her grandparents were Jewish," Alma said in a neutral voice. "Just like Margarete Slezak's, the Berlin opera star and Hitler's favorite." Ignoring Sofia's stunned look, Alma picked up her bow, her eyes gazing into the distance. "Margarete—Gretl as we all used to call her—was my childhood friend… She used to vacation with us every summer, at our summerhouse near the Black Forest. We used to be so inseparable, *Vati* liked to joke that we were attached at the hip. But when I tried contacting her again in 1938, right after my father was fired from his position at the Vienna Philharmonic, she refused to help us. Was afraid for her family's fragile position, I suppose. She travels all over occupied Europe, entertaining the troops, from what I last heard." As though suddenly awoken from a dream, Alma struck her bow on the wall in the absence of a music stand and commanded, "Ladies, 'Blaue Husaren'!"

Within seconds, the very atmosphere in the ward changed. A merry tune swept over the infirmary inmates, waking them from their fitful daytime sleep.

Alma thought it to be a travesty to play such cheerful music in the barrack that stunk of death and where condemned women lay on the bare floor just outside this ward, ignored even by the medical staff. But the SS declared that the music raised morale and so they played—for the dying women in the sickbay and for the outside gangs heading out of the gates every single morning to their brassy marches as though on some grotesque parade.

Slaves themselves, they played for the enslaved people, in a world that must have gone completely mad if such concepts as music and unimaginable suffering could peacefully coexist in a hell like Auschwitz.

While they played, a few women dragged themselves off their bunks and shuffled, barefoot, just to stand against the wall near the orchestra girls, clutching their pitiful imitations of blankets next to their caved-in chests. From time to time, they reached out with their nearly transparent, blue-veined hands and touched the instruments, faint smiles full of tender melancholy lighting up their exhausted, ash-white faces.

A nurse appeared with a single roll of aspirins and distributed it among the patients that were ready to trade their rations for the little relief the pills could provide. Most of the medicaments came from the local black market, according to the all-knowing Zippy. Morphine was the most expensive, but even that could be organized from the SS hospital, where it could be had in abundance. One only had to know the right infirmary inmate to bribe.

An impatient honk from the outside and familiar German shouts sent the medical staff and the healthiest inmates that could still move about scrambling. The inmates who had been listening to the music, resting the weight of their bodies on one elbow, flattened themselves on their bunks and pulled the blankets up to their necks, their frightened gazes riveted to the corridor. In it, some sort of an *Aktion*—a typically German euphemism for an extermination operation—was happening, for the frantic screams soon replaced faint moans and desperate pleas, in all European languages imaginable. That still-invisible, Babylonian orgy of violence nearly drowned out Alma's orchestra with the sheer volume of it. Stiff with fear, the girls picked up the tempo without any command, propelled by some animalistic instinct of sheer self-preservation.

From the corridor came an incensed shout in German. It was the voice of someone who was used to giving commands and having those commands obeyed. "The SS medical office gave you an order to put seventy inmates on today's list. I've only counted forty-three. Where are the rest?!"

The inmate doctor—body positioned firmly on the threshold of the ward, blocking the SS man's way to her charges, the brave woman—responded something to the effect of the rest being able-bodied workers in recovery, tried demonstrating some charts to the uniformed man, in a pitiful attempt to save a few patients from him and his *list*.

Germans loved making those, Alma recalled Zippy saying. They also loved putting numbers on them, numbers to which they had reduced the camp population. The main office in Berlin had put a request for twenty thousand to be liquidated in August; Auschwitz Kommandant Höss ensured that precisely twenty thousand were put to death by the end of the month. Sick or healthy, Jews or communists, men or women—that mattered not. What mattered was that the lists were correct and numbers in order.

The inmate doctor was still saying something, her pleading eyes trained on the guard, but he simply backhanded her with such force, she stumbled into the wall and sank onto the floor, still clasping the clipboard to her chest.

The SS man stepped over her legs and regarded the ward, eyes narrowed, a truncheon in hand. In less than an instant, he yanked a flimsy blanket from a patient who had the misfortune to lie closest to him. "What's the matter with you?"

"I'm recovering from malaria, Herr Unterscharführer." Eyes wide open, the entire body trembled with dread on her bunk.

"Are you still sick?"

Unsure of her reply, the woman risked a glance in the doctor's direction. The latter didn't meet her gaze; only stood, rubbing her temple, with a doomed look on her face.

"I asked you a question, you *Scheiße-Jude!* Have you gone mute with fear?!"

"*Jawohl,* Herr Unterscharführer." Her answer was a mere whisper.

"*Jawohl,* what?!"

"*Jawohl;* I'm still sick, Herr Unterscharführer."

With a vicious grin, the guard raised his truncheon and hit the woman on her bare legs. "How about now? Still sick? Shall I give you some more medicine or shall I help you onto that truck outside? The Reich has no need of sick Jewish vermin that can't work and contribute to the war effort."

Two painful welts were already rising on the woman's legs. As though in some terrible nightmare, Alma stared at them, unable to look away, all the while her hands produced the joyful music of their own volition. She suddenly felt herself to be a powerless marionette in some grotesque puppet theater performance conducted by an invisible madman. Her fellow terrified puppets followed her tune just as mechanically, as though their hands were being pulled by the same hidden strings.

The woman scrambled off her bed and swayed at once, almost collapsing from the effort. "I can work, Herr Unterscharführer!"

The SS man burst into laughter, spreading his arms wide. Behind his back, two male inmates in striped pants but civilian jackets joined in. Standing in the door, they were shifting from one foot to the other, awaiting their master's orders. Turning to them, the guard motioned his truncheon in the trembling woman's direction. "It's a miracle healing! Have you ever witnessed anything like it? Let us see how many more of these Jewish cows have been vacationing here at the Reich's expense. I still need those twenty-seven inmates to make my list."

The two hulking inmates swiftly moved through the ward, sending more women scrambling off their bunks. The ones who could stand pulled themselves upright, their shaking hands clasping at the walls and each other for support. The ones who couldn't manage even that were roughly pulled off the beds and dragged into the corridor by their ankles or wrists.

In her corner by the door, the doctor silently ticked off their numbers on her list. Her face was entirely wet with tears.

Outside the barrack walls, the wailing had grown to an unbearable level. Fighting the desire to press her ears with both hands, Alma continued to play under the SS man's curious gaze. He strolled among the emptied bunks and approached the orchestra. Stopping within mere steps from Alma, he began whistling the song she was playing in perfect tune with her violin. She closed her eyes, unable to stand the sight of his handsome, vicious face in front of her.

Suddenly, something landed on top of her right hand, startling her. Alma's bow cut across the strings in sharp protest. Inside her chest, her heart was pounding so loudly, she could swear it would break her ribs any moment now. The rounded end of the truncheon touched her bow hand once again—a playful tap, not a painful blow.

"That's my favorite song," the guard announced amicably. The sudden change from a raging beast to a Zara Leander music lover was more than disturbing. "Are you a professional?"

"*Jawohl*, Herr Unterscharführer."

"What's your name?"

"Alma Rosé, Herr Unterscharführer."

He scrunched up his face, searching his memory. "Are you that new violinist Lagerführerin Mandl won't stop bragging about?"

"I suppose, Herr Unterscharführer."

"Now I see what the fuss was all about. You play very well." Alma didn't detect any notes of sarcasm in his voice. He appeared genuinely impressed.

"Thank you, Herr Unterscharführer."

In the silence that followed, animalistic screams coming from behind the barrack walls turned outright deafening. All of a sudden, Alma couldn't get her breath. It was all too much, too loud, too terrifying—this SS man with his truncheon, the helpless doctor, the emaciated bodies shivering next to each other along the wall, the condemned humanity that wailed like a herd of trapped animals led to slaughter and the fact that there was no escape from it all.

"Hey, stinkers," the SS guard called to his inmate underlings, "have you heard how well she can play?"

"First-rate music, Herr Unterscharführer!" They rushed to nod in agreement at once, their faces a unanimous picture of servility. "Such talent!"

"You wouldn't know talent if it hit you in your ugly mugs," the SS man grumbled, just to hear a deferential, *Jawohl, Herr Unterscharführer,* in response to the insult. Disgusted, he slapped one of his underlings half-heartedly as he passed them by.

Whatever propelled her to move after him, Alma didn't know. The floor of the eerily empty corridor, where dying women had lain mere minutes ago, was already being hosed down by an inmate-nurse. Alma regarded her with reproach. Sofia tried calling after her, but Alma's feet carried her forward as though of their own volition.

Outside, a truck was parked. Two well-built inmates in white undershirts and striped caps were presently hurling the women into it by their legs and arms, ignoring their petrified shrieks.

"There are corpses here! Corpses! You're putting us together with the dead people! We aren't dead yet!"

"You shall be, in about thirty minutes," the SS officer explained good-humoredly, after consulting his watch.

Gradually, the protests gave way to the sobs, forlorn and profoundly miserable.

Without thinking, Alma brought the violin to her shoulder and rested her chin on it. She had no power to change their fate; neither could she help the condemned women any other way and so she did the only thing she could think of—she played the Hatikvah for them. It was a capital offense, playing the national song of the Israelites in Auschwitz and yet, it suddenly didn't matter to Alma that she would land in the back of the same truck for such insolence, adding one more name to the SS man's list.

He stood there gaping at her in stunned silence, which could be followed by a violent eruption any moment and Alma knew it. But still, this was the right thing to do; she felt it deeply inside, and the right thing was always worthy of risking one's life for.

Inside the truck with the Red Cross on it, the women gradually quieted down. Alma's violin roused something in them; something that the Nazis had tried to eliminate and erase from their very memories for all eternity—the national pride of the long-suffering people that had survived for thousands of years against all odds.

With resolute, noble dignity, they rested their shaved heads on each other's shoulders and sang the song of the Promised Land with their eyes closed. Most cried silently without a single muscle on their faces moving; some regarded her with gratitude for bringing them peace during the last minutes of their lives.

Taking her violin off her shoulder, Alma saw that it, too, was wet with her own tears. She didn't even realize that she had been crying this entire time.

When Alma turned to face the SS man, she noticed his truncheon hanging motionless by his side, as if he suddenly wasn't sure of what to do with it.

"Herr Unterscharführer," she addressed him softly and this time with a measure of respect in her voice. "Allow me please to go with them. They'll go more peacefully if I keep playing for them—"

"No." Recovering himself at last, he interrupted her with a categorical shake of his head. "That's not allowed. Only the *Sonderkommando* are allowed inside the—" Stopping himself abruptly, he pursed his lips as if he had let on more than he was supposed to, put his cap back on and marched off. The doors to the truck were locked with an ominous clang, but this time not a sound could be heard from the inside. Soon, it drove off in the direction of the crematorium, leaving Alma alone in front of the deathly silent barrack.

Chapter 7

"You don't have to go to the ramp," Sofia said. By now, Alma was familiar with a camp slang the inmates and the SS used for the railroad unloading platform. "It's just idiotic march music that they expect for us to play for the new arrivals while the SS doctors sort them out. I have just enough conductor's talent to supply that."

Sofia was standing on the threshold of Alma's room, watching her struggling with the hairbrush. Alma's hair was growing out and curling into short, silky ringlets that positively refused to be assembled into any sort of order. In the washed-out light of the morning, the violinist's eyes shone brighter than usual—black, radiant, alert with intelligence. They were her most striking feature that commanded attention at once. She was painfully pallid; her cheekbones stood out far too much in her face and yet, those marvelous, liquid eyes of hers glowed with such hidden strength, it was impossible not to fall under the spell of their quiet power. Sofia found it amazing how, even in such horrid conditions, Alma managed to carry herself with the dignity of royalty, no less. It appeared as though she simply refused to be touched by the baseness of camp life and kept her head high and shoulders squared almost in defiance of the degradation they all had been forced to embrace.

It was a fortunate thing for the orchestra that Mandl had appointed Alma as a Kapo, Sofia thought without an ounce of resentment for the lost position. Alma was much stronger than her; she would teach the girls how to survive.

"I've heard that you-don't-have-to-go-there song before." Alma gave her a certain look. "Last time, it came from Zippy. I'm starting to fear you two are plotting against me in the hope to usurp my hard-earned *Kapo*'s power."

In spite of herself, Sofia chuckled, grateful for the humor, gallows or not. "Even Zippy doesn't go to the ramp if she can help it. Why would you want to?"

Having given up on the brush, Alma covered her head with a kerchief and gathered her violin case along with the conductor's baton from the table. "I don't *want to,* but I shall go all the same. If the entire orchestra is there, it's only suitable for the conductor to be there as well."

"Ramp is hell."

"This entire place is hell, if that idea is new to you."

"Some of its parts are more hellish than the others."

"Perhaps so. Even more reason for us to go there and play music."

"Dr. Mengele will be conducting selections. His presence alone would be enough of an incentive for me to stay away from the place."

Herr Doktor's reputation preceded him. The camp rumor was, compared to Dr. Mengele, Dr. Clauberg from the Auschwitz Experimental Block was a simple scoundrel. Unlike his colleague, Dr. Mengele's imagination wasn't limited to bloodless sterilization. Sterilization was, in fact, below him. Dr. Mengele had much grander ambitions than that—he was working on a paper on Aryan racial theory and thought it to be a marvelous idea to use Auschwitz inmates as guinea pigs to prove its thesis. He'd arrived in the camp only recently, after being injured on the Eastern front, but had already secured the entire compound of Birkenau experimental blocks for himself—separate barracks for twin boys and twin girls, a barrack for gypsies and dwarfs, a facility for inmates with deformities, whom, according to Zippy and the documents she was sometimes forced to type in the camp office, Herr Doktor dissected with envious regularity and the fanaticism of a mad scientist. Sometimes, he didn't bother with the anesthesia. Sometimes, he put chemical dyes in children's eyes in the hope to change their color. So far, he'd been unsuccessful, Zippy had told Sofia; Zippy knew it because it was her and Mala, her Jewish colleague from the camp office, who packed jars with those eyes swimming in them in different solutions, into boxes that bore "Handle with Care: War Material—Urgent" labels on them. All were shipped to the Institute of Biological, Racial and Evolutionary Research at Berlin-Dahlem.

Something clicked in Alma's mind. She was still shaken after what had occurred in the sickbay and she had sworn to herself, as soon as they returned to the block, that she would do anything in her powers to prevent her girls from being thrown onto one of those trucks in such a despicable manner. And now, she stood before Sofia, thinking feverishly. It was something uttered by that SS man, just one phrase that kept working itself in circles in her mind—*the SS medical office gave you an order to put seventy inmates on the list...*

Alma's head snapped up. She was looking at Sofia sharply, a beginning of a smile forming on her lips. "Is Dr. Mengele only in charge of the ramp selections?" Alma inquired with sudden interest when Sofia didn't budge from her position in the door, as though physically blocking it with her body.

"No. He conducts them around the camp as well, whenever he's bored. Which is almost every other day."

"Can Mandl override him in his decisions?"

"He's a medical doctor, so no. If he chooses to send someone to the gas, that inmate is licked. His authority is almost limitless when it comes to selections. Mandl can try and intervene, but he makes the ultimate decision."

Alma stood and considered something for a moment, nodding to some thoughts of hers. Under her brow creased with utter concentration, two dark eyes shone, sharp and steady. "Then, he can grant pardons as well, I assume?" She glanced at Sofia, still calculating something in her mind.

"He can," Sofia acknowledged, regarding Alma with suspicion. She didn't like the look on the violinist's face one bit. "Though, he'll only do it if he has a personal interest in it. Make no mistake, he's a regular monster. But only on the inside." She grinned darkly. "Outwardly, he's handsome like a movie star and polite to the point of ridiculousness. Until he stabs an inmate's heart with a direct shot of phenol just to dissect the body while it's still warm."

"Sounds like a charming fellow," Alma jested grimly with a perfectly straight face. "Now, move. I assume, he wouldn't appreciate us being late."

Without hesitation, Alma walked past Sofia in her resolute step—shoulders squared, violin case in hand, head held high.

A soft grin playing on her lips, Sofia watched the girls follow their new leader promptly without a single command given. She trailed Alma outside; lined up along with the others in front of the barrack; as Alma inspected her little troop carefully and with the cool eye of a professional: "Go back and clean your shoes; they're dusty... Retie your belt; it's much too low..."

Sofia nodded with approval. Alma was a quick learner.

A single tube of lipstick—wherever Alma had smuggled it from—soon made its way among the Music Block ranks. As Alma was rubbing some of it into their pale cheeks in the ingenious substitute for rouge, the girls' expressions transformed as though by magic.

"Maria, look at you. A regular film star!"

"Like in the old times, at the dances!"

"Karla, how pretty you are. Just like in your old pictures."

"Hilde, if only your Werner saw you now..."

When Sofia's turn came, she made a wry face at her successor. "Where did the goods come from?"

From Alma, an unimpressed shrug. She was more concerned with her orchestra's looks than logistics. In Auschwitz, rouge and lipstick went for the price of gold. Rosy cheeks and lips that still had color in them were far from fashion statements; they were a matter of life or death. Zippy had already recounted to Alma how the inmates, who couldn't afford such luxuries, slapped their own cheeks as hard as they could and bit into their lips till they drew blood to make themselves appear healthier than they really were before the selections. Alma had been saving the precious tube precisely for that purpose, but now, considering that Dr. Mengele would be watching them, she needed for her girls to look their best.

"The *Kanada*; where else? Their overseer permitted me to take it if I played a song for him."

"What song?"

"Some sentimental affair to which he and his lady friend danced before he was transferred here. He says he misses her dearly."

Sofia arched a skeptical brow. "So, they can feel something after all, the SS?"

"They must. Only not toward us."

High above their kerchiefed heads, the sun was beating down unmercifully. In neat rows of five, they marched along the *Lager-straße*, the little army in blue parading down the street. Past empty barracks that stood with their doors open like ancient beasts with gaping mouths, ready to swallow their human prey each evening without fail. Past watchtowers with elderly SS napping atop their machine guns. All the young flesh had long been fed to the beast of the Eastern front. Now, it was the dead sons' fathers' turn to don the uniforms and guard the people they had no feud with, but which *der Führer* loathed and announced to be their enemy. In days of their youth, on a different Eastern front, there was a different enemy—armed and dangerous—not these women and certainly not these skeletal men. Unlike their ideologically reliable dead sons, they failed to comprehend this all and so they napped or smoked their pipes, lapsed in some languid abstraction, and watched musicians march like soldiers on parade.

Soon, the infamous ramp came into view. From inside his booth, an SS guard barely granted the girls another look before waving them through the narrow enclosure of the barbed wire. Deceived by its gentle humming, birds sometimes landed on it. The SS's Alsatians took great pleasure in playing with their stiff corpses the instant they hit the ground.

The train hadn't arrived yet. The ramp stood silent and empty; only two SS officers of a low rank loitered there, looking dreadfully bored, while their inmate subordinates waited, with arms along the seams, in the respectable distance.

Moving as quietly as possible so as not to disturb the guards, Alma began to organize her little troop.

Stifling a yawn, an SS man in charge of the transport reception checked his wristwatch. "The blasted thing is late again."

His comrade, lanky and bespectacled, was patting himself for cigarettes. "Must be letting a *Wehrmacht* transport through."

The first one squinted at the horizon. "You noticed *Wehrmacht* transports only go one way lately? Always east. Back—only Red Cross trains with wounded soldiers heading to the army hospitals if the Soviet bombers didn't drop a few eggs on them and erased such a need."

"Rot." The second one obliterated him with a sweep of the hand. "*Wehrmacht* transports take this route home all the time. Else, how would the soldiers on leave get home?"

"Do they now?" The first one narrowed his eyes maliciously. "When was the last time you saw a *Wehrmacht* transport full of soldiers on leave? Ever since we lost Stalingrad and the entire Sixth Army along with it, we've only been retreating."

"Shortening the front," the second one argued unconvincingly.

"That's the very strategy!" The first one laughed derisively. "Pull out all the way to Berlin so that we can attack them on our own land with our miracle weapons! It doesn't matter that their numerical superiority had swelled to about ten Soviets to one

German, but since we're such fierce Aryan warriors, we'll obliterate them all solely on the superior blood principle." He spit on the ground with disgust. "Keep listening to the Propaganda Ministry political addresses; they'll be insisting that we're winning this war even when one Ivan or the other is sleeping in your bed with your wife and you're locked up in this very camp as a prisoner of war."

The second one drew himself up but said nothing, only extracted a cigarette from a beautiful silver case and also spat on the ground before lighting it. "One ought to report you to the camp Gestapo; see where you end up for your long tongue."

Much to his annoyance, his comrade burst out laughing again. "Where? On the Eastern front? Go and report me then; I'll write to you personally about Russkies slaughtering our kind right and left!"

"Defeatist."

"Half-witted idealist."

With the exchange of courtesies out of the way, both turned their heads toward the train tracks. The rails began vibrating slightly. Soon, a shrill but still-distant whistle pierced the air.

Having assembled her orchestra in the assigned place, Alma raised her baton, waiting for a signal from one of the SS men. Both kept stubbornly staring in the direction of the approaching transport.

It had passed the infamous Auschwitz gates now and was slowing down as it was pulling toward the ramp. Her hand frozen in mid-air, Alma was following its progress, a vague feeling of angst and tense anticipation surging up in her, dragging her to the dark well of recent memories. The airless insides of the eerily similar cattle car. Countless pairs of eyes glistening with terror in the permanent twilight of that coffin on wheels that had left the transit camp in Drancy, only to pull them to the veritable hell on earth—Auschwitz. Days and nights mixing together on their torturous journey. No water. No food. Only a single bucket in the corner that was meant to be used as a toilet that had long been overflowing with filth. Death in people's eyes; they dropped where they stood and expired right there. Death in the air; the stench from the decomposing bodies beginning to mix with the stench of the spilled excrement. Death waiting just over Alma's shoulder; delirious from thirst and hunger, she could swear she could smell its foul breath on her very skin. It took her some inhuman willpower not to succumb to it. With an almost commendable obstinacy, Alma had stared through the cracks in the planks, memorizing the railroad signs as they flashed by, first French, then German, then Polish and German together, until the very last one came into view and the train had pulled to the ramp: Oświęcim—Auschwitz.

The same ramp on which she was presently standing.

Alma felt a shudder run through her. Death. It failed to claim her on that train, but its presence nearby was much too tangible. It watched. It waited...

A pitch-perfect, melodic whistling was now accompanying the laborious chugging of the cattle train. Without once turning her head, out of the corner of her eye, Alma spied a new officer, who was presently mounting a small podium to her right. She couldn't quite see his face—it was obscured by the visor of his cap—but she distinguished the elegant, form-fitting uniform, two Iron Crosses, the Reich's most coveted awards, pinned proudly to the left breast, tall boots polished to such mirror perfection they shone in the sun as though made of gleaming black obsidian, and the tailored gloves he was pulling unhurriedly off his palms. Somehow, Alma had missed both of the newcomer's SS underlings snapping to attention; only later saw them standing, frozen with their hands along the seams, while the officer himself ignored them with a wonderful nonchalance about him.

She had never met him personally, but she had heard enough of him by now to recognize him without once meeting him face to face. Dr. Mengele, the Angel of Death himself, had made a personal appearance to collect his share of souls that painfully beautiful morning.

The train was pulling to a stop. The ramp *Kommando,* in their striped uniforms, were already waiting for it, cudgels in hand.

Slowly and deliberately, Alma lowered her baton. The Angel was still whistling, the Brahms sonata she knew so well. Under Sofia's uncomprehending gaze—*what are you doing?*—Alma took the violin in her hand and picked up the melody in G major.

The whistling had stopped abruptly. Aware of the Angel's hawkish gaze on her, Alma continued to play from memory.

She needn't worry—she could play this particular sonata in her sleep. She had learned it so well to impress her husband, Váša, on their last joint tour. She had learned it by heart, so he would hear how well she played and fall in love with her once again. The marriage was already falling apart by then. In Germany, the Nuremberg Laws had just been passed and, all of a sudden, it was very bad taste to be married to a Jew. Váša suggested it would be best if they cancelled their joint performances.

Alma had swallowed the insult and took her revenge by creating the most successful women's orchestra, Vienna Waltzing Girls, that became an overnight sensation and which toured the whole of Europe, meeting with thunderous applause in every major city. Her husband had found a very convenient fault with that as well—"All of your constant absences, truly, Alma!"—and asked for a divorce, thoroughly pretending that it had nothing to do with his courting Germany's music scene that wasn't receptive to the musicians who had spouses of the wrong racial status. She had signed the divorce papers happily.

Back then, she had played it as best as she could to impress her husband; now, she played even better so that the Angel would let her girls live.

After she'd finished, the ramp *Kommando* moved to open the doors to the first cattle car. With a languid motion of his hand, the Angel stopped them.

"Alma Rosé, are you not?"

Lowering her violin, Alma turned to face him. He had addressed her by her name and in the polite manner, *Sie*. She hadn't expected it. Or, on the contrary, that was precisely what she had expected. From the shadow thrown by his uniform cap's visor, two dark eyes observed her with great interest. Sofia didn't lie; he was very handsome indeed. All sharp jawline, flawless skin, raven brows, and a certain air of arrogant, cruel magnificence about him that commanded awe and instilled mortal fear at the same time.

"Yes, I am, Herr Doktor."

He cocked his head, permitting himself a faint smile. "You know who I am?"

"Of course, Herr Doktor."

He nodded, satisfied. "Your camp leader won't stop bragging about you. But brag is all she does. Even the *Kommandant's* wife wished for you and your little orchestra to play for one of her soirees, but Mandl wouldn't be moved. Your *Lagerführerin* insists the orchestra is not ready for the big public yet."

"It isn't, Herr Doktor." Alma regretfully inclined her head. "I have just taken over the duties of the conductor and, I'm afraid, it will take us some time to get into presentable shape. Now, we shall keep playing simple marches my girls are familiar with and popular songs, but if you would like to hear anything sophisticated, I'm afraid you will have to give us a few months."

Mengele regarded her with great mistrust. "You believe you can teach them how to play Brahms in just a few months?"

"Brahms, Beethoven, Dvorák, Tchaikovsky, Sarasate—whatever you like, Herr Doktor."

"You seem to be very sure of yourself, Frau Rosé." His expression, just like his tone, was unreadable.

"I have already trained a female orchestra under my charge and it had great success in Europe. Yes, I believe I can train these young ladies as well." In the pause that followed, Alma finished as carefully as possible, "Naturally, it would make my work much easier if the staff remained permanent. I would prefer to have more members in my orchestra—say, forty people instead of just twenty—and if they are professional musicians just like I am..."

She ignored Sofia, who was outright poking her in the leg with her own conductor's baton.

"I understand that you need able-bodied workers first and foremost, but women-musicians are gentle creatures." Alma cast Dr. Mengele a probing glance. After he didn't object, she went on, her voice gathering conviction, "They won't last long in one of those outside gangs at any rate; why not give them to me, Herr Doktor? And I promise you that I shall make such an orchestra out of them, the main Auschwitz one won't rival it. Under my direct responsibility, of course. In case you aren't satisfied with the quality of music they produce..." *Send me to the gas; I reserve that right after you, as my punishment.* Alma didn't finish, simply smiling at the Angel through overpowering dread. Inside her chest, her heart was beating itself to death.

For a few excruciatingly long moments, Dr. Mengele was regarding her with his head still tipped to one side. To be sure, it was a gamble to make such bold propositions to him; yet, he appeared almost amused by it. It had a quality of a scientific experiment to it and scientific experiments always excited him the most.

"Very well, Frau Rosé. Your orchestra is exempt from selections until..." He considered with his eyes slightly narrowed. "Until Christmas. A perfect date for you to give a first-class performance and for us to see what your virtuosos have achieved, don't you agree?"

Alma's breath hitched in her throat, but her face betrayed nothing. Four months under Dr. Mengele's personal protection was a lifetime in a place like this. "Perfectly agree, Herr Doktor."

"Then, we have a deal." He looked very pleased with himself.

With the same effortless languidness, Dr. Mengele signed to the inmates.

At once, the heavy latches of the cattle train were unlocked, and the doors slid open to spill its frightened load onto the ramp. The inmates' hands were already tugging at their sleeves, yanking them roughly out of the wagons; the SS men's whips prodded them into packs—"*Raus, raus; los, los, los!*"—and separated them into two columns—men on the right, women on the left. All around them, violent shouts in German, SS dogs straining themselves on their leashes, lunging at the terrified crowd.

Stunned and instantly blinded, the newcomers could only stare around with a wild look about them and do as they were told. Too terrified to cry, children clung to their parents, trembling with fear. The *Kanada* men were already pulling their suitcases straight out of their hands and throwing them into one big pile, thoroughly ignoring pleading looks and whispered questions directed at them. A few women began to scream in protest when they were being separated from their husbands, but a crack of a horsewhip across their mouths swiftly put an end to the beginning of a rebellion.

Roughly shoved and threatened into silence, the crowd hushed itself. Soon, all eyes were riveted to the only figure who towered over them like some ancient, all-powerful god. Despite being prodded in their backs, they were in no rush to approach him, as though sensing the acute, inexplicable danger he was emanating.

Alma's orchestra played a cheery German marching song.

With a benevolent smile, Dr. Mengele observed the crowd in front of them. Soon, the usual ritual began—"*Links, rechts*"—left, right; "Are you with child, my good woman? No? A shame... Left. Anyone with twins report to me personally. Anyone with physical deformities also..."

With a simple flip of his tailored gloves, he granted life or condemned to death. Only, this time, he demanded for female professional musicians to step forward as well. To Alma's immense relief, both young women who claimed to be such, were sent to the right.

Chapter 8

September 1943

Like a woman possessed, Alma was digging wildly into a veritable mountain of papers that was piled up in the middle of one of the *Kanada* warehouses. Just beside her shoulder, Rabbi Dayen looked on, infinitely patient, a small cart in his hands. He was familiar with the women's orchestra conductor by now; on the days when the fresh transports arrived, she spent every afternoon here on her hands and knees, hunting for scraps of sheet music among mounds and mounds of photocards, passports, birth certificates, diplomas, personal letters and children's paintings.

On the very first few days, he saw her wipe her wet face in helpless anger. Gradually, she had learned to remain coolly detached from the grisly work she was doing—much like he did. A Rabbi, made to burn the memory of his people while the SS burned the people themselves in their industrial ovens. The camp was a ruthless teacher. There were only two choices—to adapt or to perish.

Without noticing, Rabbi Dayen began reciting the Kaddish for the ones who did.

"Could you postpone your prayers until I'm finished, please?" Alma threw over her shoulder. In irritation, she swiped aside another pile of photographs, pushing them closer to Dayen's cart. The task of digging through dead people's possessions was gruesome enough; less than anything she needed to hear the Rabbi's mournful recitals in addition to that.

The Rabbi didn't take offense; only smiled softly in understanding. He gathered the photographs as gently as possible and placed them into his cart. It was painful for him to look into each one of these faces daily; he could only imagine what it must have been like for her.

"You ought to try that new camp they have just installed," he said at length. "I heard they have well-known musicians there. It is my profound conviction they will gladly share their sheet music with you."

"What new camp?" Alma glanced up at him.

"The SS call it the Family Camp. Jews from the model ghetto in Theresienstadt."

"Why the Family Camp?" Alma was back to digging.

"Because they live there all together, in families," Dayen explained with a smile that was both full of hope and disbelief. "Wives, husbands, their elderly, children—everyone in the same barracks."

Alma paused her search just to give him a look full of mistrust.

"I was amazed too, when I learned of it," he admitted. "And they weren't even subjected to a selection on the ramp. The SS sent them to the showers for disinfection, but that was the extent of it. The SS permitted them to keep their civilian clothes, didn't shave their hair, and didn't separate them from their children. Pregnant women are entitled to additional rations of milk and white bread."

"Did the world turn upside down and the SS suddenly develop a sense of human decency?" Alma still wasn't convinced. In a place like Birkenau, it sounded like a fairy tale.

"Don't count on that."

Alma turned to the sound of the derisive snort and discovered Kitty standing there with a pile of passports in her hands. After dumping them unceremoniously into the pile before Alma, the *Kanada* girl made a vague motion with her head toward the camp.

"They're only treated with such distinction because the Nazis use them for their propaganda purposes. I have already gone there to make my inquiries. Don't look at me like that, Rebbe; when something of that sort happens, one ought to investigate. To survive this place, an inmate must be well-informed and well-connected."

Kitty shifted her attention back to Alma, who was kneeling next to the pile. "At any rate, I asked them what was so special about them that the SS don't even use them for forced labor and have pretty much left them to their devices as though they're on a vacation of some sort. Our local *Kanada* men have all decided they must have been under the protection of the Red Cross or some such. But what do you know? Those new arrivals' local leader—he was some big shot in their ghetto—tells me very confidentially that there were people with cameras making certain films there, in Theresienstadt, several times. It was regular Hollywood, he told me; the SS had brought the entire film crew there, put bows in children's hair, set up tables outside with food and drink like in an outdoor café, brought books into the hastily erected barracks and put signs, *Library, Chess Club, Music Club, Theater,* and what have you above several entrances and made them—Jews—stroll around arm in arm and smile into the cameras as they rolled. Naturally, as soon as they were done filming, they took the food and drink from the ghetto people, just like the books and the chess sets and the toys from the children. I'm thinking, the camp administration holds them here for the same very purpose—to shove them under some Swiss bigwigs' noses if they come here to inspect the SS's humanity."

"Do you not think the Red Cross or Swiss politicians will notice those monstrosities?" Alma jerked a thumb in the direction of the crematoriums, arching a skeptical brow.

Kitty only laughed with great derision. "Do you not know the SS? They will tell them those are pork processing factories or some such and those Swiss big shots will eat it up and ask for a refill." She compressed her lips and gave Alma a knowing look. "As soon as the SS have no more use for them, they'll off them all like spring lambs; mark my words."

Next to his cart, Rabbi Dayen shifted restlessly. "I sincerely hope you're mistaken," he whispered.

"Well, I sincerely hope the pigs shall start flying so I can hop on one and set off to real Canada," Kitty countered, unimpressed. "Until that happens, there's nothing else for it but to count on myself and try to stick it out for as long as possible, Rebbe."

Kitty had just made a move to leave when Rabbi Dayen's question, uttered in the mildest of tones, "You don't believe in God, do you?" made her stop in her tracks.

"Do *you?*" Swinging round, Kitty regarded him wrathfully, as though insulted by such a suggestion. "In *this* place?!"

He made no reply. Who knew what she had to go through and whom she had to lose... He always thought it discourteous to preach God's word to people who didn't wish to hear it. In this place—that part she was right about—it wasn't just in bad taste; it was an insult. Once, an inmate had spat in his face when Dayen had refused his ration in observance of the holy day of Yom Kippur. The Rabbi had offered the fellow his bread as an apology for upsetting him.

"God is dead," Kitty declared darkly, looking him squarely in the eyes. There was an audible challenge in her voice. "The SS killed him."

"Perhaps so," the Rabbi conceded surprisingly easily.

Kitty looked as though she was about to say something, but the argument that was already coming, sharp and full of scorn, was met with such passive, all-forgiving love in Rabbi Dayen's eyes, she swallowed it with difficulty and stormed off, hissing a "Sentimental old fool" under her breath.

Rabbi Dayen was already whispering one prayer or another as he rocked gently forward and backward, following Kitty with eyes full of the helpless sorrow of an adult who had somehow failed the entire generation.

Alma kept studying him with great interest. He had stood out from the immaculately turned-out *Kanada* detail *Kommando* like a sore thumb. Thin as a rail, for half of his rations went over the barbed wire and to the less fortunate inmates, he was the only person in the entire Birkenau whom the SS permitted to grow out a beard. Many inmates found such favoritism rather puzzling—unlike the *Kanada* old numbers well versed in local trade and infamous for their organizing abilities, Dayen never bribed a single guard, never as much as exchanged a single word with a *Kapo*, never displayed any talents that the SS could find useful or entertaining. Perhaps, that was precisely the reason for their interest in him. Out of the entire camp population, he never asked for anything and only gave and gave to the less fortunate ones and the SS found such a display of humanity to be a local curiosity of sorts. Perhaps, after growing bored with watching a young son tearing a piece of bread out of his frail and dying father's hands, the SS hoped to decipher what Jewish magic kept Dayen so untouched by all that degradation and death around him.

"You know, you're very different from the priests I had to deal with my entire life," Alma noted. "They would call you a heretic just for saying such things about God."

"Were you baptized as Catholic?"

"At birth, as Protestant. Later, as Catholic, because someone speculated that it would protect me from the persecution. Fat lot of good it did, too." With a cynical smirk, she tugged at her inmate's blue dress. "We were your typical assimilated Jews, Herr Dayen. We celebrated Christmas and helped ourselves to pork chops on Fridays. We never considered ourselves any different from the regular Viennese population until the Nazis came in 1938 and explained to us how we were all worthless vermin and a drain on the German society."

"Everything happens for a reason."

There was a pause.

"Aren't you going to say something to the extent of my being sent here by the hand of God or something of that sort?" Alma inquired, half in jest.

The Rabbi only shook his head. "I'm going to say, I ought to take these papers you have already sorted outside to burn them, if I don't want to get lashed by the SS."

"Do they ever beat you at all?" Alma asked, curious.

"No. Not since I began working here."

"How long has it been?"

"About a year and a half now." His beard concealed another gentle smile. He wasn't an old man by any measure, but there were thick streaks of gray in its black mass. "They think me to be some sort of a saint."

For some time, Alma gazed at him without moving. "Maybe, you are."

"Maybe, we all are here," he conceded and picked up his heavy load.

"Again."

Inside the Music Block, it was impossible to breathe, even with all the windows standing open. Oppressive heat continued to suffocate the camp population confined to their airless barracks. Water had become a luxury once again; Zippy reported that, mad with thirst, inmates traded their pitiful bread rations for a cup of it right in the open.

Wiping the droplets of sweat off her brow, Alma struck the music stand with her baton a few times. She had purposely chosen Emmerich Kálmán's *Countess Maritza* as the first official musical piece of a higher level. Anyone who could read sheet music could master that simple operetta fast enough. Yet, Lota, a German flutist, had just missed her entry—again; Maria, a Polish mandolinist, managed to hit so many false notes during the first two minutes, Alma began cringing openly. The look of utter concentration creasing her brow, Sofia tried her best to follow the score but ended up entering in the wrong place and botching the entire part.

Tense silence hung over the room, interrupted only by the buzzing of the flies and occasional sniffle coming from one of the girls. They all knew what was at stake. It appeared that, not only through Alma's mind but through theirs as well, the recent exchange with Dr. Mengele passed:

"You seem to be very sure of yourself, Frau Rosé."

"I have already trained a female orchestra under my charge and it had great success in Europe. Yes, I believe I can train these young ladies as well."

Exasperated, Alma placed her baton back onto the stand and walked over to Sofia. "Give me your guitar. Watch my fingers closely."

In the two hours that followed, she physically repositioned the girls' inexperienced fingers into correct positions; demonstrated how to keep the right tempo; made them repeat the parts they had trouble with until they burst into tears and pleaded with her for a break.

"Frau Alma, I'll never get it right!" Maria was the first one to openly protest in her accented German. "I only played music at school. I'm not a professional like you. No one here is. Kálmán is too difficult for us. We know how to play songs and marches; not classical pieces."

"It's not a classical piece; it's a simple operetta," Alma grumbled under her breath to no one in particular. She was suddenly aware of a vague sense of panic that was just beginning to mount somewhere deep inside.

A simple, lighthearted operetta and even that they couldn't grasp. She had promised Dr. Mengele a Christmas concert with Bach and Wagner; she would be fortunate if they learned the first three pages of the blasted Kálmán by that time. Crude cursing was very much frowned upon in her aristocratic household, but at that moment, a big fat *Scheiße* was ready to fly off her tongue. Their lives depended on that concert. The invisible clock was ticking louder and louder in Alma's head, turning into outright panicked pounding, and the orchestra's progress remained virtually nonexistent.

Alma collected herself with great effort. She marched resolutely to Maria once again and made her pick up her mandolin. Placing her fingers on top of the girl's, she slowly, note by note, began going through Maria's part. But she soon discovered that the Polish girl's shoulders were shaking with silent sobs. She wasn't even paying attention to Alma's ministrations with the instrument.

"Alma, quit it," Zippy said, setting her own mandolin aside. "All this useless tormenting won't do anyone any good. You won't teach someone with superficial knowledge of music how to play a complicated musical piece of the *Countess Maritza* sort."

"Yes, I will." Alma refused to surrender.

"No, you won't. And neither can you play for the entire orchestra like you're doing now."

Defeated, Alma let go of Maria at last and walked out of the barrack. Inside her dress pocket, a half-empty pack of imported cigarettes still sat, generously thrown at her by the *Kanada* SS *Rottenführer*. They had a barter going on—she played sentimental songs for him that reminded him of his fiancée and he permitted her to dig through the riches of his detail. Musical instruments and sheet music in exchange for the memories. Both sides had somehow silently agreed that it was a fair exchange.

Alma lit one up and inhaled deeply, scowling at the horizon. An offense punishable by death, smoking during work hours, but that day, it suddenly made no difference to her if she lived or died. She was in one of those moods of black desperation and reckless bravery that led to her arrest in the first place, but it appeared life hadn't taught her how not to test it, after all. Let them shoot her, for all she cared.

"Alma."

Zippy. Alma didn't turn around, just took another long pull on her cigarette.

"Alma, look at me."

"What?" Alma cringed when it came out harsher than she had intended.

Zippy pretended not to notice. "Let's just get back to playing what we can. That march from *Rosamunde*—the girls know it quite well—"

"No."

"Just because you don't want to admit your professional defeat to Mengele?" Zippy purposely stood in front of Alma, blocking her view. A soft smile was playing on her lips.

Forced to look her in the eyes, Alma gave her a hard glare. It was idiotic taking it out on anyone; she did it to herself. But the infamous Rosé temper reared its ugly head, as it always did in situations like this one.

In an attempt at an apology, Alma offered Zippy her pack. Her friend took it, not offended in the slightest. For some time, they smoked in silence; only, unlike Alma, Zippy actually watched for the SS patrols.

"Even if you fail to present him with the music that is up to his high Nazi standards, he's not going to send us all to the gas," Zippy continued after some time. "I've been here longer than you. I know him. He'll cut people open without anesthesia, but he won't kill off the entire orchestra just because its conductor didn't deliver him Bach on time. He's like Mandl, a sentimentalist when you least expect it."

Alma rolled her eyes expressively.

"Oh, I know what you think." Zippy cleared her throat—or stifled a chuckle. "She's a vicious she-devil to be sure, but sometimes her maternal instincts resurface."

"*Maternal instincts*? In Mandl?" Alma regarded her with great disbelief.

"Yes. Mandl." Zippy exhaled the smoke away from Alma's face. "One time, during one of those surprise inspections of hers that she is so fond of, Mandl discovered me in bed in my room in the *Schreibstube*. Needless to say, I was petrified out of my wits and all but expected for her to drag me out of there into the street and shoot me in front of the others, just to teach them a lesson on what happens to such saboteurs who decide to take a nap in the middle of the afternoon. But instead of doing that, she only asked me—very calmly, too—what was the matter. I told her honestly that I had bad menstrual cramps. Not that it was ever considered to be any sort of excuse in the camp. Women who work in the *Aussenkommandos* have to hurl gravel for twelve hours straight, time of the month or not, and they'd better trade their single piece of bread for a few sheets of newspaper to keep themselves somewhat clean during their shift. Heavens forbid if an SS warden or a *Kapo* notice blood streaming down an inmate's legs or if their delicate Aryan noses smell it—they'd beat that woman for being a filthy sow who can't take care of her own personal hygiene. It doesn't seem to occur to anyone that it's next to impossible for those inmates to do so when they have no running water in their barracks, let alone a piece of soap or underwear...At any rate, I was so startled, I blurted it out before I could invent a better excuse. And what do you know? Instead of beating me, Mandl smiled at me tenderly, put her hand on my forehead, just like my mother used to do, and told me to stay in bed until I felt better. Long after she had left, I kept staring at the door in great wonder, thinking that now I'd definitely seen everything in this life."

Alma appeared to consider something, taking deep pulls on her cigarette.

"Those two new girls from France are very good," she finally said.

Zippy looked at her in surprise. "Did you hear a word of what I just said?"

"Yes. I heard everything. It's just, I don't agree with it. I don't agree with half-hearted repertoire just because it's the easy way out. I don't agree with anything less than excellence." She gave Zippy a pointed look. "I'll make a professional orchestra out of this band, whatever it takes. Mengele has permitted me to take on more professional musicians. We already got two out of the last transport. Now, I'll go through barracks and try to scout more. Perhaps, more shall arrive with the new transport..." She was gazing ahead, smiling faintly to herself.

Zippy only stared at her in horror. "That's all fine and well, that 'excellence' idea of yours, but consider the Music Block veterans' position! What do you suggest they do, after you replace them with professionals? To the gas with them? Dismiss them and reassign them to the outside *Kommandos* so they can die within a week?"

Alma looked at Zippy as though she had just said something incredibly idiotic. "No, of course, not. In order to run the Music Block effectively, I'll need copyists who will draw musical staffs and copy musical parts I write out. A secretary, to manage our rehearsals and performance schedule. A few decorators who shall look after our costumes and the stage. I'll definitely need a few runners."

A wavering grin appeared on Zippy's face.

"You're right," Alma conceded, stubbing out her cigarette on the block's wall. "I can't play for the entire orchestra. And neither can I teach them how to play serious music in such a short period of time. But what I can do is gather as many professional musicians as possible—forty, if we're lucky—under the pretext that we don't have enough instruments in the low range, something of that sort. I'll invent an excuse. And the girls who have been with the orchestra from the beginning will be simply reassigned to other duties but remain with the Music Block. I'll make it sound as though they're indispensable. We'll save as many girls as possible; I'll see to it. While I'm in charge, no one is going back into main camp and neither are they going to the gas. And I'll drop dead, but I'll deliver Mengele his blasted Bach on Christmas."

Chapter 9

The girl was pitifully scrawny and trembled like an orphaned sparrow.

"She's a very good violinist! Very good!" Hélène repeated once again in her strongly accented German. "We arrived on the same transport from France, but she was sick, and Frau Czajkowska rejected her. She can play any classical music you like! You just try her, Frau Alma. Frau Czajkowska refused to take her before, but it's because she was sick. High fever, couldn't play. She can play now. You just try her!"

The news about the auditions for the Music Block spread like wildfire around the camp. Starved, desperate women crowded in front of Alma's barrack every evening after the roll call, hoping for a place in the privileged detail. Every single one claimed a former musical career that was more amazing than the other. Unfortunately, as soon as they picked up the instruments they claimed they could play so well, the noises such "virtuosos" ended up extracting from them were the furthest thing from music one could have imagined.

"I'm sorry." Alma lost count of all the rejections she'd had to announce in the past three days. "I'm looking for professional musicians only."

The worst parts were the tears and the gut-wrenching pleas that came right after.

"Frau Alma, just give me a chance. I shall learn how to play! You just show me how! I shall be the best student."

"Frau Alma, I beg you, don't send me back. I won't survive another month in the outside *Kommando*."

"Have pity on me. I shall do whatever you need! There is an outbreak of typhus in the barrack next to ours. If it jumps on us, they shall send us all to the gas! Take me temporarily, Frau Alma. You can send me back later, if you like, but please, take me just for these few weeks. I can't go to the gas! My mother is in the camp also; who shall take care of her?"

Some satisfied themselves with wringing their hands before their chests; some threw themselves on the floor before Alma and clutched at the hem of her skirt or even her ankles and only let go when Sofia, who was used to such tactics, hit them on their hands with the *Kapo*'s baton that Alma positively refused to use.

"Everyone is suffering!" the Polish woman declared sternly, escorting the rejected women out. "You're not the only one. The order was given to find professional musicians. Are you a professional? No. Out with you then. Or do you wish to deliver your complaints to Dr. Mengele in person?"

The mention of the dreaded doctor's name was enough to put the fear of God into the inmate women. It caused Alma almost physical pain, seeing them shuffle dejectedly out of the barrack like transparent apparitions in their threadbare dresses, but there was a point to Sofia's reluctant cruelty. If Alma wished to keep the girls who couldn't play as Music Block staff, she had to fill their positions with such talents that neither Dr. Mengele not Maria Mandl would oppose such an arrangement.

Lost in thought, she didn't hear what the French girl had said.

"Sorry, what did you say?"

"I said, I can play *Countess Maritza* for you."

Already sensing what the result would be, Alma silently handed the girl her own violin. "Here, child."

"Her name is Violette," Hélène suddenly announced.

Alma looked at her sternly, but she only squared her shoulders more.

"Her name is Violette," Hélène repeated. "She's from Paris. She's eighteen years old, like me, and her favorite composer is Vivaldi."

And suddenly, the trembling sparrow in front of her had a name and a favorite composer. Alma couldn't help but snort at the dirty trick with a certain measure of approval. Rejecting nameless women was a much easier task. Sending a *Violette-from-Paris* to certain death was quite a different matter. Hélène knew that it would haunt Alma for the rest of her life.

Violette-from-Paris could play but, just as was Alma's suspicion, certainly not on the professional level.

"That's enough." Alma stopped her with her hand.

Holding her breath, Violette was expecting a verdict.

"I'll take you on a one-week trial. I'll arrange your temporary transfer from the outside work detail to the Music Block, but don't expect it to turn into a resort of any sort. It'll only mean that you shall practice from early morning till late night, until you feel as though your fingers will fall off. And since your friend is so supportive of you, I'm assigning her as your personal tutor. Understood, both of you?"

"*Jawohl.*"

Violette-from-Paris even curtsied.

Alma shook her head when the girl tried handing her the violin back. "Keep it. I don't need to practice; you do." Her good-natured grumbling was aimed at both girls, but the tone was somehow kind and almost motherly.

The sparrow had finally ceased trembling. For the first time, Alma had seen her smile.

Overnight, the temperature had suddenly plummeted. Clouds of mist rolled over the camp, obscuring the barracks and watchtowers from view. In it, the distant barking of dogs echoed. The dogs were

SS too, purebred and vicious. Sometimes, when their handlers grew bored, they let them off their leashes and amused themselves with watching their Alsatians chase and maul inmates who couldn't run fast enough. Even though such entertainment was ordinarily reserved for the men's camp, Alma still paused and listened closely. The high-pitched, nervous barking, amplified by the fog-shrouded vastness around, came steadily from the same place.

Alma heaved a breath of relief and proceeded on her way. From time to time, phantom-like, uncertain shadows moved in the fog—a striped army of ghosts caught in the limbo. The dogs must have been barking at the shadows, too.

By the time Alma had reached the Quarantine Block, her head-scarf was soaked through. In her eyelashes, droplets of mist hung. Her eyes were trained on the SS warden. Alma had an *Ausweis* with her, signed by Lagerführerin Mandl herself—a passport in this land of displaced persons—and could therefore move freely around the camp on her Music Block business. Still, in the territories where she was unknown, Alma took great care to stay away from the SS as much as she could help it. They had a nasty habit of shooting inmates first and asking questions later and Alma hoped to avoid becoming such a statistic.

She heard the warden curse under her breath—the mist carried words long distances. The weather was certainly muddy and wet, that much they both agreed on, but instead of cursing at it, the warden cursed at *the blasted Jews, the dirty swine. Because of them she had to slog through the muck for hours on end, filthy pigs, the lot of them...*

Alma didn't find it all too surprising; what else was one to expect from someone whose education came from the Führer and eight years of school, where race classes had replaced history of nations, where such a term as Jewish physics was very much a real thing, and where Jewish students' noses were "scientifically" measured in front of the entire class to prove their racial inferiority to the so-called Aryans.

Watching such an "Aryan" slip in the mud and curse even cruder under her breath, Alma suddenly discovered that she both despised and pitied her. But mostly pitied. The war wouldn't last for eternity. No wars ever did. It all would pass, and they, the Jews, would return to their arts, professions, and trades. Once again, they would pick up their pens and write sharp-witted articles for international newspapers; direct plays and films that would gather international recognition; write novels that would turn into instant classics; make music that would be played for years to come...And she, the nameless figure in her black waterproof cape, would still trudge through mud for the rest of her miserable life, for hatred never substituted talent or skill or intellect, and for that reason alone, Alma pitied her with a gleeful, malicious self-satisfaction.

From the small window of the Quarantine Block, a thin arm appeared, holding an aluminum mug missing a handle. Alma watched the warden pause in her tracks.

The entire month of August that she had spent here, Alma had heard moans and pleas for water coming from that very block. In Birkenau terms, it was dubbed the gateway to hell, and rightfully so—despite being sent here on the pretext of the quarantine, most of the block's inhabitants were left without food or water for two weeks. A good two thirds of those who survived the quarantine were sent to the gas.

That day, the quarantined inmates had caught their break at long last. The mist descended upon the camp and was rolling in delicious droplets from the roof and straight into the inmate's mug. Alma could very well imagine how the entire barrack's mouths pooled with saliva at the promise of the water. It came to them straight from heaven, the sweet blessing—

The warden's baton struck the hand, knocking the mug out of it. The SS guard kicked it further away with the tip of her black boot and struck at the windowpane that separated her from her invisible victims.

"Not even two weeks in and you're getting sly already, Israelite tramps? Back into your bunks and keep your fat behinds there! Sly, dirty monkeys!"

She was still grumbling as she turned the corner.

Swiftly, Alma retrieved the cup from the mud and wiped it clean with the end of her headscarf. The window was too high for her to see into the barrack, but she lifted the mug that she had filled with water to it. "Here, take it, quick! Don't fret; she's gone."

A hand snatched it from her within an instant. From inside, excited voices and commotion followed.

"Are there any accordion players among you?" Alma asked, holding her hands out for the mug to refill it. She knew they would down it in seconds.

This time, two big brown eyes appeared above the window's edge along with the mug. They regarded Alma with a measure of mistrust. Alma couldn't tell what color the girl's hair used to be—her head had been closely shaved.

"I'm not a warden. My name is Alma Rosé," she said, refilling the mug. The girl who'd given it to her didn't appear to hear anything at all; her gaze was firmly riveted on the precious water. Alma tried again, louder this time, "I'm from the Music Block. I'm looking for an accordion player." She passed the girl the newly filled cup.

The girl disappeared once again. Hands thrust in wet pockets, Alma began tapping her foot, throwing anxious glances over her shoulder. The warden could return any moment now.

"You said you're Alma Rosé? *The* Alma Rosé, from the Vienna Philharmonic?" Another set of eyes—blue this time—peered at Alma from the window.

"Yes, I am."

"My father was a member of the Amsterdam Philharmonic! I play the piano, but I can play the piano accordion, too."

"What's your name?"

"Flora Schrijver."

"Where did your transport come from?"

"Westerbork in Holland."

Alma nodded, committing the name to her memory. "Just hold on for a day or two more, Flora. I'll come and get you soon."

Murmuring the name and the transport origin under her breath like a prayer, Alma hurried to Mandl's office, slipping in the mud and nearly blind in the thickening fog. Turning the corner of the camp office building, she nearly lost her footing again and gasped when, instead of air, her arm clutched at some stiff material as she tried to recover her balance. She was still grasping at it as she slowly raised her gaze to the SS man in front of her. As though moving of their own volition, her lips uttered, "Flora Schrijver, Westerbork, Holland," all the while her eyes stared, without blinking, in the scowling man's eyes. Next to him, Maria Mandl stood.

"Forgive me please, Herr…" Alma suddenly realized that she couldn't make out his markings under his waterproof cape. "It was not my intention to…"

She was desperately groping for the suitable explanation. It was a miracle he hadn't backhanded her yet for such insolence—steadying herself using his arm as a prop. Realizing that she was still holding on to him, Alma quickly dropped her hand. The guard's expression didn't change; only the eyes began to crinkle slightly in the corners as if he was trying to conceal the beginning of a smile.

"You were saying?" he prompted her in an exaggeratedly civil tone. It occurred to Alma that he was enjoying this little game.

Alma licked her wet lips that positively refused to cooperate and passed her hand over her forehead, also damp, but all at once she wasn't sure whether it was due to the mist or the sweat that had broken on it. She felt hair under her fingers that must have come loose during her wild sprint and was now sticking to her skin; tried tucking it away under the wet kerchief but couldn't—her hand was trembling something shameful. "The mud, Herr Kommandant…"

All that was left to do was hang her head in surrender and wait for the dressing-down or slap to come.

"Herr Kommandant?" To her astonishment, the man before her broke into a smile. The raincoat's hood was pulled over his uniform cap, but she saw that he must have been in his late thirties or early forties and had a dark coloring and inquisitive eyes. "Why, thank you kindly for the promotion. Long overdue, I must say."

Next to him, Mandl also began to chuckle. Both of them looked as though Alma appeared thoroughly amusing to them at that moment. "This is Obersturmführer Hössler. Herr Obersturmführer, this is Alma Rosé. My new orchestra conductor I've been telling you about."

"Ah, the star of the Vienna Philharmonic." He shifted his gaze back to Alma, regarding her with a different sort of interest now.

"You're much too kind, Herr Obersturmführer," Alma mumbled, still struggling with her kerchief. Mandl was obsessed with appearances; she had given them new uniforms for that very reason, to look pretty before the audience and generally to distinguish her new mascots from the pitiful camp population. And here she was, the supposed venerated leader of that orchestra, looking like a savage in front of Mandl's—Alma stumbled upon the right word—superior? He had to be, with his high rank.

Suddenly, Hössler reached toward her face. Alma flinched instinctively, expecting a blow, and froze when, contrary to that expectation, he calmly tucked the loose strand of hair she'd been fighting with under her kerchief and adjusted it neatly on her head as though it was the most natural thing to do.

"There. All better. Pretty as a picture." He presented her with another good-natured smile. "Pleasure to make your acquaintance, Frau Rosé. On behalf of the administration, I welcome you to Auschwitz-Birkenau and I can hardly wait to hear you and your virtuosos play."

He offered her his hand. Alma looked at it before giving it a hesitant shake. The entire situation was positively surreal, and she didn't know what to make of it. Despite being treated rather courteously so far by their kind, Alma still had seen what these people were capable of. He held her narrow palm in his and all she could think about was all the occasions he must have held his service gun in that same hand, all the people he must have shot—

"Herr Obersturmführer loves music," Mandl announced with another long glance in the man's direction.

"Oh yes," he confirmed readily, releasing Alma's hand at last. "Very much."

Alma couldn't help wondering if they were lovers.

"What were you saying before?" Hössler's question caught Alma off guard. Seeing her confusion, he went on to clarify, "When you bumped into me, you were saying something."

"Oh...yes, Herr Obersturmführer. I have just had the great fortune to find an accordion player in the Quarantine Block and I was repeating her name so I wouldn't forget it."

"She's so dedicated." Mandl was beaming like a proud mother displaying a favorite child before the school headmaster.

Alma decided to make use of her good disposition. "I was going to ask your permission to transfer her to my block, Lagerführerin."

"Of course. Tell Spitzer. She'll do the paperwork and I'll sign it as soon as it's ready."

"Thank you, Lagerführerin." Alma hesitated, waiting for permission to be dismissed. The entire time, she was aware of Hössler's eyes on her.

"You're all wet and shivering something frightful," he said, looking concerned. Alma hadn't even noticed that she was. "If you keep running about the camp in the same state of undress in this weather, you'll catch pneumonia or worse. Surely, we don't want that." He half turned to Mandl.

"No, of course not, Herr Obersturmführer," she rushed to agree.

"Go to the *Kanada* and pick out a raincoat for yourself." Once again, his gaze was trained on Alma. "And a regular warm coat and boots as well. The summer is gone and, here in Poland, it gets cold very quickly." He permitted himself a quick smile. "And we need you healthy, Frau Rosé."

Chapter 10

The Music Block had long gone to sleep. The only person still awake, Alma was working on the music score for the following day, when an urgent rapping came from behind the door. It was one of the girls assigned to the Reception Block.

"Do you still need a cellist?" she asked, out of breath. "I have one among the new arrivals. Anita Lasker is her name. But you have to come quick; Herr Doktor is holding a second selection among the new arrivals outside the Sauna. The girl is still inside with the last batch to go through disinfection, but as soon as she's out, there's a big chance he'll throw her onto that truck before she knows what hit her."

"Herr Doktor" meant Mengele, of course.

Alma groped for her new camel-hair coat in the semi-darkness of the room and pulled it right over her nightgown.

"Is she a professional?" Alma asked, tying the headscarf at the nape of her neck.

"I wouldn't know. She's a political and was deported from France. She even survived their French Gestapo interrogation," the girl added, obviously impressed.

She may have survived the Gestapo, but Mengele was an entirely different matter altogether, Alma thought to herself, pulling on her rubber boots.

Alma had "survived" the French Gestapo herself, after some bastard at the French–Swiss border promised to smuggle her from occupied France and into neutral Switzerland but instead sold her off to the German agents for a fee. Caught red-handed with a fake passport supplied by her Dutch friends, Alma had already been mentally preparing herself for some vicious third degree and instead was met with a dreadfully bored-looking German official. He had indicated a chair across his desk for her to take. "Real name?"— "Alma Rosé." "Nationality?"—"Austrian." From the German, a certain look under an arched brow. "Stateless person," she had quickly corrected herself. All Jews by then had been reduced to that dehumanizing definition—stateless people, a nameless herd. It was easier to kill them that way. The German had half-heartedly asked her where she got the passport from. Firmly set on keeping the names of her friends out of it, Alma had quickly made up some story about purchasing it from some Frenchman already there, in France. The Gestapo official had pretended to believe her, showed her where to sign the statement his secretary had typed out and sent Alma on her way to the Drancy transit camp, seemingly glad to be rid of her. "It was the Resistance members that they were after," one of the Drancy fellow sufferers had explained to her later. "With us, stateless people, they don't bother all that much."

No, they didn't bother with them all that much; simply sent them to extermination camps like Auschwitz to be worked and starved to death, as Alma had learned since.

"She is still inside the Sauna, you said?" Alma demanded, already in the door of the block.

"I should imagine. I ran as fast as I could." The girl searched Alma's face, suddenly concerned. "Are you permitted to go inside while the disinfection is in process?"

"It depends on the guard," Alma replied honestly and rushed outside.

After passing several checkpoints without any trouble—few privileged inmates had the permission to move freely around the camp and the SS knew most of them by now and waved them through without bothering to check their *Ausweis*—the women arrived at the Reception Block. Having processed its human load, it stood silent and almost deserted. Two Red Triangles were sweeping what remained of the shorn hair into industrial-type sacks. Three filled ones already stood by the wall, ready to be transported for disinfection and further processing. *Kanada* men were digging through the piles of discarded clothes lazily—the SS must have all gone to their barracks outside the camp for the night, leaving the inmates to their own devices. Looking utterly bored, another *Kanada* inmate was sitting at the table, sorting through a mound of wedding rings, watches, and jewelry. In front of him, several boxes stood—*Watches, Rings, Earrings, Diamonds, Precious Stones.* The *Kapo*, who was supposed to be supervising him, was napping insolently in the corner, his back pressed against the wall and arms crossed over his chest comfortably.

The girl led Alma toward the thick, double doors with the words, *Sauna and Disinfection,* written above them. Leaning against them, a *Kapo* was smoking.

"My name is Alma Rosé," she announced, presenting the burly man with her *Ausweis.* "I'm from the Music Block and I'm here for the cellist."

"Good for you," the man responded with a derisive snort, hardly glancing into her pass. "And I'm here for a ballerina, but she's still washing up for me."

"Are there women still inside then?" Alma demanded, ignoring his innuendo.

The man measured her icily. "What do you want with them?"

"I want to ask them what hats are in fashion this season in Paris," she retorted poisonously. "What do you think? I told you, I need a cellist. Dr. Mengele and Obersturmführer Hössler made a request for a full orchestra to play for them on Christmas. Shall you let me in or should I go outside and fetch Herr Doktor from the *Appellplatz,* so he can give you direct orders? Or shall I wake Obersturmführer Hössler, perhaps? Would you prefer to speak to him?" She raised her voice on purpose. It was important to sound convincing.

The lecherous grin slipped off the *Kapo*'s face as though by magic. Just one of those names would be enough to instill terror into anyone who knew what was good for them; threatening with both of them produced an immediate effect. Swinging swiftly round, the *Kapo* began turning the handle of the locking mechanism with impressive speed. "I was only joking. They've been waiting there for some time now... We have just run out of the disinfectant, so the last batch hasn't been processed yet. See if your cellist is among them." With an effort, he pulled the heavy door open.

The sauna room stood before them, silent and immersed in semi-twilight. In spite of herself, Alma felt a chill creeping down her spine, rising hairs all over her body. The memory of her own experience with it was still fresh. As she stared at the dark, gaping maw of the familiar vast room, she recalled the day of her arrival, how she was digging her heels into the cold, concrete floor on its threshold—*A real shower room or a gas chamber? There was talk, already on the train, that some camps had those, and crematoriums as well; major farms used human ashes as fertilizer; German factories purchased sacks of human hair to use for upholstery and as mattress stuffing and a lot more horrors to that extent*—just to be swept off and carried forward by the pressing wave of human bodies, prodded in their stiff backs with horsewhips and cudgels. The door had slammed shut after them with an ominous clang. The darkness. Heavy, terrified breathing around her and the harsh, sickening scent of human fear. No one had screamed. No one had dared to utter a single whisper. Instead, a thousand eyes had fastened on the showerheads mounted to the ceiling in a unanimous prayer. Hissing. Grunting of the metal. The breathing had ceased altogether. Everyone was holding it, eyes glistening in the darkness, too terrified to blink. And then, suddenly, water. Torrents and torrents of it, ice cold, pouring down their bodies and mixing with the tears of relief.

With a tremendous effort, Alma forced herself to step inside—of her own volition this time.

"I'm looking for Anita Lasker." Even her voice sounded strange in this damp sarcophagus, as though it didn't belong to her any longer. Alma cleared her throat and moved toward a wall of white, trembling bodies that were barely discernible in the darkness. They parted around her like a human sea. Wary eyes followed her every move, bewildered and too frightened to reply. "Is Anita Lasker among you? A recent transport from France? Anita Lasker, the cellist…"

"I'm Anita Lasker."

From the depth of the room, a girl advanced toward the light. Her head was freshly shorn and bleeding where the blunt shaving machine had nicked it. In front of her chest, she was clutching a toothbrush in her closed fist as one would a knife, wherever she had snatched it from.

Gently, Alma reached out and took the girl's wrist in her hand. "My name is Alma Rosé," she introduced herself, speaking as softly as possible. "I'm from the Music Block. Come with me. You shall play cello in my orchestra."

She gave Anita's wrist a gentle tug, but she wouldn't budge. The girl stood, riveted to her place, like a stone statue that couldn't be moved even with the best will in the world.

"It's over now," Alma said, wrapping her arm around the girl's shoulders. They were stiff, as though made of lead. "All over. Come. You'll only play music from now on. What can you play for me first thing tomorrow morning, after the *Appell*? Can you play Schubert's '*Marche Militaire*'?"

Slowly, Anita managed a rigid nod.

"Good. What else did you play when you were in France? I was deported from France, too. But I couldn't play anything there. I left my violin in Holland."

"I didn't play anything in France either," the girl finally spoke hoarsely. "I was falsifying the documents for the Resistance."

Under Alma's arm, her shoulders began to shake with silent sobs. She allowed herself to be led outside, into the brightly lit room where the Reception Block girl was already waiting for her with the striped dress and a pair of shoes in her hands.

"I told you, Frau Alma would help you, didn't I?" She pulled the dress over Anita's head and guided her hand, with the toothbrush still clenched in it, through one of the sleeves. "This is something temporary for you. Tomorrow morning, Frau Alma shall get you an orchestra girl dress—you shall look like a regular princess!"

Under the *Kapo*'s stunned look, Alma removed her coat and placed it over her new cellist's shoulders. The girl looked at her. The tears were still rolling down her cheeks, but she finally lowered her toothbrush, which she'd been holding like a weapon the entire time.

"All over now," Alma repeated, smiling.

The girl nodded. Terror still clung to her skin like a dirty film one would never be able to wash off entirely, but her eyes were human once again, having lost the haunted look of a cornered animal about to be slaughtered.

The new orchestra's first concert given in the officers' mess resulted in thunderous applause. Though, perhaps, such an unexpectedly warm reception was due to the orchestra's new benefactor—Obersturmführer Hössler—who was the first one to rise from his chair and clap with such frank enthusiasm. Alma hadn't changed her opinion of them; few of the SS officers, let alone regular guards, understood anything about music. But as their Prussian character dictated, they looked up to their superiors for instructions whenever they couldn't process something themselves.

My honor is loyalty, as their motto went. No, it wasn't loyalty; it was blind, dog-like obedience, which Alma despised with every fiber of her soul. Nevertheless, she smiled and bowed ceaselessly and pressed her hand to her chest—*Thank you kindly, Herren, much obliged; may you all drop dead, you miserable, uniformed herd.*

Hössler approached the makeshift stage and requested a violin solo. Alma obliged him, as deferentially as possible. *Kanada* Kitty's words had stuck with her—*To survive this place, an inmate must be well-informed and well-connected*—and so, Alma had made her inquiries about Mandl's strangely civilized companion.

The superficial investigation yielded the following: Schutzhaftlagerführer (his official position in the camp administration, according to Zippy) Hössler was Mandl's immediate superior and was responsible for the operation of the Birkenau women's camp. Above him—only the camp *Kommandant*. Immediate duties included selections and crematoriums management—*gassings and cremations,* in Zippy's straightforward terms. That was the extent of what the girl could supply; she didn't work directly under Hössler after all. The *Sonderkommando* did.

Making use of her access to the *Kanada*, Alma had successfully cornered one of the *Sonderkommando* men who was busy unloading the truck full of gassed people's belongings.

"Hössler?" He'd scratched the stubble on his neck. "The sweet-talker," came the reply. "Well-mannered and proper, very polished, like some Prussian Count…Shot a man with his revolver the other day for insubordination." An indifferent shrug. "But, overall, a just enough superior. As long as you don't get on his bad side. If he blows his lid, it's best for one's health to make oneself scarce. Music? Oh yes, he likes music a lot! Knows a lot of those big-shot composers. How is he with women? All right, I suppose. Depends on the woman. Jokes with *Kanada* girls a lot. The women from the camp, on the other hand…" A telling grimace. "They don't really look like women. I imagine, he doesn't consider them as such."

It had sounded promising enough. To be sure, Hössler was still a ruthless killer, but compared to others, he at least inspired some confidence as someone who could be reasoned with and that much Alma could work with.

Now, the radiant smile of a well-trained performer blossomed on the violinist's face as she leaned toward him. "What would you like to hear, Herr Obersturmführer?"

From Hössler, a well-bred and gracious, "Whatever you wish to play, Frau Alma."

Alma searched his face, wondering how far she could push it. "May I play Wieniawski's 'Oberek,' Polish Dance?" she probed as gently as possible.

Most of the non-German composers were frowned upon. All Jewish ones were outright banned from the orchestra's repertoire. The question was essentially a test of his ideological flexibility. With eager eyes, Alma was watching for Hössler's reaction.

After a moment's consideration, his cultural inclinations appeared to triumph over his antisemitism. Hössler smiled benevolently. "I will listen to a nursery rhyme if it is you who plays it."

With that blessing, he went back to his seat.

Giddy from a small victory, Alma picked up her violin. It was a gamble, testing the authorities in such an insolent manner, but by some miracle, it had paid off. She smiled even wider when her uniformed audience began tapping their tall boots to the gay melody. This time, after she had finished, they didn't wait for their commander's signal to applaud her.

Only Sofia wasn't too thrilled with her choice of solo music.

"What were you thinking?!" she hissed in Alma's ear immediately after the orchestra took their final bow. "To play a piece composed not only by a Pole but a Jew on top of it!"

"Don't fret. Hössler didn't mind and everyone else is too ignorant to realize whose music I was playing. Here, they're considered musical connoisseurs when they can tell Mozart from Bach; do you truly believe they know who Wieniawski is?"

"It was still an idiotic idea."

Alma didn't argue. What Sofia failed to comprehend was that it hadn't been some reckless act of defiance for the sake of defiance itself. All Alma wished was to see if the soft-spoken and well-mannered officer could be relied on when it came to protection. Having Mandl on their side was good; having Dr. Mengele was even better. But it was Hössler who was the ultimate authority over both. If she could secure him as a protector, and particularly for her Jewish girls, Alma felt she would finally be able to breathe freely, or at least as freely as one could breathe in a place like Auschwitz.

The cultural part of the evening was over. The SS stood and smoked with their backs to the stage, chatting animatedly among themselves. The lower ranks consulted their wristwatches—they heard the waiters setting the tables in the adjacent banquet hall and kept throwing impatient glances in that direction and annoyed ones at their superiors who didn't seem to be in any rush.

Ignored by them, Alma's girls were packing their instruments, making as little noise as possible. Alma hoped to get them out of the SS quarters before the tantalizing aromas would start spreading from the feast the inmate waiters were presently organizing for their uniformed masters. No need for the girls to remember what glazed ribs smelled like.

In the general rush, Violette-from-Paris caught a music stand with her elbow. Alma, her hands full with the violin and sheet music, caught it with her ankle before it could crash onto the floor.

"Excellent reflexes."

For an instant, Alma started. One of the SS men stood on the stage, bespectacled and blond. Across his left cheek was a long dueling scar. One of the nationalist fraternity types; Alma was well familiar with the kind, back from the days when Vienna was still a free city. Having recovered herself, she pushed the stand back into its position and forced a smile.

"Thank you, Herr Scharführer."

His colorless, cold eyes behind the lenses shifted to her chest, noted the absence of the star; absence of any markings, in fact. Just like *Kanada* girls, Alma was spared the humiliation of a personal number and a classification mark sewn onto her clothes.

"Are you political?"

Some ancient instinct in Alma prompted her to say yes.

He nodded, satisfied. "What were you arrested for?"

"Contempt for the government," Alma gave him a vague reply.

It wasn't, technically, a lie. It was contempt, pure and intentional, that inspired in Alma the decision to travel to Holland in the first place, even when the German army was already creeping toward its borders. Influential friends in England had secured her and her father's positions as friendly aliens with full permission to perform and earn a living. It was contempt that prompted Alma to accept the invitation from the Amsterdam Philharmonic after the Germans had forced her and her family out of the Vienna one. It was contempt that kept her in the country overrun by the gray-green uniforms. It was contempt that prompted her to play until the victorious end, right under the Gestapo's noses, until the deportations started, and her friends and hosts began to plead with her to run to Switzerland via France for her own safety's sake. One of them even married her in the hope to help her with the papers, despite the fact that he had no interest in women whatsoever in the romantic sense and only did it out of the goodness of his heart. Alma always remembered his deed with an invariable surge of the most profound gratitude.

"Your orchestra is very good," the SS man said, calling Alma back to herself. She saw him narrow his eyes at her girls with the detached look of a bank accountant about him. He was calculating something to himself. "But you have far too many Jews among your musicians."

Alma's face grew very still. "They're all professional musicians," she said, holding his gaze.

Out of the corner of her eye, she saw Hössler and Mandl climbing the stairs to the stage.

"That is all fine and well, but the orchestra was first organized as an Aryan *Kommando*," the officer pressed, growing annoyed with her staring.

"The Aryan musicians weren't professional," Alma explained with an icy smile. "All they could play was simple military marches and popular songs. Frau Lagerführerin and Herr Obersturmführer expressed their desire for an actual, professional orchestra. Now, we can play Bach and Vivaldi. However, if you still have complaints about the quality of their playing…" Under Sofia's mortified gaze, Alma turned to Hössler and beamed at him. "Herr Obersturmführer, could you perhaps allow a couple of your men's camp orchestra's members to come and tutor my new Jewish girls? Herr Scharführer has just expressed his concerns about the quality of their performance and I wouldn't want to disappoint him next time we perform."

In the periphery of Alma's vision, Sofia rolled her eyes toward the ceiling in pure torment.

"I don't see how it would harm anyone." Hössler produced an elegant silver cigarette case and, under the blond Austrian's incredulous look, offered it to Alma.

Now, thoroughly ignoring her compatriot, Alma was speaking to Hössler directly: "As a matter of fact, the orchestra could use a double bass player, so we could expand our repertoire even further. I have two new arrivals from Greece—Lily and Yvette—and Yvette was just learning how to play a double bass at her hometown, Salonika, when her family was deported. Perhaps, Herr Obersturmführer has someone who could continue teaching her how to play it?"

"I could certainly free someone of their duties for a couple of months." He held his lighter to her cigarette. The Austrian officer was staring at him as though his superior had completely lost his head. "Will a couple of months be enough to…"

"Of course, Herr Obersturmführer!" Alma rushed to reassure him. "Just in time for Christmas." She smiled charmingly at him.

"Just what we need, Jews performing at Christmas," the Austrian commented with a derisive snort, searching Mandl's face for support.

But the leader of women's camp was looking at Hössler instead, her expression unreadable.

It took Hössler a few moments to react. At first, the benevolent grin slid off his face. His features hardened like plaster; the eyes turned black with growing rage as color mounted in his cheeks. Slowly and deliberately, Hössler turned to the SS man, squaring his shoulders, uncoiling before the Austrian like a poisonous snake. The SS guard was taller than his superior, but he somehow shrank, contracted before this threatening presence that suddenly appeared to tower over him, ready for slaughter.

"Perhaps you wish to perform yourself then, you miserable idiot?" Hössler roared, his face distorted with ire. Alma's shoulders jerked from the pure violence of his shout. "If you believe that you can play better than *the Jews,* go straight ahead. Pick up an instrument. Entertain us. Well?! Why are you so silent all of a sudden? Have you gone dumb with fear? Frau Alma is doing her best trying to conjure up a real orchestra for us to enjoy and you question her qualifications and judgment? SS cultural evenings aren't mandatory. If Jews playing music offends your delicate senses so much, march out of here before I help you find your legs. Self-righteous raven with epaulets! Stand to attention when your superior addresses you. Or don't they teach you that anymore in your schools? Has the racial theory replaced military drill, what?!" he bellowed in the young man's face.

The latter had gone white in the face. Shoulders squared, palms pressed against his jodhpurs, he stared straight ahead as though on the parade ground in front of a drill sergeant.

"I said, what?!" Hössler's incensed shout immersed the entire hall in tense silence.

"No, Herr Obersturmführer."

"I didn't hear you."

"No, Herr Obersturmführer!"

"No, what?"

The young man stood there at a loss, already trembling. "No, they didn't replace military drill," he managed at last.

"And what else?"

"No, Jewish music doesn't assault my delicate senses, Herr Obersturmführer."

"Get lost, you louse with a rank! Whoever signed that promotion for you?!" Hössler snarled viciously at the sight of the hastily retreating officer.

Meanwhile, Maria Mandl was stroking his sleeve, saying something softly to him, but he appeared to be entirely oblivious to her presence in his infuriated state.

Alma caught Sofia's reproachful glare directed at her. *Well? That's the benevolent Herr Benefactor of yours. A fine temper; just what we need to play with.*

The former Polish *Kapo* was right, of course. The SS were all the same. The Berlin office didn't send charitable souls here; only savages for whom human life was worth nothing, and after seeing how Hössler had treated his own kind, Alma could only imagine what he could do to hers.

She looked away in embarrassment. A jolt went straight through her nerves, already strained to the utmost, when a hand landed on top of her arm, under which she was still squeezing her violin by its neck.

"I hope you can forgive my unacceptable behavior." Hössler was back to his well-bred self as though nothing had transpired. "It was in no way my intention to insult you with all that..." He sighed, annoyed. "They're young and stupid. For the most part. Aren't they?" He turned to Mandl. She nodded readily, a pacifying hand still on his cuff. "What of the banquet? Is everything ready?"

"I shall go and inquire at once." The women's camp leader disappeared, and Alma suddenly felt exposed and in great danger without their *Lagerführerin* in proximity. A forgotten cigarette trembled imperceptibly in her ice-cold fingers.

"Yes, young and stupid," Hössler repeated and smiled at Alma somewhat tiredly. The lines around his mouth and eyes grew more pronounced. "Are you Jewish, Frau Alma?" he asked suddenly.

She didn't know what Mandl had told him, but for some reason, after a moment's hesitation, Alma acknowledged that yes, she was. *A full Jew. Baptized first as a Protestant, then as a Catholic, but a Jew nevertheless.*

Hössler shook his head, the same melancholy smile never leaving his face. "No, you're not a Jew. You're a Viennese, and that's an entirely different race of people. Educated, refined, cosmopolitan... How I should love to sit down and share a cognac with you and talk about art and music and whatnot. If you only knew how starved I am for intellectual conversations here, Frau Alma."

"I'm sure that Lagerführerin is a fine conversationalist..." Alma's voice trailed off when Hössler broke into soundless chuckles.

"Ah, yes. You ought to say that about your camp leader. Very savvy of you. I'll tell her you said that." He gave her another wry look. "Are you married, Frau Alma?"

"Jawohl, Herr Obersturmführer."

Hössler made a face. "Don't say *Jawohl* to me. I can't bear hearing it, from you, at any rate. Just say, yes or no, like normal people do."

"Yes."

"Where's your husband?"

"In Holland, Herr Obersturmführer."

"A gentile?"

"Yes."

He nodded his approval. "Marriage didn't protect you?"

"No, Herr Obersturmführer. A new decree came out..."

"Ah. I see. Always the new decree." He looked away as though in embarrassment. When he turned back to her, an expression of genuine regret was on his face. "I'm sorry you ended up here,

Frau Alma. You're a fine violinist and a fine woman. You don't belong here."

"I'm happy here, Herr Obersturmführer. We have a very nice barrack and we're treated very well. We have nothing to complain about. And if I didn't end up here, who knows what would have happened to my girls?"

For a very long moment, Hössler regarded her with an unreadable expression on his face. "Yes, a fine woman indeed," he said softly at last. "Well, if you're happy, I'm happy too. Tell me, Frau Alma: after the war is over, will you have that glass of cognac with me?"

Caught off guard, Alma wasn't sure of how to react. But she quickly recollected herself and smiled brightly at the man, who was holding not only hers, but her entire orchestra's lives in his hands.

"It will be my pleasure, Herr Obersturmführer."

"And my honor, Frau Alma. Thank you for your splendid playing this evening. Don't leave just yet. Wait behind the stage. When the banquet is over, and the uniforms are gone, the waiters will serve you dinner on my orders. There shall be plenty of food for you and your girls."

That was the last thing she had expected.

"Thank you, Herr Obersturmführer." Alma discovered that she actually meant it this time.

Chapter 11

"I regret to inform you, but our pianist is gone."

Alma stared at her counterpart. Just like her, the *Kapo* of the Birkenau men's orchestra, Szymon Laks, wore civilian clothes and would have looked like a regular intellectual, if it weren't for the striped cap appearing oddly out of place with his made-to-measure jacket. His dark hair under it also wasn't shaved, Alma noticed, but neatly brushed and smoothed with water.

She had caught them just in time, he had informed her mere moments ago; they were just about to set out for the main *Appellplatz* to play during the execution. "The camp resistance fellows again," he had sighed dejectedly. "They say the camp Gestapo chief Grabner fried one of the poor devils' faces off on one side entirely to get the names of the accomplices from him, but the fellow said nothing. What were they even trying to accomplish, the poor sods?"

Perhaps nothing, Alma mused to herself, watching the men gathering their instruments. Or, perhaps, at least this way they wouldn't die compliantly, like sheep, for nothing and that was worth all the torture and the noose.

"Gone?" Uncertain, Alma jerked her thumb in the direction of the crematorium, hoping to steer Laks away from the subject that would certainly give her nightmares.

Laks grinned. "No. Gone home." Under Alma's incredulous glance, he pushed his steel-rimmed glasses back onto the bridge of his nose. "He had served his six-month term and was released back to freedom. He was a *Reichsdeutsche*, you see," he went on to explain. "First-rate German blood. Unlike our kind, they can actually get out of here."

"Looked like a Teutonic knight," a double bass player, Heinz Lewin, inserted. "Fit for their propaganda movies, no less."

On Alma's request and with Hössler's blessing, Heinz had been freed from his secondary duties as a watchmaker and appeared to be very enthusiastic on account of spending his days among the orchestra girls for the next two months. Summoned by the runner from his watchmaking work detail, he had already assembled his things and was patiently waiting for Alma while she was trying to negotiate another couple of tutors for her girls. There was no immediate need for a pianist; in fact, Alma's Music Block didn't even have a piano, but she had Flora struggling with her piano accordion and if Alma could find a tutor for her, she felt it would improve the girl's chances significantly.

"To be truthful with you, he was a lousy pianist," Laks went on, "but a good fellow."

"He'll be back before we know it." Heinz smirked good-humoredly.

"Why would you say that?" Alma asked.

"He's too much of a humanist to know what's good for him," Laks explained. "That's how he got himself into this *fine SS resort* in the first place. His father is one of those Golden Pheasants: the top Nazi brass. What do you know? Instead of going to one of their Napola schools for the future leaders of the Reich, the idiot decided to make music and, along with it, false papers for our kind."

Alma noticed that not only Laks, but at least half of the male orchestra members wore yellow stars sewn onto their clothes. All at once, Hössler's lenience toward Alma's taking in more and more Jewish girls began making a whole lot of sense. He'd been practicing the very same thing in his male orchestra for quite some time. It was refreshing, having the SS man in the camp, for whom the quality of music was more important than the musicians' racial status.

"He only spent a few months here," Laks said. "It's thanks to him that they organized the entire male orchestra in Birkenau."

"Unseemly for the Nazi bigwig's son to bend his back at some detail unworthy of His Grace's pedigree." Heinz chuckled, but without malice.

"He hated it when we would tease him about it," one of the violinists inserted. "I've seen many people being ashamed of their race in my day, but I've never seen anyone get ashamed on account of being a *Reichsdeutsche*."

"Perhaps he hated being teased about it because he knew that he had a reason to be ashamed," Alma reflected. "Other races are innocent. If my race was presently slaughtering the others indiscriminately, that would make me ashamed of it too."

Laks didn't argue the point. "Is your *Ausweis* good for the main camp?" he asked instead. After Alma nodded, he produced a piece of paper and wrote a short message on it. "Try Auschwitz orchestra for the pianist. Show the conductor this note; they're Poles there for the most part—the *Kommandant* doesn't care all that much what we do here in Birkenau, but he'll drop dead before he permits any Jews into his Auschwitz orchestra—and they may get difficult with you."

"Why would they get difficult with me?"

"You're a Jewess who has replaced their fellow Pole as a *Kapo*." Laks shrugged as though it was a sufficient explanation.

Alma snorted softly. In this *fine SS resort*, it was.

After taking Heinz to the Music Block and leaving him to his new tutoring duties—although there would hardly be any tutoring that day, Alma thought with a smile, just lots of chatter and that was fine by her—she made her way back to the men's camp, thoroughly avoiding the *Appellplatz* with its gallows. Having considered Laks's warning about the Polish members of the orchestra, Alma thought it wise to supply them not only with the *Kapo*'s note, but with something more substantial. A direct order from the camp leader, for one instance.

"Obersturmführer Hössler?" she inquired at the checkpoint, after presenting her pass to a bored-looking SS guard, reading the entertainment section of a newspaper.

With a voluminous sigh, he reached for his ledger and checked the time. "The transport has arrived two hours ago. He must be supervising the *Aktion* at the *Krema*."

"Which one?"

The guard rolled his eyes. "The fourth one." He was back to perusing a picture of a film star, and Hitler's favorite movie director, Leni Riefenstahl skiing in her bikini before Alma had a chance to thank him.

The doors to Crematorium IV stood wide open, swallowing entire families within seconds. It was the SS's pride and joy, the most modern facility fully equipped to exterminate "subhuman" nations in a truly German orderly fashion. There were four of them in Birkenau and they certainly surpassed their Auschwitz counterpart both in size and efficiency. It was thanks to these four monstrosities that the two former gas chambers that stood in the field slightly away from the camp and bore the innocent names of the Little White House and the Little Red House were abandoned. Two former village huts, they weren't efficient enough as gassing facilities. It took the gas too long to take hold; people cried and pleaded something terrible behind the doors, banging at them and upsetting the SS on duty with their prolonged agony. Then the bodies had to be taken to Auschwitz for cremation, and every few days the walls of the chimney would crumble from the overuse, much to Kommandant Höss' dissatisfaction. Open graves would have to be dug out to bury the corpses while the walls were being fixed, but then they would crumble again and more graves had to be dug and the SS gradually began running out of space for those. And then the ground began to rise, expelling toxic fumes and liquids, poisoning the water in the vicinity.

But now, the ingenious Aryan race had solved all of those troubles. The four crematoriums could run a nonstop operation, processing thousands of people daily. No more mass graves; no more transportation problem. They even installed elevators inside the two-storied facilities for that very purpose. Now, it only took the *Sonderkommando* minutes to transport the corpses from the gas chamber in the basement upstairs, where their teeth would be checked for gold fillings, orifices for hidden gold, hair shaven off and neatly packed into sacks. Someone was already waiting for the processed ones with the gurney. Sometimes, the *Sonderkommando* men, those unfortunate slaves of the SS forced by their uniformed masters to perform the grimmest of duties, recognized their own relatives or friends in the still-warm corpses. Sometimes, they went to the wire afterward. Sometimes, they got drunk and wept, hidden behind a sorting table in the *Kanada* detail, and told what they had to see to anyone who happened to be near.

One day, Alma had happened to be near. She couldn't sleep for several nights in a row after what she had heard from him, haunted by the images of the open graves, corpses with shaved heads, and the weeping gas chamber attendants pulling the golden fillings out of their relatives' mouths. Now, she would have to see it all with her own two eyes.

Alma found Hössler precisely where the SS man had promised. Well-groomed and absolutely unarmed, he stood near the entrance and spoke to the apprehensive crowd of about a thousand people in front of him in his well-regulated, pleasant voice.

"You have now arrived at Auschwitz-Birkenau. This is not a resort, but a working camp, and we expect you to do your duty as our soldiers are presently doing theirs on the front. Just like they are, you shall be contributing to the final victory. As soon as the final victory is achieved, you shall be rewarded for your loyalty to the Reich and released back to freedom. And now, please, proceed for the disinfection. It is essential that you undergo it, along with your children, to ensure that you don't bring any diseases into the camp. Once inside, please undress your children before you undress yourselves and remember the number of the hook, on which you place your items so that you may retrieve them later more easily. The members of our *Sonderkommando* shall then provide you with soap and towels. You may keep your jewelry on yourselves, so you don't lose it."

Despite his reassuring tone, the crowd faltered. Women's eyes were directed upward, toward the chimney, from which columns of foul-smelling, black smoke was presently rising. Arms draped around their children's shoulders protectively, they hesitated to make another step.

Hössler's subordinate, the only other SS man present, placed his hand on top of his horsewhip as he looked at his superior questioningly. Hössler stopped him with a barely perceptible shake of the head. He stepped closer to one of the women and brushed the hair on top of her child's head with a kind smile.

"What is your profession, my good woman?" he addressed the mother in the same soft-spoken manner.

"I'm a seamstress," she replied, her back stiff with apprehension.

Hössler looked positively delighted. "A seamstress? But that's precisely what we need! We have just expanded a sewing detail, where women like yourself make uniforms for our brave *Wehrmacht*. We even set up a nursery there, so you don't have to be separated from your child during your working hours. Speaking of which, we need women with experience who can look after small children while their mothers are working. Anyone here worked in a kindergarten?"

Two hands appeared in the air.

Hössler broke into another blossoming smile. He turned to look at his orderly. "It appears we are in luck today! All essential workers on one transport!"

"Indeed, Herr Obersturmführer."

Hössler was back to stroking the child's hair. "Are you hungry, my little fellow? As soon as your *Mutti* and you take a shower, there will be hot soup and coffee or tea for everyone. Oh, and before I forget, will diabetics report to the medical staff after you undergo your disinfection, please? We shall need this information to adjust your diet."

Alma looked on, horrified, as the crowd moved through the doors of the crematorium and down the steps of its own free will, pacified by the *kind Herr Obersturmführer's* words. A gust of wind descended upon the column of the new arrivals and threw a flurry of white ash into their faces.

Frantically, Alma wiped it off her skin with the end of her headscarf, but the smell of the churned flesh and burned hair was still there, sickly-sweet.

One of the men stepped forward, regarding the ash on his palm with great mistrust. "What's with the chimney?" he openly challenged, loudly enough for the crowd to pause in its tracks again.

Unbothered, Hössler gave a nonchalant shrug. "Boilers for the showers. Each shower room is designed to provide water for a thousand people. Surely, you don't wish for your wives and children or your elderly parents to bathe in ice-cold water?"

"Why are you so concerned about our well-being all of a sudden? Pardon me, but it sounds a bit inconsistent coming from the nation that swore to annihilate us all."

Once again, the SS guard made a move forward; once more, Hössler stopped him with a nonchalant sweep of the hand. It occurred to Alma that this was precisely how he had earned his promotion to such a high position. He was skilled in mass murder. He had learned from experience that gently coaxing worked much better than threats and blows.

"We need healthy workers, not an infirmary full of sick ones," he explained simply. "I've already told you, we're a labor camp, not some sinister extermination facility the enemy propaganda was trying to frighten you with. We need you in order to win this war. Our soldiers are fighting presently on the front. We need men and women to replace them for the time being. Why would we kill you all? That's simply counterproductive." He spread his arms in a defenseless gesture.

Noticing Alma, he beamed even brighter and went to her with his arms outstretched.

"Ah! And here's our irreplaceable conductor of the women's orchestra, Frau Rosé. Any Austrians here? Any music aficionados? I am one, myself. If you know anything about music, you know who she is. I still can't fully believe Frau Rosé decided to join us to lift the spirits of not only our brave guards but inmates as well. You have heard her girls play the welcoming march at the ramp; give her a round of applause! Well? She came to ask what music you would like to hear tonight. Yes, we always welcome the new arrivals with a concert on the first evening…" He wrapped his arm around her shoulders and turned her toward the crowd.

Pale-faced and trembling inside, Alma smiled at the faces that surrounded her and swallowed tears, trying not to betray Hössler's charade. It was a damnable business, going along with the SS man's despicable game against her own fellow sufferers, and yet, what choice did she possibly have? Betray Hössler's secret, shout at them to run just to prolong their agony, just to send them scrambling with terror and throw themselves against the electrified wire or get mowed down by the machine guns aimed at them from above? There was no chance for an escape from the crematorium's maw. The only choice here was between death by bullets and death by gas and Alma understood it and therefore, powerless and miserable, she was smiling at them through the tears. She loathed Hössler with all her heart at that moment; loathed him for making her into an unwilling accomplice—she was perfect proof of his facade. Attired in a warm, camel-wool coat that came off some Parisian fashionista's dead shoulders, with a matching headscarf covering glossy locks of dark hair, wearing tall boots and even stockings, she was just what he needed to shove into the apprehensive crowd's face. *See? This is how well our inmates are taken care of.*

The effect was instant. Reassured by the sleek-mannered SS officer and the inmate he was hugging with a fatherly look about him, the new arrivals forgot all about the chimney and almost hurried inside the facility.

Alma felt her entire body shaking. Hössler's fingers dug into her arm as he pressed her closer.

"They all would die, regardless," he spoke softly into her ear. "It was worse before, when they were herded inside with cudgels and fists. I give them a few more minutes of peace. By the time the gas takes hold, they won't even realize what's happened."

Alma nodded stiffly.

"How about a little Mozart tonight?" He addressed the crowd out loud this time. "Anyone here have anything against Herr Wolfgang Amadeus? No? I thought so. Mozart it is then, ladies and gentlemen. Make sure to look presentable—a violin virtuoso shall be playing for you tonight." He looked at Alma. "What is it that you wanted?" he asked her quietly.

"Permission to bring a pianist from Auschwitz as a tutor. The Birkenau one—"

"Is home with his father; yes, yes." He chuckled. "I'm keeping his position open for him. He'll be back here before Christmas," he repeated the very same thing the *Kapo* had professed. "He's exactly that kind of an idiot. Of course, go and fetch one from the main camp. Tell them I ordered it, if they start being pigheaded."

"Thank you, Herr Obersturmführer."

He was still holding her, his poster child, by her shoulders. "If you need me, next time go to my office. Don't come back here ever again, please."

Chapter 12

In front of Block 24, Alma stopped and listened with her head cocked to one side. One of the guards had directed her to this two-story, red-brick building when she asked for the Auschwitz Music Block. Only, aside from the faint piano melody that seemed to caress her very skin with its light, feathery touch, she could hear no other sounds.

One of the windows was pushed open on the second floor. A young woman with a heavily made-up face leaned out of it and rested her elbows on the windowsill. Alma saw that all that the girl was wearing was a silk slip of some sort.

She noticed Alma looking at her as she was lighting her cigarette and nodded at her. "Are you lost, bird?" She spoke German with a strong Swabian accent.

Alma brought a hand to her forehead to shield herself from the sun. "Is this Block 24?" she asked, even though the number was right there, above the entrance.

The scantily dressed girl established the fact with an affirmative nod. "Are you here for an audition?"

"What audition?"

"You know what." The girl grinned shrewdly. "You contribute to the prosperity of the Reich for twelve months while lying on your back and they let you go home. It's the latest re-education idea."

"They won't let me go home. I'm Jewish. We can't be re-educated; only eradicated."

The girl simply nodded sagely to that and gave Alma a sympathetic look as she pulled on her cigarette.

The door to the barrack swung open and a powerfully built woman appeared on its step. Almost at once she turned to the girl in the window and demonstrated her fist. "What did I tell you about hanging out of that window? Shut it at once!"

The girl scrunched her face. "I need to air the room for five minutes at least!"

"So air it without sticking your silly head through it!"

She grumbled something unintelligible and pulled back, but just so the woman downstairs wouldn't see her.

A man in a civilian jacket but with striped trousers slipped past the severe-looking matron, crushing his cap in his hands and thanking her profusely. But the woman wasn't interested in him; she was busy inspecting Alma.

"Are you new?" She motioned for Alma to step closer. "Who sent you? Are you full-blooded Aryan? Asocial?"

"No; no one; no and no. I need a pianist."

A snort reached her from upstairs. The girl was leaning out of the window again, observing the scene with great interest. "A pianist? That's something new! Did they finally open a brothel for women where you can request such peculiar things? Long overdue!"

"Get back inside before I drag you there by your hair!" the woman shouted and once again shook her fist at the Swabian girl.

Her fits of rage were swift, automatic and impersonal; harassed mothers were prone to those whenever their children misbehaved, it occurred to Alma, and for some reason, it made her smile.

"The tongue on that one," the matron grumbled under her breath. Alma grinned sympathetically. The woman crossed her arms on her chest. "Who are you again and what do you need a pianist for?"

"I'm Alma Rosé, the *Kapo* of the Birkenau Music Block." Alma demonstrated her armband to the woman.

The latter nodded her acknowledgment; though disappointment reflected in her eyes for a moment. Alma was an attractive woman with large, soulful eyes, glossy dark locks, and long legs—a fine addition to the matron's operation.

This time, Alma discovered that she was, in fact, grateful for her Jewish blood; if this block housed what she suspected it did, she wished nothing to do with it whatsoever and to the devil with all the promises of the swift release after twelve months of such "labor" on one's back.

"Obersturmführer Hössler ordered for a pianist to be temporarily freed of his duties so he can tutor one of my girls," Alma explained.

"Tough luck for you then, old girl. The orchestra is not here. They're at the Kommandant Höss' villa, entertaining his guests. Come back tomorrow. But not at this time either; they are busy at the kitchen during the day, peeling potatoes."

Her ear trained on the door, Alma searched the woman's face. "Who plays the piano right now? I can hear it. Is it a recording?"

"No, not a recording." The woman seemed to consider. "That's our Miklós playing, but he's not a member of the orchestra."

"Too bad," the girl from the window commented. "He should be. Such talent, but the blood is all wrong."

This time, the woman ignored her. "He's Jewish," she explained to Alma in a confidential tone. "Jews are not allowed in the Auschwitz orchestra. But they let him play all the same when the music room is empty, out of the goodness of their hearts. He already tried hanging himself once because no one would allow him to play his music. He's some big-shot pianist from Hungary—"

"He's a composer, too," the girl from the second floor interrupted her once again. "Wrote an opera when he worked at his Budapest Philharmonic—"

"Rot!" the woman shouted at her. "He didn't write any operas. He just played them."

"Yes, he did. I'm telling you this on the most reliable authority!" The girl was all but hanging out of the window now, set on driving her point across. "Sándor told me all about it when he visited me two weeks ago. He even brought an old magazine with an article about it. It had Miklós' picture in it, too—on stage, in tails, all business as it should be. Such a handsome fellow..."

"Wipe your drool; he's a refined sort and not interested in you. And even if he were, you two are racially incompatible."

"I would much rather go with someone *incompatible* like him than with those *Sonderkommando* apes."

"What do you have against the *Sonderkommando* men now?" the woman demanded. "They're the ones who supply you with all the goods. Where are you getting all your hairclips and stockings and all sorts of underwear from?"

Once again, the girl screwed up her pretty face into a disgusted grimace. "They take it all off the corpses while they're still warm."

"No, they don't!" the matron argued.

"Yes, they do."

"No, they don't," Alma inserted, staring blankly through the woman in front of her. "They undress the people first. They go naked into the gas chamber. They think it's a shower room. They even give them soap and towels..."

Both women suddenly fell silent. It felt as though a full minute had expired when the matron moved from the door she was blocking and gestured Alma inside without meeting her eyes. She was frightened in a sort of a superstitious way, as though Alma had just said something that oughtn't be said in the camp; as though death, even through words, was contagious. "The music room is on the first floor, at the very end of the corridor."

"Thank you."

Alma went inside and caught the matron crossing herself as the woman hurried along the dingy hallway muttering something softly to herself—a protection prayer, perhaps—the further from the violinist, the better.

The block stood silent, with the exception of that faint melody rolling in soft, soothing waves from the half-shut door at the end of the long passageway. Treading as silently as possible—a professional courtesy from one musician who didn't wish to disturb the other until he was finished—Alma approached it and paused on the threshold. The pianist sat half-turned to her, swaying slightly in time with the music. It was a haunting melody Alma failed to identify, complex and fluid at the same. At once, Alma recognized a true virtuoso at work. She played the piano well enough, but it would take her weeks to learn such difficult passages that seemed to flow from under the pianist's fingers. And yet, he made it appear effortless, as though the piano itself sang under the gentle caress of his beautifully sculptured hands, like a female body perfectly attuned to her lover's touch.

From where she stood, Alma saw that his eyes were closed. Long, dark eyelashes threw shadows over his sharp-featured profile. Over his slightly hooked nose, two vertical wrinkles lay—the only lines marring the otherwise relaxed, noble face. It suddenly occurred to her that the Swabian girl was right; he was indeed a composer. And if this was one of his creations, Alma would fall to her knees and kiss his hands, for they belonged to a true genius.

Eventually, she also closed her eyes and allowed herself to be carried away. He continued to play and, before long, she was back in the Vienna Philharmonic, an elegant, silk evening gown cascading down her tall frame. The house was full, but it was only the two of them on stage. Bringing the invisible violin to her shoulder, Alma began to follow the melody the best she could. It was no easy feat—the soft parts gave way to the forceful and dynamic ones and then shifted once again and all but died, dissolved into pensive silence just to gain force once again and shake Alma to the core with the profound emotion of every passage.

She didn't just hear it; she *felt* the music inside of her. It spoke to her in a way that she couldn't explain even to herself. Without once opening her eyes, without exchanging a single word with the pianist, she learned his entire life story through his music—his work and successes, the women he loved and lost, the life he celebrated and which was stolen from him in such a bastardly manner. He somehow managed to express it all—a broken man to a broken woman—and Alma understood him without understanding his language.

All of a sudden, the melody stopped. Alma's eyes snapped open. She stared at the pianist in the inexplicable fear of being caught at such shameless snooping, but he sat, still as a stone, with his pallid eyelids closed. For an instant, his face was twisted with a terrible emotion; he raised his hands as though to strike an invisible enemy, but instead he banged on the keys with such force, the floor under Alma's feet trembled.

His face wet with tears, he began playing Chopin's "Funeral March," savagely and without any mercy for the instrument that cried under the assault of his beautiful, white hands.

Alma felt herself shaking. It was all too much for one day. First, the *Aktion,* the fearful, unknowing crowds, Hössler's arm around her shoulder, the feeling of the warm ashes on her cheeks. Then, the music so magnificent, it reminded her that there was life after all this, there were stages and pianos and elegant gowns somewhere very far away, but real nevertheless. The pianist had given her hope and then obliterated it in the cruelest of manners and she suddenly couldn't take it any longer.

Swinging round on her heel, she ran out of the music room, out of that cursed block, and to hell with the private lessons for Flora. She would find someone else for the girl, someone who knew how to play, pleasantly and correctly enough, but not in such a way that their music would churn the guts of the ones who would listen and make them want to muster a noose out of their own stockings just not to feel this haunting beauty and desperation all at once, the promise of the paradise and the vision of Hades all wrapped in one.

Such music should be banned—here, at Auschwitz, at any rate.

Alma wiped her face angrily and only slowed her steps when she approached the guard's watchtower—running was a dangerous sport in this *fine SS resort*.

Almost as dangerous as permitting oneself to feel something once again.

Chapter 13

The inmate was beside herself with excitement.

"She didn't lie—it truly is you. Alma Rosé, the violinist virtuoso!"

Grinning, the woman shifted from one foot to another, still standing in the door of the block and staring at the freshly mopped floor almost with admiration. She wore the women's camp regular uniform of a dress of sorts that was three sizes too big. From a string, tied around her painfully thin waist, a food bowl hung and even a spoon. Alma had a suspicion the woman had to part with her ration bread for someone to make a hole in that spoon for her. But that was camp life for regular Birkenau prisoners—even the smallest favors had to be purchased, as charity and goodwill were alien concepts in dingy barracks where life had been reduced to the fight for survival. The very first ration was ordinarily traded for a personal bowl. The new arrivals quickly learned that the rations distribution *Kommando* didn't care one way or the other if an inmate had one or not. The kinder types could make an indifferent offer to pour a portion into one's cupped hands; mostly though, an inmate would receive a whack with a ladle on one's forehead and no-nonsense advice to piss off. *No bowl, no food. Now, off with you, you filthy carcass; you're holding up the line!*

The second ration was usually traded for a piece of string to tie around one's waist to carry one's scarce possessions on it. The new arrivals discovered soon enough from their own experience that this was the only way to prevent the precious items from being stolen, as theft was just as widespread among the camp population as disease. Handing another ration to an inmate carpenter in exchange for making a hole in one's spoon so that the spoon's owner could sleep soundly without fearing it would be pinched from her by a fellow barrack-mate was a small price to pay for one's peace of mind.

Regarding what constituted the woman's belongings reminded Alma once again of her own detail's privilege. Suddenly, she was overcome with shame for her clean clothes and for having an actual plate in her personal quarters that she never had to worry about.

"If you're here for an audition—" Alma began, noticing a music magazine the inmate was pressing against her chest.

"No, no!" The woman uttered a brisk, embarrassed laugh. "I wouldn't know from which side to approach a piano, let alone any other instrument. I'm not here for that. The *Kanada* detail has been a bit overwhelmed recently and their superiors called for additional manpower..." She tossed her head impatiently. "No matter. I was working there today and one of the *Kanada* girls, the regular ones, she gave me this." With great ceremony, she held out the magazine toward Alma, a triumphant smile playing on her face. "She said, you'd give me bread if I gave it to you," she finished in a barely audible whisper, her eyes downcast in embarrassment.

Mystified, Alma turned the magazine this way and that in her hands. It was old, dated 1931, and in Czech.

"Was the *Kanada* girl's name Kitty? The one who gave it to you?"

The woman nodded with great enthusiasm. "She said you would love to have it. She would give it to you herself, but she didn't know when you were coming next and couldn't wait for you to have it. She said such things lift the spirits immensely."

Old music magazines in a language she could barely read?

Not wishing to disappoint the inmate, Alma thanked her politely, brought her a piece of bread from her room and whatever hard cheese she had left—

"But you didn't even look at it!" Instead of the food, the woman took the magazine from Alma's hands and began leafing through the pages. At last, she produced a victorious, *aha!* "That's you, isn't it?" This time, she nearly shoved the well-thumbed periodical into Alma's eyes.

At once, all color drained from the violinist's face. With a trembling hand, she slowly reached for the publication. From the centerfold, her old self was gazing back at her, smiling serenely as her hand rested gracefully on the neck of her Guadagnini—royalty posing for a portrait without a care in the world despite the ominous clouds already gathering over her sheltered world. Somewhere in Germany, Hitler—still not a Führer, just a raving right-wing agitator that the general public refused to take seriously—was calling for a revolution and for a guillotine erected for her kind and there she sat, oblivious and in love, in her silver dress, her hair cut according to the latest fashion and framing her sharp profile in elegant dark waves.

Alma Prihoda-Rosé. She was still married to Váša then. How quickly that marriage crumbled under the new regime unraveling its dark wings in the neighboring Germany.

In the bottom right corner of the article, an illustrator had drawn a sensual sketch of her—back turned to the public, exposed in a low-cut concert gown; an outline of a breast just under the violin; short waves of hair obscuring her face as though blown by the wind; a tiny foot peeking from under the hem of her dress in its elegant pump, the material hugging her tall, lean frame like a second skin pooling around her...

A crystal drop landed on the Czech words full of old glory, right next to the sketch. Alma touched her face and was astonished to discover that it was wet.

"You don't like it?"

Dazed by the memories, Alma had all but forgotten about the inmate, who was presently searching her face with a tragic look about her.

"I thought you would like it..."

"Oh, I love it." Alma forced a laugh and pressed the anxious woman's hand with great emotion. "I love it very much. I'll cut it out and put it on the wall above my table..." *So it can remind me of who I once was.*

Alma disappeared into her room and, after a frantic search, returned with a pair of warm socks for the inmate.

The latter was already shaking her head and pushing the pair back into Alma's hands. "I can't take them."

"What nonsense! Of course, you can. Don't be silly."

"But you need them yourself. The winter is coming—"

"Precisely. And you're barefoot." Alma looked pointedly at the woman's bare feet, stuffed into rough wooden clogs with a single leather strap holding them in place.

At last, pacified by Alma's assurances that she had warm winter boots and woolen stockings, the woman relented. Bread and cheese wrapped in the soft warm wool against her chest, she was backing away, bowing her head ceaselessly in gratitude. *If they sent her to the* Kanada *again, she would turn it upside down to find more photos of Frau Alma; Frau Alma could rely on her. She would see to it that Frau Alma had all the photographs of herself one could only find—*

"Wait!" Alma called out to her, overcome by a sudden idea. She hesitated before she could voice it. It was much too strange, even for her; whatever the inmate would think—

To hell with what she would think. Having this piece of her lost life in her hands was much too precious. She wanted to give the Auschwitz pianist a piece of his. Alma knew that there were magazines with his photos in it—the girl from the Auschwitz brothel had seen one with her own eyes. She was sure that there were more around, buried somewhere among the *Kanada* riches.

"When you're searching for my photographs next time," Alma began carefully, "could you perhaps look for someone else's too? I don't know his last name, but his first name is Miklós. He's Hungarian and he used to play the piano at the Budapest Philharmonic."

"Miklós, Hungarian, pianist, Budapest Philharmonic," the inmate repeated and play-saluted Alma with two fingers at her forehead. "Will do, Frau Alma!"

"Thank you." Alma smiled warmly. "Your bread and cheese shall be waiting for you here."

The woman turned swiftly on her heel and trotted awkwardly in the direction of the women camp's barracks.

Alma shook her head in disapproval at the disgraceful wooden footwear the inmates were forced to wear. Shivering against the cold, she shut the door and pressed her back against it, her eyes riveted once again to the photos.

Suddenly, a shot rang out, much too close. Growing cold with suspicion, Alma turned slowly toward the door. When she brought herself to open it, a groan of torment escaped her parted lips.

Hössler stood next to the body that lay still and flat against the ground, his gun still in his right hand. In his left one, he held a pair of Alma's socks with bread and cheese wrapped in them. He waved them in the air triumphantly. "Caught a thief red-handed!" he announced with a proud smile. "Good thing I happened to be coming round for some wonderful Mozart of yours. If I was a minute late, she would have made away with her haul and we would never have found her. Here," he said, approaching Alma and handing her the items.

Alma recoiled, staring at him in silent horror.

"Oh! I beg your forgiveness." Misinterpreting her ashen-white face and her eyes staring wildly at the gun in his hand, he quickly replaced it back into his holster. "It wasn't my intention to frighten you. Here are your socks and your rations."

When Alma didn't stir, he scowled incomprehensibly. "She stole them from you, didn't she? From your room, while you were busy with rehearsals?" Now, there was a trace of uncertainty in his voice.

Alma slowly shook her head, feeling her lips quivering. "She didn't steal it from me. I gave them to her," she managed at last.

"Why would you do that?" He appeared to be outright puzzled with such behavior.

Because she was a human being who was hungry and cold, but you wouldn't understand such reasoning, would you?

"Because she brought me this." She showed him the magazine.

She brought me my life back and you took hers away from her. For nothing.

The night had come but sleep didn't. With her head in her hands, Alma sat at the table with music scores scattered all over it, immersed in her thoughts, for quite some time. Darkness had flooded the room, along with a sense of growing despair and anguish; darkness, which even the scant light of the table lamp could not disperse.

From every corner, along the walls and floorboards, shadows were stealing toward her, brushing Alma's ankles with their ghostly touch, threatening to drag her into the dark abyss. It was best not to think of what had transpired, of the woman's body still lying outside while she played Mozart for Hössler with hands that were strangely steady, but now that the day was over, the horror had caught up with her. Her turn would come sooner or later. It was inevitable; she saw it clear as day now. Her eyes stared fixedly into the void, black and haunted, just like the night outside.

Lapsed in some apathetic, outwardly abstraction, she didn't notice the commotion outside her door until a startled scream jolted her out of her dark musings. Music scores forgotten on the desk, Alma leapt to her feet and pulled the door open.

At once, an overpowering stench of alcohol fumes assaulted her senses.

"Who's there?" she demanded with all the authority she could muster, despite her hand clenching on top of the door handle. She couldn't discern anything in the dark barrack; she could only hear heavy stumbling steps and the girls' frightened breathing. "Leave at once or I will report you to the administration!"

Only privileged inmates and the SS had access to alcohol in this place, but Alma had never seen an inebriated inmate wandering around the camp after the curfew. Although she had heard plenty of stories about drunken SS men looking for entertainment.

A shadowy form materialized in front of her, swaying slightly, like some dark, evil apparition. The scant light falling from her room reflected off the familiar belt buckle.

Our Honor Is Loyalty. An SS guard.

Her mouth suddenly felt very dry. She took a step back. He advanced toward her. Now, she could just see the leer on his freckled, round face. He hiccupped once, twice. His eyes, narrowed in a typical fashion of a drunkard, traveled up and down Alma's frame, hidden only by a thin slip.

In spite of herself, Alma forced herself to square her shoulders. Her extremities turned into ice. Inside her chest, her heart was beating wildly, but her face remained dispassionate and stern.

"I said, leave at once!" She almost shouted this time. "Or you shall find yourself on the Eastern front, in one of their disciplinary battalions, for *Rassenschande*, before you know what hit you. In case you forgot, race defilement is still a criminal case for you Aryans."

For an instant, he appeared to hesitate. Then, his ideological education must have triumphed. A scowl replaced a lecherous grin. "Threatening an SS man?" he slurred, making a grab for Alma's arm.

With the agility of a cat, she jumped to the side and snatched her coat from the nail on which it hung.

"Insolent Jewish slut!" he bellowed. "I shall teach you how to obey!"

They both stood inside her room now. Holding the coat in front of herself like a protective shield, Alma watched him without blinking. All of her muscles tensed with extreme alertness, like a spring ready to be released.

"Jewish slut..." he repeated, and fell backward, against the metal frame of Alma's bed. "It's a big honor and you don't appreciate..." The gaze of his bloodshot eyes landed on her violin. "A musician then... Figures... You're all arrogant, stuck-up bitches..." He hiccupped again. "Must have been going with every Jew banker who came to your concerts... That's where all of your jewels are from. Robbing honest Aryan folk to dress up their Jew bitches in diamonds and silk."

"Both of my husbands were Aryan," Alma hissed spitefully and made another leap back when he swiped with his hand to catch her wrist. "And I never accepted presents from anyone. I earned all of my money myself, unlike you; it's you and your comrades who dig into our hard-earned money in the *Kanada* every day because you, yourselves, don't amount to anything, you ignorant, pathetic bunch."

"You insolent whore!" he roared and went for her again.

Alma jumped onto her bed and all but made it across and to the safety of the exit, when a hand closed around her ankle and yanked hard. She yelped in pain when her forearm hit the metal frame; she could swear she heard the bone crack. Her bow hand, her most precious possession, broken by some drunken SS pig!

Suddenly infuriated to the point of blind, savage rage, she twisted and kicked with all her force, digging her heel square into the guard's face. He cried out in surprise and released her at once, clutching at his broken nose instead. Alma was already on her feet, on the other side of her bed. In front of the door, she paused, threw a quick glance at the enraged man, who was getting up using a wall to steady himself, and then slammed the door after herself, leaving him inside.

"I'm getting the guards!" she screamed over her shoulder as she charged, barefoot, toward the front barrack door—both for the frightened girls' sake and for the SS man to hear. She could only hope that he would have enough sense to disappear instead of going after one of her charges instead.

Holding her right arm pressed tightly against her chest with her left hand, Alma made it past two neighboring barracks when she came to an abrupt halt. For a few moments, it was just darkness, her heart pounding with violent force and her breath coming in harsh, erratic gasps. In another instant, she suddenly burst into hysterical, shrill laughter that refused to stop, even when she clasped her mouth with her good hand.

She was getting the guards! Indeed!

Alma shifted her weight from one foot to another so that they wouldn't sink too deeply in the freezing mud. Her shoulders were shaking uncontrollably. All around her, eerie darkness lay on the long, rectangular shapes of the barracks, like some grotesque, giant coffins in which their victims were buried alive. Alma's eyes watered. A searchlight swept the ground in front of her. She knew that in this grave stillness her laughter could be heard for tens of meters and yet, for the life of her, she couldn't bring herself to stop.

Did she imagine, for one moment, that she was back in Vienna and had human rights for the local police to protect? It was one of them, the guards, who was just about to assault her, and she wished to invite more of them into the barrack?

The searchlight blinded her for an instant, slipped past her but returned at once and fixed her with its bright yellow glare. Standing in a pool of light in the middle of the blackest night, Alma laughed in its face and opened her arms in an insolent gesture.

"Shoot!" She didn't recognize her own voice as it echoed wildly around the compound.

But no shots followed. Only the sound of two pairs of boots running through the wet mud.

Alma's arms dropped. The throbbing in the right one intensified. It was swelling with blood; she could feel it, just as she could feel the icy needles beginning to prickle at her fingertips.

Broken, to be sure.

Everything was broken. There was no coming back this time.

Just as abruptly as it started, her laughter had ceased. She was waiting for them with calm resolve as one waits for a hangman on the gallows.

Against the blinding light, they were two black shadows closing in on her. Alma stared at their faces but could see nothing except translucent vapors coming out of their mouths in short, quick gasps.

Not quite reaching her, they came to a stop as though the circle of light itself didn't permit them within its limits. With a muzzle of his rifle, one of them probed at her left sleeve.

Scowling, Alma turned her head to see what he was studying with such apparent interest.

Blasted Kapo's *armband.*

She closed her eyes against her own stupidity. If it weren't for the band, they would have executed her on the spot and it would be all over with. Regular inmates were fair game. *Kapos* were appointed either for their ruthlessness or other advantageous attributes the SS could use. It was an unspoken rule among the camp administration—whenever it came to punishment, *Kapos* were subject to certain consideration. Shooting a senior camp officer's pet Jew certainly wouldn't earn one a promotion.

"Music Block?" one of the shadows demanded, recognizing the number of the block on her armband.

For a moment, Alma considered confessing to it, telling them the entire story, but stopped herself. "I need to see Dr. Mengele," she said instead. Her voice was hoarse and hollow, still not her own. "It's urgent."

"That's putting it one way," the second shadow remarked to his comrade in a certain tone. Alma saw him twist his finger next to his temple a few times, clearly implying that the broad was off her rocker.

The first one merely waved the tip of his gun at her to follow him.

"Shut the blasted thing off!" he shouted in the general direction of the searchlight. "The Soviets can see you from their airbases!"

Once again, the night had enveloped them and this time it was even darker than before. The sky itself had disappeared, along with the gigantic coffins. Before Alma's eyes adjusted to the black, all she could see were the two small yellow circles of the SS men's pocket torchlights chasing one another in the mud like two deranged fireflies.

She didn't remember for how long they walked and in which direction; she only came to herself before the displeased Herr Doktor. His arms crossed over his chest, Dr. Mengele stood in front of her in his immaculate white gown and stared at her feet with disapproval. Still dazed and not in full possession of her faculties, Alma lowered her gaze and saw, for the first time, that they were bare and covered in mud.

"We found her near one of the barracks in this state," the older guard reported. Just like his younger comrade, he looked as though he wished to be as far away from Dr. Mengele's quarters as possible. Just then Alma noticed a body, with its chest open, lying on a slab behind Dr. Mengele's back. A man of about fifty stood beside it, his gaze downcast, holding an instrument of some sort in his bloodied, gloved hand. "She just stood there asking to be shot."

Dr. Mengele finally shifted his gaze from Alma's feet to her face and searched it carefully. "Is that so?"

Alma made no reply. Her right arm was throbbing painfully, but despite it, she felt nothing at all. It suddenly mattered not if she replied to him or not; if he ordered the guards to beat her just for his own pleasure. He could dissect her alive for all she cared. She was finished with this place.

Something shifted in Dr. Mengele's countenance. His signature, slightly mocking expression was gone, replaced by something different.

"Dismissed until further orders." He waved both guards off. "And send someone here to mop the floors!"

A snappy "*Jawohl*" came from the door, along with a click of the heels. The men were gone as if the entire Soviet army was chasing them.

"Now will you tell me what happened?"

Dr. Mengele's calm tone had the opposite effect on Alma. Before she could get one word out of herself, a violent spasm shook her entire body, turning into dry, heaving sobs. This was worse than the laughter. This new attack terrified her, for, all at once, everything inside her body felt as though it had come loose. Some chord that had held it all together this entire time had finally snapped and out came the terror and the tears and the grief and everything else that she had kept bottled up for much too long.

She felt Dr. Mengele's hands dig into her shoulders as he squatted next to her. Alma was sitting on the floor now, leaning against the wall and didn't remember how she came to be here, in this pool of mud and tears—a ragged doll that he was trying to shake, none too gently, back into its working state.

"You're having a nervous breakdown. You ought to breathe." But his rational explanation didn't help.

He slapped her hard across the face. Startled, Alma clasped her reddening cheek and stared at him with wild eyes.

"What happened?" he repeated, rubbing his palm in annoyance.

"An SS man broke my forearm."

"One of those who brought you here?"

Alma shook her head. "He came into our block after the curfew..." The scene began to replay itself before her eyes. "I was in my room. I heard one of the girls scream. He must have tried getting into her bunk or dragging her out of it—I don't know. He was very drunk. I told him to leave and then he came after me... Came into my room." A ragged breath escaped her. "I only wanted him to leave, but he wouldn't go. I was trying to get past him, but he caught me by my foot. I fell on my bed and hit my forearm on the metal bedframe." The tears were back, still silent for now, but

Alma could already feel another attack coming. "I kicked him in his face. I think I broke his nose; there was a lot of blood...And then I ran. I wanted to get help and—" There it was again, the violent, uncontrollable sobbing. "I can't be here anymore. I can't go on like this...That drunken pig—" She couldn't finish. *She would never play anymore; not on the professional level, at any rate. Her life was effectively over.*

Alma clutched at the sleeve of the doctor's pristine white gown with her good hand. "Give me an injection of phenol, Herr Doktor." Her eyes were gleaming feverishly. "If there's anything human left in you, give me the injection. Put me out of this misery. I won't be able to perform anymore anyway. I'm of no use to you now. Please, do this one favor for me, I'm begging you."

"Which did he break? Left or right?" His tone was oddly businesslike.

Alma pulled up the sleeve of her coat and turned her bruised arm toward him. He seized it at once and began prodding at it, completely disregarding the fact that his patient was screaming in pain.

She was slapping at his hands, yanking herself free of his grip with the desperation of a wild animal struggling its way out of a cast-iron trap. "I said it was broken. Do you not have a heart at all? Just give me that shot!"

Without another word, he suddenly released her, rose to his feet and went to a medical glass cabinet containing neat rows of ampules and jars.

Aware of the inmate doctor's tragic eyes on her, Alma watched Dr. Mengele fill the syringe with a clear liquid.

Before long, he was crouching beside her once again. "Last chance to change your mind."

It was an odd moment. Alma didn't expect him to agree so fast and to proceed so quickly. Although, what else did she expect from the one whom they called the Angel of Death? Sympathy?

Compassion? A promise to look into the case? To protect her from harm, as in the oath he must have given in exchange for this white gown of his?

Alma saw the crystal drop collect on the end of the needle. It gleamed, seducing and terrifying at the same time.

Dr. Mengele was watching her with some unhealthy interest in his eyes. Alma couldn't shake the feeling that he was conducting an experiment of sorts with her just then; only which sort, she couldn't tell for the life of her.

Slowly, she pulled the edge of her slip down, offering him her heart. Dr. Mengele placed her left arm on his knee instead. Confused with the change of the protocol—everyone in Auschwitz-Birkenau knew that phenol executions were performed only straight into the heart muscle—Alma watched him insert the needle into her vein.

"Sweet dreams."

Those strange words and his sly grin were the last things she remembered before the darkness suffocated her.

Chapter 14

When Alma came to, the sun was bathing the entire room in a soft glow. She was lying in a bed, which wasn't hers, covered by a woolen blanket that bore a faint smell of disinfectant and someone else's body. Besides the bed, a small desk and a chair stood next to the window. On the chair, her coat was laid out, brushed and neatly folded. Underneath stood a pair of her boots.

Her head still swimming slightly, Alma pulled the covers off her legs and saw that they were perfectly clean, and that a bandage was wrapped around her forearm as well. Thoroughly confused and trembling, she stumbled toward the door and pushed it open.

The same inmate doctor, whom she had seen previously with Dr. Mengele, straightened next to the dissecting table of polished marble. A new body lay on it, pasty white and still untouched.

"Good morning." The doctor greeted her with a gentle smile.

For some time, Alma merely stared at him.

"It didn't work," she spoke at last. "The phenol didn't work."

The doctor shook his head with a grin. "It wasn't phenol. It was a regular sedative."

In that second, Alma felt both mortally betrayed and infinitely relieved.

"Why would he do that to me?" she managed at last. "That's just cruel..."

The doctor only shrugged. His kind, lined face seemed to say, *He enjoys games of that sort.*

Still stunned, Alma kept staring at the body on the dissecting table. It lay on its stomach, in some odd, twisted position.

"The deformity of the spine," the doctor explained with the impassiveness of a scientist, motioning toward the body with his scalpel. "Herr Doktor brought him this very morning. A new transport..."

That's who had gotten her dose of phenol in the heart. *Poor devil.*

"Why did he do that?" Alma repeated, still failing to understand Dr. Mengele's warped logic.

"Herr Doktor is very interested in deformities of all sorts," the inmate doctor replied, misinterpreting her question. "He always brings them to me for dissection, so later he can forward the results of the autopsy to the Institute of Biological, Racial and Evolutionary Research in Berlin. He's writing a scientific work for them of sorts... About the inferiority of degenerate races, like ours." He glanced up at Alma. "You're Jewish, aren't you?"

"I'm asking why he did that *to me*," she repeated without replying to his question.

"Did what? Gave you a sedative? You were having a nervous breakdown. That was the only logical solution in this case. I would have done the same."

"No; why he didn't kill me like I asked."

"Oh. Your arm is not broken. It's just a nasty bruise. He even had the inmate X-ray it while you were asleep to ensure that it was indeed the case. You will be playing your violin in no time. He said you're a very good violinist. He enjoys listening to you play."

In resignation, Alma lowered herself onto the only free chair that stood beside the desk piled with journals and books. Only when the inmate doctor covered her gently with a medical gown did she come out of her reverie.

"Forgive me, please." What had this place done to her? She was sitting in the presence of a man she didn't know wearing only a thin slip and wouldn't have even noticed it if he hadn't brought her attention to it. "I didn't mean to offend or embarrass you."

The doctor merely waved her apologies off. "Your head will be fuzzy for some time. Why don't you lie down? That's my personal room over there. And there's a library in the adjoining room, if you wish to occupy yourself with something. It's mostly medical journals and books, but the editions are all recent, and if you're interested in that type of literature..." As though remembering himself, he pulled the glove off his palm and thrust out his hand. "I'm Doctor Ránki, pathologist."

"Alma Rosé, violinist."

They smiled at each other. It felt alien and oddly pleasant, introducing oneself by name in the place where they had been reduced to mere faceless numbers.

"Perhaps, I should go back to my block. My girls—"

"No, no!" Dr. Ránki cried, alarmed. "You can't leave here without Herr Doktor's direct orders." Seeing Alma's expression, he softened his tone, tilting his head apologetically to one side. "He wants to ensure that you're...safe to be released to the general public, so to say. Surely, you understand, after last night...You can't quite run around the camp and make such a ruckus. One inmate starts doing this and soon they shall have a revolt on their hands. He doesn't want that."

"Of course not," Alma answered mechanically.

"Would you like more sedative?"

"No. Can I just sit here with you? I won't bother you. I can't be alone just now."

He appeared to hesitate. "I need to dissect the body."

"All right."

"It's a rather frightful sight for the unprepared eyes."

Alma released a sigh and pressed the back of her head against the tiled wall. "Living people scare me, doctor. This poor fellow is already dead."

*

Alma was helping Dr. Ránki with his notes when Dr. Mengele walked in, briefcase in hand. He halted in his tracks as he noticed Alma at the inmate pathologist's desk and blinked at her attire of the white medical gown.

"Have you decided to take up a new profession?" he asked nonchalantly, concealing his initial surprise at the fact that she sat in such close proximity of the dissecting table. "Or has Dr. Ránki decided to make you into his forced labor assistant while I'm not here?"

Dr. Ránki stood frozen to attention before the slab, his face now displaying the same cadaverous tint as the body on the table in front of him. "I didn't think it would do any harm if I permitted her to take notes as I was performing…" The pathologist's voice trailed off. He was suddenly aware of the kidney he was holding in his right hand. Not quite knowing what to do with it under Dr. Mengele's penetrating glare, he dropped it into the medical scales and began to peel off his gloves. "Please, allow me to take your overcoat, Herr Doktor."

Alma rose to her feet too but, unlike the pathologist, didn't salute the SS man.

"I hope you don't mind, Herr Doktor," she said, wiping her hands down her gown. "I couldn't bear sitting locked within four walls like in some mental institution. It was me who asked Dr. Ránki to assist him, if it was within my capabilities. He was kind enough to grant me his permission, solely for the sake of occupying my time and hands with something. If anyone here is to be punished, it should be me."

His head cocked slightly, Dr. Mengele was watching her with interest. A wry smile appeared on his face as he observed the pathologist's discomfort. Shifting his gaze back to Alma, he tutted in mock reproach. "Frau Alma. The noble martyr. Ever the protector of the defenseless." He broke into chuckles. "What am I to do with you?"

"Release me back to my orchestra, please."

He snorted at that with even greater mirth. "Still want to get shot? Or poisoned?" he asked in a casual tone.

Alma shrugged indifferently.

Dr. Mengele approached her, deposited the briefcase on top of the desk and took her face in his hands without removing his gloves.

"You didn't give her any more sedative," he spoke to the Hungarian pathologist after examining Alma's eyes closely.

"She said she didn't want it."

"What happened to the things that I want or order for that matter?" Dr. Mengele demanded, only half-in-jest, judging by Dr. Ránki's anxious expression. "Do they not bear authority all of a sudden?"

"Of course, they do, Herr Doktor. I only thought . . . she appears to be perfectly calm today and in full possession of her faculties."

"Is she now?"

"You can see for yourself, Herr Doktor."

At last, Dr. Mengele peeled off one of his leather gloves and pressed his thumb against Alma's wrist. Excruciatingly aware of his fingers on top of her skin, Alma forced herself to remain still while he watched the hand of his wristwatch make a complete circle.

"Hm. Not bad, considering," he announced his verdict. "Open your mouth."

Alma did. He inspected her gums by forcing his thumb under her lips.

"Beautiful teeth."

After he took his hand away, the faint taste of nicotine and disinfectant of sorts remained in her mouth. It took Alma great effort not to spit on the floor to rid herself of it.

"How's your arm today?"

"It's all right. Sore, but I can even write with it just fine. As long as it's not broken, a little pain I can deal with."

Dr. Mengele nodded his approval. "Flex your fingers and wrist."

After she did what she was told, he prodded at her muscles around the bandage.

"I wrapped it tightly to decrease the swelling. If you don't overexert it, we'll remove it in a couple of days."

"Thank you, Herr Doktor."

"You wish to go back to your girls?" he asked, unbuckling his briefcase and extracting charts and papers out of it.

"Yes, Herr Doktor."

"Not for the next few days."

"Why not?" The words flew off her lips before she could stop herself. "You have just examined me—I am perfectly fine!"

"So it appears. The trouble is, I don't trust you yet."

"Herr Doktor, I promise you—"

"I said no and that's the end of it." Despite the refusal it clearly wasn't up for any further discussion, and his tone remained just as conversational as before. "If I release you back to your block and you begin throwing tantrums again, it shall be me who will look like an idiot before the administration. We don't want that, do we?" He finished quietly and ominously, lifting his eyelashes in a sideways glance, and Alma saw that there was no humor in those dark eyes of his anymore.

In spite of herself, she pulled back. "No, of course not."

"Good." Back to smiling from Herr Doktor.

For some time, Alma watched him sorting his paperwork.

"Can I at least keep helping Dr. Ránki with his notes?" She licked her lips anxiously and added, as though an afterthought, "Please? I really need to occupy myself with something. I can't just sit here without action. Then I'll really go mad."

Dr. Mengele straightened next to the desk. "You aren't squeamish, are you? Not even next to that open carcass?" He gave her a teasing look and smiled, displaying a gap between his two front teeth. "My wife faints at the sight of a simple needle and you, you sit here in front of a cadaver with his chest pried open, write down

all the gory details of his autopsy—not even an elevated heartbeat."
He regarded her with some unhealthy, newfound admiration.
"Yes, you may help Dr. Ránki if you wish. In fact, the doctor and
I shall be rather busy tonight, if these temperature charts don't lie.
A temporary secretary will be most welcome."

Either it was the charts or Alma's progress, but he had left in
excellent spirits, whistling a tune to himself.

Outside, the motor of the staff car roared to life, its sound soon
fading in the distance. In the silence that followed, Dr. Ránki stood
motionless and pale, not quite daring to touch the papers with the
photographs of the identical twin boys attached to them that Dr.
Mengele had left on his desk.

At last, he muttered, almost without moving his bloodless lips,
"You have not the faintest idea what you have just volunteered for."

The twilight stole through the windows with their green anti-
mosquito screens and colored the whitewashed walls of the
pathologist's quarters drowned-blue. The inmates came and took
away the latest body. Dr. Ránki watched them go with an unreadable
expression, released a heavy sigh and went to clean the dissecting table.
It occurred to Alma that the table never remained unoccupied for long.

With some grim obsession, Dr. Ránki kept polishing the nickel
taps and the basin, all three porcelain sinks that were immaculately
clean even without his attentions, the glass on the medical cabinet,
the microscopes in the adjoining room—harsh, unforgiving strokes,
as though he was trying to wipe away his own presence from these
quarters to which he was confined against his will. His own hands
he washed just as obsessively; scrubbed them raw with soap and
a medical brush as his eyes stared, unseeing and doomed, at the
white tiled wall in front of him.

"If I weren't such a coward, I would have long ended it all," he
said suddenly, in a very quiet and bitter voice.

Alma looked at him, startled. "But you're a pathologist only. I mean...all you do is dissect bodies for him. They're already dead when they arrive here. The *Sonderkommando*, they have to assist the SS in murder."

He gave her a very strange look, as though he considered saying something but changed his mind and went back to his frantic scrubbing.

Alma thought she heard him mutter, *I'll never wash all that blood off my hands,* but the running water muted his words and she thought it rude to ask him to repeat what must have been plaguing his mind ever since his arrival here.

When the inmate brought their dinner—potatoes with blood sausage, two generous portions—Dr. Ránki hesitated and suggested that perhaps it was best to leave it for...*after,* he finished, refusing to meet Alma's eyes.

"I have a strong stomach," she assured him with a grim grin, gesturing toward the marble table on which a body lay not an hour ago.

Not for what you are about to see, his sad eyes seemed to read. Yet, he said nothing, only picked up his fork and began to eat in small, delicate bites. Alma bit into a piece of sausage, tasted copper on her tongue, realized that she didn't have much of an appetite, and proceeded to chew mechanically simply because sausage and potatoes were a delicacy in camp terms and snubbing it would be an insult to the ones who had to make do with a pathetic piece of sawdust bread that night. She wondered what her girls were eating for dinner. Hopefully, sausage as well.

Tense silence, interrupted only by the sounds of their utensils on the plates, made the air heavy. In the corners, the shadows were gathering, creeping toward the table with its green lamp, the only island of light in a world of darkness.

Abruptly, Dr. Ránki rose from his chair, marched across the room—a mere shadow himself—and groped for the light switches on the opposite wall. He turned them on, one by one, and all at once, the room was flooded with white, sterile light. Now, it was possible to get the rest of their food down. Alma smiled at him in gratitude. In an awkward, paternal gesture, he reached out and patted her hand.

It was ten past eight when they heard a child's wails outside.

"Herr Doktor has arrived," Dr. Ránki whispered, his eyes riveted to the still-closed door with an anguished look in them.

The door flung open. An inmate walked through it first, carrying a child's lifeless body in his arms. Dr. Mengele followed right after, his black eyes never leaving the corpse. He scarcely noticed a boy of around seven who clung to his sleeve and yanked at it, demanding for him to give him his brother back.

"Right there, on the dissecting table," Dr. Mengele commanded to the inmate. "And remove all of his clothes."

"Don't touch him, you vile Nazi!" The little boy positioned himself firmly in front of the SS doctor and pressed his tiny hands against Dr. Mengele's belt with its holster in a futile attempt to ward him off his dead brother's body. He was screaming in German, with a faint trace of a regional accent Alma couldn't quite place. She saw that he wasn't shaved, just like his brother; his wheat-blond hair was tangled and dirty and his cheeks, streaked with tears, hadn't lost their healthy, round shape.

"Wolfgang and Wilhelm Bierlein, seven years old, Sudeten Germans; parents—political; children aren't suitable for re-education on the conclusion of the *Reichsführer's* office of Race," Dr. Mengele announced by means of introduction and chuckled, positively delighted, when the boy hit him in the chest with his tiny closed fist.

With great effort, Alma forced herself to remain still and impassionate despite her limbs turning into ice at the horror of the unraveling scene.

"That's the spirit!" Instead of shoving him aside, Dr. Mengele ruffled the child's hair. He hardly felt any impact from the child's blow. "The *Wehrmacht* could use you on the Eastern front, little fellow. Now, hop onto that table next to your brother and give your shirt to kind Herr Doktor." He motioned his head toward Dr. Ránki.

The latter had just finished pulling on his medical gloves and now stood, miserable and helpless, with his shoulders stooped.

"I'm not doing anything you tell me. Wilhelm let you give him that shot and now he's dead!" The boy broke into sobs. "I will shoot you!"

It was a pitiful picture, watching him paw at the SS man's holster.

With his arms folded behind his back, Dr. Mengele watched him with an amused expression on his face as though observing a harmless pup at play. The boy wasn't strong enough even to undo a tight button to get to the weapon.

Alma felt a lump growing in her throat.

It appeared, Dr. Ránki couldn't bear watching it either. He scooped the child in his arms and set him on the edge of the dissecting table, holding him firmly in place.

The boy squirmed and screamed something frightful; even the inmate who stood by the wall with the dead boy's clothes in his hands began to wince from all the agony that they all felt, as though they were connected to the child by some invisible thread.

Only Dr. Mengele remained perfectly unfazed. Having removed his overcoat and cap, he donned the medical gown and gloves and went to the medicine cabinet, from which he had fetched a sedative for Alma the night before. She remembered clearly which shelf he had taken it from. The twenty cubic-centimeter glass container he had extracted now came from a completely different shelf and box.

Chloroform, Alma glimpsed the blunt black letters running across its side. *Danger: poison*. The skull and crossbones framing the warning bore an eerie similarity to the ones on Dr. Mengele's uniform cap that lay, forgotten, on top of his overcoat, thrown carelessly onto the desk.

The boy's shrieks turned outright animalistic. He struggled against Dr. Ránki's arms and tried kicking at the hand in which Dr. Mengele held a syringe filled with clear liquid.

A feeling of lightheadedness swept over Alma. Dazed and trembling, she saw the SS doctor give the boy a wolfish grin.

"Now, now, the more you struggle, the less chance I have to bring your brother back. You do want him back, don't you?"

The boy stilled at once, staring at the doctor with suspicion and something else. Hope.

It was that look of hope that had ignited in his swimming eyes that tore at Alma's heart.

"He's dead," the boy spoke with uncertainty. "You can't bring him back."

"Oh, but I can. This is the new medicine I have developed, but it works only on twins. Did your mother and father tell you how twins are connected?" he asked, holding the syringe upright. After the boy nodded, still unconvinced but listening carefully, Dr. Mengele continued, "I have discovered that if a twin dies and I give the other twin this shot straight into his heart, the other twin wakes up as though nothing happened. But it has to be done within an hour and only inside the heart, otherwise, the medicine won't work. We ought to hurry. You will be brave for your brother, won't you?"

Alma nearly choked at the resolve with which the little boy removed his shirt and handed it to Dr. Ránki. He wasn't looking at the syringe or the SS doctor any longer; half-turned toward his brother, he was clasping at his hand and saying something to him in a pacifying voice of an adult as Dr. Mengele was probing at his chest. He flinched for one instant when the long needle pierced his skin and muscle tissue and turned toward Mengele, a flash of mortal betrayal passing through his eyes. They widened; a small, inaudible gasp escaped his mouth. Then, he slackened in Dr. Ránki's arms.

When the Hungarian pathologist laid him out next to his brother, Alma saw that the boy was still holding his brother's hand.

"Children are so gullible," Dr. Mengele commented, smiling and shaking his head.

Alma lifted her head toward the ceiling and blinked rapidly a few times until the tears were gone. When Dr. Mengele turned to her, she met his gaze, perfectly calm and unrattled. Inside of her, a war was raging, but her face betrayed nothing at all. She'd made a grave mistake of showing her weakness in front of him before. Alma swore to herself that no matter what it took, he would never see it again.

Chapter 15

Dr. Mengele reappeared early the following morning. He walked in with a medical case instead of a briefcase and ordered Alma to a chair near the window. From his case, he produced an odd instrument with which he began measuring her face with such profound concentration as if all other scientific research had suddenly ceased to exist for him along with Dr. Ránki. The latter regarded him silently and motionlessly from his usual post by the dissecting table, relieved to be left alone.

For a time, Alma sat in her chair compliantly while Dr. Mengele was transferring all the measurements into a paper file. She had to thank the Hungarian pathologist for her passive state and the fact that she didn't feel the natural urge to recoil at the touch of Dr. Mengele's hands. Despise her protests, Dr. Ránki had injected her with yet another dose of a sedative the night before and gave himself one right after—"to keep the nightmares at bay," he had explained with a tragic imitation of laughter, which, it was Alma's profound conviction, concealed the sobs crowding in the pathologist's throat just as they were crowding in hers after the horrors they had witnessed. No, not just witnessed; participated in.

"It's best to forget it for now. It's best not to think altogether," he'd told her. "You'll drive yourself mad if you do. Later, after the liberation, we'll remember it all. But not now. Not just yet. We'll all fall apart if we start mourning everyone who we have lost."

That morning, Alma was grateful for his words and for the sedative, the effects of which still lingered. It made Mengele's ministrations almost tolerable for her dulled nerves. But it was when he extracted a metal plate with a number of hair samples of all possible colors attached to it out of his medical case and began comparing those samples to Alma's hair, she finally couldn't contain herself any longer.

"What are you doing, Herr Doktor?"

He made no reply, preoccupied with his hair-color chart. At last, when he had finally discovered a perfect match—*V, braun-schwarz*—he pulled back with a self-satisfied look on his face, as though he had just found physical proof of the Theory of Relativity. "Are you aware that you and I, we have the same exact hair color?" he asked.

Alma regarded him, puzzled. "What are you saying, Herr Doktor? That we're some long-lost brother and sister or something of that sort?" With the best will in the world, she couldn't keep the sarcasm out of her voice.

He exploded into laughter at that. "No, I'm not saying anything of that kind," he replied, his shoulders still quivering with chuckles. "I'm saying, you have the features of an Aryan. Alpine racial type, to be precise, according to your facial measurements. The same type I fall under."

"But I'm Jewish." Alma's desire to make him see the ridiculous logic of his statement overpowered her instinct of self-preservation.

"I know."

"A full Jew."

"Yes."

"And you're Aryan."

"That's correct."

"And yet, according to your scientific parameters, we fall under the same racial category."

"That's what I just said." He was playing with the chart's hair samples, curling and uncurling them with his fingers.

Alma read the name on the metal plate, *Fischer-Saller*.

A smile began to grow on her face. It would be idiotic to laugh just then; it would be even more idiotic to say out loud precisely what she was thinking, but Alma couldn't help herself.

"Well, doesn't it render your and *Herren* Fischer and Saller's racial science...nonsensical?"

Dr. Mengele drew himself up, his expression turning defensive. "Science is science. It doesn't make mistakes. And doctors Fischer and Saller are an established eugenicist and anthropologist, respectively. In fact, Professor Fischer's ideas inspired the Nuremberg Laws."

Once again, Alma should have kept quiet and once again, she didn't. "But what you're saying contradicts your own Führer, Adolf Hitler. He declared that there is such a thing as Jewish physics after Einstein had fled Germany for the United States in order to discredit Einstein's work. According to your Führer, Jewish physics was not a real science. But if you're saying that science is science, and physics is certainly science, then—"

Out of the corner of her eye, she saw Dr. Ránki signing to her to stop it right that instant by making cut-throat gestures behind Dr. Mengele's back.

There was a tense pause.

"Perhaps, you're not a full Jew after all," Dr. Mengele concluded and began prodding at Alma's face with renewed vigor.

"My late mother would take great offense to that, Herr Doktor."

"I wasn't insinuating anything," he muttered, feeling the bridge of her nose. "This is not a natural deviation. Your nose has been broken, and broken recently."

"You're very observant, Herr Doktor."

"Not while you were in custody?" He pulled back, regarding her with disbelief, as though it appeared unconceivable to him that one of his fellow SS cronies would stoop so low as to hit a woman. Perhaps, in his imagination, it was indeed a behavior unworthy of an SS man. He had no qualms about killing them personally or by ordering them to the gas or murdering twins in cold blood, but he had never hit anyone, not in front of Alma, at any rate.

A real chivalrous gentleman, Alma mused to herself with great sarcasm.

"No, not in custody. I broke it myself, by accident."

"How could you break your own nose by accident?"

"I tripped and fell down the stairs at my hosts' house in Holland. Landed straight on my face and smashed it rather badly. There was blood everywhere. I looked like a right beauty for a couple of weeks afterward." She snorted softly at the memory. "My eyes were black as pitch and swollen to slits."

"How does one land on their face when they fall?" He regarded her skeptically. "A natural human reflex is to—"

"Bring one's hands forward to break the fall, yes," she interrupted him with a smile. "But I'm not a regular human, Herr Doktor. I'm a violinist. My hands and arms are my everything. I held them behind my back on purpose when I was falling in order not to break them. My face doesn't matter all that much."

Dr. Mengele was looking at her in astonishment. "What admirable self-discipline," he muttered at last. His eyes brightened when a realization dawned on him. He began to smile. "So that's why you were in such a hysterical state when those two SS fellows brought you here. That's the reason for all that Herr-Doktor-Give-Me-A-Shot-Of-Phenol blooming nonsense. I didn't realize how important it was to you, the ability to make music. I thought you staged that scene solely due to weak nerves, but now I see that yours are made of steel, Frau Alma." He motioned his head toward the dissecting table, now thankfully empty. "I apologize."

That was the last thing Alma had expected. "Thank you, Herr Doktor." She searched his face. "Am I free to go then?"

"Stay here for a few more days. You ought to rest your arm at any rate. And, besides, I like having you here. You interest me. Scientifically," he added a tad too hastily, as though to clarify a misunderstanding.

*

In the afternoon, Zippy arrived carrying a violin case and a wrap under her arm. After hugging Alma briskly, she deposited the wrap on top of the doctor's desk.

"I brought you a change of clothes and your violin. How is your arm?"

Alma was already pushing her away from the desk and toward the door. "You shouldn't have come; he'll be here any moment and if he sees you—"

Zippy seized her shoulders, smiling. "Almschi, it's all right. He knows I'm here. It was him, who sent me. Specifically ordered me to bring you your violin, too." She drew closer and lowered her voice, "He didn't do anything to you, did he?"

Anything meant experiments, most certainly.

"Oh, no. Just gave me a sedative on the very first night and bandaged my arm."

"It's not broken, is it?"

"No. It's just a bad bruise."

Zippy nodded in apparent relief and, after throwing another look over her shoulder at the Hungarian pathologist (to his credit, after the initial greeting, Dr. Ránki had retired to the furthest corner and pretended to be preoccupied with checking the labels on the vials in the medicine cabinet), extracted a folded note from inside her dress. "I have something for you. From Auschwitz."

Mystified, Alma stood for some time staring at the paper in her hand blankly. At last, she approached the window and opened it. It wasn't a note; a letter, if anything, written in an elegant cursive. As soon as Alma began reading it, the lump in her throat returned at once and the charcoal lines soon began blurring in front of her eyes.

Dear Frau Rosé,

I hope you shall forgive me for introducing myself in such an unorthodox manner; my only excuse is that I don't presently possess an Ausweis *and therefore can't move freely between the camps.*

My name is Miklós Steinberg. I'm afraid, it is my music that you had the misfortune to hear today. I should like to apologize to you for being so rude and not paying any attention to my surroundings; else, I would never have played that atrocious march, if I only knew that you stood there the entire time. I can see how it upset you...

If it's of any consolation to you, Frau Gerda, the Block's Kapo—*I believe you two have already made your acquaintance—has already let her sentiments on my account be known to me and has thoroughly chastised me for my inexcusable behavior and unfortunate choice of repertoire.*

Please allow me to assure you once again that it was unintentional. Sometimes it all overcomes me, and I start playing things that oughtn't to be played. I hope you will find it in yourself to forgive me.

Sincerely,
Miklós Steinberg.

"When a runner brought it from the main camp, you were already gone. I carried it on myself the entire time." It was obvious that Zippy was itching to see what was inside. "What is it? A love letter from a secret admirer?"

Alma tried to smile but couldn't for some reason. "No. I don't even know him personally."

"Who is he?"

"A pianist." Alma pondered something and added in a very soft voice, "One of the best pianists I've ever heard."

After Zippy was long gone, Alma still sat, re-reading the letter countless times, on top of the pathologist's bed in his private quarters. For the first time, she didn't mind being alone.

Miklós Steinberg. Of course, he would write a letter of this sort. Mirthless laughter escaped Alma's throat and died almost instantly. Inadvertently, he would go and make it all even worse by reminding her of her past life where chivalry wasn't dead and buried somewhere in the field behind the Little Red House, where human decency was still worth more than a slice of bread, where Jewish musicians didn't have to apologize for mourning their kin with a funeral march.

Alma folded the letter, then her arms on top of the pillow and let her head drop on top of them. It suddenly felt as though it weighed a ton.

He was right. She didn't know him, but all at once he had become someone much more familiar than anyone here. Alma felt an inexplicable closeness to him that she didn't feel even toward Zippy or Sofia or any other of her girls. He came from the same place as she did, without coming from the same country. He played music which she felt reverberating inside of her still, touching every nerve, bringing back memories she so thoroughly tried to bury. He was a piece of her past and her future, the only living reminder of something intangible, but so impossibly important.

Desire to live, it suddenly hit Alma with such force. He was the first person who gave her the desire to live.

Up until now, her own fate mattered little. She was pondering taking her life back in Drancy, long before all this detestable Auschwitz business. It was her upbringing that inspired such dark, anguished thoughts—it was better to be dead rather than live in this German-imposed slavery. Ridiculous as it sounded, she envied the Eastern-European Jews who shared the crammed quarters with her in the French transit camp; they had each other and their religion and, to them, it appeared to be enough. They'd been chased through Europe for years, from the revolution-ravaged Russia to Germany to Poland, Austria, and France. *Passports?* They had laughed heartily at that. They hadn't had those since 1917. Temporary papers from police headquarters was all they could show to their names. They'd grown used to such a sad state of affairs.

Alma had envied them, and they had pitied her in return. Pitied her elegant clothes growing gradually dirtier and her high-heeled shoes (what torture those had turned out to be in the box car! Alma ended up removing them altogether and standing barefoot throughout the entire journey). Pitied the very fact that she came from a household with a governess and a small army of servants and now, all of a sudden, she had to cook raw potatoes for herself on the communal stove. "When you have nothing to begin with, there's little they can take away from you," one of them, black-clad and Orthodox, had wisely noted. As long as their family members were alive, they were perfectly content with the little that they had.

They bore their sufferings nobly and with pride. "Our ancestors suffered for two thousand years and so must we." Earning the heaven on earth or something else to that extent—Alma knew very little of their traditions or religion and understood them even less. With the best will in the world, she couldn't find comfort in their ideals. A cosmopolitan Viennese, she was too much of a cynic and an aesthete to reconcile herself with the idea of suffering and surviving just because it was their—Jews'—lot in life, to suffer and survive. The entire trouble was, ever since she was a child, she was taught how to *live*—lavishly and with great taste. *Surviving* wasn't something that was taught in the Rosé household. The only reason she hadn't taken that poison she had managed to secure from one of the Drancy black-market dealers was the thought of her father. He was an old man. The news of his only daughter's death would kill him.

In Auschwitz, where death was quite literally in the air, twirling softly in great, ashen flakes, it was all for the girls' sake. If it weren't for them, fat chance Alma would be so deferential with Mandl and so purposely feminine with Hössler. It was for them, her little sparrows, for Violette-from-Paris, for camp-savvy Zippy, and for blunt but kind-hearted Sofia, that Alma dug through the heaps of dead people's papers to fish a music score from under a pile of smiling children's photographs. It was for them that she exchanged pleasantries with the SS men she despised and praised the music taste of SS women who understood virtually nothing about it. If it weren't for the girls, she would have long sent the entire show to the devil.

But now, there was this pianist and his letter in her hand. Alma hadn't the faintest idea about his existence just a few days ago, but now he had stirred something in her with his music and his words and she sat and dreamt of playing alongside him on stage—the composer, the creator, the man who could play what she only felt inside and couldn't put into words.

Her eyes were staring ahead, bright and shining. A radiant smile was slowly growing, blossoming on her face, erasing the years of suffering, smoothing the harsh, bitter lines around her mouth. For the first time since her arrest in France, Alma was glad to be alive.

Chapter 16

Alma was released back to her girls by the end of the week. Prior to escorting her out of the pathologist's quarters, Dr. Mengele handed Alma an official form of some sort, filled with his tangled handwriting.

"This is for Drexler or Grese, if they ask for it during the roll call. You were officially in my care this entire time. Tell them it is imperative that you rest your arm as much as possible. If you're not up to performing for their cultural evenings and whatever songs they demand from you whenever they grow bored during their shift, then you aren't, and that's final. If anyone needs further explanation on that matter, send them straight to my quarters."

It was Alma's profound conviction that no one in the camp lacked common sense enough to question the sadist-in-chief's orders. Still, she was grateful for the precaution; both wardens shared a reputation of cruelty for the sake of cruelty and although Mandl personally forbade them to inflict any sort of physical harm on the orchestra inmates, they had long made their sentiments on the Music Block's account known.

"If it were up to me, all of you, useless tramps, would have been put to work in the *Aussenkommando* instead of wasting the Reich's resources for nothing," Drexler had snarled at Alma just a couple of weeks ago, after the latter handed her the extended roll call list.

"All new additions to the orchestra are here on Dr. Mengele's authority," Alma had replied evenly, her eyes trained on the ground as Sofia had taught her.

Sometimes, Alma wondered if Drexler would indeed shoot her if she raised her gaze to her—a capital offense in the SS warden's eyes. Grese, her lieutenant, only aspired to her mentor's level of viciousness. She was still very young and unexperienced in the SS business and mostly satisfied herself with lashing the inmate women with her whip across their breasts until the skin would split under her blows, but she wasn't known for shooting inmates indiscriminately solely for daring to look at her, not just yet.

With those two "fine" representatives of the Aryan race, it was never too prudent to be able to present a written protection from one of their male superiors, Alma considered on her way to the block, studying the form with its gothic script and Dr. Mengele's signature on the bottom.

You interest me. Scientifically, he had said. That was the only reason she was still alive, Alma realized with disgust. That *scientific* interest of his and his fondness for classics. It was truly a travesty, the extent to which the value of a human being's life had been reduced in this new Thousand Year Reich. "Usefulness" and someone's personal interest.

The form clutched firmly in her hand, Alma trooped through the muddy parade ground fantasizing, with unexpected sadistic cruelty she had never expected from herself, about the day when their liberators would come and when the SS wardens' bodies would be swinging from the gallows of the women's camp instead of Jewish "useless eaters'."

Overcome with shame, she had to stop for a few moments. No, this was not who she was. Alma slowly passed her hand over her forehead where the beads of sweat had gathered despite the cold. She was better than this. She wouldn't let this place's poison work its way under her skin and turn her into one of them—cruel, heartless, openly enjoying the sufferings of the others. It would be both a moral and professional death at any rate—an artist ought to *feel* to create anything worthy of attention. Any music was produced out of love, never out of hatred or cruelty. That's why there was no new culture born out of Hitler's new Germany. They slapped dusted-off Wagner atop outdated Nietzsche, peppered it with bastardized Darwin, stamped it with the seal of approval by the Ministry of Propaganda and passed it off as Great Germanic Culture and New Racial Science and the public was no wiser.

It was good that she could still feel it all—fear, desperation, guilt, shame. Sympathy. Hope. Love?

Alma's fingers brushed the pocket of her coat where another note, much more important than anything that Mengele could possibly write, was tucked away discreetly. She stopped contemplating the mud under her feet, raised her head higher, and resumed her walk. As long as she could feel, all was not lost.

Warden Drexler openly cringed at Dr. Mengele's form but said nothing this time; Grese only demanded if Alma would play for their cultural evening on Sunday.

"Dr. Mengele ordered me to rest my arm until it heals completely," Alma replied, not without inward pleasure.

She could play her violin just fine, if not for prolonged periods of time; after all, she had played it for Herr Doktor himself. He had sat with his eyes closed at Dr. Ránki's desk, the chair turned away from it and toward Alma, his head inclined slightly and his right hand caressing the air in front of him in soft, languid strokes in time with her music, a blissful, serene smile fleetingly touching his lips whenever she played his favorite parts. His requests, Alma couldn't reject. But the wardens, with their little dance parties featuring Alma as the main entertainment, could all go and hang themselves. She would much rather spend her time and effort rehearsing with her girls.

Grese, a pout already forming on her porcelain, doll-like face, was just about to interject something to that, but Lagerführerin Mandl herself made an appearance at that moment, stared at Alma's still-bandaged forearm in terror and declared, in a no-nonsense tone, that Alma was to rest her arm for as long as needed so it would heal properly.

"As for the drunken SS men looking for a good time," she made a disgusted face, "the orchestra needn't worry about them anymore. The new *Kommandant* has already sent a few offenders on their way East."

With that, the matter appeared to be dismissed.

"The new *Kommandant*?" Alma asked Zippy as soon as Mandl left, along with the wardens, wondering just how much she had missed while she was away.

Zippy made big eyes at her. "Kommandant Liebehenschel. He was here the very next morning after you had disappeared and interrogated us all for a good hour. From what I heard from the wardens in the *Schreibstube*, he assembled all SS men later and told them explicitly that such behavior would not be tolerated any longer. He also told them that all beatings are to stop from now on, both coming from the SS and the *Kapos*. He said it's counterproductive for the camp's purpose. Announced some new reward system for the prisoners. The harder you work, the more privileges you get or something of that sort. An odd fellow, I must tell you. How he made it into a camp administration is beyond me!" She lowered her voice confidentially, "There's gossip that his mistress, or fiancée, or whoever she is, has been accused by the Gestapo for her associations with the Jews and that's the reason why he was transferred here, to Auschwitz-Birkenau, from his previous position. Supposedly in punishment for standing up for her and her views," she finished in a grave whisper, obviously impressed by such an unorthodox—for an SS officer—achievement. "She followed him here. They live just outside the camp."

Alma regarded her in genuine amazement. A sympathetic camp *Kommandant*? That was something new entirely. "What happened to Kommandant Höss?"

After a fleeting glance over her shoulder, Zippy resumed her whispering: "They say, he was stealing too much even for the SS's liking. Some Berlin higher-ups came here with the inspection last week. Some SS bigwig, Dr. Morgen I think his name was, turned the whole of the camp office upside down and subjected SS wardens and us, inmate secretaries, to such interrogations, I almost told him everything I didn't even know just so he would leave off. Something to do with corruption in the camp among the SS. Well, it appeared that Morgen fellow, and whatever inspectorate he's working for, didn't appreciate the fact that Höss was appropriating *Kanada* goods for personal use and employing inmates for personal pleasure. Auschwitz orchestra, in particular. They spent more time playing for his guests in his villa than doing work they were supposed to be doing. They're employed elsewhere, unlike us. Potato peeling detail, truck driving... Instead, he made them into his personal band of sorts. It looks like it rubbed even his own superiors the wrong way and they shipped him off someplace before replacing him with Kommandant Liebehenschel."

Alma met the new *Kommandant* soon enough. He simply walked in one afternoon, accompanied by Mandl and two of his adjutants, took off his uniform cap and found a chair in the back of the music room, waving for the orchestra to be seated as they leapt up to greet him.

"Kommandant Liebehenschel," Zippy whispered helpfully at Alma from her front row seat, and made expressive eyes at the conductor. *Play something nice for him!*

"I had no wish to disturb you," he spoke in a soft voice and smiled pleasantly. "Please, continue your rehearsals and don't mind me."

From her conductor's stand, Alma could only discern that he had a pale handsome face, dark hair and the large brown eyes of a sad deer. Partly out of politeness and partly prompted by Zippy, she inquired if Herr Kommandant wished to hear something particular.

He only shook his head again and offered her another embarrassed smile, as though in apology for inconveniencing her with his presence. "Please, don't bother on my account and pretend that I'm not even here."

Zippy didn't lie. He was an odd fellow, for an SS man.

Alma was astounded even more when, after the rehearsal was over, Kommandant Liebehenschel approached her and very politely inquired if her orchestra needed anything.

"A piano would be nice, Herr Kommandant," Alma ventured, encouraged by his amicable disposition. "If that's at all possible, of course."

"Naturally, it's possible! There are three of them at the villa," he announced. Alma guessed that he most likely meant Höss' former quarters. "I'll arrange for the special *Kommando* to deliver one of them to you at once. What sort of orchestra is it without a piano anyway?" He laughed, looking round for support from his entourage.

The adjutants and Mandl began nodding enthusiastically at once.

"Anything else?" He turned to Alma again.

And why not? Alma considered. *One must take the good as it comes, and in this place especially.*

"An iron stove, Herr Kommandant, to warm the quarters." When he appeared to hesitate—it was an unheard-of privilege among the inmates—Alma quickly signed toward the instruments, "In cold months, they require a constant temperature to stay in tune, and particularly the stringed ones. The wood on most of these instruments is very sensitive and the strings may simply snap from negligence, if one doesn't treat them accordingly—"

"Yes, yes, I understand. You'll get the stove. I assume you'd prefer one on which you can cook your own food as well?" He made a sign to one of his aides.

The young man took out a small black notebook and began scribbling in it under Alma's astonished gaze. She could hardly believe her good fortune.

The new *Kommandant* was looking at her benevolently with those big deer eyes, his generosity seemingly knowing no bounds.

Alma remembered Drexler and her recent *useless tramps* comment and was suddenly overcome with a desire to stick it to the warden with yet another privilege granted by the camp *Kommandant* himself.

"Herr Kommandant, perhaps now that the winter is approaching, it would be sensible to conduct a roll call inside the quarters instead of outside?" Alma probed, offering him a tentative smile. "We're a small block and surely the wardens would prefer it as well…"

Mandl looked at the new administration questioningly.

Alma nearly fell over with astonishment when Kommandant Liebehenschel only nodded amicably again.

"Perfectly sensible. And, if you please, I would rather you not address me as Herr Kommandant." He grimaced slightly as though the title itself tasted foul on his tongue. "Herr Obersturmbannführer will do just fine."

"As you wish, Herr Obersturmbannführer." Alma inclined her head, putting as much deference in the gesture as humanly possible.

"Anything else?"

Alma almost laughed with mad, hysterical joy. *Surely, she was dreaming!*

Behind Mandl's shoulder, Sofia was shaking her head at Alma, signing to her wildly to stop trying her luck.

Alma only grinned at her, an insane, vicious grin of someone who had been to the other side and back, looked the devil in the eye and wasn't afraid of anything any longer. "You have a Jewish pianist in your main camp who's not allowed to play in the orchestra. Would it be too much trouble to transfer him here, to Birkenau men's orchestra so he could play the piano there? And if he could come here and tutor my girls, that would help us tremendously."

Sofia stared at her, positively mortified.

But the new *Kommandant* merely asked for the pianist's number. "I don't know his number," Alma confessed. "I only know his name. It's Miklós Steinberg and he was very famous in Hungary."

Instinctively, her palm passed over the pocket where she carried his letter with her at all times. For some reason, it felt insanely good just to say his name out loud.

As soon as the delegation had left the Music Block, Sofia swung round toward the beaming Alma. "Have you completely gone off your head?! Höss would have shot you for that!"

"Höss is gone." Alma shrugged, perfectly unimpressed, and picked up her baton. "I hope they court-martial him and shoot him like he deserves."

The very next day, a new, shiny piano was brought into the Musical Block. The day after, a big iron stove made its way into the corner, along with a full sack of coal—"From Herr Kommandant, with best wishes," the special *Kommando* men tipped their striped caps theatrically and left, exchanging jests among themselves.

And, on Wednesday, Miklós Steinberg appeared in the door. He stood there indecisively, crushing his cap in his long, beautiful fingers, like a saint with the halo of the sun against his head and, all at once, the barrack itself appeared to be lighter.

Chapter 17

"That F you just played was supposed to be an F-sharp." With an abrupt rap of the baton, Alma stopped the rehearsal.

"I'm sorry, Frau Alma. It's difficult to concentrate when..." Violette-from-Paris didn't finish, motioning with her bow toward the grand piano instead, at which Miklós was tutoring his new charge, Flora.

At once, the pianist lifted his gaze from the keys. "If we're bothering you—"

"You're not bothering anyone in the slightest, Herr Steinberg." Alma fixed Violette with a glare instead. "Are you able to concentrate with the new arrivals screaming in the background as the SS tear their families apart at the ramp? Are you able to concentrate when the outside gangs are marching back in through the gates, carrying their dead with them from the fields? Are you able to concentrate playing against the screams and moans of the dying in the sickbay? Well then, the piano, playing a different tune from your own instrument should be the least of your trouble. From the beginning!"

In the course of the past couple of months, Alma's orchestra had significantly swelled in its number. Making use of Dr. Mengele and Obersturmführer Hössler's permission, Alma was pulling them out of selections and quarantine blocks at every chance she had. But now there were forty of them, not counting the ones whom she turned into Block staff, like copyists and runners, and out of those forty only twenty were professionals. The SS, who began to drop in in the middle of the day more and more often and request certain songs, appeared to be more than pleased with the new, improved orchestra. Mandl reported the Music Block's progress with visible pride to everyone who agreed to listen and even ordered the sewing detail to fashion a new uniform for their concerts. Now, Alma's girls performed in pristine white blouses, dark blue skirts and with their heads covered by beautiful lavender kerchiefs. Their *Lagerführerin* even commandeered black silk stockings for her mascots, much to her female underlings' astonishment and displeasure. Prior to that, only SS wardens were allowed such luxury.

But the more the SS were giving, the heavier the pressure was growing. Alma felt it on her leaden shoulders—an invisible, yet oddly physical burden to create an orchestra of the Vienna Philharmonic type out of the pitiful Birkenau motley lot. The SS didn't have the habit of being charitable without a reason. For each new privilege, they expected a more complicated piece. For each new extra ration or item, they expected a veritable concert given in their honor. If it was just Alma, on whom it all depended, she would have never complained. From her early childhood, she had been trained to play, play without stopping and on the level of a virtuoso; she had been disciplined into this lifestyle and it came naturally to her. Even now, she stayed up late in her room long after lights-out—another personal privilege given to *Frau Alma,* to leave the light burning on her desk after the curfew—and worked on the scores for the following day.

There were forty girls and, for most of them, life had only begun. They didn't understand much of it; they cried at night and scratched at her door shyly and announced, out of the blue, that they missed their mothers, and cried even harder when she held them and stroked their hair and assured them that everything was going to be all right and the day when they would be liberated would certainly come and, as soon as it did, she would take them all on a Victory Tour all over Europe.

There were forty girls, who tired quickly from playing for ten and twelve hours a day and couldn't bend their fingers properly the next morning. There were girls who were constantly hungry even though their rations were much better than those of the regular inmates. There were girls who regarded her with silent reproach whenever she would demand perfection from them and who refused to understand that their conductor only tormented them for their own good; that, in case something happened to her, they would be able to fend for themselves and remain alive until the liberation.

All that made Alma's work much more difficult.

"You're very strict with them," Miklós remarked to her, pulling his short jacket on top of his sweater with two holes in it rimmed with brownish-red, right over the heart. He didn't appear to mind the bloodstains and the fact that the goods had come off some poor bastard's corpse; having a sweater in the first place was too much of a blessing to question its quality.

His first tutoring shift was over. It was time for him to return to his new orchestra and their evening duties—greeting the returning outside gangs with a cheery march. Alma suspected that in view of the impossibility of bringing the piano to the gates, Miklós was on the permanent music stands carrying duty with Laks's orchestra.

"I have to be. They have to play excellently, so that the SS can't send them to the gas," Alma explained, a bit more defensively than she had intended.

Miklós grinned, fixing his striped cap on top of his shaved head. "I never said it was a bad thing."

"Yes, well . . ." She cleared her throat slightly, suddenly tongue-tied and not quite knowing what to say. "I'll walk you out."

"You don't have to. It's freezing out there—"

"No, it's all right."

Outside, the snow was falling. Searchlights swept lazily over the still-empty compound, piercing the gathering darkness and obliterating misshapen shadows with their yellow-eyed glares. The air was wet and misty, and their breath was coming out in translucent vaporous clouds. At once, Miklós pulled his jacket off and threw it on Alma's shoulders. She looked at him, somewhat embarrassed, and felt her cheeks grow warm.

"I heard you playing in Vienna," he suddenly announced.

"In the Philharmonic?"

"Twice in the Philharmonic. You played chamber music with your father. And other times at the Prater."

"With my Waltzing Girls?" Alma felt a smile blossom on her face at the memory. She loved her first orchestra dearly. Much like the Birkenau one, she had conjured it up out of thin air and turned it into an overnight success. No longer in the shadow of her father's name, she had unfurled her wings and become a force of her own, the name people repeated with awe and admiration. Her marriage had gone to the devil, but Alma had discovered that she was almost grateful that it did. While they were married, it was always Váša's career that mattered; Alma's was scarcely ever discussed, and condescendingly at that. But with the Waltzing Girls, this was no longer the case—now, it was Alma's face that looked on from every wall and magazine, looking proud of her success, and rightfully so. And if certain men couldn't take the competition, it was their loss, as far as Alma was concerned. She had wanted *a partner*, not a mere husband. A partner who would share both the spotlight with her and all the hardships as well. She hadn't met him, but she had still nursed a hope that he existed.

"The very same. I didn't miss one concert whenever I visited. Sometimes you were on tour, though. On those days, I couldn't see you."

There was a pause. Alma discovered that she was afraid that he was about to say something corny: *All those girls around you on stage, but I only saw your face. You were so impossibly beautiful...* That's what her lover Heinrich used to say. That's what her ex-husband Váša had been attracted to—a beautiful face and a famous last name. Sometimes, her brother used to joke that Váša married their father and not Alma. Alma had laughed out of politeness but deep inside, she always suspected that Alfred was right.

She started when Miklós spoke again, something quite different from what she had expected: "When I first heard you play, it touched something deep within me. Ten violinists can play the same piece, but it's the manner in which they play it that counts, if you know what I'm trying to say?" He cringed slightly at his own words, as though embarrassed that he couldn't express himself more eloquently, and rubbed his neck, hiding his eyes from her, chuckling bashfully. "You must take me for veritable mutton just now. I hope I'm not offending you with all these revelations; I assure you, it was never my intention..."

"No, no; please, continue," she urged him. *Tell me everything you heard in my music.*

"Yes, well...You were very restrained with your instrument, almost austere. And yet, there was such passion hidden deep underneath that austerity, I couldn't quite take it in, how it was even possible to play like that. I was sitting there at my table, looking round and thinking to myself, 'They're not hearing it, these people around me, all they hear is simple music,' but I heard what you were trying to conceal from all that crowd; I felt it, it gave me literal chills on my skin, that force, that raw talent you were carefully hiding behind the meticulous technique." He rubbed his arm as if the chills were still there, his eyes flashing about with excitement. "I'm not sure if you understand—"

"I understand," Alma rushed to assure him, feeling a smile growing on her face. She understood him better than he thought. She had the same chills all over her skin when she heard him play.

"After I heard your violin that day, I was wondering what it would be like to know you as a person, as a fellow musician. I was hoping that I could meet you one day just so we could sit down and talk about music and life and art for hours. I guess I ought to thank the SS for making my dreams come true."

The jest broke the gravity of the moment and Alma was almost relieved that it did. It was difficult standing next to him when he was saying all of those things and not allow herself to be affected by them. *A talent. A person. A fellow musician.* Nothing about her beautiful face or her beautiful dress, and thank God for that! How infinitely disappointing it would have been, if he had turned out to be just as superficial as the others. Alma released a breath she didn't realize she'd been holding the whole time.

"You could have approached me after the concert," she said.

"I considered it," Miklós admitted. "But then I thought that if my guess about you was correct—you see, you look like a woman who never suffered from the lack of men's attentions and who would, in fact, be insulted by such a crude approach—you would have most likely told me to get lost with my compliments and that would be the end of it."

Alma had to laugh, even if something caught in her chest at those words. "That's what I would have said. Most likely."

"Yes?"

"Yes."

"See? My deductions were correct then," he announced, unsuccessfully trying to conceal another grin.

"Disappointed?"

"I would have been disappointed if you said no just now."

Alma was looking at him. He had eyes the color of steel, and yet, to Alma they appeared to be the warmest eyes she'd ever seen.

"I have never been to Hungary," she said, changing the subject. The previous one was growing much too personal and she didn't want it. Not in this place, at any rate. "And never heard you play before. And now I regret it. I feel I have missed out on so much."

"I suppose it's good fortune then that we're both here and can play for each other every day."

In the distance, a dog was barking. Against the indigo of the sky, the orange fires of the crematorium raged. In the glare provided by them, Alma held her hand, palm up. Some of the flakes melted instantly. Some didn't. Alma wiped them on the jacket, remembered that it wasn't hers and looked at Miklós in sudden profound misery.

He only smiled sadly and shook his head. *Don't apologize. I understand everything.*

"You should be going. It's getting rather cold and you mustn't be late for your marching out. We have to head out too." She handed him his jacket. "I hope you're not mad at me."

"Why would I be mad at you?"

She gave a small shrug. "For you, a renowned pianist, training my charges must feel like a university professor teaching kindergartners the alphabet."

"You're joking. You made my transfer possible; you arranged for me to become a member of an actual orchestra. Now, I can do what I love doing most—play the piano all day, and you say I ought to be mad at you?"

"Are they treating you well there?"

"Yes. Like a king."

"I'm serious."

"Me too. They put me in the Family Camp on my request."

"They did? That's wonderful news!"

"It is. I met so many former acquaintances there—musicians, journalists, directors—you name it. We have the best cultural evenings in the entire camp. The SS should be jealous of us."

"I might know some people there, too. Could you, perhaps, ask around for me? Do you know anyone by the name Röders there? They're my Dutch friends. Also, James H. Simon could be there as well."

"I will ask this very evening. I'll turn the entire barrack on its head, but I shall find them for you, if they're there."

"Just tell them that Alma Rosé is here. Some people I didn't mention may know..."

"You have ties to former Czechoslovakia?"

"My first husband was Czech." Alma looked away.

There was a pause, during which Miklós was trying to search her face. "I'm sorry...Did he die?"

Alma looked at him at last and smiled. There wasn't much joy in that smile. "No. I died for him. You see, I was Jewish, and he had a very promising career."

Miklós didn't say anything, but the expression on his face did.

"Just like Heinrich after him," Alma continued to enumerate. For some reason, it was so easy to talk about it all with this man she had just met. "Just like Leonard, my Dutch fiancé after that... But it also didn't go further than that. He had a career and I was still very much a Jew. A homosexual man married me in the hope of saving me from deportation. Funny, isn't it? The Nazis call them perverts and put them in camps, but those so-called 'perverts' turn out to be much better people than those 'upstanding' Aryans."

"Perhaps, you should start seeing Jewish men."

His nonchalant announcement threw her off guard. Looking at him in amazement, Alma broke into mirthless laugher in spite of herself. "Where? Here?"

"Here is just the place. All of the European Jewish elite has gathered here, haven't you noticed?" Standing against the crematorium chimneys, he gestured widely around himself. "But be quick about it before they gas us all."

All at once, Alma couldn't get her breath. A sudden fear had seized her; the irrational, wild fear that one day he would walk inside that crematorium and the world would lose him and his glorious talent forever.

"It's all right to laugh about death." As though sensing her mood, he dropped his mock-cheerful act. "We, like no one else, have deserved this right."

He took her hand in his and kissed it as though they were parting ways after some gala or other, bowed to her sharply and elegantly, and walked off in the direction of the columns of fire.

Alma stood, looking after him, a lone figure in the creeping, silvery shadows, with sudden infinite longing. A mad idea possessed her, as though it was all predestined, as though that very meeting had been written by some omnipotent and invisible hand long before she was born, long before he was born; that they were brought here together on purpose. The past had virtually ceased to exist—the past without him in it—and that last thought terrified and excited Alma to the bone and left her trembling violently, not from the cold, but from the sudden realization of it.

Chapter 18

November 1943

At the end of November, the days grew gradually shorter. The indifferent sun shone onto the inmates' bowed heads only for a few pitiful hours a day, if it deigned to make an appearance at all. After lunch, while her girls were sleeping, Alma could see the prisoners' ghostly figures through her little window. Barefoot, they shuffled toward their barracks holding their wooden clogs in their hands—utterly useless footwear in winter that only made one slip and break the formation. Officially, the beatings had been prohibited by the new administration, but old habits died hard.

Alma used to stand outside and smoke, staring pensively into nothing, but after Dr. Mengele had caught her snubbing her naptime in such an infamous manner, Alma remained confined to her room from then on. Unlike the other girls, she couldn't sleep, but to pacify Herr Doktor, she pretended that she was getting enough rest.

He still wasn't deceived.

"You've lost more weight," he remarked to her in a businesslike manner after she finished playing Schumann's "Träumerei" for him on the Block's new grand piano.

"I'm planning to become a fashion model in Paris after the war is over," Alma replied with mock-seriousness.

She had learned by now that this was precisely what the most feared SS physician preferred—from her, at least: stony-faced gallows humor and just a bit of insolence to spice things up. He appreciated that sort of humor because he, himself, was prone to it.

"You may as well." Dr. Mengele rose to his feet and picked up his uniform cap from the chair. As always, he was immaculately turned out, not a hair out of place, handsome and just as ruthless—a perfect product of the Party. "Parisian couturiers will need new ones after we have chased through the chimney all the old ones." He motioned toward the instrument: "That piano is very good."

"I should imagine it would be. It used to belong to Kommandant Höss."

Dr. Mengele barked an unexpected laugh. "How things change in this place! Well, good riddance to bad garbage, if I'm entirely honest with you. He was the most intolerable, self-important raven one could have had for a superior."

Things did change, and they hardly changed at all.

Obersturmführer Hössler stopped by every other day with his Alsatian, which lay at his feet panting while Alma played solos on her violin for him. He always brought her something—smuggled sweets from the SS canteen or even bones for his own dog, wrapped in a napkin, so she could feed them to the dog. He began bringing them along after Alma had mentioned that she used to own an Alsatian as well and that his name was Arno and that he used to ride with her in her white convertible along the Prater, the famous Viennese public park, and people recognized her right away, just by that white car and black dog in the passenger seat. Soon, Hössler's shepherd migrated from under his master's feet to Alma's. The camp leader didn't seem to mind.

Mandl appeared one afternoon, depositing a stack of postcards on the table where the copyists worked and announced that all Aryan members of the orchestra were allowed to receive parcels from home according to Kommandant Liebehenschel's new directive.

"What about Jewish girls?" Alma looked at the Birkenau *Lagerführerin*.

Mandl simply regarded her as if she had just said something incredibly idiotic. Alma herself realized what it was just then: the

Jewish girls' families had all been gassed upon arrival and if they hadn't, they were in hiding someplace that didn't have a return address.

"Jewish inmates shall be receiving aid directly from the Red Cross, so that when the Swiss come here with the inspection, they can't say that we're not treating you right," Mandl said in response before taking her leave.

Naturally, such SS goodwill was purely self-serving—a convenient façade to present to the world through the Red Cross inspectorate's reports—but Alma was grateful for the additional rations all the same. Inside the Red Cross parcels, there were cookies, smoked sausage, bread, and even tinned sardines in oil. Alma distributed the contents of the packages evenly among the girls and shared her own with Miklós. They ate the golden sardines straight out of the tin, holding the glistening, sleek bodies by their tales and swallowing them whole, their eyes closed with pleasure. The heavenly, long-forgotten taste, rich and almost decadent after the Auschwitz austere diet, made their taste buds nearly explode with sheer delight.

"Pure luxury," Miklós commented after they wiped the oil from the tin with the bread until the metal was bone-dry. "Reminds you of the Ritz, doesn't it? Only a silver bucket with champagne is missing."

"What impertinence to say there is no bucket!" Alma play-protested and kicked the aluminum bucket that stood next to the table with the tip of her boot. "This is the Music Block; we run a high-class establishment here. And there's drinking water in it that won't send you to the sickbay with dysentery, so that classes us with the camp elite."

"That much is true. I really must apologize, Countess." Following her act, Miklós humbly pressed his hand to his heart. "It was never my intention to insult you in such a manner. Indeed, I ought to be more grateful. The SS provided me with foreign travel and free board and I'm pining for the luxuries of the past. But that can't be helped. I fear, this is my greedy, capitalist Jewish nature that upsets all of their SS reeducation efforts," he said with a heavy dose of sarcasm.

"I thought we were dirty socialists who wish to bring about the Bolshevist revolution?" she countered.

"No, we are the all-powerful Zionist organization that secretly rules the world from Wall Street and accumulates possessions by robbing the honest German folk. The Minister of Propaganda Goebbels has just made a new speech about it. By waging this war, they're trying to save the world from our clutches."

"That's odd. In his previous speech, he said that they're waging the war against the Comintern and the Marxist Jews that had invented the entire idea of communism. He said, we Jewish scum wish to take the honest Aryan folks' money and redistribute it among the masses."

"That was before the United States entered the war."

"Quite so. My mistake."

Miklós struggled to keep his face straight but couldn't contain himself any longer and exploded. He had a wonderful laugh, rich, if somewhat cynical, and almost inappropriately careless in a place like Birkenau, but Alma was secretly glad to hear it. In the golden light cast by the lamp, his gray eyes shone like shards of broken glass, piercing and clear.

"How long have you been here?" Alma asked him.

He considered. "Too long. Sometimes it feels like my entire life, and sometimes, as if I had only arrived yesterday."

"Some inmates know the exact count of days."

"The Green Triangles, because they have a chance of getting out of here."

"You don't believe you shall ever get out of here?"

"I will, one way or another." The playful manner in which he tossed his head in the direction of the crematorium turned Alma's stomach. Aware of her painful grimace, he changed his tone—and subject—self-consciously. "I got myself a new job. I was about to tell you all about it, but you seduced me with your sardines and, after that, I couldn't quite think straight. And don't fret; I'll still be tutoring your girls. I shall be working the odd shifts, from what they told me."

Alma grinned, grateful for the distraction. "A good detail, I hope?"

"One of the most kosher ones in the entire camp," Miklós confirmed. "SS kitchen detail."

Alma stared at him, unable to conceal her amazement. "Just how did you manage to get yourself there? I thought it was reserved only for the German Green Triangles?"

"It is." Miklós nodded. "Their *Kapo* approached me himself after he saw me pass through the SS checkpoint with my *Ausweis*. A rather queer fellow, let me tell you! A German Green as well; a giant of a man with hands so big, he could crush my entire skull in them. Frightened me something terrible when he descended upon me like a hawk. He was interrogating me worse than the Gestapo for a good fifteen minutes—about my status, my camp pass and the reason why it was issued, my access to different work details, my political inclinations and whatnot. But it was after I recounted the details of my arrest that he suddenly became very amiable and announced that I would be most welcome in their detail and that he would settle all of it with the SS himself."

"What is so particular about your arrest that made him so eager all of a sudden?"

"Nothing, to be truthful with you. Though, it could have been the circumstances of it…" He pondered something before continuing, "I was arrested in 1942, in Prague."

"What were you doing in Prague?"

"Playing the piano," he replied with all seriousness.

Alma discovered that she was grinning again, in spite of herself.

"In 1939, we didn't have the Nazis in Budapest yet, but we had the Arrow Cross Party and they were no better. Same song, different words. After they adopted their so-called Second Jewish Law, I was dismissed from the Philharmonic due to my racial status. Vienna was out of the question—you already had your own Nazis parading down the Prater there. I had a diplomat friend in Prague who invited me there to work for the local radio. Prague was already a capital of their so-called German Protectorate, but the acting Reich Protector, von Neurath, happened to be good friends with my friend, whose protection I enjoyed. For a time, I was pretty much left alone. On the radio, they never credited me with the music that I played, but it was fine with me as long as I could play it at all." His steel-gray eyes now had a faraway look to them. "I was arrested right after they shot that second Reich Protector, Heydrich, in his car. Or they threw a grenade at it—I don't recall exactly what happened, but what I do remember is that the SS put the entire city on lockdown and the Gestapo were at my door the very next day."

"Why you?"

"Because I'm a Jew and we're the perfect scapegoats for that sort of thing, no?"

There was no arguing the point. It was perfect Gestapo logic. Alma caught herself chuckling, despite herself.

"At any rate, they took me down into some basement and began demanding the names of my accomplices." His eyes began to shine with mischievous mirth. "Well, seeing that they were so firm in their conviction that it was I who must have orchestrated the entire affair, I didn't wish to disappoint them and gave them all the names that sprung to my mind—Berlioz, Sieczyński, Schumann, Benatzky, and I didn't forget to add Mendelssohn for the even count. They disappeared with the list but returned soon after; one of their superiors must have been more educated musically and explained to them what the joke was." He cringed theatrically. "I need hardly add, the Gestapo don't take kindly to Jews making fools out of them before their own higher-ups. It was then that my nose made a close acquaintance with their knuckledusters. They held me there for another week or so, stopping by my cell periodically to give me a kick in the ribs. But then they caught the real perpetrators and shipped me here just for being a Jew and having a long tongue."

Without the orange glares of the crematorium dancing in the room, his face stood out, pale and noble, against the shadows. Suddenly, Alma felt overcome with a desire to reach out and touch his cheek, just to ensure that he was indeed here with her. "How brave you are," she whispered, and meant it.

He shook his head, concealing yet another grin. "I'm not brave. Those Czech patriots were brave. I was simply a harmless Jew, too pitiful to even waste the bullet on." For a moment, he lapsed into silence but then suddenly said, " 'Fortunately, fate is famous for giving second chances and even a harmless Jew can prove himself useful.' That's what the SS kitchen detail *Kapo* said. And, you know, I want to believe him."

Alma didn't like that kitchen *Kapo* one bit. There was something extremely vague and secretive about the entire manner in which he had accosted Miklós. It was Greens, Reds, and the *Sonderkommando* that were never up to any good compared to the terrified and therefore passive general population of the camp. It was their kind that swung from the gallows more often than not. Unlike regular inmates, in which all thoughts had been replaced by an obsession with life-saving crumbs of bread and sheer survival, these privileged kinds still schemed and plotted against the SS with a truly obstinate determination. Their stomachs were full; they still had strength in them and thus they could occupy themselves with other matters. To be sure, they got caught and executed, but that was an acceptable sacrifice in their eyes. In place of the dead heroes, new ones invariably closed ranks, and something told Alma, the kitchen

Kapo was among them—the elusive camp Resistance—tortured, maimed, hanged and fired at, and yet, oddly immortal. She didn't like the kitchen *Kapo* one bit, but she couldn't help but respect him.

"Let's drink to that." Alma dipped her aluminum mug into the bucket of water and offered it to him.

Miklós didn't take it; only made a sign for her to wait a moment. "I have something better," he declared with a look of a conspirator about him, dug into the inner pocket of his civilian jacket and produced a small porcelain cup with a mark on its bottom Alma instantly recognized.

"*Limoges!*" she cried in amazement. "Where did you get it?"

Setting the expensive cup aside as carefully as possible, he held up his index finger once again. Under Alma's incredulous gaze, Miklós extracted a saucer to complete the set. "I'll trade you this set for your mug."

"No, I can't possibly accept it . . . It must have cost you a fortune in rations . . ." Alma tried to protest, but Miklós would have none of it.

"You will oblige me, truly. You see, I'm allergic to porcelain."

Alma looked at him and couldn't help but wonder how she survived this entire time without his jests.

"Where did you get it?" she repeated, turning the cup this way and that in her hands.

"That's not important." He gently took the cup in his hand and scooped water into it. "Here, Countess. Now, you have a suitable set to take your morning coffee. *Prost.*"

"*Prost,* Count. Here's to second chances."

"Here's to leaving this place on our own two feet."

For some time after that, the crematoriums stood suspiciously still. From the camp office, Zippy brought the rumor about the new *Kommandant* obstructing the extermination orders from Berlin.

Then, one morning, Alma woke up to the familiar smell and saw the orange glare reflecting in the glass of her window.

Kommandant Liebehenschel walked in that very evening, sat in the very back, as was his habit, with his doe eyes downcast and requested a funeral march to be played.

Miklós played it for him, a gut-churning piece that made one want to howl with despair. Liebehenschel sat for a while after it was over, rose to his feet a bit unsteadily, thanked him in a soft voice and walked out, discreetly wiping his face with his sleeve.

Things changed in the camp, and they didn't. Time itself stood still.

Chapter 19

"Typhus."

Alma stared at Dr. Mengele as though unable to comprehend the meaning of his words.

"Yes. A regular case. Nothing to be done," he repeated and motioned Violette out of her bunk. "All of you shall stay in the Sauna for a time, during which your barrack will be disinfected."

Before he could take another step, Alma moved swiftly to stand between him and her youngest charge—Violette-from-Paris, favorite composer Vivaldi. "Where are you taking her?"

He looked at her mockingly. "Where do you think?"

"I won't allow it!" The words were out of her mouth before Alma realized what she was doing. Her hands balled into fists, she stood before the most feared man in the camp. Her entire body was trembling, yet she refused to take a single step back. An image of the twin boy in Dr. Ránki's quarters appeared before Alma's eyes; she must have seemed just as harmless and thoroughly amusing to Dr. Mengele with her pitiful defensive stance. And yet, the desire to protect had surged up in her, overwhelming even the instinct of self-preservation. "She's an essential member of my orchestra and I won't allow it!"

Dr. Mengele regarded her, slightly annoyed but impressed nevertheless. "I'm taking her to the sickbay," he finally said slowly. "Not the gas chamber. And now, off to the Sauna you go. I want to see if there are more cases among you before I take her to the Revier."

Alma stared at him with great mistrust. "She's an excellent violinist. You heard her play. It won't be easy for me to replace her."

"In that case, I advise you to step away, so I can take her to the sickbay as soon as possible so she can get the medical attention she needs."

A phenol into the heart? Alma wouldn't budge from her spot.

"Dr. Švalbová shall be treating her. Well?" He flicked his riding crop against his boot impatiently. "Out with all of you, now! Do you wish to catch it too?"

With great reluctance, Alma signed for the girls to follow her outside.

In the usual formation, five abreast, they marched to the Sauna in tense silence. But it appeared their ordeal was far from over. As soon as they stepped through the doors of the anteroom with rows of hooks lining its walls, Dr. Mengele immediately motioned the women toward the benches under those very hooks.

"All of your clothes—off, now."

An anxious murmur passed through their ranks. The veterans of the camp, they knew they were inside the safety of a real Sauna and not a gas chamber; yet, the fear of something quite different was written plainly on their faces. A *clothes-off* order, and particularly coming from one whom they rightfully called the Angel of Death, meant only one thing—a selection.

As though propelled by some communal, animalistic instinct, all heads turned to Alma at once—imploring, begging for protection. She remained perfectly calm, not just for the girls' sake—fear was just as contagious here as any other deathly illness—but because she was aware that Dr. Mengele was watching her closely, grinning, with his eyes narrowed. They betrayed sheer curiosity, a mental bet with himself as to what she was about to do. He was fond of these psychological games; Alma had learned it far too well by now.

What she had also learned was that his reactions were impossible to predict. Sometimes, he listened to the inmate doctors' pleas and permitted them to treat almost hopeless cases; sometimes, he remained unmoved even when the inmate doctors promised him that their patients would be able to return to work a few days later and sent the entire ward to gas instead.

"Herr Doktor, is it really necessary?"

Dr. Mengele looked almost bored. "Lice are known to transmit typhus," he began explaining in a tone of a lecturer. "If one of you is sick with it, there's a big chance lice could get into the seams of all of your clothes. They ought to be disinfected. Just like your entire block. Just like your musical instruments. Just like you are. But before that, I need to see if any of you are also sick with it. My experience has shown that inmates can be very sly when it comes to concealing such things. That's the reason for outbreaks all over the camp, that very slyness of yours."

Slyness? There wouldn't be any slyness if certain medical SS personnel didn't send all the infected cases to the gas, Alma wanted to say.

"You are correct, as always, Herr Doktor." Without another word, she began unbuttoning her cardigan, annoyed with her fingers that were trembling slightly—from indignation, not fear.

The girls followed her example, somewhat reassured by her composure. It took Alma great effort to appear perfectly unmoved in front of them when she was seething inside.

In the last attempt to preserve at least some of their dignity, not really hoping for a positive answer, Alma inquired if the girls could leave their undergarments on.

"Everything needs to be disinfected," Dr. Mengele countered without emotion.

"I understand that, Herr Doktor. We will take everything off *after*."

"After what?" It was impossible to tell whether he was serious or playing one of his mental games again.

After you leave, Alma didn't say anything, but her expressive gaze did. "You will still be able to see the typhus spots on their chests and stomachs even if they have their underwear on," she said in the pause that followed.

"I'm a medical doctor. I'm not interested in your breasts or private parts."

"Even more reason to keep them covered."

Dr. Mengele burst into chuckles. "When did you make a sport out of arguing with me, Frau Alma?"

When she didn't reply, he simply shook his head in resignation and began walking along the line of girls, inspecting the skin on their chests and only asking them to pull the waistbands of their undergarments down whenever he saw a suspicious rash.

Three more girls, including Flora, the orchestra's only pianist, were separated from the rest in this manner. They stood, huddling next to each other and staring at Alma instead of the SS man, with the mortified, unblinking eyes of wild rabbits.

"Are they also going to the sickbay?" Alma didn't conceal her alarm.

"Yes, yes, to the sickbay."

She didn't trust a word that came out of his mouth.

"Will I be able to visit them?" Alma followed their small procession to the door.

"Absolutely out of the question."

"What about our schedule? We ought to play in the sickbay every Tuesday and Thursday."

"Not during the outbreak."

"We can play outside!" She stopped short of catching his sleeve. "We can set our instruments outside and play for them. Music therapy is important for recovery."

"I heard low temperatures are harmful for your instruments. Wasn't that the reason for the stove in your quarters?" He arched an amused brow at her.

Alma only looked at him with faint reproach.

Whatever prompted him to do it, he waved his gloves at her in a dismissive gesture before heading out. "Have it your way, if it's so important to you. Tuesday and Thursday, but only outside the block and for thirty minutes only. If I catch one of you inside, there won't be any more talking."

"You won't, Herr Doktor," Alma promised to his retreating back. "Thank you."

Alma watched him stroll in his warm gray overcoat in front of three of her girls, who had to half-trot after him, barefoot and almost naked against the howling wind and gusts of snow, and felt tears gathering in her throat from an incomprehensible mixture of gratitude and savage, violent hatred for him that nearly suffocated her with its power. The camp did strange things to one's psyche. After constant abuse inflicted upon them by the SS, such a miserable gesture as permitting the inmates to remain partially clothed, somewhat fed, not quite killed and only slightly beaten, was seen as something impressive. Everything in them had been reduced to dog-like instincts and they gladly licked the hand that occasionally threw them one metaphorical bone or another and feared the boot that could kick them under the ribs at the same time...

Collecting herself once again, Alma turned to her orchestra, reduced by a few irreplaceable members, and smiled encouragingly at them. Two female inmates with cans of strongly smelling disinfectant were already waiting for them near the Sauna entrance itself.

"Well, ladies, you know the drill," Alma spoke to her frightened charges in her brightest voice. "Keep your eyes shut at all times and rub the stuff into your hair until your scalp feels as though it's on fire. I'm not losing more of you to the sickbay, so better suffer through it now than later. Undress and off you go inside. Make it snappy—no need for you to catch cold either."

Only Sofia lingered behind. She waited for the girls to be admitted inside before she approached Alma and whispered into her ear, "Do you truly believe he took them into the sickbay?"

"I don't know," Alma admitted honestly. "But the first thing I'm going to do as soon as we get our clothes back is find out."

*

Her inflamed eyes still stinging from the disinfectant, Alma crept toward the sickbay, watching for the familiar gray overcoat closely. Once inside, she breathed with relief, for she knew that Dr. Mengele wouldn't go into the block that had been turned into an infectious ward if he could help it. The Angel of Death didn't mind dissecting them when they were already dead, but living patients he mostly left to the inmate doctors' care.

Alma knew he had been transferred to Auschwitz after getting injured on the Eastern front and deemed unfit for further frontline service. He wore quite a few awards for bravery, two highly coveted Iron Crosses among them. He must have treated actual patients, in the most dangerous conditions, at some point, risking his own life for their sake. So, when did he turn from a brave frontline medic into a sadist and a murderer with complete disregard for his victims'—precisely victims, they certainly weren't his patients—fate? And how could he possibly come to her block after sending a fresh batch of human beings into the gas and listen to her violin with the look of tender melancholy on his face? Alma failed to comprehend many things in this place, but him she failed to understand most of all.

As she moved further along the corridor, Alma had to cover her mouth and nose with her headscarf. The sickbay was overrun by the recent influx of typhus patients. As it often was in the camp during outbreaks, when there weren't enough beds, half of them lay right on the dirty, cold floor. As carefully as possible, Alma stepped over the bodies, wondering how many of them were already dead. Not that the living patients looked any better. Delirious with fever and plagued with severe stomach pains, they moaned and pleaded with no one in particular in different languages in that hellish Babylon, where God himself abandoned them for reasons no one could quite comprehend.

Rats crawled freely over the bony frames covered by threadbare, soiled clothes. Some women kicked them off indifferently; some didn't budge even when a particularly insolent rodent would start gnawing on their flesh.

That's how the nurses must have recognized the corpses.

"This one also," one of them called to two inmates under her charge, kicking the rat off the woman's chest.

Flattening herself against the wall as much as the space between the sleeping women allowed, Alma let them pass with their human cargo. Outside, over the loudspeakers, some cheerful march was playing and the corpse's arm, dangling in the air, moved in perfect synchrony with it as though the dead woman conducted the march herself. Alma felt a shudder run through her at the grotesque image.

In the corner, a woman was wailing; her bunkmate had just torn a husk of dry bread out of her fingers.

"I heard what the doctor was saying about you. You won't recover!" the bunkmate was saying, stuffing the bread into her mouth. "You're a useless eater. I ought to eat. I shall come out of here and serve the Reich! The SS need me! Quit your sniveling. I'm entitled to your portion because I'm stronger. The strongest survive; it's perfect applied Nietzsche. You're too dumb to comprehend the greatness of his ideas..."

Alma stared at her in horror and disgust. *What have they done to us?* she thought, contemplating the yellow star sewn onto the bunkmate's chest. The Jew, wearing a striped robe in which countless Jews must have died before her and quoting Nietzsche to her former friend, from whom she had just stolen her last piece of bread. Reduced to animals and taught to act like ones...

"Typhus doesn't inspire charity."

It took Alma some time to turn to the voice. An inmate doctor stood before her with a clipboard pressed against her chest. She had a harassed look about her, but her face was noble and calm.

"When they recover, they get tormented with the worst hunger any of them have ever experienced, even by the camp standards," the doctor went on to explain. "It literally drives them wild. One time, they combined forces and attacked the inmates who were on soup distribution duty that evening. Nothing came out of it, of course. They simply spilled the entire cauldron on the floor and ended up leaving the whole block hungry. We reported it. They got gassed. Since then, it's just this, minor-scale stealing among themselves. Dog eat dog. A sad state of affairs." She was looking at the woman who was finishing off the bread. "She used to be a professor of literature in Prague." She turned to Alma, unmoved, as though such scenes were nothing new and didn't impress her any longer. "What can I help you with?"

"I'm looking for Dr. Švalbová."

"You're speaking to her."

"Alma Rosé, the Music Block." At once, Alma extended her hand.

Dr. Švalbová looked at it but didn't take it. "I'd rather not. Don't take offense—for your protection, not mine. You don't want to know what I'm touching all day and we can only use soap in the morning and in the evening. Rationing."

"Yes. Of course. Forgive me please." Alma hid her hand, suddenly embarrassed with her clean hands and the good coat that still smelled reassuringly of disinfectant. They were the elite block because the SS frequented it; the medical block the same SS didn't deem as essential as they didn't get any profit from it, only disease. "Dr. Mengele promised to bring my girls here—"

"He did. Made me free a separate room for them we usually reserve for the *Kapos*." She didn't sound pleased. "In the absence of any *Kapos*, I was using it for my other patients, but they had to be moved here, into the corridor, because we don't have enough beds for them inside the ward. Your girls are very comfortable though. There are only four of them, each in her own bed."

"I didn't ask him to do it," Alma muttered in self-defense, even though, technically speaking, she had nothing to be guilty of. It was the administration's fault that the sickbay was in such a pitiful state. Was it wrong of her to worry about her girls' wellbeing? Still, she softened her voice even more as she addressed the doctor, "I came to ask if you need anything for them. Medicine, food, blankets—"

"All of my patients need all of those things," Dr. Švalbová interrupted her once again. "As for your girls, they already have their blankets, a stove in their ward, and double rations. Now, if you'll excuse me."

She brushed Alma's shoulder as she passed her by. Alma took no offense. It wasn't the first time the inmates expressed their disdain at the fact that hers was a privileged detail and the "Music Block tarts strutted around in their silk stockings with curled hair under their lavender kerchiefs and played their songs for the SS's entertainment," when others had to suffer through their days with only a crumb of sawdust bread and a smear of margarine on their palm to look forward to. The camp was full of such sentiments. It was nothing new. Alma had learned to ignore it.

She should have returned to the Sauna and lounged about with her girls, who, after having recovered from their recent ordeal, were openly enjoying their unexpected day off. Instead, Alma made her way to the pathologist's quarters and stood outside for quite some time, too terrified to knock out of fear of discovering Dr. Mengele inside. Finally, she braced herself for the worst and rapped on the door.

Dr. Ránki opened it and pulled her inside at once, slamming the door behind him.

"Is he here?" Alma asked by way of greeting.

"Of course not. Would I invite you in if he were?"

"I need medicaments." Alma decided to skip small talk.

"I figured that much. Typhus?"

"Do you have any medication for it?"

"Nothing that wouldn't go unnoticed. Though, I suppose, I can give you something that he wouldn't think to suspect." Dr. Ránki went to open the glass cupboard and began rummaging through it. Soon, small vials and bigger medicine bottles of all shapes and colors began making their way into Alma's pockets. "This should reduce fever. This isn't what they typically administer to typhus patients, but it will help with stomach pains... I don't think he'll notice if we sneak this one out as well... And this little fellow; this ought to be given as an injection to a particularly difficult case. I'll write it off as broken. I can give you some morphine; to trade for an extra ration or a different medicine, if not to use it directly on the patient. Do you have a doctor you can trust?"

"Dr. Švalbová," Alma replied without hesitation. She'd only met the inmate physician once, but she had already seen that Dr. Švalbová put the well-being of her patients—all of them, without preference—above anything else.

She wasn't surprised when Dr. Ránki smiled in acknowledgment. "Ah, Dr. Mancy, as her patients call her. Manca Švalbová; she's a very good doctor. Her only concern is her patients. It's rare in a place like this. Most lose their humanity altogether..."

Weighed down with her contraband, Alma stole along the barracks until she reached the safety of the *Kanada*. Kitty was in her usual station, sorting through the mountains of clothes with a look of disgust about her. The new transport must have arrived from the ghetto.

"Look at this!" With two fingers, Kitty lifted and held a threadbare male shirt with wide yellow circles staining its armpits as one would a dead rat. "If we send this to Germany, they shall gas us on principle only and shall be right! Wherever are they sending them from? Just a few months ago, we were getting such coats—ermine collars, black fox, silk lining—all business as it should be. Rice facial powder, French lipstick in golden tubes—I still have some left—hand creams infused with Egyptian oils. And now? They don't even have suitcases anymore. They bring all this garbage here in pillowcases!"

Alma shifted from one foot to the other impatiently. "I need soap. Could you spare a few bars?"

Kitty only snorted in disdain and shook the shirt in the air. "I am telling her we're getting all sorts of garbage lately that all but crawls with vermin and she wants soap..."

Alma moved closer to the girl. "I have morphine."

As though by magic, Kitty's expression changed. Morphine was the equivalent of liquid gold in camp terms. Quite a few SS men were addicted to it and would hold the inmate, who could get their hands on it, in the highest esteem.

"Wait here."

Kitty disappeared into the depths of the warehouse and soon returned with two sturdy brown bars in her hands.

"Five for a vial or no deal." Alma wasn't stupid either.

"That's midday robbery!" Kitty protested.

"Take it or leave it."

"Are you a violinist or a stock-market speculator?"

"I can be both when the occasion calls for it," Alma replied, unmoved.

"You're extorting a fellow Jew!"

Alma regarded her with great skepticism. "The right SS man will give you his kidney for that vial and you know it. That's hardly extortion."

"Kidney is not something I can use," Kitty grumbled but finally gave in and brought Alma three more pieces.

When Dr. Švalbová saw the soap bars, two of them French lavender, lined up neatly on her desk, she appeared to lose all faculty of speech for a few moments.

"I also brought you rubbing alcohol, bandages, iodine and medicine, but the medicine must go to my girls first," Alma said.

"Whatever is left, feel free to divide between the others as you deem fit. I'll try to bring you more supplies when I can."

Without saying a word, Dr. Švalbová rose from her chair, took one of the soap bars to the rusty sink attached to the wall and began lathering her hands with it. After a thorough wash, she carefully deposited the soap next to the miserable sliver of the previous bar and walked up to Alma. "Thank you, Frau Rosé," she said in a tone very different from before, and offered Alma her hand. "Dr. Manca Švalbová. You can call me Dr. Mancy."

Alma took the doctor's palm into hers and gave it a very firm shake, her warm smile mirroring Dr. Mancy's.

Chapter 20

Each day, instead of only Tuesdays and Thursdays, Alma brought her orchestra to the front lawn of the sickbay. Each day, against the wet snow or howling wind, they played the sick girls' favorite pieces. Each day, Miklós snuck in whatever goods Birkenau men's orchestra could "organize" for their female counterparts. The goods ranged from raw potatoes brazenly appropriated from the SS kitchen to various pills and powders, just as insolently pinched from the SS medical block. Each day, Dr. Mancy delivered short notes to Alma written by her sick charges—*we are doing quite well here and recovering slowly but steadily; thank you for all the food and medicine; how delightful today's Brahms was!* Each day, Alma left the sickbay with a painful knot inside her chest, unsure if she would find the entire block empty the very next day. Each night, she sat, plagued by insomnia, and stared at the orange glow of the chimneys through her window, terribly afraid to close her eyes, as if her doing so would somehow jinx the girls' fate and send them all to that flaming inferno.

Sofia and Zippy had long given up on Alma's nocturnal ways and assurances that she didn't need more than four hours of sleep; only Miklós regarded the dark half-moons under her eyes with disapproval and soon acquired a habit of smuggling all sorts of food items into her room without her noticing it—"to lift her spirits." Two days ago, it was an apple. Before that, a bar of Swiss chocolate. Bread days were rare and occurred only out of pure desperation—Miklós preferred more refined items to the pitiful official camp rations.

Whenever Alma discovered the items before the pianist was gone, he would only shrug her reproaches off with the nonchalance of royalty about him and positively refused to take his gifts back or even split them. Hands thrust in pockets, he stood before her like a starved Rockefeller's son on whom his Music Block jacket was all but hanging and declared that he had more where that came from and wasn't hungry at all. He often played his piano during dinners in the SS canteen, he had explained. They fed him well enough.

Alma doubted that such was the case; his cheekbones stood out much too sharply in his face and the skin had a grayish undertone to it, making his resemblance to a gothic statue of some noble, medieval knight complete.

"You could exchange that bar of chocolate for a whole loaf of bread," she argued.

"Local bread is a disgrace and wouldn't make me full at any rate," he countered, unimpressed.

"And imagining me, drinking my morning coffee from a Limoges cup with Swiss chocolate you risked your life for would?" Alma arched a skeptical brow.

"Yes. That image and my piano are two things that keep me alive these days," he declared in a grave tone he ordinarily reserved for his jests, but now, Alma saw that his eyes were perfectly serious, and it made her heart miss a beat.

"But I have nothing to give you in exchange for your generosity."

"You're offering me your company and your music. That's more than enough."

"Still, I would like you to keep at least something for yourself."

"I'm giving it all because giving is what makes a human human. As long as I can give something, I feel I haven't spent that day for nothing. Don't you feel the same when you give whatever you can to your girls?"

She did. But she also guessed that he stole all of those "presents" when the SS weren't looking and pleaded with him to stop it for his own safety's sake. However, he refused to listen to reason and brought her an orange, as though in defiance, the very next day.

"I didn't steal it this time, don't fret," Miklós explained, laughing, before Alma could scold him for it. Only the SS had access to fresh fruit; being discovered with something of that sort on one's person meant an automatic death sentence, a bullet in the back of one's head without any questions asked. "Herr Kommandant's lady friend gave it to me."

Alma noted the respectful form of address, *Herr Kommandant*. Former Kommandant Höss used to be referred to mockingly as the Old Man, both by the inmates and the SS. It appeared that Kommandant Liebehenschel enjoyed a better reputation among the camp population.

"One ought to feel for him, the poor fellow," Miklós continued. "He's in love with her something mad, and his superiors won't allow him to marry her."

"Why not?"

"Rumor has it, she's politically unreliable. Much too friendly with the Jews," Miklós repeated the same rumor Zippy had mentioned not that long ago. "That's why they have shipped them both here from some high office in Berlin—for re-education. Little do their superiors know, they appear to be very happy here. He was in the kitchen with the inspection today, talking to us like a normal human being about our concerns. She accompanied him. At first, I thought she was his secretary or some such, but then I saw the way he was looking at her. Later, the head waiter explained it all to me."

He snorted as though not fully believing it.

"Imagine that? *Our concerns*," he repeated in amazement and shook his head. "Herr Kommandant wrote everything down in his little black notebook and promised to do what he could to make things easier for us. Tried to explain that every time a gassing occurs, it's due to the direct orders from Berlin, not on his own initiative. I could swear to you, he appeared almost upset about the whole rotten business, and particularly when he was talking about women and children...And his lady friend, what a nice woman! I am the only Jew on the waiting staff, the rest are German Green and Red Triangles. What do you know? She takes me aside and asks me—very discreetly, so my fellow waiting *Kommando* mates wouldn't hear—if they're treating me all right. I said yes, they treat me just fine and that they're all first-rate fellows. She smiled, took this orange out of the basket, enclosed it into my palm and patted my hand with hers."

He regarded his hand in disbelief. Alma was also looking at it, a smile growing on her face. She wished she was there to see it with her own eyes, such an unexpected display of humanity in a place where that very humanity was slaughtered by the hundreds of thousands.

"How did the head waiter come by such information?"

"You won't believe how much the SS spill when they get good and drunk." Miklós chuckled. "They would easily put any washer-woman to shame with their aptitude for gossip. Naturally, the waiting staff hears it all and uses it to their advantage."

"What advantage?"

"The regular camp affairs." Miklós turned suddenly very vague, as though he'd let on more than he had initially intended, and quickly changed the subject. "Do you want me to peel it for you?"

"Yes. And share it with me, please." Alma held out the orange to him, ignoring his sudden secretiveness out of politeness only. "Just today. Oblige me."

He hesitated, but something in her eyes moved him. "Very well, Countess. But only today and only because it was bestowed upon me by some miracle."

Alma's face had grown very still when he produced a pocketknife from his boot to cut the orange. Only the camp resistance was rumored to have access to cold weapons. The SS hanged two of its members not that long ago for discovering precisely such unauthorized items on them. Only two, for those two withstood all of the camp Gestapo's tortures but betrayed nothing else to Grabner's grisly department; Alma recalled all the chilling details of the story.

"Don't tell me Herr Kommandant's lady friend gave you the knife as well."

"No, of course she didn't." He purposely avoided her eyes; she could tell.

"Miklós?"

"Yes?"

"Did you get mixed up with the wrong people?"

Miklós looked at her strangely and gave her a smile that was both secret and proud. "No. This time, I got mixed up with all the right people. This time, I shall be brave too."

He gazed into her eyes for a long moment and then suddenly drew her to himself and kissed her, deeply and without restraint, seemingly robbing her of the very ability to breathe. Alma didn't mind the suffocating feeling of harsh, overpowering desire that flooded her body. Instead of pushing him away—it was madness to kiss in such a manner even behind the closed door of Alma's private room; Mandl had a habit of strolling inside without knocking and inmates landed in the *Strafblock*, the penal confinement barrack, for much less—Alma wrapped her arms around his neck and held him fast; pressed herself against him, feeling his heart beat wildly against her, and allowed herself to forget everything for a few precious moments. It had all ceased to exist—Mandl, danger, the camp and the entire world outside; now, there were only his long fingers tangled in her hair and his hot breath against her open lips and, for Alma, it was all that mattered.

The sun hung low and bleak over the crematorium, but the inmates had never seen it brighter. It wasn't obscured by the permanent curtain of thick black smoke and the air itself was now clear and pure. They sniffed at it greedily during the roll calls, inhaled the long-forgotten scents of earth and the breeze and melting snow. Even their own filthy clothes smelled of sweat and grime, rather than the sickly-sweet of burnt flesh, and that was a vast improvement.

The new administration demanded to shorten the time of the roll calls and two extra hours of sleep lifted their spirits immensely. They shouted their "*Jawohl*" when their numbers were called and exchanged quick, happy looks of disbelief at the fact that for the first time in years their hands were empty. On the new *Kommandant*'s explicit orders, they were permitted to keep their uniform caps on to keep their heads somewhat protected from the elements, instead of holding them in their trembling limbs as a sign of respect for the SS conducting the roll call as it used to be during Höss' ruthless rule.

In the distance, a water reservoir was being constructed. Officially, for the Birkenau fire brigade. Unofficially, for the inmates to swim in during summer for overachieving their quota. "Herr Kommandant has promised, personally," they whispered to one another and followed the tall figure in his gray overcoat with eyes full of genuine gratitude.

Kommandant Liebehenschel himself appeared to be in excellent spirits. The crematoriums had stood inactive for a week now. Alma wondered what it cost him to wage those battles with Berlin. She also wondered how long such a standoff would last.

Alma had just returned from the sickbay with her orchestra, relieved with the progress her four sick girls were making, when Maria Mandl burst into the block in utter excitement. Speaking rapidly and snapping her fingers at the composer—"what the devil was his name, but the melody goes like this"—she announced that she had just heard the most wonderful piano four-hands piece on the radio and wished for it to be included in the Christmas music program.

Miklós recognized the melody the women's camp leader was humming—Schubert, *Fantasia in F minor*—and, before Alma could open her mouth to protest, he was already assuring Mandl that *it would be their pleasure, Lagerführerin, but in view of the piece being rather difficult, it would require long hours of rehearsals...*

Mandl agreed to everything and even freed Alma of some of her *Kapo*'s duties.

As soon as the women's camp's leader was out of the door, Alma swiftly turned to Miklós. "Whatever have you just signed me up for? I'm a violinist; piano is not quite my sphere of expertise, to say the least, and he wants me to play a Schubert duet!"

Unbothered, Miklós airily waved her protest aside. "There's nothing really to it. I'll teach you in two days."

"Two days?" Alma stared at him. "You *are* mad."

"Countess, we are all mad here," he quoted Lewis Carroll with a playfully wry smile. "And now, enough with the empty jawing and at it. You heard your camp leader. She wants Schubert and Schubert she'll have. We ought to prove to our Aryan masters that we aren't useless eaters."

Sofia took the girls to the Sauna for their daily shower. Alma was much too preoccupied with the blasted Schubert Miklós had imposed on her to waste her time on scrubbing when it could be spent on rehearsing. Her friend regarded her in stunned disbelief—Alma was infamous for her obsession with cleanness and hygiene—but accepted Alma's *Kapo* armband without another word.

"I'll wash up later, from the faucet in the latrine," Alma explained, her tone almost apologetic. "I really must rehearse every waking hour I have. My piano skills are much too rusty for someone of Schubert's level."

She needn't worry; Miklós turned out to be an excellent tutor. With infinite patience, he guided her through the sheet music he wrote from memory. Alma herself wrote quite a few pieces from her own memory for the orchestra and could never comprehend Zippy's amazement whenever the girl watched her do it with her mouth agape. But, for some reason, she saw Miklós produce the entire piece in under twenty minutes and was suddenly overcome with profound admiration for him.

"No, not like that." Miklós stopped her gently now as they practiced. "You're much too hard on that poor piano. She doesn't like it and it makes her scream and whine."

"She?" Alma asked, amused.

"Naturally, she." Miklós looked at her as if it was something obvious. "All musical instruments are either male or female. Piano, just like your violin, is definitely a female. It needs to be caressed." With utmost gentleness, he began brushing the keys with his fingers. "Hear the difference? Now, she hums softly. Here, let me show you. Someone taught you a beautiful technique, but your fingering is stiff and wooden. The piano doesn't like stiff hands. You ought to relax your wrists more." Positioning himself behind her back, Miklós placed his hands under Alma's palms. "Rest your hands, completely relaxed, on top of mine and feel how my muscles move when I play this passage. You barely need any effort at all. Feel it?"

Alma felt that it was suddenly very hot in the room and that she was acutely aware of her own breathing.

"Close your eyes. Your muscle perception works better when your eyes are closed."

Alma did as she was instructed. Now, it was just the peaceful, serene darkness all around her, a haunting, beautiful melody penetrating her very skin, and someone's arms around her.

"You're still much too stiff. Relax your shoulders. Lean against me. Stop processing everything with that restless mind of yours and start *feeling* the music, at least for five minutes." His voice was low and oddly hypnotizing. "You are no longer here. This place doesn't exist. We are in Vienna, on the stage where you used to play chamber music with your father, but now it's just us and the piano and we're preparing for a concert. You shall wear a beautiful gown and I, an elegant black tailcoat with a bow tie starched to such an extent, it'll be stabbing my neck like a knife the entire time. You will curse your new unbroken shoes but wear them all the same because appearances are everything and we're two old musical veterans and can withstand anything in the name of art."

Alma grinned and pressed her back against him. It would have been inappropriate in any other setting, but here, it suddenly felt the most natural thing to do. He didn't move away, but, on the contrary, pressed his cheek against hers as he rested his chin on her shoulder.

"The entire Philharmonic was sold out in mere hours," he continued. "The posters for our performance are plastered all over the city. The Rothschilds will be sitting in their box and will drown you in roses, as is their habit, when you rise to bow to your audience as gracefully as only you can. In front of the stage, the press will be going wild with delight. All eyes, all cameras, are on you while you stand, a veritable goddess, basking in the light of their flashes and floodlights."

"I don't want to stand there alone." She'd been alone as long as she could remember. Even with Váša sharing a stage with her, she was always aware of that gnawing solitude all around her. Even with Heinrich, running from the Nazi-overrun Austria, she was alone—alone in her grief, alone in her misery, even as he sat next to her in their train compartment and swore to her that he would share whatever hardships would stand in their way. Just like her first husband, he didn't last long. It only took a few months in a foreign city with Alma supporting them both with her music for him to flee back to his native Austria, where the family business was prosperous and where his male dignity was once again restored.

"You're not alone. I'm right behind you, waiting to take your hand as soon as you're ready."

"Take it now."

Miklós took her hand in his and brought it to his lips. "You shall never be alone again."

"You all say that."

"I'm not *all*. I will never abandon you. Not of my own free will, at any rate." He was kissing each of her fingers. "They will have to send me to the gas to separate me from you."

Instantly terrified, Alma pulled away at once. "Why would you say such frightful things? Of all things…"

He was already apologizing and holding her face in his hands. He kissed her pale cheeks, her wet dark eyelashes, her lips, her neck, her hair and her hands.

She had sworn to herself never again to be involved with a man, not seriously, at any rate. She had been so determined to keep her heart closed and cold, but Miklós kissed her and suddenly, breathlessly, she had no choice.

"It won't last forever, Almschi," he whispered to her. "We shall come out of here one day. We shall come out of here together and I will be holding your hand when we walk out of those gates. And then we shall tour all over Europe and every evening I shall stand by your side and hold your hand. Do you believe me?"

She did. In spite of herself, in the middle of this death factory, she did.

Outside the block, Sofia's voice echoed around the compound as she counted her charges before admitting them inside. With great reluctance, Miklós dropped his hands from Alma's face and took his seat next to her, but this time closer than before. She also shifted nearer him, until she felt the warmth of his thigh against hers.

"So, the piano and the violin are female instruments," she said, purposely changing the subject. Possible freedom was still much too painful to dream of, let alone the idea of sharing it with this man, without whom it would lose its very purpose. "Which ones are male?"

"Why, the contrabass, of course. He's the old German burgo-master with a Kaiser mustache who grumbles, with his bass voice, about good old times when his country wasn't overrun by liberals and Jews."

A shadow of a smile stole over Alma's face. "And what else?"

"The drum, naturally. The drum is the Reichsmarschall Göring of the musical instruments. He's full of himself, despite being entirely empty inside. He makes a lot of loud noise but no music whatsoever. One can only march to it but never dance—that's why it's the Nazis' favorite instrument."

Alma became livelier. Her black eyes were now sparkling with long-forgotten joy. "What else?"

Miklós looked at her—no, not just looked, caressed her with his gray, brilliant eyes. "The trumpet. The trumpet is not just some man, it's Herr Minister of Propaganda Goebbels himself. Just like the drum, it can't create any beautiful music one can enjoy, but it shrills and shrills instead until it wakes the basest instincts in people that are listening to him. Its marching music is easy to recognize and follow. It doesn't require any semblance of intellect or sophistication. All one can do when one hears it is march to its tune."

Alma had to laugh. The characterization was much too accurate. "All right, Herr Steinberg. Enough with that Nazi rot. Let's switch to something more pleasant. We have already established the fact that the piano is your favorite mistress. Now what do you have to say about my violin?"

"Your violin? Your violin is just like you. All hard, rare wood outside; strings pulled to their utmost—they've withstood far too much but haven't snapped yet by some miracle; and the most beautiful melody comes out of it, if one only knows how to stroke it right with their bow."

At that moment, the girls burst inside with their cheerful banter and Alma didn't get a chance to tell him that, against all the odds, he certainly knew how.

Chapter 21

The velvet darkness had descended upon the camp. Somewhere inside the barrack, next to the furthest wall by which the stove stood, pot-bellied and blissfully hot, the girls were chattering in several languages at the same time as they cooked their rations. A tantalizing aroma of fried potatoes with a faint tinge of blood sausage—Red Cross supplies, no doubt—wafted through the air.

Alone in her room, Alma was gazing out of the window and into the soft, cloudy night. It was almost inconceivable to imagine that somewhere past the crematorium, past the field with its mass graves behind it, past all those layers of barbed wire, lay freedom. Somewhere within walking distance from here, some Polish woman was roasting potatoes for dinner, smiling at the voices of her children playing outside in the snow. Somewhere, not too far away, a farmer was locking up his animals for the night inside the barn that was warm and snug and smelled of hay and wool. Somewhere, in a nearby town, a man was kissing a woman right in the street, and there were no curfews or yellow stars for them, and no SS to worry about. In a surge of torturous, impotent bitterness, Alma fell into her bed and buried her face in the pillow at the injustice of it all.

In Auschwitz, she loathed the evenings the worst. The days were much too busy to inspire any opportunity to think. But then the evening roll call would come and, after that, the agonizing few hours of nothingness, of brooding thoughts that drove her to near madness, the mounting sense of despair and hopelessness and no escape from it all.

The door creaked softly.

"Thank you, but I'm not hungry," Alma spoke into the pillow without lifting her head.

They meant well, of course, her little sparrows; they never failed to offer her a share of whatever meager provisions they were roasting on that stove, but she hardly ever accepted their generosity. "You eat; your bodies are still growing," such was Alma's default explanation. The truth was, most of the time, she was so sick to her stomach with this dog-like existence, her own body revolted against it, choosing to starve itself to death rather than continue to live like a slave to the Nazis.

She felt the mattress springs sag as someone lowered themselves next to her and then, a palm in between her shoulder blades. It traveled along her spine to the small of her back and then up again, until it rested on her neck, gently massaging the muscles strained with tension.

She didn't have to see his face; she'd recognize the touch of those hands out of a million. He was caressing her, and the cold knot inside was uncoiling, the shadows were fading away; the world once again had its colors.

"Countess."

"Mm?"

"Are you asleep?"

"Yes. I'm having the most wonderful dream and if you wake me up, I shall never speak to you again."

Alma felt his breath on her skin as he chuckled softly, covering her neck with featherlike kisses.

"You don't have to wake up. You only have to take my hand and follow me."

This time, Alma turned to look at him.

"What is that?" Amused, she nodded at some sort of a rag tied around his neck in imitation of a fashionable bow tie.

Miklós fixed it with theatrical seriousness. "Countess, it's a gentleman's duty to look his best when he invites a lady out."

Sitting up, Alma broke into a grin. "Just where are you planning to take me?"

"The fanciest place around, of course," Miklós replied, offering her his hand.

Alma took it and marveled at his uncanny ability to stir her back to life when she was seriously considering going to the wire just minutes ago.

They walked through the familiar passages, but all of a sudden, the maze of electrified wire had ceased to exist, along with the guard towers and machine guns and the SS dogs and the SS brutes themselves. Their steps were light because their hands were touching and that was all that mattered, for a few minutes at least.

In front of one of the barracks, Miklós stopped and bowed to Alma with mock-gallantry.

"Countess, allow me to welcome you into my humble home, the Family Camp."

He knocked on the door in a peculiar manner and, at once, it swung open, revealing a young boy with shining eyes and a head full of unruly, dark locks.

"Herr Steinberg!"

"We aren't late, I hope?" Miklós asked.

"Not at all. They shall begin in five minutes. Herr Hirsh has saved you seats in the front row."

"Make sure to mind your post."

"Always, Herr Steinberg!" The boy clicked his heels and play-saluted the pianist with his hand at his forehead.

Once inside, Alma was looking around in amazement. In addition to the usual barrack signs in German—Your Block Is Your Home; Respect Your Superiors; Cleanliness Aids Good Health; Be Hard-Working and Obedient—this particular block's walls were adorned with colorful drawings of boys and girls and animals and even musical instruments. But what rendered her speechless was the number of children who were engaged in putting the final touches to the improvised stage in the middle of the barrack. They acted confidently and were perfectly at ease, unlike the frightened little ones Alma was used to seeing on the ramp, right before Dr. Mengele would send them, with an indifferent flip of his gloves, straight to the gas chamber.

Holding Alma by her hand, Miklós led her toward one of the bunks, next to which a young, good-looking man stood, holding what appeared to be a playscript in his hand. Just like the rest of the block inhabitants Alma had seen so far, he was attired in civilian clothing and wore tall, polished boots that instantly classed him with the privileged caste. His dark, pomade-smoothed hair shining in the dim light provided by the candles, he was engaged in directing his young charges on stage. As soon as he saw Miklós, he brightened at once and smiled even wider when the pianist introduced Alma to him.

"Frau Rosé!" he exclaimed, cupping her hand with both of his with great emotion. His German was almost as good as Alma's, only a faint trace of the Czech accent still recognizable in it. "What an honor to have you here. I'm Fredy Hirsh. We have quite a number of your colleagues here. Mostly Czech, but they all speak German, so, after the performance is over…"

Countless hands were already waving at her from the neighboring bunks. With a growing lump in her throat, Alma was thanking them for the warm welcome, for their kind commendations, for their memories of her father and uncle and exclamations—"I've never heard such excellent, perfectly sublime chamber music before!" She recognized their names and shook whatever outstretched hands she could reach and wiped the tears off her face at the mixture of delight and the most profound sorrow at the fact that all of these virtuosos were locked here, quite possibly to perish forever.

The lights were dimmed even further, leaving only the candles highlighting the stage. On Fredy Hirsh's signal, the audience hushed itself. From the corner of the barrack, two uniformed men appeared, one with a Hitler mustache clearly painted under his nose and another one carrying a pillow under his military jacket to imitate a protruding stomach. Just the sight of his buttons that were threatening to burst any moment now sent the audience giggling. Nestling next to Miklós atop one of the bunks, Alma recognized one of the uniforms as a Great War Austrian one; the second actor's attire she wasn't familiar with.

"They're both Great War veterans," Miklós, as though reading her mind, supplied in a hushed whisper. "The SS permitted them to keep the uniforms and even their military awards."

The actor with a painted mustache bent over the improvised desk littered with crudely drawn maps and began moving tin soldiers from one position to another, making childish battle noises under his breath. A few people snorted with laughter. The pillow-bearing actor knocked on the wooden plank of one of the bunks.

"Reichsmarschall Göring here, mein Führer. Allow me to come in?"

At once, Hitler straightened out and smoothed his uniform, taking on a grave air. "Ja, you may enter, ja."

Göring climbed onto the stage, slammed his heels together and straightened out his arm in the salute. "Heil Göring!"

"What did you say?" Hitler swung round, staring at Göring wrathfully.

A picture of injured innocence, Göring gave a shrug. "I said, Heil Hitler, mein Führer. Did Reichsführer Himmler give you that chamomile tea again that makes you hear all sorts of the oddest things?"

The audience burst into laughter.

"I don't know what you're talking about."

"Last time you drank that tea, you began insisting that God himself spoke to you and appointed you as his messiah to save Germany from Judeo-Bolsheviks, mein Führer. You said it on air, too, before Minister Goebbels could censure it properly. We received a lawsuit from Churchill; he claims, as he heard it on the radio, he began laughing so hard, he choked on his scone and almost died. The Pope sent a telegram to the Reich Chancellery as well and demanded we don't bring God into our affairs; they're starting to lose parishioners."

"Those are Catholics. We don't care about those. We persecute them as well."

"Do we?"

"Are you reading my persecuted groups memos at all? What do I send my weekly updated versions to you for at all?!"

"I do, mein Führer."

"Whom did I recently add to the updated list then?"

Göring appeared to be searching his memory in great urgency. "The Italians, after they switched sides?"

"That was a lucky guess. Who else then?"

"The Japanese?"

"Why would we persecute the Japanese?"

"They're barbaric Asiatic hordes?"

"Bolshevists are barbaric Asiatic hordes!"

"But mein Führer, Bolshevists are Russians, are they not?"

"No, they're international Jewry! How difficult is it to follow my line of thought on racial superiority?!" Banging his fists on the desk, sending tin soldiers flying all over.

In the audience, someone exploded, causing the entire block to howl with laughter once again. It took great effort for both actors to contain themselves as well, but they managed to keep their faces straight.

Göring, under his breath, wiping his brow with his handkerchief, "Extremely difficult, when you change it twice a day, you miserable oaf."

"What did you say?"

"I said, they shall be serving meatloaf for lunch today, mein Führer."

"What? Meat again? When will you quit that barbaric practice of slaughtering poor animals?"

"But mein Führer, we slaughter humans in droves…"

"Precisely. Those are humans. We don't care about those."

Once again, the barrack was in uproar. Immersed in this communal hilarity, Alma roved her gaze around and discovered that in the past few minutes she had entirely forgotten that she was in the camp, that this was not an actual stage, and that the actors wore their real war uniforms and not costumes.

It's all right to laugh about death, she recalled Miklós' words. *We, like no one else, have deserved this right.*

Yes, they laughed about death; they laughed, fearlessly and insolently, right in its ugly face, and this small act of resistance made Alma nearly choke with pride for these brave Family Camp people, for their resilient spirit, for their refusal to submit.

Alma grasped Miklós' hand and, in a surge of emotion, kissed it before he could stop her. "Thank you for bringing me here."

He was looking at her tenderly, drinking in the delight painted clear as day on her animated, flushed face. "I wanted to show you what other inmates feel, when you play your music for them. You make them forget where they are, just like these fellows made you forget. They did, didn't they? I can tell by the look on your face. I've never seen you so happy, so carefree before. Here, it is the biggest gift, having something that makes one forget. You give them that. I want you to remember that, whenever you feel as though your music is useless. In this place, it's almost as important as bread. And you give it away in spades, my generous Almschi."

His lips brushed hers just for an instant but, suddenly, Alma felt as if she had grown wings.

A sharp whistle coming from the boy standing sentry at the barrack's door interrupted the performance, sending the two actors scrambling. With old wartime agility Alma had never expected from two elderly veterans, they clambered atop the top bunks and were instantly buried in blankets by their fellow inmates. Children, attired as gnomes, were already marching along the stage and singing a cheerful song in German. A beautiful girl with a crown of glossy black hair had joined them and was clapping her hands when the door to the barrack swung open and in walked Hössler flanked by two SS men.

Fredy Hirsh was already saluting him from his place in front of the improvised stage.

The habitants of the block made a big show of getting out of their bunks, but Hössler motioned them to remain in their places.

"*Snow White?*" He motioned his head toward the children in their gnome caps.

"Jawohl, Herr Obersturmführer," Fredy inclined his head deferentially. "As you requested. We were just in the middle of rehearsals."

Hössler approached the stage, interested. On cue, Fredy Hirsh motioned for the children's play to continue. Apparently, the Birkenau camp leader found the young performers perfectly delightful; dipping his hand inside his pocket, he extracted a handful of candy and threw it on the improvised stage.

"Their German has improved significantly," Hössler remarked to Fredy.

"I've been tutoring them personally every day, Herr Obersturmführer."

"Commendable work, Hirsh. Carry on."

With that, Hössler and his entourage were gone.

A unanimous sigh of relief echoed around the barrack, accompanied by a few nervous chuckles.

"They're gone!" the sentry boy called from the door, his small face still glued to the hole in between the planks. "You may continue."

"Close call, mein Führer," someone commented from the top bunk and the entire barrack exploded once again.

In the middle of all that gaiety, Miklós sat gazing into Alma's eyes as one enchanted. Twilight hung over the barrack; the candlelight's frantic dance threw fantastic shadows over the bunks and painted walls. Warm light lay softly around the pianist's frame. Alma was looking at the stage and he was looking only at her, as if no one else in the world existed.

"I should have brought my violin along. I could have played for them after the play was over—"

He interrupted her mid-word, "I think I love you, Almschi."

For an instant, Alma started. The confession had caught her unawares. It was much too soon for this; much too unexpected; the setting much too inappropriate. But the passing shadow of something profoundly painful in the pianist's eyes—he couldn't have waited for the liberation to tell her this; for them, it may never come—made Alma understand his reason. In Auschwitz, each day counted. It was important to say the words while one was still alive.

Her hand shifted to the back of his neck, caressed the dark stubble of his hair at the nape of it as she regarded him with tenderest affection. "But you barely know me."

"I do. I've loved you since I first met you. I've loved you since I first heard you play on the Prater. I think, I've loved you my entire life without personally knowing you. I loved the concept of you, the dreamlike version of you I constructed for myself. I was searching for pieces of you in all those other women, but something was always missing. And now, you sit before me, whole and real, and I feel I have never been happier. I feel it was worth getting myself into this place just to meet you."

A smile blossomed on her face. All around them, people were laughing; the actors were mocking the German leader with admirable insolence, but Alma scarcely heard them all. Love was a cruel mistress; it tormented its victims more often than not. Alma had fought against it for as long as she could, but that night, she surrendered herself.

"You know, Herr Steinberg, I think I love you too."

*

As it always was with Auschwitz, one could only count on a few days of relative respite from all the horrors they had long grown used to seeing. It was naïve, of course, to hope that it would last, but Alma still did in spite of herself, until the day came—the first one when Miklós was late for their rehearsal—and obliterated all of her hopes in the cruelest of manners. Her anguish had only intensified when he failed to appear altogether that day and the following one.

When he returned at last, two days later, his face was so badly bruised, his left eye was almost entirely swollen shut. Rough stitches pulled the skin above his eyebrow together, his nose was most certainly broken, and yet, he was smiling at her with those busted lips, all the while Alma regarded him in mortal horror.

"No need to look so alarmed; my hands are perfectly fine," he declared at once, demonstrating his unmarred, beautiful palms to her as though it was her only worry. "The Christmas concert won't be cancelled on my account, you have my word. I have never cancelled a performance in my life and am not about to start now."

"Your eye!" That was all Alma could manage in reply.

"It is my profound conviction it'll look presentable by then."

"You could have lost it!"

"Fortunately for me, I have two. I can see the sheet music just fine as long as I keep my head turned this way." He had already seated himself at the piano and assumed a certain comical posture.

To Alma, it appeared tragic, if anything.

He patted the bench inviting her to take her place by the piano, but she remained standing. Her entire body was trembling with some wild emotion.

"You could have gotten yourself killed!" A cry tore from her throat. She was suddenly overcome with the violent, impotent desire to slaughter him properly. "They caught you stealing, didn't they? The SS? It was them who beat you?"

"They wouldn't kill me. Herr Kommandant's orders."

"Hössler himself shot a woman, in front of my very eyes, for assuming that she had stolen from me! Do you truly think they give a brass tack about Herr Kommandant's orders? And all for what? For some idiotic chocolate bar! Would it have been worth it? Getting beaten to death for a chocolate?"

"You're screaming," he commented softly.

"I have all the right to!" She wanted to stop, but all of a sudden she had lost all control of her voice. "How do you imagine I would have lived with myself if they murdered you for some stupid chocolate bar? Is it all some sick game to you? Is it amusing, to see how long you can go stealing from the SS and getting away with it?"

"It wasn't about the chocolate bar this time," he said very softly.

Alma stared at him, aware of the deathly chill spreading slowly through her veins. "What was it about then?" she asked almost in a whisper, almost afraid to know.

For a few moments, he appeared to consider whether to tell her or not. "They found something on me. Something I shouldn't have had."

"The pocketknife?"

"No. Not the knife." His tone grew strange all of a sudden. "I had already passed it on to someone by then."

Chalk-white and unable to speak, Alma kept searching his face but could only discern a shadow of something oddly triumphant and defiant under that purplish map of half-healed bruises and swollen flesh.

The last of her doubts were obliterated. His new comrades—the Greens and the Reds, his *Ausweis* and the ability to move freely about the camp, his proximity to the SS and his somewhat protected position—it would be idiotic of them (she silently cursed at the men who had dragged him into their dangerous machinations) not to employ his services for their goals, whatever those goals might be. Alma was aware that Zippy mixed with the camp Resistance as well, but Zippy only traded in information she gathered in her camp headquarters. She wasn't stupid enough to hoard guns or ammunition as the Resistance members were rumored to do in the hope of staging a revolt as soon as the Soviet Army drew close enough. Apparently, Miklós was. Or he simply valued his freedom and dignity over the dangers the Resistance carried along with its proud name.

"Miklós, what did you do? And don't lie to me, please. I ought to know so I can be...prepared."

"There's nothing to be prepared for," he tried to assure her. "I've already received my obligatory beating. The SS jodhpurs they discovered on me I explained by way of the cold barrack and my own ignorance. 'Some fiend from the disinfecting station in the *Kanada* traded them to me for a piece of bread, Herr Untersturmführer; he had persuaded me that they had been discarded by your office and that I could wear them under my own trousers for warmth and no one would mind...'" His look was thoroughly innocent and sincerely apologetic as he playacted the scene before her. Even Alma found herself convinced. "I did, after all, wear them under my own trousers. It looked like an honest mistake. So, they gave me a good thrashing and closed the case."

The SS may have closed it, but Alma couldn't. "What did you need the SS uniform trousers for?"

He laughed uneasily, hoping to escape further interrogation, but seeing that Alma wouldn't budge, Miklós took a deep breath and was noble and proud and grave once again. "A fellow has to escape and, to do so, he needs to be dressed as one of them. If he makes it outside and then to the Soviets, he'll give them the maps of the camp layout and the crematoriums. We're hoping that either Soviet or American bombers lay a few eggs on them or at least onto the train tracks leading up to the camp."

A fleeting grimace of pain furrowed Alma's brow; she was just about to say something, something about the Gestapo chief's sinister department and the gallows on the *Appellplatz*, something about herself not being able to survive if he didn't, but then looked into his clear, fearless eyes and ended up putting her cool palm on his cheek as a blessing.

Yes. You do what you ought to. Be brave now, when it matters the most. I wouldn't love you this much, if you were a coward like others. Be brave. Do what you must, and I shall stand by you and hold your hand just as you promised to hold mine.

She didn't say any of that either, nor was it necessary. He read it all loud and clear in her eyes and thanked her softly for understanding. It was almost insulting to be in love in this place, but for them, there was suddenly no way around it. They pronounced their feelings for each other that day like a death sentence and sealed it with a kiss that left both gasping for air.

"For all eternity, no matter how short it will be."

"For all eternity, and long after that, too."

Chapter 22

December 1943

Five days before Christmas, two of her girls were released from the sickbay to Alma's care. They appeared in the Block, pale and willow-thin, completely exhausted from the laborious walk, but shuffled toward their respective chairs in spite of themselves. With growing anxiety, Alma watched them struggle with their instruments, for even such a lightweight affair as a violin was suddenly too heavy for Violette to hold. Flora wasn't faring any better at the piano, even under Miklós' gentle guidance—an hour, one pitiful hour, of rehearsals left her drenched with sweat and even more ghostly-white than before.

"This won't do." Miklós was the first one to openly declare what everyone was thinking. "This is torture, not rehearsals. They released them because they aren't contagious anymore, not because they've recovered. They ought to be in their beds, resting and eating double and triple rations, not mastering blasted Wagner for the SS concert!"

Just as Alma was about to send her charges into their respective beds and leave them to rest, Dr. Mengele strode in, seated himself in one of the chairs in the audience and motioned for the orchestra to proceed. Alma didn't like at all the gleeful, wolfish smile that wouldn't leave his face.

A picture of composure, she squared her shoulders and tapped her baton on the stand. "From the beginning."

It took her great effort to keep her gaze over the heads of the girls with a professional indifference when all she wanted was to see if Violette would find it in herself to bring her violin to her shoulder in time. But, as though sensing some malice hanging over the room like a dark, ominous cloud, her orchestra played better than ever. The violinists in particular entered on time and in perfect synchrony, as though in a desire to protect the weaker member of their herd from the predator in his elegant gray overcoat. Still, it wasn't enough to hide a false note from Violette's instrument.

Dr. Mengele cringed visibly.

Next to Miklós who shared a bench with her, Flora was struggling with the piano. Under Dr. Mengele's gaze that was a mixture of mock horror and barely concealed amusement, the pianist sat next to his student in helpless ire until his own nerves gave out. Miklós moved Flora's hands away from the keys and picked up the melody himself, correcting the sound of the entire orchestra at once.

Alma felt tempted to do the very same thing with Violette's violin.

Beads of sweat collecting on her forehead, Violette was desperately squinting at the sheet music in front of her. With great effort, she tried to keep up with the rest, but it appeared as though her eyes and her hands refused to work together.

Another false note; she pressed her bluish lips into a tight line and clutched at her violin with greater force just to keep it on her shoulder. Her fingers were too stiff with effort; the bow cut across the strings with a harsh, screaming sound.

Defeated, she finally lowered her instrument. The look that she gave Alma made Alma's throat constrict with emotion. It was an agonized expression of utter despondency and disappointment—with her own incompetence. *Forgive me . . .* The girl's lips were quivering. Two heavy tears rolled down her ashen cheeks and dropped onto the violin that lay, useless and silent, on her lap.

Alma stopped the music. Miklós was right; it was a torture.

As though on cue, Dr. Mengele rose from his chair. "Frau Alma, may I have a word in private?"

In the grave silence that followed, Alma led him to her room. Once inside, he looked around with curiosity, pulled one of the chairs away from the small, rickety table and gestured Alma toward it with almost theatrical gallantry.

"Herr Doktor, surely, you don't expect them to be in their top shape," she began speaking against all protocols. "They have just been released from the sickbay. They're still very weak and need time to return back to normal…"

"Do you know how exactly typhus affects people?" Dr. Mengele asked her as if he didn't hear a word out of what she had just said. "Possible complications include hearing loss, sensitivity to light and general vision problems, muscle stiffness." He gave Alma a pointed look. "All are a death sentence to any musician; don't you agree?"

Alma made no reply. She was certain that his choice of words was intentional.

"Let's not bring the entire orchestra's performance down just because of a couple of weak members. The new transport shall arrive soon; you'll select new girls, fresh girls, maybe even better than these have been—"

"They are not *have been*," Alma's voice was full of ice. "They're still here and they're going nowhere; not while I'm in charge, at any rate. It's any civilized society's duty to look after and protect its weak members, not get rid of them as soon as they fall ill. This is what makes us human, *Herr Doktor*."

"Marxist ideas." He dismissed her argument with a negligent wave of the hand. "This is not how the Reich operates. And Auschwitz-Birkenau falls under the Reich's jurisdiction and ideology. All weak members of society ought to be eradicated. They're useless eaters who don't contribute anything." He gave Alma another provoking look from the corner of his eyes. "Just like those two charges of yours in their present state."

"They'll be playing just fine by Christmas," Alma asserted, holding his gaze. Her tone barely contained any emotion in it. "I'll see to it."

"But they're weak and half-blind. Such complications can last for weeks; sometimes months," Dr. Mengele continued with a certain malicious relish. "There's another issue—constant hunger that can't be sated no matter how much food the recovering person consumes. They turn into virtual animals. They begin stealing from their own relatives—I personally witnessed what such hunger does to them."

Alma had seen it too. Yet, she only stared at him obstinately with her black eyes. "My girls don't steal."

"In ordinary circumstances, no, they don't. But these are not ordinary circumstances."

"Of course not. It's an extermination camp." Alma shrugged coolly.

Dr. Mengele grinned, amused. "You're quite a word fencer, Frau Alma. I bet you had rather a number of admirers back in the day."

"Fat lot of good their number did when your racial laws went into effect and they all jumped my sinking ship like the rats that they are."

"They're mere cowards then," Dr. Mengele conceded surprisingly easily. Alma regarded him with suspicion, but there was not a trace of irony in his gaze now. "You can't blame cowards for their cowardly ways. They can't help it, like rabbits can't help not moving when faced with a wolf. It is rather sad that we have such weak elements in our Aryan racial stock…" He suddenly pulled forward, his hand, with its index finger pointing, stopping a mere inch from Alma's chest. "You, on the other hand, have steel in you, Frau Alma. Sheer steel for nerves; pure, cold mercury in your veins. In that regard, you're much more Aryan than our highly praised Teutonic Knights that tremble in their boots and drop their weapons at the mere sight of an advancing *Ivan*. I've seen it happen on the Eastern front…A pathetic picture. The 'undefeated' German war machine, waving white handkerchiefs as soon as they hear *Oorraah, pobieda—hurrah, victory*—coming from the Soviet lines, even before they see the Russkies themselves charging at them." Once again, he was back to studying her with his eyes slightly narrowed. "But I can bet any money that you wouldn't have run." He shook his head, as though in confirmation of his own thoughts. "No, you wouldn't have. You never back away from danger. You're fearless to a suicidal extent. That's a very Aryan trait and I can't help but respect that."

It took Alma great effort to prevent disgust from showing on her face. "If you indeed respect that, *Herr Doktor*, and if you do have such trust in my 'steel,' allow me to put those girls back in shape. I will make sure they will play excellently at Christmas."

"It's a big event, Frau Alma. Kommandant Liebehenschel is going to be there. All the camp's top brass."

"I understand that."

"You don't want to embarrass yourself with such musicians, do you?"

"I would never let a musician on my stage if I wasn't one hundred percent certain that they could play according to my high standards."

"Why are you being so obstinate about that particular couple at any rate? They're easily replaceable. Announce a camp audition—it is my profound conviction you shall have a new violinist and a new pianist by lunchtime."

"I don't need replacements. My girls are perfectly capable of playing." She looked at him and softened her tone. "Herr Doktor, you have already placed your trust in me once, on that very first day on the ramp. You gave me your permission to expand the orchestra and, I believe, I haven't disappointed you with the result, else, you would have long sent us all to the gas for our uselessness. Place your trust in me once more. I will get them back into shape. You have my word."

"In five days? Impossible."

"No such thing as impossible. Everything is achievable if only one applies their all."

"Commendable thinking."

He leaned back in his chair, studying Alma with great interest. Her own gaze was riveted to one of Dr. Mengele's tall boots. It was sticking from under the chair and was polished to such perfection, she was sure she would see her own reflection in it if she leaned closely enough.

"Very well." At last, he announced his verdict. "You shall keep your girls until then. But if I hear one false note during the concert—just one—not just these two but all four of your sick orchestra girls get phenol shots to the heart the very next day. I believe that's fair enough."

Chapter 23

"Right."

Facing her own orchestra suddenly felt like facing a firing squad. The weight of the entire world had all at once descended on her shoulders. Steel for nerves, her foot; why was her "steady hand" suddenly shaking as she picked up her baton? It was much too heavy for her just then; Alma dropped it into its place, lowered into one of the chairs and wiped her hands down her face. It was all too much. Too much responsibility, and not just for herself, or for her elderly father as it used to be, but for four human beings, four young girls with their lives long and promising before them, with their hopes and fears and their dreams for the future. She regarded her hands that lay limp, palms up, in her lap. Four lives. Four human lives she held in those hands.

Suddenly overcome with shame, she glanced at her charges, who'd kept searching her face ever since she'd come back from her room. They desperately needed a leader and here she was, sitting lamenting her fate when it was theirs that was at stake. Time was of the essence. Wasting it on self-pity was a crime.

From his place at the piano, Miklós gave her an encouraging smile. Just like her girls, he appeared to have faith in her even when she, herself, didn't.

"Right," Alma repeated, this time with determination in her voice, and rose swiftly from her chair. "It is obvious that both Violette and Flora need extra nourishment before they can resume rehearsals. From now on, for five days, we will be feeding them extra rations to ensure that they have enough strength to play. Five days is a very short time, so we shall start right this instant. Girls who still have food left in your parcels, bring it here. Regina, make hot tea for everyone, will you? We could all use some warming up, and the girls will eat in the meantime."

There was an almost instant rustling of chairs as the girls rushed to their bunks to bring forward whatever meager provisions they'd been rationing with utmost care. Misty-eyed, Flora and Violette watched a small pile grow on their communal dining table—dried fruits and cookies, preserves and smoked sausage, cheese and even cubes of sugar—a veritable feast few Auschwitzers had seen.

Busy dividing the food into two equal piles, Alma didn't notice at first a small group of Polish veterans conferring a bit aside from everyone. Only when Sofia's voice rose over the general commotion and descended upon the group with its rapid crescendo of incomprehensible, indignant screams, did it catch Alma's attention.

"Is something the matter?" Alma inquired, approaching the group.

The girls' voices quieted, turning to mutters. Alma couldn't understand their language, but she recognized defiant notes in them just fine. There were only five of them and each was staring at anything but Alma's eyes.

"These obstinate cows refuse to hand over their rations," Sofia reported, staring at her fellow countryfolk with cold disdain.

"Why?" Alma asked softly.

She already knew the answer but wanted them to openly say it, out of some perverse desire to confirm her own theory.

"We don't think it fair to give them our food," one of the girls replied in her halting German. "Why should we do that?"

"Because they have been sick and need food to recover." Alma managed to keep her tone calm, even though she could already feel her anger rising. "You can't blame them for getting sick, can you now?"

"We don't blame them. We're only saying that it's not fair to give them our food. They should have watched themselves better.

If their health is weaker than ours, why should we pay for it? They never receive any parcels from their relatives—"

"Because their relatives are all dead." Alma's chest was rising and falling visibly now. She was aware of Miklós' eyes on her. The very thought of him seeing her in this state revolted her, but what revolted her even more was such attitudes in her ranks. She would drop dead before she permitted this poison to spread among her girls as well. "They have all perished right here, in Auschwitz, sometimes, in front of their very eyes. Is that their fault also?"

"We're not saying it's their fault. We're saying it's socialism, taking from the ones who have something and sharing it among the ones who don't."

"Socialism, you say?" Before Alma could stop herself, her hand flew up and slapped the girl on her cheek with a resounding smack. "That's not socialism; that's called regular human decency, if that notion is new for you!"

The girl stood stunned before her; in another instant, she broke into sobs. Yet Alma didn't feel an ounce of shame for what she had just done, only blinding, overpowering rage.

"First, I had to sit and listen to that SS sod's racial theories and now you shall start repeating them to me, under my own roof? Like a good SS-trained parrot, no less! I've already seen the likes of you, right in the sickbay, tearing the last piece of bread out of her dying friend's hands and justifying it! Can you get it, once and for all, there are no Jews and Poles here, no French and no communists, there are only SS and inmates, and that's what it all comes down to. We're all equally nothing to them. Do you consider yourself superior to Violette because she's a Jew and you're a Pole? Well, let me give you this news: in the eyes of the SS, you're still dirty vermin that needs to be exterminated. The more we quarrel among each other, the better it all works out for them. The more we act like animals toward each other, the less work is left for them. That's what they were counting on when they organized this entire camp;

do you not understand that? We're all in this together. They're the enemy, not your fellow inmates."

"And you're just like them!" the girl shouted back. "Slave-driving us worse than the SS. You don't have the right to call yourself a Jew. You're a typical, cold-blooded German. No wonder they appointed you as a *Kapo*. They recognized one of their kind."

This time, it was Sofia who slapped her, much harder than Alma.

"Ungrateful sow!" the former *Kapo* roared in indignation. "Frau Alma has done so much for you lot; all of your privileges—the new clothes, double rations, Red Cross parcels, your blasted naptime after lunch, roll calls inside the block instead of in the freezing cold, a stove to warm us all, a shower every day, laundry once a week—all forgotten already? Selfish, rotten child. Today, it's Violette; tomorrow, it could be you. Would you still think it was socialism if Frau Alma shared her ration with you as you lay dying from fever?"

The girl didn't reply. She was too busy nursing her stinging cheek and sniffling.

Her comrades now appeared to hesitate and, a few minutes later, they brought their supplies to the communal table. Alma accepted them silently. When their leader approached the table with a few tins, Alma stopped her in her tracks.

"Keep your food. I don't want you running about the camp and complaining to everyone who agrees to listen how *Kapo Alma* extorted the rations from you, the socialist bitch that she is."

"I'm sorry, Frau Alma."

"No, you're not. You're afraid; not sorry. Afraid that I will take some sort of revenge on you or banish you from the orchestra altogether." Judging by the girl's startled look, the words hit the nail squarely on the head. Alma grinned crookedly. "You have nothing to be afraid of. Your own conscience will be your worst punishment. Every day, when you look at Flora or Violette, you shall be reminded of your own cowardice and selfishness. Every single day, for the rest of your life you shall live with yourself. No punishment can outdo that."

Before long, the girl was crying again. This time, it was guilty tears; she was nudging the tins into Alma's hands with a pitiful, pleading gesture, but Alma just stood before her, still and cold like a statue, with her arms crossed over her chest, blocking the table from her and her attempts to put the food into the collective pile.

At last, acknowledging her defeat, the girl approached Violette directly and gave her two tins, leaving the other two for Flora.

"Forgive me, please...I don't know what came over me..."

"It's all right." Violette smiled. "I understand perfectly. You don't have to—"

"No, please, take it. It's for you. You ought to eat."

"There's enough there for everyone—"

"No, you eat. You've been sick. You need it..."

When the *Stubendienst* girls—the block caretakers—brought in the lunch for the block, Alma divided her entire portion between Violette and Flora. They were still protesting when she headed toward the door, patting her pocket for her cigarettes absentmindedly.

Outside, it was a veritable North Pole; the frosty crust of snow crunched underfoot, but Alma secretly welcomed such biting cold as a twisted form of self-inflicted punishment. Shivering against the gusts of wind in her light cardigan, she lit up her cigarette from the third attempt.

"Hunger strike again?"

In spite of herself, she smiled at Miklós' voice. She was grateful that he hadn't interfered with the affair, but she was even more grateful for his standing next to her now. Something heavy fell on her shoulders; she brushed her fingers on it and recognized her own camel-wool coat.

"I'm not hungry. Just very tired and full of nerves."

"One should imagine." He narrowed his eyes, gazing in the distance.

"If you tell me again that I'm too strict with them, I shall first drop something on your head and then divorce you."

"I wasn't going to say anything of that sort. In fact, I think you handled the situation admirably well."

"With one exception." Alma took a deep pull on her cigarette. "I hit a person today. For the first time in my life, I hit someone." Her voice was full of disbelief at the event.

Much to her surprise, Miklós broke into soft chuckles. "An unimaginable feat for a *Kapo*, to hit an inmate for the first time after months! They ought to put your name into some local book of honors or some such. Most *Kapos* don't last as long as one day without bashing someone's head in with a baton."

"They have different batons. Mine is for conducting music, not for hitting anyone. That's the entire reason why I'm so disappointed with myself. I feel this camp is changing me into something horrible. I'm becoming much too coarse, too hard-hearted." She looked at him tragically. "I'm becoming one of them, Miklós," she finished with a note of some desolate finality in her voice.

At once, he took her face in his hands. "Nonsense! No filth, no degradation of this place, is enough to touch you—"

"It has already touched me," she interrupted him, calm and resigned to the fact. "I have become good friends with the SS. They call me *Frau Alma* and address me with the polite, *Sie*. They talk about music with me, about Vienna, and about all matters refined."

"That's not friendship. You know that you ought to show deference and keep decorum with them if you want your orchestra to survive. If you yourself want to live."

"They taught me how to be violent."

"No. You simply lost your temper. Anyone's nerves would snap, after everything you've been through."

"I slave-drive my own girls and the SS praise me for it. You know you have become a terrible human being if the SS begin praising you and admire your 'Aryan character.' Do you know what Aryan stands for, in their eyes? Ruthlessness, overachieving, and blood as cold as ice under one's skin. Mengele just told me I embody all three. He said, he admired me."

"Stop it."

"No, I won't stop. I want you to hear it, so you know what sort of person I am. She was right, my little Polish mandolinist, just like Hössler before her, and Mengele along with him. They all stated the same thing and were right about it; I'm not a Jew. I'm a German, and that's why it is so easy for me to survive here. They consider me as one of their own, the SS. They recognize the kindred spirit," she nearly spat out the last words.

Miklós didn't ask her to stop this time; merely pressed his mouth hard against hers and felt her choke on a sob she was desperately trying to stifle.

"You may hate yourself all you want," he declared with a fearless smile when he finally pulled away. "I will always love you for the both of us. No, no; no tears just now. They can't see you like this. They need you strong, all of them."

"Yes." She wiped her face with her sleeve and smiled bravely at him.

"That's better."

"Will you stay working with Flora till the curfew?"

"Of course. I will keep working with Flora and you take Violette. I'm certain that Sofia can manage the orchestra just fine. You have already trained them perfectly. Did you hear how magnificently they played before Mengele just now?"

Alma smiled through the tears. "They did, didn't they?"

"And they will play even better at Christmas. We both shall see to it."

He wrapped his arm around her shoulders to take her inside and, suddenly, the burden didn't appear to be as heavy as it used to be.

"Play just this first line, but play it perfectly." Alma stood over Violette, her hand planted firmly on the back of the girl's chair.

After a generous meal, some of the color had returned to Violette's cheeks and her eyes began gleaming brighter. When she tucked the violin under her chin, the former mortal weariness and desperation was no longer there. Under Alma's intent gaze, she played the first few notes carefully but without mistakes.

"Good. Now play the second line the same way."

Violette did so and looked up at Alma, who nodded in encouragement.

"Now play both of them."

This was where Violette's faltering hand slipped for the first time. At once, her face fell. She began lowering the instrument, but Alma was having none of it.

"No breaks until we finish the entire piece. Play just the third line where you made the mistake. Twenty times in a row."

Violette's head shot up.

Alma only shrugged with a grin. "This is what my father would tell me to do when I made mistakes. Having talent is all fine and well, but practice—and more practice—is essential for mastering the piece you're playing. When you practice something ten, twenty, thirty times, your fingers will begin playing it correctly automatically. You'll grow sick of that part, but you will never play it wrong again; take my word for it."

By the end of the first hour, they had been over only the first three pages. By the end of the second hour, Violette, her hands shaking and her eyes swimming with unshed tears, began to beg for a break. Alma fed her a few pieces of dried apple and a cube of sugar for energy but refused to be moved otherwise.

"I said, no breaks until we finish the entire piece and we will finish it. You may cry, you may curse me, you may hate me for what I'm doing to you, but you shall master that piece, Violette. From the beginning."

By the end of the day, they had finished the piece. There was blood on Violette's fingerboard, her fingers were cut raw, but she played the entire piece with only two mistakes.

Alma brought the girl to her room and began cleaning her wounds.

"You played exceptionally well today, Violette."

Much to her surprise, she discovered that Violette was smiling.

The violinist tossed her head at Alma's fingers. "Those are violin scars." It wasn't a question; a statement, if anything, with a measure of admiration to it.

"Yes, they are."

"Your father made you rehearse until you cut your fingers, too?" she asked, in her accented German.

"No. He didn't have to *make me* do any anything. He was such an excellent violinist, all he had to do was play his chamber music. I couldn't bear hearing it, it was so magnificent." Alma paused and then added with a soft smile, "I'm not a particularly talented violinist."

Violette looked at her in stunned disbelief.

Alma shook her head, grinning. "I really am not. Not naturally talented, like my father or uncle, at any rate. I trained myself well enough to pass for one. But it's all technique, for the most part. I play with my hands. He played with his heart. But you can only tell the difference if you're a music critic of the highest rank. They always called me out on that and they were right." She finished applying the salve to Violette's cuts. "If I could train myself into confusing the general population, so can you. Only, you have to confuse just one man. But it's utterly important that you confuse him; do you understand?"

If Violette was frightened by Alma's grave expression and her final words, she didn't show it. She only nodded instead and promised to start early the very next morning.

"Brave little soldier!" Alma took her face in her hands and kissed the girl on the forehead.

Chapter 24

Christmas Eve, 1943

Since the morning, the Germans around the camp were in excellent spirits; it was Alma's orchestra girls who were growing colder and colder with fear. The concert was a mere few hours away. To Alma, the time had never felt more like an ax that hung over her head, threatening and indifferent, ready to fall at any moment now. Miklós held her hands and assured her that she had done all she could for the orchestra. She had rehearsed with her girls until she could no longer feel her right arm; until the baton had grown so heavy it was a torture to hold it upright; until the spot on her back, just under her shoulder blade, began to pulse with searing pain as though the camp Gestapo was prodding her skin with a hot poker. And yet, Alma still felt as if she hadn't done enough. If Flora or Violette played badly that night, their deaths would be on her conscience. She was their conductor after all, their *Kapo*, their mother they no longer had.

All around the SS mess hall, inmates rushed to and fro in a great hurry, assembling and setting the tables, wrapping the sharply smelling tree with tinsel and little swastika flags, fixing the portrait of Hitler on the wall. Miklós' comrades from the waiting staff *Kommando* made it a point of honor to make an indecent gesture in the portrait's face whenever they passed it by. At least that appeared to lift Alma's girls' spirits. That, and double rations straight from the delectable SS kitchen fed to them by the Green Triangles, Miklós' *Kommando* mates, who guarded the girls like hawks while they ate their fill behind the closed doors.

"At least now, if we die, we've had our last meal," Violette-from-Paris jested grimly, and Alma suddenly felt very sick to her stomach.

"You won't die. I won't let him touch you." It was a promise she had no right to make and still, Alma made it, because it was something that her girls needed to hear.

At ten to six, Maria Mandl came in to check on her mascots. Alma heard her address one of her wardens, "Aren't they pretty in those blue concert uniforms?" and cringed inwardly. That's all they were to the women's camp leader. Dolls to demonstrate to her colleagues. Dolls, who played music if one pressed the right buttons.

"Make sure the girls smile when they perform." This time, Mandl spoke directly to Alma. "They look so much prettier when they smile."

Something dark and vile surged up in Alma at those words. She was overcome with the desire to walk up to this ignorant woman and slap her hard across the face. Her girls' lives were hanging by a thread and she wished them to smile, while they quite possibly lived through their last hours?

With a tremendous effort, Alma willed herself to stay calm. Not a muscle twitched on her drawn face when she inclined her head in acknowledgment of Mandl's desires. "Of course, Lagerführerin."

The mess hall began to fill, a gathering of gray-clad vultures. They clapped each other on their shoulders—*how goes it in your detail, veteran of the wars? Did you save up enough to buy your Lotte that fur coat she wanted?*—and laughed at the usual Auschwitz joke: *why buy anything when the* Kanada *has it all?* They pulled family photos out of their breast pockets and bragged about their children, just as uniformed and ruthless as their fathers. "Mad fellow my youngest one is growing to be! Has just denounced his best friend's father because the old sod refused to greet him with the obligatory Hitler salute. No sentimentality about my little scoundrel, that's for certain. A sheer Germanic spirit, loyalty to the Führer only."

Alma was glad that her back was turned to them as she conducted soft, background music before the official concert began. This way, they couldn't see her face twisted into a hateful grimace of cold, all-consuming contempt.

They would play through this night. They would play, and they would survive, so that they could come out of here one day and make it their business to hunt these gray-clad vultures down, to bring them to justice for daring to laugh when thousands suffered, for daring to boast about their children when they burned Jewish ones in stacks, for daring to celebrate in the middle of this slaughterhouse. The cold, pitiless resolve on Alma's face reflected on the girls' faces. Yes, they would play excellently tonight, because the act of survival was resistance too and they were the fearless freedom fighters.

Breathing heavily, Alma stood before her audience, her conductor's baton in hand. All the SS top brass were applauding her girls wildly, but she stared triumphantly at only one man. Dr. Mengele waited for a while, but finally unfolded his arms and began clapping as well, a bit theatrically, but that mattered not. Both Violette and Flora played remarkably well that night. Both were wet with sweat—Alma could see the sheen of it on their exhausted faces—but that was a small price to pay for the lives of four girls.

Along her own back, sweat was running down in rivulets; concerts always made one lose a few pounds from sheer exhaustion and nerves, and she had barely eaten anything in the course of the last five days, splitting her own rations between her two recovering charges. Her ears were ringing faintly, the muscles in her left arm were screaming in protest after her final violin solo—just as it was with her Waltzing Girls, she had to conduct and perform at the same concert—and her head felt oddly light. The dark spots dancing between her eyes, Alma thoroughly pretended to ignore.

Thank heavens for the *Kanada* lipstick; it tricked her audience into seeing a Viennese virtuoso standing before them in all her glory and not an exhausted woman about to collapse. No; collapsing was entirely out of the question.

Alma blinked the spots away and forced a bright smile back onto her face. Miklós and she had a long night before them—first, their piano performance, four hands, next, a concerto for a violin and a piano and, after, whatever their SS maters requested for as long as the night went on.

The SS requested a lot. Now that the official part was over, Miklós' piano was moved into a corner of the mess hall. In its center, the tables were pushed into a bracket around a tall Yule tree decorated with swastikas and tinsel. Skillfully dodging dancing couples in their dress uniforms, inmate waiters rushed to and fro, weighed down by the overflowing dishes balanced on the tips of their fingers. The mouthwatering aroma of the Christmas goose instantly reminded Alma of home and her father carving the traditional holiday dish as the entire Rosé family watched him keenly. She would kill for a chance to sink her teeth into that golden-skinned bird but refused to betray herself even with a single glance in the waiting staff's direction. Their tight white coats and starched napkins thrown over their bent left arms almost made them look like ordinary waiters, if it weren't for the absence of good-natured servility civilian waiters were prone to display in the hope of a generous tip. These men stared at their patrons with cold, deliberate hatred whenever the SS men snapped their fingers to summon them.

The SS were particularly rowdy and intolerable that night. They had their female counterparts to impress and the waiters were the ones at whose expense they decided to produce such an impression. Though, such swinish behavior didn't make them differ all that much from regular, civilian restaurant patrons, Alma thought. There were always the types who could only elevate themselves by putting others down. It was Alma's personal experience that the nastiest sorts always left the most miserable tips, unlike the quiet, dignified men. The latter never complained, even if the steak was overcooked, and invariably slid a tip that constituted half of the bill into the waiter's hand personally and with a somewhat timid smile, before shaking that hand thoroughly in gratitude for the exceptional service.

Alma looked at Miklós and saw that his eyes were closed, as though he didn't wish to see any of the uniformed herd he was forced to entertain. It was a damned humiliating experience for the virtuoso of the Budapest Philharmonic to play for a mess hall stuffed full of drunken SS men amid all the shrill laughter of the wardens and guffaws of their red-faced male counterparts, but he bore it stoically and with great dignity. Partly obscured with cigarette smoke, the mess hall stunk of stale sweat, food grease, and spilled alcohol, yet Miklós played with a serene half-smile on his face as though it was only his body that was present there—his spirit was somewhere very far away, untouched by all this baseness and Nazi-imposed perverse order of things.

Someone shouted for Zara Leander's "Under the Red Lanterns of San Paoli."

Miklós flexed his fingers and threw a concerned glance at Alma. He had the advantage of sitting, all the while she had already spent countless hours on her feet. She met his gaze, smiled at him bravely and even winked at him. *As long as I'm playing next to you, I'm not tired in the slightest.*

"One day, it shall all end," he mouthed to her soundlessly.

She couldn't possibly hear him amid that drunken chaos, but she still understood everything.

"I don't want it to end," she mouthed back to him. *I want to play next to you for the rest of my life, no matter where.*

He understood it too, for he felt it inside of him, that sentiment that welled in her eyes as she struck her violin with her bow—the beautiful song about eternal love. It seemed strangely befitting. She looked at him with tenderest affection; he had not once ceased looking at her as well, and all of a sudden, the rest of the noise died down, muted itself against the force of that invisible connection. There were only two of them in the entire hall. The gray uniforms were grotesquely insignificant and didn't belong here. Only music did and so they would play it until the last uniform was gone. And after that, they would still play, even if it was for the inmate waiters only. They were a better audience in any case.

It was past three in the morning when the last group of SS men finally stumbled uncertainly toward the exit with their arms wrapped amicably around each other's shoulders. Only one of them lingered behind to supervise the inmate waiters as they cleared the tables. The *Kapo*, also attired in a white coat for the occasion, attempted to assure the SS man that he would see to the order, but the guard only sneered with contempt and wagged his finger at the *Kapo*.

"I know what you sly apes are up to," he slurred, swaying on his feet. The edge of his tunic was tucked sloppily into his trousers—by accident, judging by the looks of it. "As soon as we're out of the place, you will gorge yourselves at the expense of the Reich, you dirty pigs."

Next to Alma, Miklós snorted softly with disdain. He sat, half-turned from his piano as his elbow rested on its closed lid and observed the drunken man with the mixture of unconcealed disgust and tolerant amusement of an adult watching a child doing something idiotic.

The waiters ignored the insult and went about their business, looking oddly dignified and polished in contrast with the uniformed "master of the world." That seemed to infuriate the SS man even further.

"Yes, lately you have all become very sly indeed. Organizing escapes under our very noses, making use of the new *Kommandant's* good disposition toward you, you filthy swine! That's all right. We'll catch that sod yet. You watch what we do to him and whoever helped him after we catch him. We'll string him up nice and high, along with his accomplices; you'll see how fast we will."

Alma turned to Miklós, aware that she was holding her breath. He only winked at her, looking immensely pleased with himself. Their efforts hadn't been in vain. *They succeeded; by some miracle, no less, but they did, the brave Resistance men!* Alma regarded Miklós with unconcealed admiration.

"Conspiring behind our backs," the SS man continued his grumbling, "strolling around with haughty looks on your ugly mugs... Even the new ones... Arrogant muttonheads! We're taking them to the gas and they're singing their national anthems and promising us that we're next!" Now, there were incredulous notes in his voice, as though such a possibility was beyond any comprehension.

Alma put her violin into its case, but when she made a move to leave, Miklós caught her by her wrist and pulled her close. She sensed it too, some sinister, invisible threat hanging in the air.

One of the waiters gathered a few plates and was clearing them over a large cauldron. Officially, the scraps were supposed to go to the SS dogs. Unofficially, according to Miklós' explanation, the food went to the starving inmates who already knew to line up along the barbed wire with their bowls at the ready. Risking their own lives, the waiters distributed it right through the wire. By the time the cauldron reached the kennels, it was almost empty.

This SS man didn't seem to be aware of the arrangement but suspected the waiters of appropriating the bits of the feast themselves. He waited for them to finish clearing the plates and then approached the cauldron with a malicious grin. Alma watched him pull a chair toward it and mount it. Miklós' hand clasped tighter and tighter over hers; his gray eyes grew progressively colder as he followed the guard's every move, already suspecting what his intentions were. The waiters dropped whatever they were doing and also waited for the man's next move with sharp, unblinking eyes.

Slowly, for his fingers didn't appear to listen to him too well, he unbuttoned his fly and began relieving himself into the cauldron. As he did so, he roved his unfocused gaze around victoriously. A self-satisfied grin turned his expression into an ugly grimace of pure spite. Alma felt Miklós' hand on top of hers tremble with rage.

The waiters drew themselves up, barely visibly. Now, they surrounded the SS man in a semicircle. A few stood in the entrance to the kitchen, observing the scene in ominous silence. Another couple closed the exit doors and locked them noiselessly. Inside Alma's chest, her heart was thumping with blunt, violent force. Her throat had gone suddenly very dry.

The *Kapo* reached for the cognac bottle that still had three quarters of amber liquid splashing in it. Alma half-expected him to bash it over the SS man's head, but the *Kapo* only poured a shot glass almost to its brim and offered it to the guard.

"That was a fine trick, Herr Rottenführer!" he said admiringly. "Only a true SS man can piss like that. Civilians can't pull off such a fine arch. They lack character." He held the glass before the SS officer, who beamed stupidly at him.

Using the *Kapo*'s shoulder for support, he clambered down and reached for the cognac to down it.

"What are you here for?" the SS man demanded, slapping the *Kapo* on his chest and handing him the glass back.

The *Kapo* was quick to refill it. "Murder, Herr Rottenführer," he explained amiably. "Here, drink another one. Civilians lack character for that, too. Only our brave SS can put down the entire cellar. We can only aspire to reach your level."

There was a certain undertone to the *Kapo*'s voice; Alma heard it clearly now.

The SS man pondered the glass in front of him, hiccupped, swallowed rising bile, but recovered himself and emptied the glass again, encouraged by the *Kapo*'s words. The latter was positively grinning now.

"Who did you do in? Your old lady?" the SS man slurred, wiping his mouth and swayed back, almost falling.

"An SA man, your Nazi Party Storm Detachment colleague," the *Kapo* explained in an even friendlier tone than before, drawing chuckles from his fellow inmates. "He came for an elderly Jewish couple who lived above us and thought it would be a fine trick to drag them down the stairs by their hair. In turn, I thought it would be a fine trick to swipe him a couple on the snout, lift him by his ankles and drop him, four floors down, onto his head." He paused for dramatic effect. "The delicious sound his skull made when it connected with the marble floor, ah! Civilians don't make such fine sounds. Like a ripe melon busting open." He kissed his fingertips with relish. "Only empty SS and SA heads make such splendid sounds."

The waiters around him weren't chuckling any longer, but their bared teeth were still there, gleaming menacingly in the darkness.

The blood drained from the SS man's face. He swallowed with great difficulty and looked about himself. For the first time, there was genuine alarm in his eyes.

"And here's Urschel," the *Kapo* continued, pointing at one of the waiters. "Also an SA killer. Only, he's a veteran, unlike myself. He offed his very first one back in 1933."

"Took his eye out with the sharp end of his own banner," the veteran declared proudly.

The murmur of approval rustled among their ranks.

"He was taking them out with his anarchist hit squad for years before the Gestapo finally caught him."

"They could only prove one." Urschel shrugged. "I'll be out of here in two months; Herr Kommandant said, I served my time and have rehabilitated myself."

"Have you really?" The *Kapo* looked skeptical.

The veteran made a wry face and turned to the SS man. "We're all murderers here, Herr Rottenführer. You, yourselves, appointed us to this privileged position because you didn't wish the docile Jews to serve you. Is something the matter? You don't look too well. You ought to drink some more."

The *Kapo* was already pushing the whole bottle—not a glass this time—into the trembling SS officer's hands. "Drink it. Drink what's left in it, you filthy hog."

After yet another frantic look around, the SS man released a wild appeal for help.

"Shout your head off, if you like," the *Kapo* laughed cuttingly. "All of your comrades are tucked nice and snug in their beds, snoring like the good little soldiers they are. But you—" once again, his face took on an outright threatening expression, "made it your business to mix with our affairs and upset our arrangement. I imagine, you deserve all too well what is coming to you. You chose to live like a pig—it's only fair you die like one."

The guard stared at him with pleading, terrified eyes.

Shoving the bottle at him again, hard against his chest, the *Kapo* nearly knocked him over and spilled some of the cognac on the SS man's tunic. "Drink!" he bellowed, his features twisting into a mask of rage.

To Alma, the *Kapo* looked positively homicidal just then and yet, it suddenly occurred to her that she had no fear of this man. On the contrary, he appeared to her as a sort of ancient vengeful spirit in his white attire, who had answered the prayers of the ill-treated, magnificent and awe-inspiring in his righteous wrath.

So, this was the camp Resistance. All of these men, and Miklós with them. She clasped the pianist's hand tighter and looked at him with infinite affection.

With a hand that shook, the SS man reached for the bottle and brought it to his lips. As he took the first few gulps, the *Kapo*'s chant—"Drink"—was picked up by the entire mess hall waiting personnel. They all stood in their white coats and shouted "Drink, drink, drink"—judges and executors craving their justice.

Feeling her feet moving of their own volition, Alma advanced closer and closer to the crowd, her black eyes riveted to the condemned man in its center. This time, Miklós didn't hold her back but followed her instead. Sensing them approach, the white coats separated and included them in their circle. Shoulder to shoulder, they stood, bright-eyed and smiling darkly.

Under the *Kapo*'s heavy gaze, the SS man retched and dropped the bottle. It burst into dozens of sparkling shards. The guard dropped to his knees and keeled forward, but the *Kapo* quickly shoved him in his chest with his boot, flipping him onto his back. He began to choke; he made an attempt to lift his head at least, but the *Kapo* stepped gently and deliberately onto his neck and sneered when the SS man began to clutch at his leg in wild desperation.

"Weidel has his wife waiting for him to bring her food. In the freezing cold, she stands by the wire in her threadbare robe. He is here because he refused to divorce her, his Jewish wife, and chose to follow her into the camp instead. And now, thanks to you, she will wait in vain. And every day is crucial here, when it comes to food. Just like every breath is crucial when you're choking on your own vomit. You know, I consider it poetic justice." He pressed his foot down harder. "She won't eat tonight, but Weidel will tell her about how you died, and she will go to bed full. Full with hope, that one day we shall have our revenge and then you all ought to look out, for we won't be merciful in delivering our justice."

The *Kapo* turned his head slightly to the side. He resembled a child squashing a bug under his heel; only, there was no innocent, childish curiosity in his face. He stared at the SS man with very rational hatred.

Alma roved her gaze around and saw that all of their faces reflected the same exact emotion. She wondered what her face looked like.

At last, after a few last moments of struggle, the SS officer stilled under the *Kapo*'s boot. The waiter removed it from the uniformed man's chest and regarded it with disgust. It was splattered with something vile; he quickly wiped it on the SS man's sleeve. "Nasty business," he muttered to himself.

Something told Alma he didn't mean the vomit on his boot.

"There's no other way around it," the man, whom he called Weidel, shrugged with resignation. "They started the whole rotten affair."

"Shall we call for a medic perhaps?" Urschel inquired, squatting next to the corpse and inspecting it closely. "Or shall we have a smoke first?"

"Let's have a smoke first," the *Kapo* agreed, patting himself for cigarettes. "He is going nowhere, and I could kill for a cigarette now." He suddenly barked out a mirthless, hoarse laughter. "Kill for a cigarette! What do you say to that? This place is making me into a regular comedian." He suddenly kicked the corpse viciously.

"Don't kick him," said one of the waiters, a bespectacled man with a pale, intelligent face. "There shall be marks on the body during the autopsy and Herr Doktor will begin asking questions."

The *Kapo* retreated from the corpse, holding both hands in the air in mock surrender.

"That's Dr. Tellman," Miklós commented into Alma's ear, pointing to the man in glasses. "He was sentenced to hard labor for refusing to perform euthanasia on mentally ill patients. They're all Germans here. Journalists, doctors, lawyers even. Some are communists. Some are simply men with consciences. First-rate men, all of them."

Alma and Miklós still stood over the body of a man those *first-rate men* had just murdered in cold blood and yet somehow that last comment made perfect sense to Alma.

One of the waiters brought Alma's violin case forward, along with her sheet music. "You'd better scram, children. It shall get very hot here very soon. It is my profound conviction that we shall worm our way out of this little predicament, passing it off as an unfortunate accident, but it will be better if we tell them that you were already gone by then, to spare you the interrogation."

Outside, the snow was falling softly. The wind tossed the flurries of snowflakes about. Some melted instantly as soon as they touched the couple's exposed cheeks; some shimmered with dull brilliance atop their wet eyelashes. Shadows loomed all around them, yet they sensed no threat in them that night. The air was clear and crisp, and their hearts were filled with hope and an odd, savage joy. They walked for a time together, Miklós carrying Alma's violin case. They had just witnessed a murder and yet, Alma felt strangely serene. It was wrong and disgusting, but that night, she had no choice. She couldn't force any remorse into herself no matter how much she searched her soul for it.

"Merry Christmas, Alma," Miklós suddenly said. She didn't notice how they reached the gates that separated the men's camp from the women's. Just one more barrack and the guard's booth would come into view. "You do celebrate Christmas, don't you?"

"Yes. I told you, I was baptized a Protestant and, later, a Catholic. I celebrate double. And today, triple."

"Merry Christmas then," he repeated again. "Tonight turned me into a believer as well. If the Christian God decided that enough was enough, I shall believe in him from now on. He made a Christmas miracle. He has proved it to me tonight that He does exist. I think, I actually like the fellow."

Alma grinned lopsidedly. "Do you want to hear a joke?"

"Tonight is just the time for it."

"Jesus' mother was Jewish. According to the Nuremberg Laws, it makes him the first official *Mischling*."

Miklós snorted, looked at Alma incredulously and closed his mouth with his hand to stifle his laughter. Her shoulders were shaking as well, but she wasn't sure whether it was from laughter or tears. The latter found their way out at last, big and heavy. She wiped them with the back of her hand, annoyed, and hid her face in Miklós' shoulder.

Chapter 25

January 1944

The new year came and, with it, relative stability. Not much by the world's standards, but a matter of life and death in the hell of Auschwitz. The joint Sunday concerts given by both Music Blocks gained more and more popularity among the SS. Even Kommandant Liebehenschel attended each one. He was in excellent spirits now; according to Zippy's reports from the camp office, Berlin approved of his new, "soft" approach and even authorized the system of rewards the new *Kommandant* had suggested for the inmates. Sofia scoffed at the news and shook her head in disgust. At last, someone had gotten it through his skull that rewards offered better results than punishment. *It was all the same, though,* she also concluded in resignation. *The new* Kommandant *wouldn't last long. He was too lenient for his higher-ups' liking. Someone would spoil it for him yet, they would all see.*

The words turned out to be prophetic. The news of some upcoming inspection spread around the camp like wildfire. Before long, everything was getting dusted off and put into presentable shape. Even in Alma's barrack, the inmate carpenters showed up and began patching up the leaking roof around the skylight.

"What extravagance!" Zippy regarded their work in amazement. "Shall we truly have a solid roof now? I'll be!"

"Some big shot must be coming then." Sofia was much less enthusiastic. "That never ends well."

"Oh, shut it, will you?" Zippy swung round to face her. "You'll jinx us all!"

"It's not a jinx; it's experience speaking," Sofia countered calmly. "Some official bigwig is coming—expect mass selections."

"Rot!" Zippy snapped.

Sofia merely regarded her with pity and made no further comment.

Alma watched it all with a vague feeling of unease and could only smile helplessly whenever Miklós tried to shrug it off as well.

"We'll worry about it when it happens. And now, let's forget everything and play music. It's the best way to spend Sunday afternoon."

The SS were in exceptionally good humor that day. Even the carpenters were allowed to come down from the roof and sit on the floor, legs crossed, at the very back of the barrack, and enjoy their share of Beethoven. It was them who caused a commotion in the middle of "*Sonata Pathétique*." Alma scowled at the noise; she never tolerated it among her audience and was known to stop the performance, even if it was the SS wardens who produced it. But Miklós, who was presently playing a solo, didn't seem to even notice. Alma's frown deepened when she saw the inmates jumping to their feet and making way for an SS guard and an inmate—or at least someone who appeared to be an inmate—who had just entered the barrack.

"Von Volkmann!" Laks, the men's camp Music Block *Kapo*, muttered incredulously.

The inmate still heard him and strode straight toward the conductor of the men's orchestra to shake his hand. "The very same, you veteran of concert halls!" He was visibly pleased to see Laks and grasped at his palm with great emotion.

Holding her violin by the fingerboard, Alma observed the scene in stunned silence. The inmate, if he was one, was hardly twenty years old and was so handsome, it was impossible to look away from him. He was all sunshine, with golden hair that wasn't shaved but cut by an obviously skilled and expensive barber; forget-me-not eyes with long lashes; sharp cheekbones and a square jawline that belonged on the SS posters for Aryan purity and race. But what astonished Alma the most was the pure adoration with which the present SS members were looking at the newcomer. Even in Hössler's eyes there was a fatherly emotion, as if he were glad to be welcoming a prodigal son back into his embrace.

The young man walked up to him, and Hössler rose to his feet. The two exchanged warm handshakes.

Alma nearly dropped her violin and searched Laks's face, feeling positively at a loss.

"That's our former pianist," Laks whispered to her, barely moving his lips. "The Berlin SS bigwig's son. The local administration is terrified of his father. SS Gruppenführer von Volkmann is their superior and can make things very hot for them if they mistreat his little golden-haired scoundrel while he's in their care."

"Told you he'd be back before long," his fellow orchestra member nudged his leader, making use of the commotion among the SS. "You owe me a pack."

"The bet was that he would return before Christmas. It's January."

"You arch-crook! Trying to weasel your way out of an honest bet?"

"I'm not and you have lost. It's January, so you owe me a pack."

"But he *is* back!"

"I never said he wouldn't be. It's the date that is important."

They were still bickering amongst themselves, but their words didn't register with Alma any longer. She was looking at Miklós in alarm. Oblivious to the news, he was also observing the unraveling scene with a look of surprise on his face, his palms lying flat on his lap.

"Whatever have you gotten yourself involved with this time?" Hössler asked, patting the strapping fellow's chest. "These are not your own clothes, are they?"

"No, they're disinfecting mine. The fellow said he'll bring them to me, deloused, washed, and ironed, tomorrow morning. They gave me this sweater and a suit at the *Kanada*."

"Is it your size?"

"It's fine enough, Herr Hössler. Don't worry about me."

Herr Hössler. Alma exchanged looks with Zippy.

"So, what was it this time?" Hössler repeated, satisfied with the matter of the youngster's clothing.

"Distributing of the antigovernment propaganda in the area of Greater Berlin. Leaflets and oral agitation. Six months hard labor," von Volkmann announced brightly with unmistakable pride in his voice.

"Hard labor, my foot," someone grumbled behind Alma's back. A few knowing chuckles followed.

"You just can't stay away from us, can you?" It was Hauptsturmführer Kramer's turn to shake the young fellow's hand. Kramer was another camp higher-up whom Hössler had brought along to a Sunday concert one day and who had swiftly turned into the orchestra's ardent admirer. He was a career SS officer, with a brutal, square face, the cold eyes of a murderer under heavy brows, a slash of a mouth prone to shouting abuse at the inmates, and an inexplicable love of Chopin.

"Why would I? You have all modern conveniences here. It's a first-rate place to be. Safer than in Berlin, at any rate. Here, the Amis aren't trying to land a bomb on my head each time I venture outside!" von Volkmann finished and burst into careless laughter.

"Communist propaganda?" Hössler inquired, genuinely interested.

"Pacifist. *Lay down your weapons and surrender to the Allies to prevent further unnecessary bloodshed. Release all prisoners of war and concentration camp inmates and reinstate their citizenship and rights. We're all brothers and sisters—*"

Hössler was already waving his hand in front of his face. "That's quite enough; we all get the idea. Your six months' hard labor starts immediately. There's your piano—off you go."

Under Alma's alarmed gaze, Miklós began to rise from his seat. He had been here long enough and knew the deal. The Aryan men were dear guests; he was merely a replaceable Jew. But, much to his astonishment, von Volkmann was already pushing him down by his shoulders in the most courteous manner.

"No, no! You sit, Herr...?"

"Steinberg," Miklós supplied, blinking at the youngster.

"Herr Steinberg. You sit. This is your rightful place. I can't play Beethoven to save my life in any case. I will assist you where I can, if that's agreeable with you." Getting a somewhat wooden nod out of Miklós—just like Alma, he was still stunned by everything that had occurred—von Volkmann turned to Hössler, a bright smile on his face. "Is it all right with you if we play four hands, Herr Hössler?"

From Hössler, a languid wave of the hand.

As such, they let the youngster amuse himself, but eventually their previously hushed murmurs turned into an open discussion.

"What shall we do with the other one?" It was Kramer who posed the question.

"Why, we'll keep them both." Hössler shrugged at his colleague.

To Alma's relief, Mandl nodded her approval with great enthusiasm. She had grown to enjoy Miklós' music just as much as everyone did. After he wrote a short song for her specifically as a New Year's present, the leader of the women's camp officially counted Miklós among her personal favorites.

"We can't keep both." Kramer looked at him. "Eichmann is coming with an inspection. How are you planning to explain two pianists to him?"

"Easily, Herr Kramer!" It was the youngster himself this time. "I'm a lousy pianist and can only play popular songs; no fancy stuff like Herr Steinberg here. The orchestra needs him more than me. Send me to an outside work detail instead. I'm strong. I can work for five."

Kramer barked out a laugh. "An SS Gruppenführer's son, in the outside detail! That shall go down well when he hears of it. Next thing you know, we shall be raking the gravel together with you for that stunt."

Von Volkmann turned to Hössler, but the camp leader would also have none of it. "Forget the outside detail. You're staying in the Music Block and that's the end of it."

"Herr Obersturmführer." Alma heard her own voice as though coming from under the water. Blood was pulsing too loudly in her ears. "What's going to happen to Miklós?"

Not the outside detail. Anything but the outside detail.

For a time, Hössler considered. "We'll transfer him temporarily into the *Kanada*, under Wunsch's charge. The *Kanada* is a good detail. Maybe even better than the Music Block." He gave her a reassuring smile. "His *Ausweis* will be prolonged; he'll still be able to come here and tutor your pianist girl or practice with you for performances."

Alma breathed out in relief. The *Kanada was* a very good detail. She thanked Hössler softly.

The SS had departed first. Next, the men's orchestra began packing their instruments. It was then when von Volkmann had suddenly exploded.

"We ought to do something! This is not right!"

"What's not right, pup?" Laks asked him with amicable indulgence.

"Removing Herr Steinberg from his position simply because he's Jewish! Have you just heard him play Beethoven? Bach? I was sitting next to him; he didn't even look at the sheet music. Played the entire affair with his eyes closed, from memory!" He regarded Miklós with unconcealed admiration.

Miklós stood before the SS General's son, pale with amazement and profoundly touched, and still couldn't quite take it in that the boy addressed him, an inmate and a Jew, *Herr Steinberg* and with a polite, *Sie.*

"He ought to be in the orchestra, not me!" von Volkmann continued with conviction. "He has the talent, the requirements for it. And I ought to be in the outside detail—"

"Let's get going, *outside detail*," Laks mocked him, dealing him a good-natured clap on the shoulder. "The curfew is going into effect soon. You must have lost the habit for it while there, in the capital."

"There's also a curfew in the capital now," von Volkmann announced quietly and through his teeth. "And an order for complete blackout because we're getting bombed by the Amis and the Brits with envious regularity. *All thanks to our Führer*," he spit out the last words—a slogan which had turned into a mockery—with such hatred, it sent a shudder down Alma's back.

The SS were wrong about him all along. He wasn't rebelling against his father and neither was he horsing around with all that German resistance business; he genuinely loathed them, the system they stood for, and, most of all, the madman they followed. All of a sudden, Alma felt a surge of respect, gratitude, and hope at the sight of this Aryan poster child, who chose to stand up for what was right, no matter the consequences.

Laks only looked at him sorrowfully. "I'm sorry about your city. There's nothing to be done about it. And now, let's get moving."

But the young man wouldn't budge. "It's not fair what they're doing."

"Life is not fair."

"Something needs to be done."

"There's nothing to be done. Let's go."

"No."

Suddenly, the SS Gruppenführer's son headed toward the exit near which the carpenters were gathering their instruments, grabbed a hammer, put his palm against the wall and began smashing his own fingers. The inmates froze in their places, their mouths wide open in horror. A few of Alma's girls released frightened shrieks.

Everything was over before they knew it. Von Volkmann turned to face them, holding his hand with bloodied fingers up as some sort of macabre trophy. Tears were streaming down his face—the body's purely physical response, no doubt—but he was smiling brightly nevertheless.

"There. It's all fixed. Now, I can't play at all. They will have to send me to a sorting detail and Herr Steinberg shall stay where he belongs."

"You hot-headed idiot," Laks uttered, his eyes staring wildly at the young man's mangled hand, but his tone was somehow tender and full of some unspoken emotion they all felt but didn't know how to express.

It reminded Alma how her father was escorted out of the Vienna Philharmonic, how a similar young Aryan had instead mocked him as he went. She looked at this one and his brave, noble face, and was suddenly overcome with a profound gratitude for his keeping his humanity when he had all the reason not to.

Chapter 26

February 1944

Day and night, the slamming of the heavy hammers echoed around Birkenau. From the camp office, Zippy brought daily snippets of rumors—about Hungary supposedly shifting its allegiance toward the Allies, about someone important named Eichmann (the name repeated with a measure of fear even by the SS) and his upcoming inspection, about the possibility of the German invasion of its former ally and about the plight of the Hungarian Jews, who would surely be the scapegoats in all that mess and would soon enough find themselves among the camp population.

"It's the second ramp that they must be constructing," Sofia concluded, watching the train tracks crawling closer and closer to their block.

"From what I heard from the wardens, they're planning to transport the entire Hungarian Jewish population here. That's what that Eichmann fellow is rumored to be coming for—to give the SS exact orders about their accommodation. Five hundred thousand people. I wonder where they're going to put them all," Zippy mused, squinting at the inmates.

From where they stood, the construction *Kommando* resembled busy ants forming lines and going about their business as if nothing else mattered. The SS resembled ravens in their black capes—beady-eyed and cawing their orders at them in their harsh, loud voices.

"Those new barracks they're building by the field." Sofia motioned her head toward yet another construction site.

Alma, who stood a bit aside from them, smoking, quickly counted the barracks and shook her head with suspicion. "Those few miserable blocks? They will hardly house fifty thousand; never half a million."

"I imagine they will build some more by the time they begin deporting them," Sofia said, but without conviction in her voice.

Alma took another deep pull on her cigarette. "With the best will in the world, they will house a hundred thousand. Where shall the rest go?" She turned to face the girls.

All three pairs of eyes instinctively shifted to the chimney of the crematorium. Only a very thin fence separated them from it. From its entrance, another group of inmates was constructing a narrow passage framed by the barbed wire. Alma traced their progress with her index finger until it stopped at the point where the new ramp was supposed to be soon standing. She had just opened her mouth—*they'll gas them all, can't you see?*—but then, seeing the growing horror on the girls' faces, thought better of it.

When they marched to the sickbay—it was Tuesday, the music therapy day—they saw three more inmate *Kommandos* unraveling barbed wire from the entrances of three other crematoriums. All led in the same direction—the ramp under construction.

Kommandant Liebehenschel was walking toward them with his hands folded behind his back and eyes trained on the ground as though he didn't wish to see it all. As Alma stopped with her little troop to give him and his aides space, the wind caught their words and threw them in her face.

"...Even all five won't be enough, even if we run them continuously night and day. According to the preliminary data that Eichmann gave us, we'll be getting transports daily. Perhaps it would be wise to put the Little Red House and the Little White House to use as well?"

"Gassing is not the problem; it's the cremation that—"

Alma ordered the girls to start marching even before the grim delegation had passed them. The protocol suddenly didn't matter. She couldn't bear the thought of them hearing it all.

Worst of all, the news seemed to affect Miklós. Alma understood it well enough—it was a damnable business to hear rumors about one's homeland, soon to be trampled by fascist boots and beaten into submission. But there was something different about the manner in which he reacted. Instead of agonizing openly or lamenting the fate of his people, Miklós seemed to retreat more and more into himself. He still appeared in the Music Block to tutor Flora, but his mind was always elsewhere. With a stub of a pencil he begged off Laks, he kept scribbling something in a small notebook he carried with him and didn't even notice the mistakes Flora was making. Alma had a suspicion that whatever he was working on was a matter of paramount importance—for him, at any rate—but thought it rude to pry. In Auschwitz, people coped with their misfortunes each in their own way. She felt she had no right to meddle with that private world of his.

When Alma took him into her room and asked him gently if he needed a few days away from his tutoring responsibilities, he agreed readily, much to her surprise and disappointment. Still, for his sake, she hid it well, smiled at him brightly and told him to take care of himself. He mumbled something incoherent, walked toward the door but, suddenly, as though awakened from a dream, swung round sharply, crossed the room and kissed Alma with infinite passion on her lips. When he pulled away, the pain in his eyes almost tore her own heart in two.

"It won't take long," he promised in a rushed manner. "I'm almost finished. It'll all make sense soon!"

He grasped her hand, kissed it almost reverently, and dropped it just as abruptly before rushing out. Alma felt his fingers on her skin long after he was gone.

*

The next few days turned into pure torment. Alma had to suffer through bleak days that dragged and dragged, suddenly gray and entirely devoid of any hope. The walls of the barrack were there once again, tangible and closing in on her; the barbed wire, the camp—Miklós had shielded her from it all with the sheer power of his music and his presence and his stolen kisses, and now, it was all back once again and tenfold, desolate, alien, and terrifying.

She knew he was alive and well. Every morning a runner from Laks's Music Block brought her short notes scribbled in haste and on scraps of paper, but it was his concern that counted.

... I miss you terribly, Almschi...

... These useless chores are the most despicable thieves of the precious moments I so desperately need. It's quite all right. The nights are still mine for using and I don't need sleep all that much anyway. Just a few more days, Almschi...

... Could you possibly send your kerchief with the runner? I ought to have something of yours; otherwise, I feel I shall go mad from loneliness...

...I had a dream about you last night. When Fredy shook my shoulder to wake me up for the roll call, I smacked him, imagine? He isn't mad; he understood...

Alone in her room, behind the closed door, Alma kissed his handwriting and tucked the notes inside her pillowcase and lay wide awake for endless hours, touching the letters with the tips of her fingers under the pillow, and felt madly loved and profoundly lonely, all at the same time. She knew he wouldn't abandon her for no good reason. It must have been something terribly important, his freedom-fighting affairs perhaps. With such immense pride, he had told her about the connection the camp Resistance made with the Krakow cell; with such fearlessness, he'd admitted that he, himself, was secretly passing documents to the free Polish workers whom the

SS hired for odd jobs around the camp, completely ignorant of the fact that the shrewd Poles were gathering intelligence under their very noses. Alma understood it all too well. She was grateful that he took the time to let her know he was alive and well, but still, she felt his absence much too sharply, like a knife stuck in one's gut. Her pianist was gone and, suddenly, she felt as though the entire world had died.

All at once, Alma couldn't conduct anymore. First thing in the morning, she would grasp her violin by the neck and begin to play it with an unhealthy obsession, just to recapture the same sense of peace and serenity Miklós' hands gave her as they guided hers over the keys of the piano—*just close your eyes. You're not here anymore. This camp doesn't exist. We're on stage*...

Sofia and Zippy begged her to rehearse with them. It was official now; Eichmann was coming next Monday. Eichmann, the dreaded SS official who made it a goal of his life and career to exterminate as many Jews as possible, according to what Zippy had managed to learn about him at the camp office. "He was the latest subject of discussion at the *Schreibstube*," she reported, visibly alarmed. The camp SS higher-ups spoke about his efficiency with a mixture of reverence and admiration. "Not everyone was cut out to supervise. His SS extermination squads shoot entire families for hours on end and smile with satisfaction at the result," they claimed, marveling at Eichmann's nerves of steel. "Not everyone could stomach watching little children fall into a ravine atop their mothers' bodies, nonchalantly brush brain matter and blood off one's overcoat, and head out to dinner with local civilian authorities, eat with great relish and toast a job well done."

To the local SS, Eichmann was an example to aspire to. To the camp population, the Music Block included, he was death personified.

Even Mandl seemed nervous when she stopped by to check on their progress every day—"You ought to play the best you can, you hear me? This is the man who can give special orders without any higher authorization; even Herr Kommandant won't be able to override him!"

Alma heard her and didn't hear her at all. It suddenly didn't matter what that Eichmann fellow would think of them. *The camp didn't exist. She was on stage...*

"Alma, we're all begging you!"

Awakened from her reverie, Alma looked at the intruder in her room. It was Zippy. Her face was stained with tears; the girl whom she had never seen cry before.

"Please, come out. We must rehearse. The entire orchestra depends on you..."

That was the whole trouble. Alma lowered the violin and smiled sadly. Everyone was always dependent on her. Her very first orchestra, then her whole family, then—just her father. For far too many years she had to be strong for someone else, with no one to rely on but herself. Finally, someone had come and promised to share that burden with her, but now, he was gone, and it was as heavy as ever. Alma dragged her palms down her face. She wasn't sure for how long she could go on like this.

But there Zippy stood and there were the girls, much too young to die, and therefore she had no choice but to move, had to go through the motions.

"Let's go." She rose to her feet wearily and followed Zippy out of the room, catching her reflection in the small mirror. Why had no one told her that her hair was growing out with so many grays in it? And what happened to her aristocratic posture her mother was so proud of? Stooped shoulders, a tired old woman, at thirty-seven years old. "You all think you need me, but you don't. You think I don't hear anything, hiding in my room...I hear everything perfectly. You're doing fine on your own."

Zippy stopped and looked her in the eyes. "We do need you. We always will," she said gravely, and Alma felt something catch in her throat.

All this time, she'd believed that she was saving them, but perhaps, it was them who were saving her. Her girls. Her little sparrows. The most wonderful orchestra on earth.

The girl was crying by the fence. She sat much too close to it—Alma could hear the electricity hum when she approached the inmate from the women's camp. Shaved head covered with sores, gray skin smeared with dirt and tears, the rag-like dress of an indistinguishable color—the usual Birkenau business.

Alma knelt in the snow next to her, reached for her bony hand holding a rock. No; a potato.

"Has someone beaten you?" Alma searched the girl's face. There were no visible bruises on it; only infinite suffering. Her entire expression was the picture of it. "Has someone stolen your food?" Alma probed again, regarding the potato doubtfully.

The girl kissed the vegetable, cradled it against her chest and wept even harder, reaching for the wire just over her shoulder. Alma swiftly caught her by the wrist and pulled her away from it and into her lap. The girl scarcely weighed anything; she was all bones—bones everywhere under that dirty sack she was wearing, bones against Alma's chest—a living skeleton who still breathed by some miracle.

All of a sudden, Alma felt ashamed. People died here daily in hundreds and here she was, suffering from an aching heart and carrying her grief about her like some brooding, romantic heroine from a gothic novel.

"If you tell me what happened, perhaps, I shall be able to help," she suggested softly, rocking the girl in her lap like her own mother used to when she was a little girl.

Alma never permitted herself such affections with her orchestra girls—on purpose, not to spoil them with tenderness, for tenderness was extremely dangerous in this death factory. In Auschwitz, tenderness killed. Only the hard types survived, and, more than anything, Alma wished for her girls to come out of here alive. But this girl was already too broken; she had to be, if the wire seemed like the only salvation from whatever tragedy she was living—or dying—through. It was only fair to hold her, so she could feel warmth for the last time.

"There's nothing to be done." The girl's voice was oddly extinguished, full of ash and tears. "He's dead."

Something about those words pricked sharply and painfully at Alma's chest. She felt blood draining from her face. Naturally, the girl meant someone else, someone unfamiliar and nameless, but still . . . How ominous the pause was. Alma could hear herself breathing.

"Who's dead?" Her question was a mere frightened whisper.

"Tadek. My husband. See this?" She brought the potato to Alma's face. It smelled of earth and slightly of rot—a graveyard stench that made Alma recoil. "Every morning, he would throw me one across the fence. A potato and a note tied around it with a string. Only a few words scribbled on it—*keep your chin up, my darling, we shall meet again soon, the war shall soon be over*—but that was enough. Enough to know that he was alive . . . And today, his *Kommando* mate came instead. Came to the fence, threw me this potato, and walked away, wiping his face." Her bloodless lips trembled. "That's how I knew." A ragged breath. A shake of the head. A small smile—a gratitude for Alma's kindness. "You won't help me, but thank you for listening." She enclosed the potato into Alma's hands with finality.

Alma rose to her feet a bit too unsteadily, looked at the girl one last time, but she was already moving toward the fence.

This time, Alma didn't stop her, only walked faster and faster toward her own barrack, until the walk changed to a trot and a trot to a sprint and she couldn't get her breath any longer.

He's dead.

He's dead...

Inside her block, without shedding her coat, she grasped the violin and began to play, as loudly as possible, just to silence the words that kept echoing inside her mind.

There was a knock on her door. Alma went to open it and time itself suddenly stopped. Miklós stood before her, looking like he hadn't slept for weeks, gray-faced and much too thin, but his eyes had never shone brighter.

"I finished," he said, by way of greeting, and pushed a thick stack of papers into Alma's hands.

She regarded them, dumbfounded. It was handwritten sheet music. *Für Alma,* the title read. "What is it?"

"A sonata. For you. I composed it. Beethoven wrote one for Elise and I wrote one for my Alma. I hope it's worthy of your name."

Alma stared at him, speechless. The papers trembled in her hands. She read the first half of the page, heard the music in her head, imagined him playing it for her...

"I know what's going on. They will kill all Hungarians," Miklós said very calmly.

"No, just the new arrivals! You're an essential prisoner. Under Hössler's protection. They won't touch you." She didn't know whom she was trying to convince, Miklós or herself. She only knew that her heart was pounding almost painfully hard with mounting terror at the truth she refused to acknowledge, even to herself, and that the room suddenly felt like a coffin, from which all air had been sucked out.

He smiled at her sorrowfully. "They'll kill all Hungarians," he repeated with quiet resignation. "I am one. Hitler will never forgive Admiral Horthy his betrayal for turning on him and negotiating an armistice with the Allies. A public betrayal, at that; my waiting staff comrades heard all about the Hungarians' desire to switch sides over the makeshift radio they use to learn about the progress of the war. That's the biggest talk of the BBC as of now. Someone will have to pay the price for such treachery. The SS are already gossiping about an upcoming *Aktion* against the Hungarian Jews, but, for now, the Berlin office with that sod Himmler in charge will satisfy itself with offing the ones who are already here, and that's the Family Camp."

He cupped her cheek, regarding her with infinite tenderness.

"My beautiful, brave Alma. I hope you will forgive me for abandoning you in such a manner for the entire week, but I had to make sure I finished it in time before they round us all up. This way, you shall have something left of me, something to remember me by. Now, I shall die happy and in peace. I wrote off the rights for you too; my signature is on the very last page. You will be its rightful owner after you come out of here. You may resell them so that you have at least some money to support yourself for some time. I wrote the addresses of some Hungarian friends and colleagues of mine—they will buy them from you, if it is your wish to sell them. All of them are Aryans, don't fret. They will still be there when you come out."

"You're mad." She pushed the sheet music against his chest. "No, you are absolutely mad."

She was screaming, and was aware of that fact, but couldn't stop herself. It all surged in her at once—the desperation and wild, animalistic fear at the thought of a world in which Miklós Steinberg, a pianist and composer, the man whom she loved so selflessly that she would gladly give her own life just so he would live, didn't exist anymore.

"Take it back at once! I don't want it. He's giving me his last will and testament. I don't want it. It's a bad omen. Very bad luck—you'll jinx us all! Take it back and don't show it to me ever again."

"Alma, be reasonable."

She was struggling with him, but the more she did, the tighter he held her against his chest, the firmer he pressed his bloodless lips against her hair, stroking it, stroking her shoulders shaking with sobs.

"You don't believe in bad luck, Almschi."

"I began to believe in it here. You began believing in the Christian God."

"I was joking. I'm still very much an atheist. But I believe in lawyers and they know my signature—"

"Miklós, just stop . . . If you have a heart, just stop talking."

"All right. I will stop talking. I'll go and play it for you instead; what do you say to that?"

Before she could stop him, he went to the grand piano, pretended to flip back the tails of his invisible concert tailcoat, gave Alma a wink—*do not despair, my love, we still have today*—and began to play.

Alma listened breathlessly and thought that she had never heard anything half as beautiful as that sonata. It was composed in hell, written by an agonized hand and a half-starved mind, and yet, how soft and lyrical the melody was, how hauntingly touching the tone. She understood him just then. She held the pages close to her chest and understood his reasoning, respecting him for making this decision for both of them. He knew that if he died, tears would do little to help things. Money, on the other hand, would help her survive and that was all that was important to him—her survival, her happiness. If the places were switched, she would do the same for him, Alma realized, and felt the beginning of a smile forming on her lips.

"How beautiful."

Alma was the first one to turn to the unfamiliar voice. Her entire orchestra was huddled around the piano, enchanted by Miklós' playing. Now, they quickly scrambled to their instruments at the sight of Lagerführerin Mandl, Obersturmführer Hössler, Dr. Mengele, Hauptsturmführer Kramer, and the inconspicuous officer who stood in front of them, his leather gloves in hand.

"I've never heard it before," he spoke again, in a soft voice and with the same accent as Mandl. If it wasn't for the uniform and the high rank Alma had recognized from his shoulder boards, she would never have classed him with the SS crowd. With his slim build, small stature, hooked nose and glasses, he resembled a typical Jewish lawyer *Der Stürmer* mocked in their periodicals with envious regularity. "Who composed it?"

"I did, Herr Obersturmbannführer," Miklós admitted.

"Name?"

"Miklós Steinberg, Herr Obersturmbannführer."

"Are you a composer?"

"A pianist, mostly. I have only composed a few things in my life."

"What is it called?"

"For Alma."

"Who's Alma?"

"My dead wife," Miklós lied without blinking an eye.

Next to the newcomer, Mandl seemed to breathe out in relief. "Herr Obersturmbannführer, the women's orchestra prepared something special for your visit, with your permission," she began to speak with deference, signing to one of the girls to pull up a chair for their distinguished guest after he showed no visible inclination to take a seat himself.

Could that man, the Jewish lawyer, truly be the dreaded Eichmann who had arrived early? Alma couldn't quite believe it when she raised her baton. On Mandl's recommendation, they had gone through the pains of preparing a Wagner piece for Herr Obersturmbannführer's visit, a pompous, thoroughly German affair that cut Alma's ear with its militaristic grandiosity, but which, she was well aware, the SS considered to be the national anthem of sorts.

Eichmann, if it was indeed him, stood and listened for a few minutes, then nodded curtly, and motioned for her to stop. "Thank you. I've heard enough."

With that, he was gone, the rest of the local SS administration filing after him. Deathly silence descended on the Music Block.

"He hated it," Sofia announced the verdict after that silence had grown unbearable and just about anything would be better than it. "He hated it. We're all licked."

They remained in the same state of petrified stupor for the rest of the day, hardly exchanging two words and awaiting their official death sentence.

Still dazed and much too mentally exhausted to utter a single word of useless encouragement no one would believe at any rate, Alma sat among her girls without movement, staring into nothing, oddly content at the thought that at least they would all die together now—the Family Camp and her Music Block.

Only Miklós displayed the strangest serenity as he brushed the keys of the piano softly and pensively in the corner—a man whose affairs had been settled, who could die in peace now. The eerie, haunting melody he played suited the occasion frighteningly well. As though under a spell, they were coming to terms with the inevitable. It was a ghostly and funereal song that he played, but for some reason, oddly pacifying. Coming from under his marble-white hands, the song of death no longer appeared to frighten. The dark beauty of its eternal peace had dawned on them, settled over the block like a cloud, and granted a few precious moments of longed-for comfort. Miklós played their funeral song, and Alma couldn't be more grateful that he did. Only he could turn mortal dread of the upcoming slaughter into something so utterly beautiful.

As the evening closed in on them, Mandl marched into the barrack. Her face was nearly shining with joy. "Your block is granted one day's leave. One day's leave, in the field, outside the camp. Ober-sturmbannführer Eichmann thought it suitable to reward you for your performance."

"But he hardly heard us perform," Alma heard herself say, still unable to grasp the reality of what Mandl had said.

Mandl only motioned toward Miklós, grinned knowingly—*he had heard him, though*—and walked out.

All at once, the girls threw themselves onto Miklós, hugging him and kissing him in communal, unrestrained madness. But he had eyes only for Alma. He was smiling in embarrassment and looking at her with such profound love and devotion, she felt perfectly at peace once again. He was here, with her, and everything was as it was supposed to be.

Chapter 27

March 1944

Their promised "leave" kept being postponed due to the weather. It snowed something unmerciful the entire week, but then, in the first week of March, the sun suddenly burst through the clouds and began obliterating enemy positions with the determination of the Soviets on the Eastern front. Before long, the knee-deep snowdrifts were gone. Blades of grass shoved through the muddy, wet soil, bright-green and stronger than ever. It was a punishable offense, but the inmates still broke the protocol as they were being led to work through the gates and plucked dandelions just to stare at them in amazement—*were there indeed still flowers in this world then?*—and scarcely felt the blows of the *Kapo*'s baton for breaking the ranks.

An SS man stood in the doors of the Music Block; next to him, Miklós and von Volkmann, grinning from ear to ear.

"Get dressed and line up in front of the barrack for the roll call," the guard commanded. "Leave day. Camp administration orders."

Before they set off, still not quite believing their luck, the kitchen *Kommando* showed up with a cauldron of camp coffee—though, "coffee" was a rather ambitious name for that disgusting brew—and dealt the orchestra girls a double portion instead of the usual ration.

"Double rations? Whoever did you please so much?" the kitchen inmates asked.

"Someone named Eichmann," Alma replied and brought the cup to her lips with a hand that wasn't too steady, as though to wash the taste of that name from her mouth.

He was long gone, yet something ominous remained. It still hung in the air, along with the noise of the hammers from the ramp under construction.

Now, the *Sonderkommando* was also digging something in the field not too far from the two former gas chambers—Alma saw them each time she visited Kitty in the *Kanada*. "Not mass graves again?" Alma had regarded Kitty incredulously. Surely, the fiasco with the former mass graves that all had to be dug up had taught the SS something. But even the always chatty Kitty had clammed up and positively refused to say a thing as to what those pits were. As if to put a stop to such unhealthy curiosity, the SS soon erected tall solid screens that obscured the *Sonderkommando* and their ghastly work from the rest of the camp population.

Mind your own affairs, ladies and gentlemen. Nothing to see here. Something a sleek-talking Hössler would say. Alma had already known how such assurances ended with him.

It took Alma great effort to stop herself from contemplating those sites on that fine spring day. Counted and assembled into the usual five-abreast manner, the orchestra girls marched along the main *Lagerstraße*, accompanied only by their own *Kapo* and a single SS man. At first, no one paid them any heed, but the closer they came near the main gates, the more inmates flocked to the electrified fence, stopping just within inches of it. Shaved-headed, gray-faced apparitions in their tattered robes, they stared at the troop and their lavender kerchiefs in utter disbelief.

No one ever left camp grounds on such strolls. It was something unthinkable, much too un-Auschwitz-like. But here they were, heading out of the gates and to temporary freedom and, all at once, the inmates that were left behind broke into hoarse cheers, pumping their bony fists in the air. It must have cost them considerable effort to exert themselves in such a manner, but they cheered all the same, because finally someone had come out of this place, so it was possible after all. The field behind the barbed wire, the grass, the cows, the farmers, the houses, the cities and the countries; the planet still rotated and they weren't caught forever in this limbo for the sins they didn't know they committed until the Nazis came and read out the list of their nonexistent offenses.

"Shut your beer traps, filthy carcasses," the SS man barked over his shoulder at the inmates half-heartedly but didn't follow through with a general shot in their direction when they didn't quiet down. The sun was warm on his face and the rifle hung much too snugly on his shoulder to bother with.

The ground on the field wasn't turned yet, and the guard inquired of the local farmer as to why not.

"Too early, Herr Kommandant." Every SS man must have been Herr Kommandant to them. It appeared that this particular one didn't mind the promotion.

The farmer was a German, from Saxony, judging by the accent. All of the local Poles had long been removed, to where—no one quite knew. Some speculated that Auschwitz was precisely where they ended up.

"This is a trick the spring is playing on us all," the farmer followed up his explanation and made a sweeping gesture with his arm. "It's a safe bet that all this will be covered with snow in a week or so. Only a complete blockhead would believe that this weather has come to stay. The winter will be back before all these buds and flowers know what hit them. It'll bury them all yet; you'll see how fast it will, Herr Kommandant."

"I believe you," the SS man obliged him with a grin.

Alma stood very still beside him. *Yes, it would bury them all yet. Just a trick, all of it...*

They sat where the SS man had indicated, on a patch of grass that had already worked its way through the ground—a weather anomaly, to be sure. It wasn't a typical Polish spring by any stretch of imagination; that much the farmer was right about. The anomaly, just like them, the camp inmates lounging in the sun with their faces turned toward it—a little troop of sunflowers who soaked it in and pretended not to care one way or the other about what tomorrow would bring.

The farmer's wife soon appeared with a basket that she deposited before the guard. He made a half-hearted show of refusing it, but then accepted it after all and even threw a smoked sausage and a whole homemade bread into Alma's hands. There was a bottle of something peeking from under the linen napkin; catching the SS man's eyes on her, Alma quickly averted hers, pretending not to notice it.

The bread was still warm and smelled like heaven itself. It was far from the type that they were used to consuming. No, this was real bread, kneaded by the woman's hands, baked in an oven until the golden crust had appeared. How deliciously it broke in Alma's hands as she divided it among the girls. They chewed it with purposeful slowness, eyes closed, savoring its delectable, rich taste. The gentlemen that they were, both Miklós and von Volkmann refused theirs.

At least an hour must have passed. The guard had finished the bottle and was snoring evenly, with his hands folded under the back of his head. His rifle lay next to him; in that blinding sunshine, it had lost its menacing look and appeared to be a mere stage prop, just like the SS man himself. Alma looked at him and it occurred to her that he didn't belong here. There was no place for guns and uniforms amid this emerald grass. Nature would reclaim her rightful territory soon enough—by peaceful means, which always won over guns and bombs and heavy artillery in the end. The Germans blasted the earth with their charges; they trampled these dandelions with their hobnailed boots, and yet, every spring without fail, the grass tore through the gunpowder-poisoned ground, the flowers sprung back where bones of the fallen still lay.

It was the world order that the SS man didn't comprehend. Beauty was indestructible. It was the most powerful force on earth and would always be. As he lay there, unsuspecting, those weeds and dandelions weaved around his body; they were half-concealing it already and Alma suddenly realized just how mortal and fragile the guard actually was.

"The end is near," Miklós whispered in her ear, as though reading her thoughts. He sat with his legs framing hers and pulled her close, so she would rest her back against his chest. "Their end."

They both kept studying the sleeping guard in front of them as though he was already a relic of the past. Wishful thinking, to be sure, but that was all they had.

"He is already dead; he's just too thickheaded to realize it. All of them are."

"And what about us?"

"What about us? We shall live forever. Through our music. Every time someone plays a record with your violin concerto, you shall be reborn. Every time the radio plays my piano concerto, I shall live again. We have created something that can't be killed, Almschi. And they, they shall all perish and the very trace of them will be wiped off the face of the earth."

"Do you still believe we shall get out of here?"

"We already have." He laughed softly somewhere in her hair.

"No. You know what I mean."

For some time, he didn't answer. Only when he felt her stiffening against his chest did he kiss her tenderly on her shoulder and say the words he didn't quite believe but which she desperately needed to hear: "We will. Of course, we will. And then we shall tour the whole of Europe with just one suitcase."

"And my violin case."

"And your violin case. I'll buy you a Stradivari as soon as we get paid."

"Just how much do you expect to be paid?" She regarded him with mock-skepticism.

"Millions. We shall become a curiosity, you take my word for it. The Auschwitz musicians. Returning from a place like this is like returning from hell itself. They will come to look at us like someone who had returned from the grave. We'll be very rich and very famous; you'll see."

"Good." She didn't argue with him, only smiled and nestled against his chest. He was a fabulist, to be sure, but he was a brilliant one. She believed him every time he spun such impossible scenarios.

Just then, von Volkmann walked up to them, shielding his face from the sun with the hand that was still in a cast. His nose and cheeks had already acquired a rosy blush from the sun exposure. He must have been dreadfully bored doing nothing at all, loitering about Laks's Music Block for days on end and visiting other privileged details from time to time, so it was only natural that the SS had sent him along with Alma's girls on a little outing of sorts, likely hoping that he'd mention it in his letter to his influential parent. "Am I interrupting?"

"Not at all," they replied together.

He caught on to that and grinned knowingly.

"So, what's the plan, children?" He motioned his golden head toward the sleeping SS man. "Shall we kill him and run toward the Soviet Army? I hear, they're not too far away from here. Approaching Lublin as we speak. The local *Armia Krajowa* is an option too, if you don't fancy the Bolshevists." He laughed before they could come up with a suitable response. "I'm joking. Though, it is my profound conviction that they wouldn't execute me even if I went through with the enterprise." Once again, he contemplated the sleeping man as though sizing him up and the distance to his rifle. "I'm almost tempted to put that theory to the test."

"A splendid idea. You'll get a slap on the wrist and we'll all get shot," Miklós announced.

"There were people who escaped from here, you know."

"We know," Miklós replied tonelessly, his blank face betraying nothing.

The camp Resistance had been in splendid luck lately: the escaped fellow had never been caught and they had got away with murder on Christmas Eve. The waiting staff *Kapo* had made a big show of bursting into the SS infirmary quarters that night, screaming something frightful about *the poor Herr Rottenführer choking to his death, God damn that French brandy, didn't he warn him not to drink too much of the blasted stuff, could they please fetch a doctor right this instant* and some other utterly convincing lies to that extent. Alma remembered very well the look of delight on Miklós' face when he recounted the entire affair: "Can you believe it, they hardly interrogated us at all when they came to the canteen! Dr. Mengele refused to even touch the body, let alone bother with an autopsy. Called the dead SS man a drunken pig who had it coming, signed a document declaring it an accident, and marched off as though nothing had transpired."

Perhaps, it was splendid luck indeed. Perhaps, the freedom fighters had simply grown more professional and therefore dangerous in their techniques.

"They even gave detailed camp plans to the Allied commanders," von Volkmann spoke again, obviously impressed. "I learned about it from my father, days before they arrested me. You should have seen the state they were all in! My father's office was in wild uproar when they learned about the entire affair. Reichsführer Himmler himself gathered them all for an emergency meeting and screamed at them something frightful for permitting such damaging information to escape Auschwitz' walls. Now, the Allies know what they're up to…"

"Fat lot of good it did, from where I'm sitting." It was Sofia who gave her opinion this time.

Von Volkmann went silent. He suddenly seemed upset. "You're right. The Allies' priority is winning the war. Not us."

"Why did you come back?" Miklós voiced the question that everyone must have asked themselves who knew of the von Volkmann family.

At first, the SS General's son made no reply. But then he looked at Miklós with his bright-blue eyes and suddenly announced in a firm voice that sounded both desperate and disgusted for some reason: "Because here, unlike in my family home, I feel free."

Miklós averted his eyes, sorry for having asked. Alma felt for the poor man as well; it was a damned sad business, finding oneself more at home among the camp population, surrounded by so much horror, rather than his own blood-related kin.

The sun was rolling westward, and the guard woke up from his nap just in time for the farmer's wife to appear with yet another basket brimming with goods. This time, even more foodstuffs were thrown in the inmates' direction. They ate, chatting amicably among themselves, and didn't even hear the sound of an approaching car that stopped on the side of the road, not too far from their group.

Instantly ridding himself of the bottle he was nursing, their SS escort leapt to his feet and snapped to attention. Dropping their food as well, Alma's girls rose swiftly from the ground, propelled by sheer camp instinct.

Near the edge of the field, a tall SS officer stood in front of a black Mercedes and observed them in silence. With a wave of the hand, he dismissed their guard and walked up to where Alma, Miklós and von Volkmann were standing. The latter released an annoyed grunt, much to Alma's alarm. The officer snorted with disdain as though he had expected that much, removed his gloves finger by finger, then his cap with the skull and crossbones just above its visor.

Alma stared at his face in amazement. He could have easily been von Volkmann's twin.

"*Herr Sturmbannführer*," von Volkmann greeted him mockingly. "To what do I owe such a dubious pleasure?"

"Still consider yourself witty?"

"I can afford a long tongue. Unlike you, I don't have to watch every word that comes out of my mouth."

Von Volkmann's twin ignored the jab. "Have you had enough yet? Ready to go home to your family?"

Almost twins, but not quite. The smooth, pure beauty of their von Volkmann heritage froze, hardened like plaster on this demented reflection of his. It painted harsh lines along a stubborn mouth that was used to giving orders and having those orders obeyed. It chilled the boyish blue of von Volkmann's eyes to glacial indifference in the SS officer's ones. He was a statue of a man, hard like granite—a mere empty vessel from which someone had pulled out the soul.

"I *am* home, big brother," von Volkmann smiled and gestured with his cast-encased hand toward the orchestra. "And here's my family."

His brother slapped him across the face—with an open palm, a purposeful insult.

Von-Volkmann-with-the-cast-on-his-hand only smiled and offered him his other cheek. Von-Volkmann-the-SS-man obliged him with a second slap, harder this time, actually meaning it.

Von-Volkmann-the-pacifist wiped the blood off his busted lip and laughed in his face. "You can slap me about all you like. It will change nothing. You can drag me by my collar to that Mercedes of yours and bring me home—I'll only embarrass you and Father even more the first chance I get."

"Father has different plans for you. Now that you're of age, you're going to the front, with the *Wehrmacht*."

"No, I'm not. I'll refuse to put on the uniform and to take up the weapon. They will have to ship me back here again, this time on actual pacifism charges, not just for some pitiful leaflets," the younger brother explained amicably.

"Obstinate idiot!"

"One yourself," von Volkmann countered calmly and received another slap.

"Why do you keep acting out?"

"I'm not. I want to be here; what's so difficult to understand about that?"

"Among these filthy Jews?!"

"They're not filthy. We all shower every day and our clothes are being washed weekly."

"Stop speaking to me as though I'm an idiot."

"How else am I to speak to you if you say idiotic things?"

Another blow, and this time with a closed fist that made von Volkmann stumble back a step. He stood a while, holding his nose and letting the blood drip freely onto the grass; then straightened and wiped his face. The smile was back on his face and, for some reason, the sight of it made Sturmbannführer von Volkmann swallow uncomfortably.

"How much I pity you," the younger brother suddenly said.

Sturmbannführer von Volkmann stepped back, alarmed.

"Yes, I pity you. I'm looking at you now and I pity you; do you want to hear why?"

Sturmbannführer von Volkmann looked like he didn't.

"Because you're a slave, big brother. You're a slave and I'm a free man. You're a slave to this uniform—" He caught the lapel of his brother's overcoat; the latter slapped his hand away and took another step back. "To your rank and your office and, what's worst of all, to your beloved Führer. You're chained to it all good and fast, big brother, and you have put those chains on all on your own and now you won't get out of it, oh no! You have chosen to be a slave. You voluntarily gave your oath to the dictator. You surrendered your pride and your voice to him. You have virtually ceased to exist. Now, you're a mere faceless uniform that means nothing to him. Do you not understand it yet? He doesn't care about people. He doesn't care about you. He only cares about himself and he will willingly sacrifice you all in the name of some idiotic idea that had sprung into his demented head. And you will all march to your deaths bleating his slogans—*greatness to Germany!*—the brainless herd that you are. Why are you looking at me in such horror? Because I spoke against your leader or because I spoke the truth that you're too afraid to admit? You're a coward, with your gun and your uniform. A coward and a slave. And I'm a free man and shall always remain such. And now, go. You have no business to be here. This is the land of the free, *Herr Sturmbannführer.*"

Von-Volkmann-the-slave almost ran back to his car. Von-Volkmann-the-free-man stood against the sun and watched him.

Chapter 28

March 8, 1944

Alma began to suspect that something was wrong when Zippy didn't return to the Music Block from the *Schreibstube*. The sense of foreboding grew when SS warden Drexler declared coolly that such was the directive from above and didn't go into details. It turned into outright panic when, after conducting the evening roll call, Drexler and Grese locked the door to the Music Block from the outside with an ominous clang.

Alma flinched; the sound instantly reawaked the memories of the cattle train.

Even Sofia, the camp veteran, looked alarmed. "That can't end well."

Alma heard her whispering—under her breath, so that the girls wouldn't hear.

"Are they bringing the Hungarians?" Violette asked.

Sofia obliterated her with a withering look.

"Have they ever locked you up before?" Alma looked at the former *Kapo* with pleading eyes, hoping for reassurance.

Sofia made no reply, thoroughly avoiding Alma's searching gaze on her.

"They're planning a liquidation, aren't they?" Alma could barely hear her own voice; the blood was pulsing too violently in her ears.

Her friend's silence spoke volumes.

Rushing to the only window in her room, Alma wiped the moisture that had accumulated on it. As suspected, the SS were bustling about in a manner that could only suggest one thing—an *Aktion* was coming. Powerful floodlights had been switched on, contrary to all blackout regulations; they highlighted the guards and the entrance to the crematorium like a stage being readied for some ghastly, grotesque performance. Glued to the glass, Alma watched the *Sonderkommando*—death chamber attendants, as they were dubbed by the camp population—rushing to and fro as the SS shouted their orders at them. Soon, *Sanka* trucks began to arrive in the yard. In the artificial pallid light, the Red Cross on their sides appeared to be bleeding.

The SS rushed to the trucks; tore at the tarpaulin and the tailboards and all at once began yanking the people that huddled inside and clubbing them savagely.

"*Raus, raus, raus!!!* Out everyone, now!"

A woman's hysterical voice, "He's just a child! Don't hurt him!"

Someone elderly, trying to reason with the club-wielding SS, "I am an essential worker—" His explanation ended abruptly.

"We're under the protection of the Red Cross!" A younger male voice; a sharp, surprised yelp—then, silence.

Alma watched as two *Sonderkommando* men dragged someone toward the stairs leading down to the changing room by his legs. The unconscious man—*or was he dead already?*—was dressed in civilian clothing.

They were all dressed in civilian clothing, men and women and children and elderly; it had suddenly dawned on Alma with bone-chilling terror. It was the Family Camp.

Her entire body covered with cold sweat at the ruckus in front of her, she realized why she had never before heard anyone screaming even though the crematorium stood right there, just across the fence from their block. The new arrivals were tricked by Hössler and his speeches; reassured by the signs on the walls—*Shower and disinfection,* written in different languages; lulled into submission by the numbered hooks on which they left their clothes—*Don't forget to memorize the number so you can find your belongings easier after you shower, ladies and gentlemen.* She had seen it with her own eyes.

The new arrivals went willingly to their deaths for they suspected nothing. It was the Family Camp that had to be clubbed and forced down the stairs and into that changing room for they knew what it was. They resisted and protested that they wanted to work, that they were under the protection of the Red Cross, called for Lagerführer Schwarzhuber, who had given them his word of honor that they would be safe under his charge.

The man arrived soon enough; only, he didn't stop the SS guards. Instead, he laughed openly at the Jews and their gullibility. His orderly, Oberscharführer Voss, stepped forward.

"Now, whatever is the matter, you Jews? Your time has come. There is nothing to be done about it. Why make your last moments so unnecessarily distressing for yourselves and your loved ones? Why all this pitiful spectacle now? Show some dignity; get undressed and move on to the next room in orderly fashion, as you should."

The next room. The gas chamber.

Frantically, Alma began searching the crowd for the familiar face. Surely they had transferred Miklós into Laks's Music Block prior to the *Aktion*. Surely, they knew he didn't belong with the rest of the Family Camp. Her cheeks grew hot with shame for being so selfish. Before her eyes, entire families were being led to slaughter and she was searching for only one man amidst them all. But didn't those mothers beg for their children only and not for all of them in general? Grief and fear were selfish emotions; there simply was no way around it.

In a spasm of some violent emotion, Alma burst out of her room and hurled herself against the door padlocked by the wardens, banging on it and slamming into it with her shoulder. As though through a haze, dazed and disoriented, she felt Sofia's arms restraining her, heard the Polish woman's soothing voice assuring her that *he wasn't there, he wasn't there, she shouldn't do anything daft or she would get herself killed for nothing—*

Alma was in front of the window again, eyes searching, palms flat against the glass. Next to Lagerführer Schwarzhuber, Dr. Mengele was now smoking, slender and elegant as always. That reassured Alma somewhat. Still, she took a step back and sized the window up with her eyes. It was very small, but there were no bars or mesh on it and she was thin enough to squeeze through it. Alma made a grab for a chair, but Sofia was there to stop her once again.

The former *Kapo* pulled the chair away from Alma's reach before she could get hold of it. "Oh no, you don't! Do you not see what's happening there? Do you want us all to join them? The SS will oblige you for this stunt!"

"They won't liquidate the entire block. We're essential."

"Ha!" Sofia's laugher came out in the form of a one-syllable, cynical bark. "Look outside. There go your essential inmates. The most privileged ones in the entire camp. Red Cross protection and all that fancy business, my foot. Now, either you get hold of yourself or I'll tie you up with my own kerchief and leave you like that for the rest of the night. I understand your concerns very well, but I have the orchestra to mind. I love you and respect you for what you have done for the girls, but I won't have you jeopardizing their safety."

Alma felt the tears collecting under her chin and only then realized that she was crying. "Sofia, if he's there, I will never forgive you," she sobbed, feeling small and helpless, like a child with the weight of the entire world on her shoulders.

It was ridiculous to blame Sofia for anything, of course; she understood it perfectly well. Sofia understood it too. She gathered Alma into her arms and held her fast and rocked her gently from side to side, repeating her assurances that *everything would be all right tomorrow, she would see for herself.*

Of course, nothing would be all right. More trucks pulled toward the entrance as the SS chased their screaming victims through the door of the crematorium. Soon, the familiar orange shadows began to dance on the floorboards of Alma's room. The ovens were working. The first batch of inmates had been gassed.

A sickly-sweet odor seeped through the cracks in the planks of the Music Block's walls; it hung like death over the room, clung to Alma with its sickening embrace. Death, death everywhere. She was inhaling it, it stung her throat, her eyes, her very soul, obliterating everything in her, destroying the last defenses, turning blood into acid. Inside her chest, her heart was bleeding itself white.

Good. Let her die right now; let her take her last breath along with him, no matter the distance between them. It would be the easy way out. It was bad enough that Sofia's arms were around her, reminding her of the arms the touch of which she would never feel again.

They were now sitting on Alma's bed. A few times, driven by impulse, Alma made an anguished move to get up and go to the window, but Sofia held her tight.

"What's the use? It's torture, watching them all, regular torture…"

But even if they couldn't see them, they could hear them well enough—the wails of the children and the weeping of their mothers, the indignant demands of their husbands and the pleas of their elders—all of them drowned out by the mad howls of the SS dogs and the vicious bellowing of their uniformed handlers.

"We want to work. Herr Lagerführer, tell them; we're all very good workers! Put us to the outside detail, you'll see how well we can work!"

"Mama! Mama!!" Like razors, children's high-pitched cries split the night's veins open. The little gnomes, whom Hössler was feeding candy for their marvelous *Snow White* performance, were being torn away from their mothers' arms on his orders.

Every breath a painful struggle, Alma clawed into Sofia's shoulders. It was all too much to bear. She almost wished she had never visited the Family Camp, never met all those people; it would have been easier to live through this all had she not known them personally, the proud, brave people who mocked, with wonderful derision, the feared German leader himself.

But most of all, she wished she had never heard Miklós' words. *I think I love you, Almschi*. But he had said those words and, from that moment on, she was connected to him by an invisible and yet almost tangible cord, and now, if he should perish, she would have no choice but to follow; she realized it with harrowing clarity.

Outside, the Nazi orgy of destruction was still raging.

"Get inside, you bloody shit! Inside, you shit-Jews. Make it snappy before I help you find your legs."

"Herr Doktor, tell them I am exempt! I'm pregnant, Herr Doktor! You ordered them to give me milk in addition to my rations because I'm pregnant! Herr Doktor, I'm right here."

Something in that woman's words made Alma go very still in Sofia's arms. "Go and see if he pulled her out of the line." Her voice sounded oddly soft.

"What?"

"That pregnant woman. Go and see if Mengele pulled her out of the line."

Sofia rose to her feet with great reluctance. She stood by the window silently for a time, while Alma stared at the orange shadows slithering along the floorboards like great deadly serpents.

"I don't see any pregnant women," Sofia spoke at last.

"Do you see Mengele?"

"Yes."

"What is he doing?"

"Just standing there with Voss and Schwarzhuber."

Alma nodded slowly to herself. All light seemed to have gone out of her eyes. They stared, black and empty, into a void, unseeing and already dead.

"You have cheated us!" a woman shrieked outside. She had nothing else to lose. "But your Hitler will lose the war! Then will come the hour of revenge. Then you will have to pay for everything, murderers!"

A shot rang out. Suddenly, in the silence that followed, someone began to sing. Alma recognized the former Czechoslovak national anthem.

The SS must have tried to stifle such an unorthodox form of protest, for the very first voice had died down very quickly, but now more had picked up where the first man left off. It was coming from the underground, from the changing room and the gas chamber into which they were being herded, deep and sonorous. It rose above the enraged shouts of the SS and spread over the camp, a powerful reminder of the inmates' unbroken will.

From the darkness of the barrack, more voices joined in. Alma's girls were signing, joining the revolt. Alma stood up. Her legs weren't too steady, but her hands were when she took her violin from its case. She brought it to her shoulder and looked at Sofia.

"I know he's there. I know he's singing with them now. I want him to know that I hear. That we all hear."

She closed her eyes and began to play—for Miklós, her fearless freedom fighter; for the brave little gnomes; for Fredy Hirsh, their guardian angel; for two Great War veterans who mocked Hitler himself, and for everyone who watched them and laughed when they did so.

The Family Camp inmates must indeed have heard the first few notes of her violin. Revitalized by its support, their voices grew louder, more condemning, more defiant, more deafening. Behind the wall, Flora slammed the piano keys with righteous anger. She wasn't singing the anthem along with the others; she was screaming it and, oddly enough, it fitted the occasion just fine. Before long, the entire orchestra was playing with the feeling that was always absent when they played for the SS. They were playing the farewell song.

Chapter 29

Alma sat in Maria Mandl's office, where Zippy had personally escorted her.

Alma felt infinitely sorry for her poor messenger—her eyes rimmed with red, Zippy hadn't stopped apologizing to her friend for not being able to warn her, for failing to find a way... "Mala and I, we overheard Schwarzhuber's conversation with Berlin when he discussed the upcoming liquidation... Mala, she had already conjured up the plan—where to run first, whom to warn, how to turn the liquidation into an uprising. She knows women from satellite camps who smuggle gunpowder into Birkenau, for the Resistance. The *Sonderkommando* have weapons; they also store makeshift grenades right in the crematoriums. They would have helped; Mala was certain of it..." Zippy's voice had trailed off, full of tears. She had stood before Alma, miserable, her shoulders stooped and quivering with sobs. "But Schwarzhuber realized that we heard it all when he exited the office. They locked us both there for the rest of the day and night, so we wouldn't be able to warn anyone... Will you forgive me?"

Alma had tried to smile at the girl and tell her that she had nothing to forgive her for, but the words wouldn't come. The smile, that was something beyond her power entirely. Miklós' death the night before had drained her entirely; the official confirmation of it came in the form of a dull pain at the place where her heart used to be. All that was left of it was a mere broken husk, unable to feel anything any longer.

Mandl had met them, uncharacteristically soft-spoken and visibly uncomfortable. She had asked Alma to sit. Alma had done so, without a word, without looking at the camp leader.

"Helen, you may go." She even called Zippy by her first name instead of the usual, *Spitzer*. The other girl remained in the office, by the file cabinet. "Mala, you too. No, actually, wait. Bring us coffee."

Ordinarily, such an order would amaze Alma. Now, she just sat and stared apathetically at the potted geranium on the windowsill.

Mandl seated herself opposite her, shifted a few times in the chair. There was a long pause.

Mandl was visibly relieved to see Mala bearing a tray with coffee. "Ah, there you are! I had begun to think that you had lost your way."

Mala did not once look at Alma, her eyes fixed on the silver tray. She stood next to Alma's shoulder perfectly silent, and yet, there was such profound sorrow in her entire posture, her head bowed as though in mourning, that even Mandl felt it, and averted her eyes swiftly in shame. The accusation in that silent stance of the inmate must have stung the camp leader like a red-hot branding iron and now, there was no ridding of the mark. *Murderer.*

"Just put it down and go. Go! I can do everything myself. No need to loiter here." Mandl busied herself with organizing the cups on the table fussily; picked up a creamer and searched Alma's face. "Cream?"

When Alma didn't answer, she put it down as noiselessly as possible.

"Wise choice. We both need something stronger today." Mandl produced a flask, gave Alma a conspirator's grin, and generously poured rich amber liquid into the cup. "Drink."

Alma didn't budge. It wasn't a deliberate statement with the intent to insult or anything of that sort; she simply didn't have the strength to move her arms. The walk here had taken too much out of her. No, not the walk; Zippy's words. They reminded—

"I understand that you are upset. I'm upset myself, believe me. You know how much I liked him. We would never have done it intentionally. It was an honest mistake; you have my word of honor. He wasn't on the list. Here, look for yourself." Mandl pushed some useless paper with names and numbers on it toward Alma, which Alma also ignored. "It's just they were liquidating the entire Family Camp, and he was the only one out of the entire orchestra who lived there, God only knows why."

"He knew people there. Fellow musicians. From before." Alma barely recognized her own voice. It was hoarse, sounded strangled.

"Both Obersturmführer Hössler and I offered to transfer him to Laks's Music Block permanently, but he didn't want to."

"I know. Thank you for allowing him to stay in the Family Camp. He was very happy there."

"I don't understand why he didn't identify himself when they were being transported…or led to…Obersturmführer Hössler wasn't there yesterday, but Dr. Mengele was. He would have pulled him out of the line at once."

Would he? Alma finally gathered enough strength to take the cup and took a big gulp. As soon as she put it down, Mandl refilled it with coffee and more cognac.

"Maybe he wanted to go with them. Patriotism and all," Mandl mused out loud, meanwhile. "One of the *Sonderkommando* men also went into the gas chamber along with his compatriots, just to die with them, imagine that? Good thing the inmates had good conscience to pull him out from behind the column where he was hiding and put him before his SS supervisors. They gave him a couple of slaps for getting such an idea into his head and sent him upstairs, back to the ovens, but what I'm trying to say is, they do strange things sometimes, even privileged inmates. You know the *Sonderkommando*; they live better than anyone there, in their crematoriums. Separate bunks for all, mattresses and pillows, food and alcohol in abundance. You saw how hulky they all are?" She shook her head in amazement. "And that one fellow still went inside."

Did Mandl really think that feather pillows and food in abundance somehow made up for the fact that they had to burn humanity on the SS men's orders day and night? Alma took another big gulp from her cup; remembered the Limoges one that was still standing on her table, back in her room, and felt her stomach contracting with almost physical pain.

"He simply couldn't take it anymore," Mandl continued, oblivious to Alma's anguished state. She didn't clarify if she meant the *Sonderkommando* fellow or—

Alma pressed her teeth so tightly together, she heard them grinding against each other. She still couldn't say his name, even in her mind. Wouldn't be able to, for a very long time. It flooded her chest with agony and her eyes with tears that washed out Mandl's image at once.

The camp leader's swimming image reached across the table to pour more cognac into her cup, this time no coffee, pure liquor.

"Do you need anything?" Mandl sounded almost sincerely compassionate.

Alma forced herself to look at the SS woman. "May I get a black dress from the *Kanada*?"

Mandl appeared relieved. "Of course! What a silly question to ask. Go straight from here if you like and tell them I allowed you to take five black dresses."

"Thank you, Lagerführerin."

"Anything else?"

Alma considered. "Your word that nothing will happen to my girls."

"You have it. As long as I'm in charge of the women's camp, nothing shall happen to them."

"Thank you," Alma repeated, much calmer this time. Her affairs had been settled. There was only one thing left to see to.

"It was an honest mistake," Mandl said. "Truly."

Alma nodded. Mandl was saying something else, but her words didn't register any longer. She was considering how many vials of morphine one potassium cyanide vial would cost on the *Kanada* market.

*

Appell. The block, unpleasantly silent. Alma, lining up her girls for the roll call, as was their daily custom. Black dress, black eyes, expressionless and empty, black poison coursing through her thoughts. She hadn't spoken to anyone since—neither did she cry. Only went through the necessary daily motions of camp life like an automaton, already winding down, ready to expire any moment now.

"Bizarre, isn't it?" Even her voice displayed a chilling lack of feeling. The girls started at the sound of it. "The entire camp has just been gassed, and yet, life goes on. All of those people perished, and we shall be playing music as though nothing had transpired." She snorted softly with laughter that was cynical and much too cold and reached out for Zippy's morning report.

From the first row, Sofia was watching her in open alarm. It went against all laws of nature, such frightening apathy, such a lethargic state. But what worried Sofia the most was the air of unnerving serenity that Alma carried about herself like a dark mantle, as though she had set her mind on something and only the promise of that something got her through the days. The violinist's eyes were so utterly devoid of any remnants of life, not even tears could flow out of them to mourn her loss. To Sofia, it was the first warning sign, the most frightening one. Besides Alma, only the camp *Muselmänner* had the same haunted look about them right before they succumbed to their fate. The *Muselmänner*, emaciated shadows from the outside details, who chose death over their daily struggle, for death suddenly appeared to be a much better option. They too never cried. They simply possessed no strength to care about anything any longer.

Rapportführerin Drexler walked in, accompanied by Grese. Alma greeted the wardens with the usual salute and handed Drexler the report, looking her square in the eyes. They turned out to be hazel, with specks of yellow and brown in them. With fascinating calmness, Alma continued to study the eyes of the warden who shot any inmate that dared to raise their gaze at her.

Drexler's hand reached for the holster and paused there. Alma followed its progress with disturbing indifference.

At last, Drexler found her voice: "Have you forgotten your place, what?!"

From Alma, the same blank look.

"Answer when your Rapportführerin addresses you!"

Alma kept staring silently.

"Make no mistake, I'll dispatch you where you stand, you insolent sow."

Not a muscle moved on Alma's face, only a faint shadow of relief passed fleetingly through her eyes.

Drexler's hand flew up, preparing for a slap; her lieutenant, Grese, caught her wrist mid-air, against all regulations. She whispered something softly and urgently in Drexler's ear, something about Mandl and Hössler and Mengele as well, and the entire block watched in amazement as one of the most feared wardens lowered her hand and took a step back.

"You won't last here long at any rate," Drexler muttered spitefully and with great hatred and snatched the report from Alma's lifeless hands.

A dark grin twisted the violinist's features. "From your lips to God's ears, *Rapportführerin*."

For an instant, Drexler appeared unnerved by such a response. "Dumb Jewish bitch," she grumbled under her breath and stalked off, forgetting to count the musicians.

From the swamps, the fog was rolling in silver waves. Alma felt the dampness creep into the block through the door left open by Drexler, who had beat such a hasty retreat. Once again, she had looked death in the eyes, and once again, it was death that had averted its gaze first. Alma stood and stared after it, disappointed.

*

In the evening, Alma called Zippy into her private quarters. Instead of the lamp, a single candle was burning on the table. All around the room, shadows loomed, silent and mournful. Surrounded by them, Alma's face looked extinguished, entirely devoid of life.

"Here. I want you to have it." She handed Zippy a tight roll of sheet music she could no longer bear having near. The very presence of it was a painful reminder of the grim reality, of the fact that the man who had composed it, would never play it again. Having it by her side had turned into pure torture. Oblivion was the only solution to get through the days, until she could find a way to be reunited with the one without whom the world had gone completely silent. "I know that you'll put it to good use once you get out of here."

As soon as Zippy saw the title—*Für Alma* by Miklós Steinberg— she began shaking her head, pushing the sonata back into Alma's hands.

Alma regarded her with sympathy but refused to take it back.

"I know." Alma's colorless, dry lips pulled to a sad, pitying smile. In the dull light of the room, her skin had a ghostly pallor to it. Under her eyes, dark half-moons lay. "It's a damned swinish thing to do, to hand someone your last will and testament in such a manner. I told him that much when he gave it to me, but I took it all the same, because rejecting a condemned person their last wish is also a damned swinish thing to do. When someone dies, it's always much more difficult for their loved ones. The person who is about to die, they know that their suffering is about to end and they're at peace. It's the loved ones who have to live with that loss, with that unspeakable tragedy in their hearts for a long time after." She paused, once again lost in her memories. Outside the window, just over the crematorium's chimney, a pallid slice of a moon clung to a single cloud. "He knew that he would die soon."

Just like Alma knew that she would; Zippy saw it in the violinist's eyes—dark and impenetrable, two bottomless wells—and choked with emotion. "Almschi…"

"I hope you will find it in yourself to forgive me for burdening you with this responsibility, but I have little choice," Alma continued.

She pressed her temple against the wall and began to play with the candle's flame, putting her fingers through it in an oddly hypnotic gesture—right to left, left to right. Zippy watched her fingers closely, wondered if the violinist felt any pain and suddenly discovered that she didn't wish to know the answer. Perhaps, Alma no longer felt anything at all. Perhaps, she did, and was tormenting herself on purpose, for the physical pain provided at least some sort of distraction from the utter devastation she so carefully hid inside.

"Else, when I'm gone, it will end in some undeserving hands and the world shall lose it forever. And it's such a beautiful piece." There was tenderness in Alma's voice. Her face was very pale and very still.

"It is a beautiful piece. But why don't *you* put it to good use…" Zippy's voice betrayed her; trailed off. Next, the tears came. Alma's ghostly shape was swimming in them, slowly dissolving into nothing, along with the walls surrounding them, along with the table and Alma's violin case and a small vial lying next to it. *It is only morphine,* Zippy repeated to herself with some desperate obstinacy. *Only morphine. To help Alma sleep.*

In a surge of emotion, Zippy grasped Alma's thin, blue-veined hand and pressed it against her cheek. It lay against her skin, lifeless and cold, as though already belonging to a corpse, only the fingers were warm and smelled faintly of fire. But that warmth was artificial, short-lived. It was gone before long and Alma's hand had grown colder than ever.

They killed Miklós, but left Alma mortally wounded, Zippy realized with sudden painful clarity. One would never recover from such a blow.

With utmost gentleness, Zippy lowered the violinist's hand back onto the rough surface of the table and left the room and, in it, Alma to her world of shadows.

Epilogue

April 1944

The Music Block stood silent for the first time since its opening in the spring of 1943. The entire front wall of it was flooded with wreaths. In the center, a single chair stood, draped in black. On it, Alma's violin and a conductor's baton lay. Sofia asked Lagerführerin Mandl for Alma's picture to place beside the instruments, but it turned out, the SS hadn't taken any for their files starting with mid-42. As though in apology for that, the camp administration permitted the girls to pay their respects to Alma's body in the sickbay where she had passed away. Dr. Mancy did everything possible to save her. Dr. Mengele was summoned; he came astonishingly fast, armed with his medical case, but Alma was already taking her last breath. She died with a smile on her face, looking somewhere past the faces crowding over her bed, as though finally recognizing someone familiar she hadn't seen in a while.

Dr. Mancy helped Zippy dress Alma's body in her favorite black dress. Sofia helped brush Alma's hair until it lay in soft waves around her pale, peaceful face.

First, the musicians came to the sickbay where Alma's body was laid out, both from Auschwitz and Birkenau. His cap crushed in his hands, Laks stood for a long time before the simple plywood coffin the *Sonderkommando* quickly made on Hössler's orders—perhaps, the first one in the camp's history.

Hössler himself sat on a chair in the corner, bent over his folded hands with his head hanging so low, no one could see his face. He paid no heed to the inmates or the SS men who snapped to attention at the sight of the shoulder boards on his stooped shoulders. His Alsatian was whining sorrowfully at his feet.

Von Volkmann wept openly on his knees before the coffin. The fingers of his good hand were clasping at the dead violinist's palms, which appeared to be made out of marble, with the net of bluish veins under the white skin, and repeated in a broken voice only one word—*murderers*...

Mandl brought flowers and lay them at Alma's feet, before placing a hand on Alma's forehead. The camp leader's face was powdered deathly white, but even all those layers of makeup didn't conceal the red tip of her nose or her puffy eyes.

In the corner, almost entirely obscured from sight, Rabbi Dayen stood, his lips moving ever so slightly as he whispered the words of the mourner's prayer. It mattered not that the woman he was praying for belonged to a different faith or that it was the deceased's family's duty to recite the Kaddish; he still prayed as he always did, for there was no one else around to mourn all of these people.

When the *Sonderkommando* men came to retrieve the body the next morning, Hössler came very close to their leader, Voss.

"You'll cremate her as she is, dress, shoes and all, in this coffin. Under no circumstance are you to disturb the body in any way; do you understand?"

"*Jawohl*, Herr Obersturmführer!"

"And you shall put her on that gurney alone. No other bodies next to her."

"*Jawohl*."

"If I find out that you disobeyed me..." Hössler's voice descended into a barely audible, ominous whisper that didn't promise anything good.

"Your instructions are perfectly clear, Herr Obersturmführer."

In the end, Hössler decided to go to the crematorium himself and only left after he saw it with his own eyes that his orders had been followed precisely.

The procession of the inmates continued well into the following day, this time to the Music Block. The SS wardens and guards mixed with them—the oddest spectacle that would leave even Sofia, the camp veteran who had seen it all, speechless. Auschwitz didn't hold memorial services for its inmates. It was simply unheard of and yet, here they were, filing in, silent and respectful, the victims and the executioners alike, pausing reverently before that chair draped in black. Somehow, during her very short stay in Auschwitz, she'd managed to touch them all, the one whom they addressed respectfully as Frau Alma. The violinist of Auschwitz. The woman who had left on her own terms, and they couldn't help but admire her for it.

At last, when the night drew in, the Angel of Death himself made an appearance. The room hushed itself at once as he walked toward the chair wreathed in flowers and black drapes. In front of it, he took off his uniform cap, straightened, and clicked his heels in salute before bowing his head.

"In memoriam."

It was long past curfew. The night hung, velvet and mild, over the Music Block. Inside the stove, the fire crackled softly, highlighting pale, pensive faces gathered around it. Only a few of the girls slept soundly in their beds. Most sat, against all regulations, in a semicircle around the fire, craving its warmth—children orphaned for the second time.

Zippy's head rested on Sofia's shoulder. In her hands, the former *Kapo* held Alma's lavender kerchief.

"I still can't believe that she's gone," Sofia spoke in a voice that seemed robbed of all its strength. She brought the kerchief to her face and inhaled deeply. "Lilacs." A faint smile on her face wavered in the uncertain light of the stove. "There's still a piece of her favorite soap left," she told Zippy. "You should have it. She would love for you to have it."

Zippy made no reply; only wiped her face subtly with the back of her hand.

"I wouldn't be here if it weren't for her."

Sofia turned to the voice with a familiar French accent. Violette-from-Paris was biting her lips to stop them from quivering.

"I would have never survived if she didn't give me a chance," the French violinist repeated with suppressed emotion.

"Forgive me, please, for rejecting you when you first came to the audition," Sofia began to apologize, but Violette only waved a hand in front of her face as though to indicate that it mattered not, that she held no grudge against the former *Kapo*.

"You had good reason for it. I played atrociously." Violette laughed through the tears.

Sofia tried to smile but felt her own face twisting into a painful grimace as well.

"Frau Alma only took me because she felt sorry for me. Hélène begged her to give me a chance." Violette glanced at her freight-train friend, who was presently rubbing her back. Hélène's face was wet with tears as well. "Frau Alma did; it was Kálmán, *Countess Maritza*, I still remember it as if it only happened yesterday. How did she manage not to cringe openly when I played it for her!" Another peal of strangled laughter; another round of suppressed sobs from the orchestra girls. "And still, she took me on a one-week trial. I had to walk every single morning from my block to the Music Block and practice with the orchestra. I remember, on the third day I think, someone from my block stole my galoshes and I had to walk barefoot, and it was so cold that morning! Cold and muddy and wet…"

"It was. And I didn't allow you inside the block until you washed your feet at the door." Sofia reached out for Violette's hand and Violette took it in hers, squeezing it tightly. "Forgive me."

Once again, the violinist shook her head. "You were only doing your block elder's duty."

"I remember how you began to cry."

"I cried because my feet were so cold and because I was upset that someone stole my footwear, not because of you," Violette assured her. "Without footwear, your days are numbered in a regular block. How was I to get a new pair? I knew no one in my own block; not a soul cared about my well-being. So I sat here and cried, and Frau Alma came out and asked what the matter was. After I told her, she said she'd take me on a permanent basis." Violette released a ragged breath. "That was the first time she saved me." It was still difficult to talk about it. She passed her hand over her forehead, forcing her emotions under control. "The second was when I got sick with typhus. Dr. Mengele would have sent all of us sick girls to the gas, if it weren't for her."

"He was ready to send us to the gas even after we recovered, just because we were so weak," Flora spoke. Her voice was hoarse with tears. "If Frau Alma didn't intervene on our behalf, he would have done just that." For a few moments, she was silent. "She saved me too, from the Quarantine Block. I had all but given up on life. We were locked there for over a month, with almost no food or even water. I was so weak, I sincerely thought I had four or five days to live. And then Frau Alma came and asked if anyone played the accordion. I told her that I knew how to play the piano, but she still took me. I will never forget the day when an SS man unlocked the door and called out my name." She nodded several times to herself and finished very quietly and gravely, "she saved my life."

"She pulled me right out of the Sauna," Anita said, her eyes big and mournful against the gathering shadows. "I stood there with a toothbrush in my hand—I have not the faintest idea who gave it to me or why—stood and waited for the gas to come out of those showerheads and kill us all. And then the doors suddenly opened, and she walked in, tall and elegant in her camel-hair coat and headscarf, like a movie star, and demanded if Anita Lasker, the cellist, was inside. When I first saw her, I thought she must be the SS or someone important. And she took me very gently by my hand and said, 'It's all over now, Anita. You shall come with me and play cello in my Music Block. All over now, don't fret. I will protect you.'" She drew her eyes up to the ceiling and blinked rapidly a few times. "And she did," she managed at last, but the tears still spilled down her cheeks, round and heavy like pearls.

"I could scarcely play at all, but instead of turning me away, she made me into a runner and saved my life," another voice from the back joined in.

"I couldn't play either, and she made me a copyist, even though she already had a dozen of them."

"My fingers were crippled with arthritis and she managed to persuade Hössler that I was a violin virtuoso and would play marvelously once I recovered. He ordered me double rations, so I would recover faster."

"She split her rations with me when I just arrived at the block and was so weak, I would faint each time I would rise from my chair too swiftly."

"She organized a warm cardigan for me from the *Kanada*."

"She allowed me to sleep in her room when I learned that my mother had died. She held me all night in her arms and sang me some lullabies. If I didn't have her then, I think I would have gone to the wire. The only thing she asked of me was to be silent about it. She wanted to keep a stern face before the others at all times. She didn't want to mother us too much, so it wouldn't weaken us. Here, weakness kills. Frau Alma knew it. That's why she was so demanding of us—to make sure that we would be able to survive if something happened to her."

"She made Mandl, Mengele, and Hössler give her their word that the orchestra shall remain an essential detail for as long as they're in charge," Zippy supplied suddenly. "Made them swear that there will be no selections for us for as long as this blasted camp stands."

"Do you think they shall keep it?" Sofia turned to look at her.

"They will," Zippy replied with conviction. "There are few sacred matters for the SS, but, fortunately for us, Alma was one such sacred matter for them. It will be the most swinish thing to do to break that promise to her. I can't quite explain it, but... They will keep it. You all shall see. We'll all come out of here alive, and when we walk through those gates, I want you all to remember the name of the woman who made it possible, for as long as you live. I want you to remember her name and I want you to tell your children and your grandchildren that it's Alma Rosé, the Birkenau orchestra conductor, whom they owe their lives to as well. And, in turn, I promise that I—" her hand found the board that had been recently replaced by her own, Zippy's hand, "will make sure that she lives forever. Through music, just as she would have wanted." Her fingers stroked the wood almost with affection.

Under the board, in the aluminum box, wrapped in several layers of cellophane, Miklós Steinberg's *Für Alma* was concealed—until liberation day, until it was safe to carry it out through those cursed gates of the Auschwitz hell and show the entire world that not even the SS's hobnailed boots could trample human spirit; that love would always triumph over hatred; that music was stronger than death itself.

January 1945

The real, physical liberation was the furthest thing from the idealized affair Zippy used to dream of for years on end. There was no pomp, no flowers, no press, no overjoyed heads of states welcoming them back to freedom with open arms. The only camera crews were Soviet and even they weren't really interested in ordinary inmates; they were too busy filming Mengele's twins being led out through the gates by the Polish Red Cross nurses and Soviet doctors. Herr Doktor himself was, naturally, nowhere to be found.

Just like the rest of the SS, Dr. Mengele had fled as soon as the thunder of the Red Army's artillery crept dangerously close to the camp's borders. His colleagues followed suit soon enough, but only after they had burned all documentation that could have been found—first in the crematorium ovens and then, right in the open pyres in front of their headquarters. Zippy knew it firsthand; a former camp administration worker, she helped destroy the evidence. Choking with impotent fury, hiding whatever precious few papers she could, but she did as she was told. It was the last time they ordered her to do something.

Whatever she had managed to salvage, Zippy handed to a senior Soviet officer from a political department of sorts. *SMERSH* or whatever his section was called; Zippy didn't remember and cared even less.

Comrade Kommissar perused the papers, nodded gravely, shook her hand, and told her not to worry. "We'll string them all up soon enough," he promised through an interpreter. "And now, go home, *grazhdanochka*. I bet you've seen enough of this place."

Zippy smiled at the strange Soviet term of address, *citizen*. Smiled and felt her lips quivering in a sudden surge of gratitude and tears. A citizen. Not an inmate any longer. She threw her arms around the astounded commissar and gave him a resounding kiss right on his razor-sharp cheekbone.

"*Ladno, ladno,*" enough, enough, he was muttering, visibly embarrassed, wiping his cheek with the back of his palm, but grinning all the same, just like the interpreter in the corner, just like Zippy herself.

As soon as they stepped through the gates of Auschwitz, all rules were suddenly cancelled for these stern-faced men. Before long, the battle-hardened warriors were crying along with inmates who hugged them, kissed their faces, hands, uniforms; crying and kissing the tops of children's heads and distributing whatever rations they had on themselves and shouting for *those bastards manning the field kitchen to hurry the hell up, people here are all starved to near death!*

They had already liberated Majdanek, the Soviet soldiers explained in their hoarse, tear-stained voices. But they were not prepared to see the scale of annihilation that they encountered here, in Auschwitz.

The camera crew was finished with Mengele's children. The gates were no longer occupied. Now, Zippy could finally walk through them. Alone. The rest of the orchestra had been evacuated to an unknown destination in October 1944, accompanied by their camp leader, Mandl—another camp, deep within German territory, as was Zippy's suspicion. Only Zippy herself was allowed to stay and only due to her position in the camp administration.

She made the first uncertain step toward freedom. In a suitcase she had recovered from the surviving *Kanada* barrack—the Nazis tried to burn even those, along with the crematoriums, along with everything that could testify to the extent of the atrocities committed—she carried generous Soviet-provided rations, a temporary paper stating her name and place of liberation, and a tight roll of sheet music still wrapped in cellophane.

Birkenau had virtually ceased to exist by January of 1945; most of the inmates, who hadn't been evacuated, had all been transferred to the *Stammlager*—the main camp, Auschwitz. But Zippy made it her business to recover the piece she kept concealed under the floorboards of her old Birkenau block.

Für Alma, by Miklós Steinberg.

They both had perished, but the memory was immortal and Zippy carried it in her suitcase, back into the free world. She carried the memory of a true hero.

She was almost out of the gates when something prompted her to pause. Out of the corner of her eye, Zippy spotted two sparrows sitting atop the barbed wire and watching her from their perch. The wire was no longer deadly. The electrical current had long been cut off. Shielding her face from the sun, Zippy studied the birds, a grin growing slowly but surely on her face. It was idiotic, of course, to imagine that it was Alma and Miklós seeing her off, but in Auschwitz, one had long grown used to believing the most fantastic things. Lifting her battered suitcase with one hand, Zippy patted it affectionately in front of the sparrows.

"It's safe with me, Miklós, don't fret. And, Almschi? The world will learn your story yet; you have my word. The world will learn and we, the ones you saved, will ensure that it will never forget. You two, like no one else, deserve the right to immortality."

A letter from Ellie

Dear Reader,

I want to say a huge thank you for choosing to read *The Violinist of Auschwitz*. If you did enjoy it, and want to keep up to date with all my latest releases, just sign up at the following link. Your email address will never be shared and you can unsubscribe at any time.

EllieMidwood.com

The Violinist of Auschwitz is a novel inspired by the true story of Alma Rosé, the famous Viennese violinist virtuoso and the conductor of the Birkenau women's orchestra. She was in charge of the camp orchestra for less than a year, but it was thanks to her skillful interactions with high-ranking SS members of the camp administration that the girls under her charge were given more and more privileges and became such an essential part of the camp's life that even after her death, they were spared the dreaded SS selections. Nearly all of them survived the incarceration and were liberated in 1945.

I first read about Alma Rosé and her orchestra in H. Langbein's study, *People in Auschwitz*, but it was when I began researching her properly that I realized what a fascinating person she was and what an impact she made on the lives of those young women, whom, according to their own testimonies, she indeed saved from imminent death—and, in some cases, on a few occasions.

Some readers may be familiar with Alma Rosé from Fania Fénelon's memoir *Playing for Time*, which was later made into a movie. In it, Fénelon portrays Alma as a harsh, cold, and arrogant woman, prone to violence and hysterical outbursts; however, according to other surviving members of the orchestra, Fénelon's memoir was full of "fantasies" (Anita Lasker-Wallfisch, the orchestra's cellist and, later, a famous English musician) and inaccurate portrayals of not just Alma, but other orchestra members as well. "It is a pity that Fania created such a misleading impression about the camp orchestra when she wrote her memoirs which were subsequently made into the film. For reasons best known to herself, she indulged in the most preposterous distortions of the truth about practically everyone who took part in this 'drama' " (Anita Lasker-Wallfisch).

As a matter of fact, some of those survivors even wrote to different newspapers and magazines in order to protest such fictionalizations of facts. According to Alma Rosé's biographer R. Newman, Helen "Zippy" Spitzer (later Tichauer), also an orchestra survivor, wrote to *Jewish Week* and *The American Examiner* protesting Fénelon's account.

Anita Lasker also expressed her protest to the London Sunday *Times:* "In the film, Fania Fénelon emerges as the moral force who bravely defied the Germans and held members of the orchestra together, while the conductor, Alma Rosé, is depicted as a weak woman who imposed a cruel discipline on the orchestra from fear of the Nazis and who was heavily dependent upon gaining Fénelon's approval. It just wasn't like that; Fania was pleasant and talented, but she was not as forceful as Alma, who helped us to survive. She was the key figure, a woman of immense strength and dignity who commanded the respect of everyone."

For that reason, while writing this novel, I relied mostly on Alma's official biography and other survivors' accounts rather than Fania's. Based on those sources, I tried to create as accurate and objective a portrait of Alma as a person and a musician as possible.

Alma Rosé came from a privileged musical background, but instead of relying on her family's celebrated name, she decided to follow her own path and organized a highly successful women's orchestra, the Vienna Waltzing Girls—not an easy feat by any means for a woman living in a predominantly patriarchal society. When the German troops marched into her native Vienna in March 1938, Alma refused to submit to the new discriminatory order that prohibited Jews from performing in the occupied territories. After taking her elderly father to the safety of England, she returned to Europe where she played—sometimes openly defying regulations—until her arrest in late 1942.

After a short detention in the French transit camp Drancy, she found herself on the transport heading to Auschwitz—the extermination camp in which an inmate's life expectancy was around two months. Grueling work, crammed and extremely unsanitary living conditions, constant abuse by the SS and the *Kapos* (inmate functionaries appointed by the SS to supervise order), meager rations, widespread diseases and regular selections turned each day into a fight for survival.

Only the inmates from the so-called "privileged" details could enjoy the semblance of normality. Their barracks weren't too overcrowded and sometimes even heated; often they had their own latrines attached to their block instead of having to use the communal ones; they slept in separate bunk beds with their own bedding; their rations were much more generous than those of the regular inmates; they could wear civilian clothes and grow out their hair; they could take showers daily and have their clothes deloused or washed once a week—a privilege which was often a matter of life and death in a camp plagued by epidemics of typhus spread by lice. Mostly the inmates belonging to the so-called "camp elite" worked either in the *Kanada* (the sorting detail, where the belongings and the valuables of new arrivals were processed and later transported to Germany), crematoriums (to compensate for the horrific work they had to do for the SS, the *Sonderkommando* inmates were fed excellently and were generously supplied with alcohol by the SS), camp offices, or orchestras. Fortunately for her, Alma found herself assigned to one such "privileged" detail.

According to eyewitness accounts, Alma was an excellent strategist when it came to dealings with the SS. She managed to secure the protection of quite a few high-ranking members of the camp administration beside her immediate superior and benefactor, the infamous women's camp leader, Maria Mandl (sometimes spelled Mandel). Alma completely reorganized the band that used to be able to play only a few popular songs and simple marches, expanded it from twenty to forty members, and turned it into a highly successful orchestra, admired by such camp SS higher-ups as Franz Hössler, Josef Kramer, and even Josef Mengele. However, unlike some other privileged inmates who purposefully chose the path of voluntary servitude, Alma Rosé was a far cry from a typical camp collaborator. She openly despised SS wardens and on one occasion even stopped her performance due to the noise in the audience and demanded absolute silence from her uniformed audience.

Using her talent and personal charm as a means to improve her orchestra girls' living conditions, Alma managed to secure such privileges for her charges as daily showers and post-lunch naptime, a stove to warm the quarters and to cook food, the privilege to receive parcels from home (for Aryan members of the orchestra) or from the Red Cross (for the Jewish girls), a grand piano for the Music Block and new uniforms, which were different for daily wear and performances. And—perhaps the most important privilege—the orchestra's exclusion from the regular selections held by SS wardens and Dr. Mengele; a privilege which remained in power even after Alma's death.

According to Flora Schrijver Jacobs, one of Alma's orchestra girls, "She (Alma) was a goddess to the SS—a goddess, who hated them."

Thank you for reading the story of this truly remarkable woman. I hope you loved *The Violinist of Auschwitz* and if you did, I would be very grateful if you could write a review. I'd love to hear what you think, and it makes such a difference helping new readers to discover one of my books for the first time.

I love hearing from my readers—you can get in touch on my Facebook page, through Goodreads, or on my website.

Thanks,
Ellie

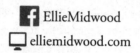 EllieMidwood
elliemidwood.com

Acknowledgments

I want to thank the wonderful Bookouture family for helping me bring Alma Rosé's story to light. First of all, huge thanks to my incredible editor Christina Demosthenous for guiding me through the process so expertly, for cheering me along the way, and for all of her insightful suggestions that helped me greatly. I'd also like to thank Sarah Whittaker for the gorgeous cover design that captured exactly what I wanted to deliver through my story. Thank you Kim Nash, Noelle Holten, Ruth Tross and Peta Nightingale for all your help and for making me feel welcome and at home with your amazing publishing team. It's been a true pleasure working with all of you and I already can't wait to create more projects under your guidance.

Special thanks to my family for believing in me and supporting me on every step; to my fiancé for being there for me on every step of this journey and for inspiring my best male characters; my two besties, Vladlena and Anastasia, whom I neglected while working on this story and who have been so understanding and incredibly supportive of me; to all of my fellow authors whom I got to know through Facebook and who became my very close friends—you all are such an inspiration! We have never met in real life, but I consider you all a family.

And of course, huge thanks to my readers for patiently waiting for new releases, for celebrating cover reveals together with me, for reading ARCs and sending me those absolutely amazing I-stayed-up-till-3am-last-night-because-I-just-had-to-finish-your-wonderful-book messages, for your reviews that always make my day, and for falling in love with my characters just as much as I do.

You are the reason why I write. Thank you so much for reading my stories.

And finally, I owe my biggest thanks to all the brave people who continue to inspire my novels. Some of you survived the Holocaust, some of you perished, but it's your incredible courage, resilience, and self-sacrifice that will live on in our hearts. Your example will always inspire us to be better people, to stand up for what is right, to give a voice to the ones who have been silenced, to protect the ones who cannot protect themselves. You all are true heroes. Thank you.

Reading Group Guide

Discussion Questions

1. Discuss the role of the orchestra in Auschwitz. Why do you think their music was perceived with antagonism when they played at the gates and with gratitude when they played at the sickbay?

2. How did Alma manage to change the orchestra? Was it only the change in the quality of their music and living conditions or the change in the girls' attitudes toward one another, as well?

3. Why do you think it was possible for Alma to openly challenge so many high-ranking SS members, including Dr. Mengele and Maria Mandl?

4. How did Alma's upbringing and her successful career help her navigate the camp life? Where do you think her resilience came from?

5. Discuss Alma's encounter with the drunk SS man from chapter 13. Why do you think she was asking the guards to shoot her and later begging Dr. Mengele to give her a shot of phenol? Why do you think he refused to do so?

6. Talk about Miklós Steinberg's role in the story. Was he only a romantic interest, or was something deeper behind his character? Discuss his role in the camp resistance. Why do you think he joined it?

7. What did you think about Alma's relationship with Dr. Mengele and Obersturmführer Hössler? Why do you think both favored her despite their otherwise ruthless behavior with other inmates? How did Alma use their favoritism to aid her orchestra? What were the conflicted feelings it awoke in her? Did you have your own conflicted feelings? If yes, what were they?

8. Discuss the orchestra's only day outside the camp's walls. Did Alma at this point still believe that she could have a life "after"?

9. Talk about the encounter between the two von Volkmann brothers. Why do you think each chose such a different path from the other? What did von Volkmann mean when he said about Auschwitz, "Here, unlike in my family home, I feel free"? Why do you think he refused to return home with his older brother?

10. Think back on the *Aktion* in chapter 28. Why do you think the SS decided to liquidate the Family Camp that was under the protection of the Red Cross? Discuss the Family Camp inmates' last act of defiance. What role did music play in the last minutes of their lives? Do you think Mandl's explanation that Miklós's death was an accident is true?

11. Historians still don't know exactly how Alma died. Do you think she indeed chose suicide, given her documented history of at least one suicidal attempt when in French captivity? If not, how else do you think she could have died? Why do you think she became the only Auschwitz inmate who had an actual funeral with high-ranking SS officials attending? How did her death affect her orchestra girls? What about other inmates? Talk about Alma's legacy and the fact that almost all her orchestra girls survived the camp.

Author Q&A

Q: What inspired you to write *The Violinist of Auschwitz*?

A: Alma herself and the fact that it was thanks to her that nearly all of her orchestra girls made it out alive because of her and her efforts. I felt like the incredible story of her bravery and selflessness just begged to be told. Risking her own life, Alma defied the authorities and carefully navigated difficult relationships with the vilest of the vile of the SS administration just to ensure that her girls would be fed, clothed, and spared dreaded selections. It really is a great tragedy that the world was robbed of her admirable, resilient spirit and her magnificent music far too soon. But it is my hope that through this novel her memory shall live on.

Q: What role did Alma's backstory play in her character development during her incarceration?

A: Long before her incarceration, Alma learned to fight for herself and her women's orchestra in a heavily male-dominated world. Instead of relying on her famous father's and uncle's names and playing a second violin (pun intended) in their shadow, Alma created and managed her own women's orchestra, which soon became such a success it easily overshadowed even her famed husband's name. She learned how to become a leader in an era when the leader's role was reserved only for men, and this undoubtedly helped her during her incarceration in Auschwitz. I firmly believe that it's due to her experience as a conductor and her orchestra's manager that she instantly knew how to organize a real orchestra out of the motley crew of inmate amateurs in a matter of a few months and impress Eichmann, to such an extent that he even granted a day outside Auschwitz's gates to the women's orchestra—an unbelievable feat in the slaughterhouse that Auschwitz was.

Q: Why did Alma become such an essential figure in the camp orchestra's life?

A: Without Alma, the orchestra didn't really exist in the true sense of the word. It was just a band of amateurs with minimal experience in music hastily thrown together on Maria Mandl's whim. But it was only after Alma arrived and established discipline and grueling rehearsals that the girls under her charge began playing on an almost professional level. Also, Alma was the glue that held them all together—Jews and gentiles, French and Dutch, Germans and Poles. The coexistence between such different cultural and ethnic backgrounds wasn't always seamless, and there were many conflicts, but it was thanks to Alma that food was always evenly distributed, duties rotated so that no one was unduly overburdened and someone got off too easily, and generally the spirit of camaraderie was soon established as soon as the girls realized that it was not them against one another but them against the SS and death itself. It was Alma who opened their eyes to that fact, and it was thanks to her that they kept together instead of falling prey to petty squabbles long after her death.

Q: Is it true that several high-ranking SS officials favored Alma and her orchestra girls?

A: Yes, it's a very much documented historical fact. Beginning with the experimental block and ending with Mandl, Hössler, and Mengele himself, the SS administration were so enamored with Alma's music that they pretty much treated her as someone very special and not just an ordinary inmate. Maria Mandl went as far as commissioning new uniforms—very handsome civilian clothes—for Alma and her girls instead of the rags that regular inmates wore. They had much better rations, were spared hard physical labor, had their own latrine, and were permitted to take showers and generally lived a life that was very different from the rest of the camp inmates'. Camp leader Hössler was known to visit the music block often with his dog, just like Dr. Mengele. All of them mourned Alma pretty much openly after her death— a fact that remained emblazoned in many survivors' memories, which proves once again just how special Alma was that even the heartless SS realized what a loss her death was to their camp and to the entire world.

Q: What is one interesting piece of information you learned when researching for the book?

A: The fact that Alma didn't mind risking her entire face just to save her hands! When in hiding in Holland, she had an accident when she fell down the stairs, and instead of putting her hands out to break her fall she purposely held them behind her back, landing on her face instead. She broke her nose and described the incident to her father in her letter, humorously mentioning that she looked like quite a sight with black and blues all over her face. Naturally, I just had to include this in the story. It goes to show just how much music and her ability to make it was imperative to Alma.

Q: What was the most challenging part about writing *The Violinist of Auschwitz*?

A: Writing scenes involving gas chambers and medical experiments to be sure. I didn't shy away from any ghastly details or gloss anything over on purpose to preserve the accuracy, but writing about it in such detail definitely affected me greatly, mental state-wise. But also—you'd be surprised to hear that probably—one of the most challenging parts was trying to describe music. I mean, how do you actually describe notes, right? Each time the violin played, it took me quite a while to write that particular scene. I never thought that searching for words to make the reader *hear* the music would be so difficult!

Q: As a historical-fiction writer, how do you handle historical accounts contradicting each other?

A: I try my best to find the truth by putting together all the accounts that mention one version of events and see how they're compared to those that mention the other version of it and go with the majority. But if it's virtually impossible or nearly all of the accounts contradict one another, I go with the version that I feel fits my heroine's personality best. For instance, there was a lot of controversy with Fania Fénelon's account of events, which contradicted other survivors' accounts. So in this instance, I went with the majority of the orchestra girls' accounts and only included things from Fénelon's memoir on which all survivors agreed. Naturally, I mentioned this to the readers in the note on history at the end of the novel, explaining what sources I used as primary ones and why certain ones took precedent over the others.

Q: If you could go back in time and say one thing to Alma, what would it be?

A: Almost all of your orchestra girls made it out alive thanks to your efforts and care. I thought you'd want to know it.

Q: What one interesting fact do you want the readers to know about your writing process?

A: My dogs are always nearby whenever I write. Sometimes they nap curled next to me. Sometimes they play-wrestle and body-slam me and bump into my laptop as I'm trying to type. Sometimes they walk over the keyboard when I leave it for a minute to refill my coffee mug. I firmly believe some of my best scenes were written by them, ha-ha!

A Note on the History

Thank you so much for reading *The Violinist of Auschwitz*. Even though it's a work of fiction, most of it is based on a true story. While writing it, I tried my best to stick to the actual historical facts surrounding Alma Rosé's life—and death—and only took creative license to enhance the reader's experience.

Alma Rosé arrived in Auschwitz in July 1943 and, after undergoing the obligatory processing, was placed in the infamous Experimental Block, where SS Dr. Clauberg was conducting his experiments in bloodless sterilization. The circumstances of Alma's arrival, her initial reaction and behavior, her interactions with the block elder Magda Hellinger and inmate nurse Ima van Esso are all true to fact and based on testimonies given by both women. After Magda Hellinger procured a violin for Alma through Helen "Zippy" Spitzer, the Experimental Block's "cultural evenings" became such a success among the inmates and nurses, Dr. Clauberg's assistant and inmate nurse Sylvia Friedmann took Alma off the SS physician's list, thus saving her from the horrific fate of his multiple victims.

The notorious Block 11, the so-called "Death Barrack" where the camp Gestapo imprisoned, tortured, and executed its victims, indeed stood right next to the Experimental Block. According to the survivors' testimonies, they could see the so-called "Black Wall" in its courtyard if they peeked through the shuttered windows—the wall by which the Gestapo executed the condemned inmates by firing squad.

The circumstances of Alma's transfer to the Birkenau Music Block are also true to fact, though versions of it sometimes differ. Some historians, H. Langbein among them, claim that Alma was transferred to Birkenau after performing for one of the camp wardens on her birthday. Alma's biographer R. Newman offered a slightly different version, in which he claimed that Alma caught Maria Mandl's attention after the SS began attending "social evenings" in the Experimental Block. Whatever the case was, Alma was soon discovered by Birkenau women's camp leader, Maria Mandl, and appointed as a *Kapo* (prisoner functionary) of the Birkenau Music Block.

The Birkenau Music Block was a relatively new installation, only organized by Mandl in the spring of 1943, just a few months prior to Alma's arrival. At the time of Alma's appointment, it consisted of about twenty women, most of whom weren't professional musicians and who could only play the so-called *Katzenmusik*—cacophony—according to the survivors' admissions. "No conductor in the world ever faced a more formidable task. Alma was charged with making something out of sheer rock" (Helen "Zippy" Spitzer).

Zofia Czajkowska (Sofia in the novel), the Music Block's first *Kapo* and conductor, was indeed demoted to the position of the block elder so that Alma could create a semblance of a real orchestra out of the band, or at least such was Mandl's plan for the violinist. Instead of asserting her immediate authority, Alma chose to create something more of a partnership with the former *Kapo*. According to Zippy, "Alma at first had difficulty with the Polish players, but Czajkowska in stepping down and taking on the position of block senior was able to help Alma overcome those early problems. Alma did not speak Polish, and very few Poles knew German. Instead of sulking and making Alma's work more difficult, Czajkowska proved to be a great help."

The descriptions of the Music Block, including Alma's room, are also true to fact and based on testimonies given by the Music Block survivors. The daily routine of the block is also based on the survivors' testimonies. There were a few changes to it after Alma's taking charge of the orchestra—the girls were indeed given the privilege of taking a one-hour nap after their lunch, a daily shower in the camp's Sauna, and having their clothes washed once a week.

The circumstances surrounding Alma's saving Flora Schrijver from the Quarantine Block, just like the fact that she pulled Anita Lasker from the shower room of the Reception Block, are all based on fact and were described by both survivors in their interviews. Alma also took in Violette Jacquet, a violinist from France, on the insistence of Hélène Scheps, who arrived together with Violette on the same transport from France, despite the fact that Violette, on her own admission, was only a mediocre violinist. After Violette contracted typhus during the outbreak in winter of 1943–44, Alma saved her a second time, claiming that Violette was her best violinist and thus sparing her from being sent to the gas chamber. Unfortunately, the conflicts between Polish and Jewish girls concerning the rations, particularly during the typhus outbreak, are also based on fact and were reported by several Music Block survivors. According to their testimonies, Alma tried her best to be a mediator among different nationalities and didn't favor any particular group, relying on a fair approach instead and doing her utmost to bring the girls together.

The descriptions of other work details, including the famous *Kanada*, are all true to fact. The inmates permanently assigned to this sorting detail, who were considered among the most privileged ones in the entire camp, were allowed to wear civilian clothes, wristwatches, grow out their hair, and take showers in the same Sauna. Corruption in the *Kanada* was rampant and the inmate prisoners made use of it, trading goods for favors both with the SS and other inmates. H. Langbein, an Auschwitz survivor and historian, described it in detail in his study, *People in Auschwitz*: "Many precious things were hidden in the clothes and shoes left behind by the destroyed Jewish transports. The *Kanada* inmates who sorted those objects brought secretly and daringly very valuable things into the camp. In return for these they received food, clothes, shoes, alcohol, and cigarettes that were smuggled into the camp by civilian employees and SS men. An inmate who was doing 'organizing' was instantly recognizable, for he was better dressed and better nourished" (based on testimonies given by Ota Kraus and Erich Kulka).

Szymon Laks and René Coudy, both members of Birkenau men's orchestra, reported the following after their visit to the *Kanada*: "The girls who work there have everything—perfume, cologne—and they look as if their hairdos were the work of the top hairdresser of Paris. Apart from freedom, they have everything a woman can dream of. They also know love; the proximity of men, both inmates and SS men, makes this inevitable…Ten meters from their barracks, on the other side of the barbed wire, rise the rectangular chimneys of the crematoriums that burn constantly, burn the owners of all the goods that these admirable creatures sort in these barracks."

The character of Kitty is based on the real Auschwitz survivor, Kitty Hart, who indeed worked at the *Kanada* sorting detail, just like the character of Rabbi Dayen, who was a real inmate tasked with burning the papers and photographs of the gassed people. Kitty Hart described her experiences in her memoir, *Return to Auschwitz*. It was that widespread corruption that led to the investigation conducted by SS Dr. Morgen and which resulted in several arrests and trials of SS personnel, demotions and transfers, and the immediate removal of the first camp Kommandant Höss, who was replaced by Kommandant Liebehenschel.

The new Kommandant Liebehenschel was really known as "the humane Kommandant" among the inmates and he, in fact, brought quite a few welcome changes to the camp's daily routine. He immediately removed the so-called "standing cells" that were used as a form of torture by the camp's Gestapo from Block 11; forbade the beatings by the SS and the *Kapos*; created a practice of personally touring the camp and speaking to the inmates about their concerns; permitted the inmates to keep their caps on during the roll calls in order to somewhat protect them from the elements; proposed a new reward system for the inmates who were granted certain privileges for overachieving their quota at their work detail, including permission to visit the camp's brothel (it was indeed housed in the same block as the Auschwitz orchestra, as described in the story).

Arthur Liebehenschel was transferred to Auschwitz-Birkenau in punishment for divorcing his wife and standing by his fiancée Anneliese Hüttemann, who was accused by the Gestapo for her associations with the Jews. It is true that he was somewhat successful in stopping the systematic gassings for at least some time, constantly fighting with Berlin about the "Final Solution" and only following Berlin's direct orders under pressure. In contrast, former Kommandant Höss was more than willing to gas both fresh arrivals and old inmates who failed to pass selections on his own initiative. In the spring of 1944, right before the so-called Hungarian *Aktion,* Liebehenschel was removed from his position for being "too soft," and once again replaced by Kommandant Höss, who had no qualms about eliminating almost the entire Jewish population of Hungary unlike his SS counterpart Liebehenschel. Arthur Liebehenschel's personality, interactions with the inmates, and his policies are described in detail in H. Langbein's *People in Auschwitz*, and B. Cherish's *The Auschwitz Kommandant*.

SS wardens Margot Drexler (also spelled Dreschel or Drechsler) and Irma Grese indeed attended each roll call at Alma's block. Their descriptions, personalities, and attitude toward the orchestra girls are all based on survivors' testimonies.

In contrast to them, Maria Mandl showed much more respect and favoritism to her Music Block mascots, designing new uniforms for the girls and granting them more and more privileges at Alma's request. Zippy's interactions with the women's camp leader, including Mandl permitting her to stay in bed when Zippy wasn't feeling well and allowing her to take a present for herself after Zippy inscribed a book for Mandl's SS comrade Kramer, are all based on Zippy's testimonies. Also, according to her, Mandl indeed changed Alma's classification from "Jew" to "Mischling" (mixed-blood) in the registration book, thus elevating her status among the camp population and granting Alma certain protection. You can read about it in more detail in R. Newman's biography, *Alma Rosé: Vienna to Auschwitz.*

Dr. Mengele, known as "The Angel of Death" among the camp population, was, in fact, a big admirer of Alma Rosé's talent. He was known to visit the Music Block quite often to hear his favorite music pieces, which he sometimes requested to be played several times in a row. The descriptions of his appearance, personality, and his obsessive fascination with the pseudo-scientific experiments he conducted are all true to fact. The occasion when Teresa W, an inmate prisoner working for Dr. Mengele, discovered "glass jars, in which were human eyes" in a box that was supposed to be shipped to the Kaiser Wilhelm Institute of Anthropology and Human Heredity and Eugenics in Berlin-Dahlem was reported by her after her liberation.

To portray Dr. Mengele as accurately as possible, I relied on R. J. Lifton's study *The Nazi Doctors*, in which he provides multiple survivors' testimonies of those who worked with Dr. Mengele personally and were forced to participate in his ghastly experiments and killings. One such inmate doctor was a pathologist, Dr. Miklos Nyiszly, who served as inspiration for the fictional Dr. Ránki. The description of his pathologist's quarters and the work he was forced to perform under Dr. Mengele's command are all based on fact and were described by him in his memoir, *Auschwitz: A Doctor's Eyewitness Account.*

Just like Dr. Mengele, Obersturmführer Franz Hössler also was among the orchestra's ardent fans. He visited the Music Block regularly and was known to bring his dog along. The fact that Alma herself had had an Alsatian, who used to ride with her in her open car when Vienna was still a city free of the Nazi reign, is also based on truth, just like the fact that it was Hössler who permitted Alma to take a few tutors for her girls from his men's orchestra's ranks.

In my descriptions of Hössler's personality and his infamous sleek handling of the people about to be gassed, I relied on the reports of one of the *Sonderkommando*'s survivors, Filip Müller, who worked under Hössler for years and was therefore quite familiar with the SS man's character. In his memoir *Eyewitness Auschwitz*, Mr. Müller described how Hössler deceived the new arrivals with promises of decent treatment and work and made them go into the gas chambers almost willingly, as they were reassured by Hössler's civil manner. So, what fictional Alma witnessed while watching Hössler giving his speech before the doomed people is based on fact.

The installment of the so-called "Family Camp," where the *Theresienstadt* Jews were allowed to live in family units and were spared back-breaking work in the outside details is also based on truth. The fact that it was used mostly for propaganda purposes by the SS and liquidated later when such a necessity disappeared was described by both H. Langbein and F. Müller in their studies.

The liquidation of the camp is also based on F. Müller's personal eyewitness account. As a matter of fact, the *Sonderkommando* inmate whom Mandl mentions walking inside the gas chamber during the liquidation of the Family Camp is based on Müller's personal story. He indeed wished to die along with the condemned inmates and was only saved when those inmates forced him toward the door and alerted the SS that one of their *Sonderkommando* men was inside.

The character of Miklós Steinberg is based on a real Hungarian pianist virtuoso whom H. Langbein mentions in his study. According to him, the Auschwitz musicians indeed allowed him to play the piano when the music room was available (Jewish musicians were essentially banned from the Auschwitz orchestra, contrary to Birkenau's lenient policy that allowed Jewish musicians to perform along with the Aryan players). His fate remains unknown, and creative license has been taken in creating his character based on a true person.

As for the camp resistance, they were a real clandestine organization as well. It mostly consisted of privileged prisoners who could move freely around the camp (much like Alma and Zippy with their passes—*Ausweis*) and had access to different work details. It was they who constructed self-made radios to inform the camp population of the news from the front (mostly, they listened to Allied stations, since all the German ones provided at that point was mostly propaganda), who smuggled and stored weapons, and organized a few successful escapes. One of the most famous acts of the camp resistance was the *Sonderkommando* revolt that occurred on October 7, 1944 and resulted in the destruction of Crematorium IV. The planned uprising failed, the revolt was suppressed, most of its participants executed, but the fact remains—Auschwitz inmates were ready to fight for their freedom no matter the cost. F. Müller, who participated in the revolt and miraculously survived, also described it in his memoir. As for the inmate's escape that was also organized with the help of the camp resistance, it really took place a few days before the New Year, just as it's described in the book.

Incredible as it sounds, the Music Block was truly given a one-day leave, with the permission to leave the camp's territory—a thing unheard of prior to that in the camp's history. It indeed occurred after Eichmann's visit; in describing it, I relied on the Music Block survivors' testimonies.

The construction of the second ramp, the new "Mexico" camp that was originally designed to house the Hungarian inmates, but which was never finished, is all based on fact.

There's still controversy surrounding the circumstances of Alma's death. Some historians claim that she committed suicide just a few weeks after the Family Camp liquidation, some claim that she contracted a virus or some other disease that killed her almost instantly, some speculate that it was the SS wardens who poisoned her out of jealousy. In my story, I decided to keep with the suicide version as several Music Block survivors testified that

Alma spoke of suicide on a few occasions and carried prussic acid on her which she had smuggled from the camp in Drancy. Dr. Mancy, who became very close friends with Alma, also testified to the fact that after the liquidation of the Family Camp, Alma had lost all will to live and often spoke of suicide with her.

Dr. Mengele indeed came into the sickbay to consult on Alma's case—an extremely rare occasion for that particular SS physician, who was mostly interested in his experiments and not inmates' well-being. Despite all of the efforts to save her, Alma died on April 5, 1944.

What is even more incredible is the fact that Alma's body was indeed clothed in a dress and "laid out atop a catafalque fashioned of two stools set side by side in an alcove next to the examining room" (R. Newman). According to the survivors, both the SS and the inmates were allowed to pay their respects to the dead violinist. Maria Mandl, according to Alma's biographer, mourned her most celebrated mascot's death openly. Obersturmführer Hössler indeed demanded to dispose of Alma's body in the most respectful fashion, given the circumstances, and ordered it to be laid out on the gurney alone and still clothed. Szymon Laks reported that after Alma's death, the SS administration also ordered that Alma's conductor's baton and a black crepe ribbon be hung on the wall of the Music Block in the violinist's memory. According to Fania Fénelon, a Music Block survivor, Dr. Mengele also came into the Music Block to pay his respects to the dead violinist: "Elegant, distinguished, he took a few steps, then stopped by the wall where we had hung up Alma's armband and baton. Respectfully, heels together, he stood quietly for a moment, then said in a penetrating tone, appropriately funereal, *In memoriam.*"

Not a single prisoner in the history of Auschwitz-Birkenau, before or after Alma Rosé, was treated with such respect after their passing. Alma's talent and integrity touched many hearts, not only the hearts of the inmates, but, it appears, the SS as well.

I feel, Alma's Auschwitz life and legacy is perfectly summarized in Zippy's words:

"She was achieving something she could never have achieved in normal life. Nothing became something in her hands. Alma's genius was that she could bring a group of amateurs to a level where they could perform acceptably. For her, it became the triumph of her career. She never would have believed it possible. She also achieved something no other conductor she had known would have tried. She told me she could never go back to her origins. That the Viennese society in which she had grown up was totally destroyed. In Birkenau she was creating something of which she could be proud. A handful of people hated her, but there are many more who loved her then, and still love her. Some could never understand there could be only one leader for the orchestra."

Thank you so much for reading this amazing woman's story.